THE YELLOW-HAIRED BRAVE

Only with the proud Absaroke Crow did Ben Tree feel the call of his Osage mother's blood. In this earthly paradise, a shaman's ominous prophecy changed young Tree's life forever. It warned of ten long years of strife—a nightmare that began with the treacherous murder of his father and twin brother, and then took his wife in an act of prejudice and hatred.

As he fought for his tribe's survival in the mountain wilderness, and moved like a deadly phantom of vengeance through the gold towns and trails of the West, Ben Tree became "Man Called Tree," a legend that would never die. . . .

THE LEGEND OF BEN TREE

THE LEGEND
OF
BEN TREE

Paul A. Hawkins

A SIGNET BOOK

SIGNET
Published by the Penguin Group
Penguin Books USA Inc., 375 Hudson Street,
New York, New York 10014, U.S.A.
Penguin Books Ltd, 27 Wrights Lane,
London W8 5TZ, England
Penguin Books Australia Ltd, Ringwood,
Victoria Australia
Penguin Books Canada Ltd, 10 Alcorn Avenue,
Toronto, Ontario, Canada M4V 3B2
Penguin Books (N.Z.) Ltd, 182-190 Wairau Road,
Auckland 10, New Zealand

Penguin Books Ltd, Registered Offices:
Harmondsworth, Middlesex, England

First published by Signet, an imprint of New American Library,
a division of Penguin Books USA Inc.

First Printing, July, 1993
10 9 8 7 6 5 4 3 2 1

To my grandson,
Henry Little Hawk.

Special thanks to Marian Geil,
the greatest of librarians.

When justice is done, it
is a joy to the righteous,
but dismay to evil-doers. . . .
                    Proverbs

THE ROUTES OF BENJAMIN TREE 1856-1864

INTRODUCTION

Little Santa Fe, near Independence, Missouri.
October, 1868

The two men sat across from each other at a round
oak table, one a young professional man, his trousers
tucked neatly into the tops of his field boots, his suit
coat and vest sorely in need of cleaning and repair.
He had been on trains, stages, and wagons, traveling
the western frontier for almost six months. In front of
him were several notebooks; he jotted in one of them
with a long pen. Across from him a gray-haired man,
slumped in the back, the wrinkles of time creased in
his leathery, tanned face, alternately nodded and
puffed on a clay pipe, pausing occasionally during the
conversation to make a point with the pipe's stem.

His name was Jim Bridger, and he was dressed in
faded blue denim. He was home again, what he called
"civilized home." For most of his last forty years
home had been almost anywhere in the wilderness
where he chose to spread his blanket, and for that rea-

son the Indians who knew him called him "the Blanket Chief." His present companion was Harold Stebbins, a correspondent for *The New York Tribune,* who had come to talk, not about Jim Bridger, but another person by the name of Ben Tree, an elusive man whom he had sought to interview for almost a month while at the most westward point of his journey, old Fort Hall, in the Idaho territory.

Stebbins was intrigued by the name Ben Tree, for during all of his newspaper work in the West, whether it was writing dispatches about Brigham Young and the Mormons, or the most recent Fort Laramie peace negotiations between the Sioux and Cheyenne Indians and the government, the name of Ben Tree had frequently come up in trailside conversations. But throughout Stebbins' long trek, he had only met two men who personally knew this mysterious, legendary man, and Jim Bridger was one of them.

The other was James Digby, a wealthy, semi-retired merchant and freight line operator in Fort Hall. Unfortunately, Stebbins told Bridger, the last time Mr. Digby had seen Ben Tree was almost five years ago, and while there were other people along the trail who knew Mr. Tree, or claimed they did, none of these had seen or heard of him for almost ten years. And, not only that, some of the stories they told were outrageously unbelievable. Also, Mr. Digby had been somewhat reluctant to divulge much information about Ben Tree. Bridger was Stebbins' last hope, for the newsman was en route to St. Louis, from whence he would return home to New York City.

Bridger, his flinty blue eyes brimming with nostalgia, smiled faintly at Stebbins. "I kin do you one better than ole man Digby, son. The last time I saw Benji Tree was mebbe the summer of Fifty-nine up in the Montana territory, and that figgers nigh on to ten years ago. I was scoutin' up that way with some army boys, engineers, showin' 'em how to link up with the Fort Benton trail.'' He chuckled for a moment, in recollection. ''Benji came down off the side of a mountain that went straight up, like a billy goat hill, I recollect. Damn near scared half of those bluecoats outta their boots when he came into camp. I headed up north after that, and I never did see him again. Oh, I heard about him, off and on, livin' up there like one of the ole boys, but seein' and hearin's two different things, 'tis, for certain.''

Stebbins, nodding and writing, looked up inquisitively. ''And do you believe he's still up there? But where? And doing what?''

''Don't know, for certain,'' Bridger said with another little, somewhat evasive smile. ''But I know Benji and his brother, Will, from when they was about yea high, mebbe seven or eight years old. And Benji, well, that boy was *born* for the mountains and he'd make do, no matter where, no matter what.''

Stebbins paused thoughtfully, thumbed back through one of his notebooks. ''Mr. Digby says that you were like a father to Mr. Tree. As I see here, he even rode with you several times when he was quite young, once during the Mormon uprising.''

''Kee-rect,'' Bridger said, puffing out a long blue stream of smoke. ''Benji knew the trail from here to Fort Boise like the palm of his hand. I reckon you could put him down 'most anywhere along the line in the middle of the night, and come sunup, he'd likely as not tell you where the nearest waterin' hole was, and how long the ride was to it.''

''Then, Mr. Tree is a knowledgeable man?''

Jim Bridger nodded, saying, ''Aye, that he is, both knowin' the sign, the land, and speakin' a few tongues. And he does me one better, too—he kin read and write with nary a pause.''

Stebbins looked surprised. "Are you telling me this man is literate . . . ? Is that what you mean?"

"Kee-rect, again," said Bridger with a smile, his eyes twinkling. "Had good schoolin' with his kin in St. Louis durin' the winters, mebbe up until sixteen years old. I'd say that's somethin' you kin look into on your way home. Had an uncle there, I recollect, hardware business. Same name, Tree."

Scratching his beard, Stebbins said, "Mr. Digby didn't volunteer much information, but it's strange he didn't mention anything about Mr. Tree's education."

"Problee figgered you wasn't much interested in that part of Benji's story," Bridger commented dryly. "Y'see, Mr. Stebbins, there's more than meets the eye, here. Benji was no brag, not even when he was a little tyke, and seems like he was always a step ahead. Big heart, the boy. Lot a gumption in him, too, quick to rile sometimes, and downright finicky about the country out here, 'specially what the whites are doin' to his Injun brothers; more particular, how they's doin' it. 'The Manifest Destiny,' he calls it, and all the papers they're writin' to go with it, like the latest treaty you're tellin' me about up at Laramie. Likely as not, not worth the paper it's written on, jest like all the rest of 'em, and hell's bells, I've seen 'em come and go for nigh on to forty years. That was always stuck in Benji's craw. Y'see, he figgers it this way: When someone is steppin' on his brothers, they're steppin' on him, too. He was always takin' things like that right personal. And Benji, with his learnin', is considered one of those smart Injuns, and no white man likes a smart Injun, 'cuz he kin read that small scratchin' in the paper. See what I mean?"

Stebbins nodded again. "Yes, I understand, Mr. Bridger. And then this, perhaps, precipitated some of the tall tales about him?"

"Tall tales?" Bridger said, slowly rising from the

table. He set his pipe aside and went over to a cupboard where he pulled down a worn ledger. Placing his hand reverently on the cover, he said, "This here is Benji's bible, so to speak. Preachin' in it. Facts too, and plenty of 'em, pure gospel, 'tis. Came down the river to me two years ago, I recollect. Think I was somewhere up around the Powder River at that time, doin' a little work along the trail for Colonel Carrington at Fort Kearny. No matter. When I gets back, all done in from that Fetterman mess, this-here's waitin' for me. Some of my kin read it to me, my eyes not being all that good anymore, and me not being able to cipher all that well, either." He placed the ledger in front of Harold Stebbins, saying, "Take this back to your hotel room in the city and give it a look. Mebbee it kin say more about Benji than any two men. Mebbe it's time some of it needs to be said. Jest be sure I git the consarned thing back! Sorta sentimental, I reckon, cuz it brought a few tears to these ole eyes."

Thumbing through the first few pages, Stebbins said in quiet surprise, "You're telling me that he kept a journal? A record of everything he did?"

"Aye, that he did."

By then Harold Stebbins had turned to the back of the journal, and he suddenly exclaimed, "My God, man, this is almost twelve years . . . twelve years of the man's life!"

"Kee-rect," returned Bridger. Relighting his pipe, he puffed a few times, then grinned down at Stebbins. "Benji mentions me in there a few times, but pay no mind, cuz those ain't the tall tales. Said you wanted to meet Ben Tree, didn't you? Well, that's him, right there in all that scratchin', and that's the only one you'll ever know, cuz I reckon that's the last of Ben Tree."

BOOK ONE

ONE

Fort Laramie, Dakota Territory. April, 1856

The long haul into Fort Laramie had been arduous, muddy at times because of the early rains, but free of serious trouble, even with hostiles. By late afternoon on this early spring day, Thaddeus Tree and several of his muleskinners were almost finished with the unloading of four of their ten freight wagons at the garrison store. The cargo, mostly civilian staples—dried and tinned foods, flour, grains, and tobacco—would be bought later by either Sioux or Cheyenne who came to trade, or by immigrants who frequently replenished supplies at Fort Laramie before heading on west to the gold country or the big Blue Mountains of the Oregon territory. Thaddeus Tree's other six wagons were destined for Fort Bridger and Fort Hall, trading outposts months away on the long, tortuous route west through hostile country along the North Platte and Green Rivers.

For members of the Tree family—father Thad, and

twenty-two-year-old twins William and Benjamin—it was just the first leg of a yearly journey across the rugged land, one that they had made many times. Almost everyone, including the various Indian tribes along the Great Medicine Road, knew the freight merchants—honest men, who often paused at trailside to share tobacco and food with their red brothers. Fort Laramie, the aged trading post, and now also a military garrison, was the first rest stop on the long trail out of Independence. Thad Tree, a frontier veteran who had been traveling the route for ten years, had a small cabin below the fort and corrals down along the creek bottom, and had built similar cabins at Big Sandy and Fort Bridger where the drivers and their stock usually took another much needed respite on the long, round-trip journey.

After running the mules and horses into the corral, Ben and Will set about the usual chores: inspecting the tack, the wagons, and ultimately, cleaning and sweeping out the old cabin. They brought up buckets of water for the ancient tin tub, for this was one of their customary rituals, a leisurely bath, unlike the hasty dips they had to take along the trail where mosquitoes and buffalo gnats most often swarmed in ferocious clouds, making bathing a hazardous event. By the time their father had completed business at the sutler's store—the place where accounts were settled and four of the six muleskinners paid off—the two young men had bathed, changed clothing, and were already making the rounds of the grounds, chatting with a few old friends and conversing in sign with a few Lakota and Cheyenne camped along the fort perimeter.

This Indian talk was routine—not only good manners, but invaluable on the trail, where friendships were rekindled during sudden, unexpected encounters with tribal relatives or the friends of these hang-around-the-fort people. Both Will and Ben had become adept at passing sign, some of it learned from their father, a one-time guide. The remainder they had picked up from the Indians themselves. So it was not unusual to see either of the Tree boys sitting cross-legged near a tipi, smoking pipe, their hands in motion, surrounded by a few old men and women, exchanging news and gossip and, sometimes, trading bawdy jokes. Not many white people knew that these two young frontiersmen were part-Indian, for there was barely a trace of it in their features. But their friends of the Plains knew it. They knew their mother had been a full-blood, a human being. Ben and Will were only six when she died of lung fever on the Missouri plains. After her death, long months of reformation followed.

Their Aunt Mary, Uncle Jediah's wife, a well-meaning, very determined Christian woman, had done her best to obliterate any trace of their origin when she took them under her wing and put them in school in St. Louis. Uncle Jediah was prosperous, considered by many to be rich. He owned a lucrative hardware business. By western standards his home was spacious and grand, hardly a place for two young savages. Schooling had been during the fall and winter months, and Aunt Mary strived so hard to cleanse their blood, to change their hardy frontier mannerisms. In the city, she succeeded. No one suspected the Osage blood in her fair-haired nephews, but once they were back at their father's mule farm below Independence the twins always reverted—they worked, played, swore, and ran free, and shed cloth for buckskin.

Even so, their Osage heritage was not that obvious. Neither possessed their mother's darker skin, only the sharpness of her features, her fine straight nose, her firm chin. They both grew straight as tamaracks just like their father, six feet tall, both sandy-haired with deep-set eyes of dark blue, little indication of breed about either of them.

Not that it mattered to Will and Ben. Independence was not St. Louis, and both boys cherished their Indian blood. On the Great Plains, anywhere from the Tree cabins at Fort Laramie to Fort Bridger, the boys were simply known as "the Tree twins," sons of Thad Tree, the great freighter and mule-breeder from Indian creek near Independence, a place few people had heard of until emigrants began using it as a starting point for the way west. The elder Tree's prominence had also come to him for another reason: He was a longtime friend of Jim Bridger, and most everyone had heard about old Gabe. And if someone on the frontier chanced upon the twin's heritage, it was like a fallen leaf upon the water, causing hardly a ripple to the knowledgeable and understanding.

The customary layover at Laramie usually took no more than two or three days—adequate time to rest, tend the stock, and make any necessary repairs on the wagons. They were now using newer Kern and Murphy freighters along with the older Conestogas. They unloaded and abandoned the Conestogas until the return trip to Independence later in the year. Thad Tree usually had one of the locals look out after the mules left behind, and authorized him to make a sale or two when the occasion arose.

Tree's operation, stretching from the plains of Independence to the mountains of Fort Hall, had made him a wealthy man within five years. For hardy work, the stock he bred and sold was considered the best money could buy. The thought that this accumulation of wealth eventually might bring him trouble somewhere down the Oregon Trail never entered the minds of his sons, as Thad Tree was a respected and honorable man without an enemy to his name.

Will was somewhat the same cut as his father—

mild-mannered, mellow, a trail veteran with the self-assurance of a man far beyond his twenty-two years. Not entirely so with Benjamin, who, although possessing some of these qualities, was more easily provoked, particularly in matters of race and prejudice. An aggressive idealist, he often found trouble; in the beginning he'd had only an argument or minor scuffle with a few bellicose bigots or bullies, but when some of these social differences had turned life-threatening, he took to wearing a revolver. After several years of practice Ben had become a true marksman, and while he never flaunted this proficiency, the Navy Colt was always there, tucked away neatly in his leather holster, at the thigh instead of the hip. Ben felt adequately prepared to defend himself, if and when the occasion arose. And, for the first time in his young life, that occasion unexpectedly arose on this early April lay-over at Fort Laramie.

Late in the afternoon, just after the men were finishing their supper, they heard a clamor on the small porch and the sound of anguished sobbing. Ben immediately leaped outside, where he discovered a young Indian woman sitting on the stoop wailing, holding her stomach, and rocking back and forth in pain. When he bent over her, he saw that she was Lakota; the blue tattoo on her forehead stood out like a beacon against her tear-stained face, and her mouth bled from a cut on her lower lip. Telling Will to fetch a damp cloth, Ben began making sign, trying to find out what had happened, who had beaten her, but her burden was too much to bear. Thaddeus, looking on, spoke Siouan, and he told Ben to bring the young woman inside where they could better tend her.

After she had regained her composure she began talking, with the elder Tree translating. Down at the creek for water, she had been accosted by a white man, a bearded man wearing a red shirt whose hair was also red. When she bit and scratched him he struck her in the face, knocking her to the ground, then kicked her in the stomach before fleeing back toward the fort. Her husband, she said, was away with troopers, helping scout the trail down the North Platte River. Only her mother was at the lodge, and the young woman was now so ashamed, she feared to go back and tell her.

Ben Tree said to his brother, "You go find her mother and bring her down her. I'll take a look for this fellow, whoever he is, see what his side of the story is."

Thaddeus abruptly spoke up, admonishing Ben. "Wait a moment, hold your horses, Benji, now, don't go making this your business! Better let the people at the fort handle it, or wait for her husband to return. It's better this way, understand?"

"I'm not going to make it my business, Pa," returned Ben. "I just think this fellow should get the word. If he knows what's good for him he better make tracks, and long ones, too, because when her people find out about this he's going to be in a heap of trouble, either way, fort or Indian. It's for his own good."

"Well, how do you even know who he is?" Thaddeus asked. "There's a dozen men or more around here with red shirts. Probably his underjohns, anyways."

"She said his shirt was colored like his hair, didn't she?" replied Ben, stepping out the door. "I'll be back directly, so don't go fretting."

"Son, I know you, dammit!" Thaddeus called. "You behave, and mind your manners! Don't go getting all hot under the collar about some little woman you don't even know!"

Giving his father a wave, Ben strode with his brother toward the distant stockade. Near the outskirts where the tipis stood, Will and Ben parted company, each one attending to his own job at hand. A few curious children tagged along after Will as he went down the row of lodges, making a few signs along the way in an attempt to find the woman's mother. Meantime Ben wandered up near the gate, and within minutes he had found his man—a tall, bearded fellow, suspenders over his red undershirt, who was wiping his face and laughing with two other men. That anyone would find humor in such a sordid affair suddenly riled Ben, and a ruddy glow came to his cheeks. Certainly the affair at the creek was their topic of conversation, for the red-bearded one was nodding toward the Laramie thickets as he talked. And true to what the woman had told Thaddeus, this man was marked, the long welt of a scratch tracing his cheekbone just above the thick growth of his red whiskers. Ben quietly stood aside from the three men, waiting for their laughter to subside. Finally introducing himself, he said calmly, "My name is Ben Tree."

Placing a wet towel over a shoulder, the tall man stared down at Ben and said, "Is that so, boy? And what might you be wanting?"

"I was wondering if you can tell me about this woman down at our place? What happened to her? She's been whomped pretty good, and carrying on a bit about it."

The red-whiskered man's brow hiked in surprise. He exclaimed, "Well, if this don't beat all! I was just telling the boys here about that little to-do." He gave Ben a stony glare. "It's no matter to you, boy, is it? She your woman? Something like that?"

"No, Ben answered easily, "never saw her before in my life. But I was just curious why someone would beat her like that."

"She had it coming, that's why!" he retorted testily. "For certain, she did, the little Injun bitch! Look what she upped and done to me!" Jerking back his undershirt, he displayed the dark, reddish-blue imprint of teeth in his shoulder. "Bit me clean through, she did, goddammit!"

Ben nodded at the obvious and quickly agreed. "By jingo, she marked you pretty good, all right. Sure must have had a good reason to do something like that." Returning the sullen stare of the gaunt man, he finally asked, "What's your name, mister?"

"Name's Jed Bullock, if it's any of your damned business."

The name was familiar, but it took Ben a moment to place it. Bullock, a high-plains drifter, a man notorious for numerous altercations with both Indians and whites along the trail, reputed by some to be a robber and a thief although from Ben's knowledge, no one had a call on him. From Bullock's unkempt appearance, his indifferent and surly attitude, Ben now found himself wondering if it was even worth imparting a friendly warning, for if this trailside ruffian ended up with a permanent Sioux haircut, it was only what he deserved. "I suppose you're right," he said at length. "This is no matter to me, but it might be to some of the Sioux when they find out who roughed up that young woman. I'd say that doesn't make it too healthy for you around here. Just some friendly advice, that's all. They might take a notion to make amends."

"They wouldn't lay a hand on me here," Bullock said gruffly. "Yes, and you damned well know it! Hell, these little wenches are always going around wagging their butts, trying to fetch a coin on the side! If you're so nosy about it, I'll tell you what happened. I was just up to a little funning with her and she angered with me. Just wasn't in the mood for me, that's all."

Turning away, Ben said, "I can sure understand that, Mr. Bullock."

"Now, just what are you meaning by that, boy?"

"No more than what I said," Ben said, smiling back at him. "Seems to me that you're forgetting it's a long

way out of here, both directions. If you value your
hair, I'd advise you to clean country before the sun
sets, or else sleep with one eye open." And with that
much said, his mission accomplished, Ben Tree started
to walk back toward the cabin. By then Will was coming along with the young woman's mother, followed
by a string of children, both Indian and white.

"Hey there, boy!" Bullock called after Ben. "I
don't much like your sass, telling me what I can do,
butting in like I'm some kind of greenhorn! Why, you
ain't even dry behind the years yet! What are you,
anyways, a goddamned Indian-lover? A squaw man, is
that it?"

Pausing, Ben heard Will say quietly, "Come on,
Benji, just ignore the ignoramus. He ain't worth a lick
of salt, so don't go wasting your time on him, hear?"

"I hear," Ben said, suddenly smoldering inside.
"But I'm trying not to."

Persisting, Jud Bullock nudged one of his companions and laughed derisively. "Look at that, boys, there
he goes, a damned fool kid with a big mouth and nothing to back it up with. I should have taken him down
a notch or two just like the little wench; kicked his
Injun-loving ass, that's what." He guffawed, slapped
his thighs, and looked to his two friends for approval.

Ben Tree, struggling for composure, turned slowly
around. His voice was calm. "Mr. Bullock, just how
do you propose taking me down a notch? Do you want
to brawl in the dust? Do you want to use that pistol on
your side, or do you want to take the friendly advice
I gave you?"

Bullock, taken aback by the unexpected challenge,
gawked at the young man across the grounds. "Well
now, boys, look at that cocky little rooster over there,
got his feathers all puffed up. He must be a squaw
man, for certain." Spreading his arms, he moved the
two men beside him away. "You listen here, boy. I

just finished washing up, and I ain't no mind to getting myself all dirtied up with a kid the likes of you, no siree. And your advice don't set well, either, and I sure ain't tucking my tail, so just where do you want me to mark you?''

Will, sensing the worst, let out another frantic plea. ''Dammit, Benji, come on! The man's daft, can't you see? He's egging you on, just trying to get your dander up!''

''Get the people out of the way,'' Ben said aside, his eyes keenly on Jed Bullock. ''I'm not calling this man, Will, but I'm not backing away or turning my back on him, either.'' And he addressed Bullock again. ''Mister, I'm ready to leave, but if you so much as make a move to that sidearm, I'm warning you fair and square, it will be a fatal mistake. I'm not so generous. I won't mark you, I'll kill you. Now, you and your friends ease off. Get back inside the gate, and we'll forget this whole matter.''

''Why, you ornery little Injun-loving shit, you!'' shouted Bullock. ''I'm going to bust your wing! Teach you a lesson!'' Suddenly his hand went down and grasped the handle of his revolver, but the weapon barely cleared the holster. One shot rang out, and Jed Bullock flew over backward from the impact of a lead ball ripping through his skull.

Horrified, the men to his side stared down, then looked helplessly out at Ben Tree. ''Jesus,'' one shouted, ''you kilt him, knocked him right dead!''

The girl's mother, screaming, flailing out with her arms, went running away toward the Tree cabin, and Will, shaking his head in futility, cursed, ''Dammit, I told you to come on! You *killed* the man! Now you've gone and got us in the duck soup, you surely have! Damnation, you could have got yourself all shot up, too!''

The children were standing around in hushed silence, gaping at the fallen Jed Bullock. Several troopers were running toward the gate to investigate the commotion.

Ben called over to one of the men kneeling over the body. "Whose fault, mister, mine or his?"

Shrugging, the man looked up and replied, "His, I reckon."

Jed Bullock, drifter, was buried the next morning in a pine box outside the fort, a small wooden marker with only his name and date of death placed over the hillside grave. As with most frontier deaths, it drew little attention in the white garrison, but the hang-around-the-fort Indians would remember, for they made such events a part of their legends—stories that would be retold time and again in differing versions around the night fires of their lodges. This young man called Tree, even though a breed, was one of their kind, and he would not be forgotten.

Ben himself was sorely distressed by the horrible incident. Taking another man's life, even a man so despicable, was not a matter easily dismissed. Guilt-stricken, he was well aware that his own selfish sensitivity had prompted the killing, not the woman's misfortune, and that much of it had been trivial, for such incidents were a common occurrence around the outposts. And so, as they prepared to leave on the third morning, Ben found himself still agonizing and cursing under his breath over the shooting.

Brother Will sympathetically gave Ben a pat on the back. "It wasn't your fault, you know. The man just didn't pay a bean to what you were trying to tell him, to get the hell out before the girl's kin put a knife to his gullet."

"I should have walked away," Ben lamented. "No matter what that man said, I should have walked away."

Will shrugged. "Well, you tried, anyway. Sometimes a fellow can take only so much. And hell, you were only defending yourself. You can always look at it that way, can't you?"

Thaddeus Tree, sorting out a singletree, interjected, "It's your damn pride, Benji. You're always letting it interfere with your better judgment. Have to take more time to think about these things . . . the consequences. Now, what the hell if that had been *you* lying in the dust instead of that buster? Good God, son, it scares the hell out of me just thinking about it. Gets right to my belly, it does."

"I'm sorry, Pa."

Thaddeus sighed mightily, and then he, too, rationalized. "Well, there's one less evil-doer on the prairie. I reckon I'll have to agree to that, anyways." But Thaddeus had another thought, one that he didn't disclose to either Ben or Will. A needless killing like this could very well be the beginning of a crooked trail for his son. Other such episodes might easily follow, because he well knew that frontier reputations only existed until they were buried. Jed Bullock's lonely marker on the distant hill attested to that.

Whatever, the three Tree men and the remaining muleskinners, Jethro Collins and Lucas and Wade Simms, were on the trail again, heading up the ruts along the North Platte River to faraway South Pass, the gateway down to Fort Bridger and the Utah and Idaho territories. They had merchandise to deliver, and with all the contingencies ahead of them—Indians, contrary weather, and possible breakdowns—the death of Jed Bullock soon faded from the conversation. His death wasn't forgotten, though—not by young Benjamin Tree.

Many days later, the men pulled up the train at the Big Sandy corrals to rest again and reshoe some of the mules. At this point, Ben Tree's freight work on the Oregon Trail for the season came to a sudden, excruciating end.

While helping the old redhead, Jethro Collins, hammer on a new shoe, one of the mules shied, lashed out with a hoof, and smashed Ben in the side of his lower right leg. He went down in a tumble of dust, and knew instantly that the bone had been broken. Jethro and Will carried him into the small cabin, where Thaddeus removed his son's boot and inspected the leg. Indeed the limb was broken, but fortunately it was not a severe break. Only Ben's heavy leather boot had saved him from worse damage, for though there was an ugly bruise and swelling, the skin was unbroken, and only a slight bend in the cracked leg was visible. But there was attending pain. Ben, sucking his breath, held tightly to the bunk rails as Will and Thaddeus straightened the limb and fashioned a sturdy splint.

With Ben packed in one of the freighters, they headed out that same afternoon for Fort Bridger, everyone praying for the best and hoping against the worse—infection. Ultimately they set up for three days at Gabe Bridger's old place, carefully watching Ben's progress. When the swelling finally went down, they headed out for Fort Hall, leaving Ben behind with post friends to recuperate.

July, 1856. Journal entry. Benjamin Tree.

It has been my good fortune to have old friends from the Crow visiting, and I decided to go north with them for some hunting until Father and Will make the return trip this fall. I left word that I will meet them at Big Sandy or Fort Laramie. Since my leg is healing, I cannot abide being idle in this land when there is so much to do with my brothers of the Absaroke, the great Bird People of the Yellowstone. My good friend, Two Moons

High, is what they call "carrying the pipe" with these
Crow. He is the leader, and a very good one, too.

I write this on the eastern side of South Pass. It
has been hot and windy, and we passed 38 whitetops and 50 or so pilgrims headed for the Oregon
country. Their stock was in poor shape. Pa could
have done some fancy trading with these people, for
they looked as tired as their mules and oxen. Domino Dominguez, guide. Domino said he saw no hostiles since the N. Platte but told me to watch my
hair up north, like as I didn't know my sense of
direction. The movers looked over my Indian brothers. They seemed happy enough when we cached
and rode out with a holler. I broke the back of an
antelope (100 paces standing) with the new Maynard. We packed him on and crossed the Popo Agie
ankle-deep and made camp this night on the Little
Wind. It's hilly country here. Two Moons High
speaks—one or two more days of riding to the summer village. I talk some but mostly I make sign. We
understand each other fine. I learn more each day
about their tongue, but it seems more troublesome
than the language of the Lakota. Mosquitoes are
thicker than buffalo gnats. We took quick baths and
feasted on antelope. My leg is holding, some little
pain when I dismount, but I have no bad complaints.
I am mending. Grass is good along the river and
creeks, burning in the hills. There is big thunder
north in the Big Horn mts. Maybe dry lightning,
maybe rain. The omens say rain. With the Bird People, it is always best to have faith in the omens.
B. Tree.

By early September, frost had come to the sacred
high country, and with it the shrill mating whistle of
the bull elk, the resounding clash of the ram's horn.
ancient autumnal preludes to the white winter ahead.

And in October, the Moon of the Changing Season, the wapiti deserted their mountain harems and the sheep idled. On the great plateau below, scattered bison herds began moving toward the long valley of the Yellowstone to feed on rich blue grama, wild wheat grass still greening in lush, protected plots around the foothill sage. To the Absaroke or Mountain Crow, who hunted from bear grass to blue stem, the Yellowstone was a land of magnificent contrasts, sometimes harsh but more often forgiving. This was the *Echeta Casha,* the land of The River of Yellow Stones, untrodden hills and coulees, the river a ribbon of alternating blue and green embraced by dun-colored bluffs and forested bottoms of golden aspen, alder, and cottonwood. To the south and west, the distant pine ridges of the Shining Mountains were already capped with new snow, which by the Moon of Falling Leaves would skiff across the lowlands and lace the tight-skin tipis.

Yet there was warmth in this beloved land, the welcome touch of *Masaka* a sunny gift by day. By evening, when the shadows grew long and a breath of air turned misty, the smoke of sixty fires began filtering from the winter lodges of Chief White Mouth, tracing wispy patterns across a hunter's moon. By dawn's rosy streaks, moccasin tracks along the water path to the Stillwater were frozen rigid and women had to break thin ice at the river's bank. This marked the beginning of the short days, Indian Summer.

White Mouth, greatest of the Mountain Crow chiefs, led his tribe down the lower Big Horn River and west to the traditional hunting grounds, and so it was on the fifth dawn of the new camp that the village crier called forth the scouts of the Big Dog society. With small ceremony from the buffalo holy man, the men rode three directions—west, north across the Yellowstone, and east toward the Clarks Fork—to locate the best of the bison herds. Another party, one solely of hunters, moved south into the blue mists of *Nah-Pit-Sie,* the bear's tooth, to make meat of deer and elk. Unlike the bison scouts, they were to hunt game and to kill at random, taking anything they chanced upon without the obligation of reporting back to the village council.

This fifth morning, Ben Tree, the tall, young Missourian and brother of the Crow, reined his blue mare, Sunday, westward with three of the Big Dog Crow scouts. His presence among the tribe was not so unusual. It was by choice, but also abetted by circumstances. Long before his time, when the fur trade had flourished, there had been innumerable men in buckskin in the mountain villages, renowned runners, long hunters, trappers, the likes of Jim Clyman, Tom Fitzpatrick, James Bridger, and the mulatto breeds, Jim Beckwourth and Edward Rose. Beckwourth and Rose had lived and stood shoulder to shoulder with some of these same Crow twenty years before in the Soldiers' Lodge, the place of chiefs and braves.

Somewhat akin to these stalwarts, Ben had first seen the frontier with eager, longing eyes. And even though many trails had been broken, much of the Northwest was still fresh, untarnished, a great, foreboding plain. The huge expanse of Oregon country remained stark and untamed, mysterious in its infinitely verdant color, its strange composites—terrible yet beautiful. Like the original trailbreakers, Ben Tree, ever since his childhood, had breathed in the West's beckoning challenge. All of the men before him had come willingly, thrived grudgingly, and most often, died violently. But they came, and continued to come, whatever the luring call; and although among the last, young Ben Tree was already making his own mark and standing.

The Crow scouts traveled twenty or more miles this day to the west bank of the Clarks Fork. Within this distance, they had spotted several bands of black-horns. But these herds were not big enough, at least not of sufficient number to warrant a hunt by the customary tribal surround. The hunt, they decided, would have to be elsewhere, where the animals were closer and more plentiful, so the scouts turned away, reined west, and finally stopped in the lower foothills overlooking the big river, the Yellowstone. It was late afternoon, the autumn air clean and sharp, fragrantly fresh, and the visibility stretching to infinity. They paused and scanned their familiar surroundings. Stationary shadows became black against a rose horizon, but the vast land of the Bird People, as empty as it seemed, was far from deserted.

The small cloud of dust coming from the east—more than a mile off—was first observed by Two Moons High, eldest son of the chief, White Mouth. Alert but not alarmed, he cautiously edged his horse back toward the others. Despite the many hundreds of miles of Mother Earth between the Three Forks and the lands of the Lakota or Sioux to the east, during the months-of-making-meat other villages and riders were only two or three days distant. To the cautious Crow, these neighbors often proved to be unfriendly. The Great White Father's treaties of 1851 and 1855 had marked and divided only some of the land of the warlike tribes.

Tribal peace was elusive, as the land was vast and caution a way of life. Nomadic Blackfeet ranged down from the north, the Lakota and Cheyenne from the east beyond the Rosebud, Tongue, and Powder Rivers. From the south, across the Shining Mountains, the Shoshoni often came. Though all sought the big "curly cow," none was beyond the game of counting coup, even during this relatively peaceful but vigorous period of hunting and laying in stores of meat before Cold Maker appeared in the valleys. Now the noble Blackfeet and Piegan had made the game even more deadly, ruling much of the open land between the *Ech-*

eta Casha and the Musselshell, and all of it to the north of the great Missouri, the River Who Scorns All Other Rivers. With regularity, these people played the coup game, neither Indian nor interloping white man being exempt from the contest.

Two Moons High pulled up to the other two braves, Sound of the Wind and Antelope Runs, and beckoned Man Called Tree. After a short consultation, they headed downriver for protective cover, behind a knoll where they picketed their horses. Climbing the small hill, the scouts flattened themselves in the sage and scrub juniper to watch the approaching dust. Five minutes passed before the moving cloud materialized into a sizable herd of horses and finally, the shadows of men. For a short time, the hazy film of dust obscured the identity of the riders. It was not until the procession moved on below them into the forest bottom and approached the river itself that Two Moons suddenly made the sign of six braves. He quickly touched a lock of his own black hair and pointed to his moccasin. These men were Blackfeet, he gestured. Clenching his fist, he made the motion of throwing to the ground—bad.

Ben immediately understood. To the Crow, the Blackfeet were notorious thieves and warriors, one of the most feared tribes in the river country. Their fame for cunning, bravery, and daring, and their bitter hatred for white trespassers, were known as far south as the old trapper outposts of Fort Laramie and Fort Bent. Shielding his blue eyes against the slant of the sun, Ben Tree watched curiously. He began to sense the excitement and alarm of his companions. Practically reading their minds, he knew they were anxious to make a dangerous game of it, a raid on the Blackfeet stock. Admittedly it was a tempting sight, all of those horses stringing out below, now heading for water. Ben Tree understood, because, after all, it was a game in which the Crow excelled. They were proudly counted among the best horse thieves on the plains. And he could see that these horses were sleek and hardy, at least forty head, including two fine stallions. Ben unconsciously wet his lips in anticipation, his sharp, flinty eyes narrowing. Several of the Blackfeet riders dismounted upstream and took water themselves. Undoubtedly, they were returning from a pony raid, perhaps somewhere along the lower Big Horn or Tongue—Cheyenne country. And the Blackfeet, the first Ben had ever seen, now were only several nights' ride away from Big Coulee on the Musselshell. A hunting village there had been reported earlier by the Crow scouts who always preceded White Mouth's autumn arrival on the Yellowstone.

Two Moons was speaking again, making sign, and talking slowly for Tree's benefit. He had twice counted coup against the Dakota, but never against the Blackfeet. In the great war of 1846, ten years before, Two Moons had been only fourteen, but his people had slain many Blackfeet warriors and captured one hundred and eighty prisoners, mostly women and children. He had been too young to fight or raid. But now! He continued to talk and flash signs, confirming much of what Tree already knew.

"They're looking for the *Echeta Casha* crossing," Two Moons said. "Cheyenne ponies. The Cheyenne have plenty of fine ponies, but these are tired from running. The braves are tired from riding."

Everyone nodded; everyone anticipated; there was not a thread of doubt in Ben's mind, and he knew it was only a matter of how, when, and where this pony raid would develop.

Antelope Runs, crisp excitement in his voice, said, "There must be a way!" Only nineteen, he was the youngest of the four, and with only a few honors, for he had never killed an enemy as Two Moons High had done. But Antelope Runs had good reason to count coup on the Blackfeet. He had lost a brother to them, and his mother had cried out in anguish, slashing herself, moaning for revenge. "I would like some of those ponies," he said. "I would like a scalp, but we have only two rifles among us." He nodded at the Hawken muzzle-loader beside Two Moons High, then at the long, burnished weapon held by Tree, a new Maynard breech-loader, envied by all of the Absaroke who had watched their white brother use it. A recent gift from Ben's Uncle Jediah in St. Louis, it spoke loudly, reached out to kill like prairie lightning. Tree also owned a Navy six Colt revolver, but because he was short of loads, he had reluctantly left it in camp that morning. And now, as he instinctively moved his right hand to his empty side, a motion he was learning to perfect, a sudden feeling of misgiving swept through him.

Two Moons spoke again, "Listen, my brothers, there is a way. We shall ride behind the hills. Our horses are not tired from running. We shall wait for the Blackfeet on the river crossing." He smiled at Antelope Runs. "Ei, you may get your ponies this very night, my friend. The sun will be low in the trees, shining in their eyes. We can attack them on the river." Then, glancing over at Tree, Two Moons said, "Are you with us, brother? How do you ride?" He motioned to Tree's damaged leg.

Ben awkwardly hesitated, searching for a ready answer. He barely knew the Crow language and it was difficult, his sentences haltingly simple like the utterings of a toddler. What he often understood he could not return in kind, his tongue turning to a wooden spoon when he strained for the usual inflections. "Good, friend," he finally said with an accompanying gesture. "I'll ride with you."

Though he claimed to be bodily sound, Ben's occasional limp had been all too obvious. From the very beginning at Big Sandy, Two Moons had seen this, and had understood. And Ben Tree never complained, since that would have been against his medicine, not the Crow way. It was beneath the true mettle of a good brave to grouse, particularly of pain; that much of his mother's Osage blood he had retained, and these good friends now in his company respected and honored him. He was a brother, a human being, and they called him Man Called Tree, making his sign, a left hand to the side, fingers moving upward, branches growing to the sun, a good sign. It was precisely because of this kindredship that Ben now found himself on this brushy bluff, the pungent fragrance of sage filling his nostrils, staring down at six unsuspecting Blackfeet and a band of stolen Cheyenne ponies. His idea to return to meet his father and brother ahead of the snows was beginning to go awry; he was dawdling; he was enjoying; he didn't want this glorious retreat with his Crow brothers to end. Before the night spent itself, his plans to move south would scatter like dry seeds in the winter wind.

Two Moons was speaking. "It is good, Tree. When we return to the village, we'll dance. Ei, you shall dance with us and wear wolf tails on your moccasins. What does your medicine say?"

Ben had no medicine, no pouch around his neck, and he was wearing boots, not moccasins, but he understood: his Crow brother wanted to attack the Blackfeet somewhere below, probably at dusk, confuse them, and chase off as many ponies as they could. If they could put one or two Blackfeet in the dust, that would be good, too. Smiling at his three companions, Ben made a quick sign, forking two fingers and plunging another between them. *Yes, strike!* Such a coup would rate the wearing of wolf tails on his boots, a great honor.

Two Moons motioned them back to their ponies.
Antelope Runs emitted a small, gleeful shout as he
broke into a trot. *"Hai-yah!"* Perhaps if he was lucky,
if his own medicine was strong, he could wear ermine
skins on his shirt, the mark of a gun-snatcher, for he
owned no rifle and most of the Blackfeet did. If his
medicine held, he might even snatch a scalp.

Sound of the Wind, a renowned rider among his
people, shared his friend's optimism, for the attack
would be swift and sure. The enemy would be too
tired to retaliate, their bottoms sore, warriors and ponies alike, weary from trailing across the prairie. And
in the dusk, a chase would be futile. After all, who
stole horses better than the Absaroke?

At a gallop, the four riders snaked back into the
piney hills, winding up gulches and cresting a distant
saddle fringed with spruce. They came down through
the yellowing groves of hillside aspen, their long, circuitous route taking them close to Point of Rocks
crossing. Here, below a deep greenish pool, the Yellowstone suddenly widened to shallow white water,
baring its shiny teeth of riffle-worn rocks. At this ancient crossing, only the strongest arm could speed an
arrow to the opposite shore, and the banks were heavily pocked by the hooves of many animals.

By now, it was near dusk. Two Moons High quickly
chose their cover: a stand of cottonwood and willow
on the south bank of the river, only a small distance
from where animals usually entered the water. After
each man had taken his position, they grasped the nervous noses of their mounts and held them closely, to
keep the ponies from whinnying at the approaching
Blackfeet stock.

As Two Moons had anticipated, the enemy soon hove
into sight, barely visible in the evening light but making directly for the crossing. Two riders were in the
lead. They easily could have been shot outright, but

that would have spoiled the plan. Instead the Crow let them pass, the Blackfeet braves taking the first ponies into the river with them. Only after the leaders were well into the water would the Crow attack, split the band, and overrun the trailing herdsmen, swiftly and surely as Sound of the Wind had predicted. And moments later, at the signal of Two Moons, the scouts set up their terrible outcry and tremolo. Charging from the trees, they plunged directly into the horses trailing at the river's edge. Confusion erupted on both sides. The Cheyenne ponies already in the river panicked and bolted ahead, pushing the two surprised Blackfeet riders ahead of them, while on the shore the remainder of the herd immediately began bolting back to high ground, galloping, snorting, kicking up their heels. Two shots rent the air, and almost simultaneously two of the Blackfeet at the rear went down the rocky bank.

With a chilling yell of triumph, Antelope Runs forged ahead to safety, driving horses ahead of him, and Two Moons followed. But from behind, one of the downed Blackfeet managed to fire a ball, sending the black pony of Sound of the Wind stumbling to the ground. Unhurt, the young scout scrambled to the side, away from flying hooves. Of the remaining Blackfeet still mounted, one cried out and made a charge. Brandishing his rifle, he galloped headlong toward Ben, who had barely finished tamping a second round into the breech of the Maynard. Swinging his barrel in a cutting arc, Ben dismounted the warrior with a crunching blow alongside his head; then, turning about, he raced back until he had caught the reins of the escaping horse. Sound of the Wind was waiting for the new mount. Within four or five bounds he was riding again, kicking away to join the others.

Ben suddenly discovered that he was alone. Unlike his companions, he had forgotten the credo: Strike and run. He heard a shot to his left, the whine of a ball through the trees. One of the Blackfeet across the river had opened up on him, and he saw another brave trying to remount near the bank. Even so, for some inexplicable reason, he was compelled to rein up over the prostrate form of the man he had just unseated. Dazed and bleeding, the warrior was trying to pull himself out of the rocks and mud. He finally managed to raise himself up on one arm and stare defiantly at Ben Tree, clearly unafraid of the ultimate coup he sensed was coming. Blood was streaming down his dark face where the blow of the rifle had crushed his cheekbone.

The eyes of the two strangers met briefly, and time stopped on the Yellowstone. Tree's rifle was firmly cushioned against his shoulder, the muzzle pointed directly at the Blackfeet's chest, but, strangely, he could not pull the trigger. In that deathly moment he never had time to reason why, for this was a game of no rules, no room for quarter or mercy. Yet he did not fire. His face was emotionless, revealing no hint of pity or satisfaction and absolutely void of anger. Finally the warrior below him cried out and thumped his chest, defiant, brave, fully prepared to die.

Time's pendulum swung again, and Ben Tree lunged forward, touching only the brave's shoulder with his barrel tip. And then, abruptly wheeling about, the young white scout rode away. It was coup enough, the enemy downed, defeated, dishonored. At the hands of another it would have been a senseless murder, the ultimate coup—but one without reason, too much for a white man like Ben to accept. The drama, the excitement of the victory charged Ben like a bolt from the sky, and he let out his cry, victorious, boisterous, piercing the evening air. He was away, Sunday's ears back, hooves flying.

Ben's dynamic exhilaration, however, was short-lived, and those waning moments of merciful hesitation cost him dearly. The telltale swish, the speeding shaft! It came so swiftly, winging home, bursting into his left hip, a streaking arrow, shaking him in the saddle, stringing him with the pain of a hundred bald hornets, sucking the very wind from his lungs. There was another sensation—instinctive reaction. His heels dug sharply into the flank of the blue mare, sending her madly in pursuit of the horses ahead.

The shouts of the Blackfeet behind him were still echoing in the heavy cottonwood bottom when Ben caught up with the trailing ponies. In pain, he followed the fleeing Crow party at a steady, unrelenting pace. They rode hard southeast, away from their own village on the Stillwater, unaware that their breed brother had been hit; but the arrow was a suffering plague, an agonizing, gnawing rat in Ben's side.

The raiders finally rode into a grassy foothill coulee, at least three miles from the encounter. There had been no pursuit, nor had the Crow expected any. Back on the river the Blackfeet were badly hurt, licking their wounds—two dead, another wounded, and with twenty spooked horses to round up. This was a victory for the Crow buffalo scouts. Two Moons High voiced the sentiments of his joyous companions: The Blackfeet had lost their war medicine. Fearing no immediate reprisal, he began exulting in the success of the impromptu raid, the great accomplishments of each man. True, there were no scalps, but that was no great matter. A scalp was a minor token, anyhow. Coup had been counted, the enemy slain and humiliated, twenty-two horses captured—certainly a worthy endeavor, one in which they all could take great pride. And once they returned to the village, his father's people would go wild!

Swept by excruciating pain, Ben Tree was less enthusiastic. He listened but he could barely speak. After the first several hundred yards of riding in sheer agony, he had had to grasp the embedded shaft and break it near the point of entry. After a while the initial sting diminished to a dull, sickening throb, and with each stride of the blue mare blood had continued to seep from his hip down his thigh, saturating his legging and the woolen underwear beneath. Only now, as he slumped forward to relieve the weight on his aching hip, were his companions finally aware that he had been struck. They stopped rejoicing. Antelope Runs saw the protruding end of the broken shaft.

"*Hai-yah,* our brother is wounded!" he called, addressing the others.

Ben pretended to laugh, a brave but feeble gesture. When he eased over onto his side the pain lessened, but now a cutting chill came over him. The crisp evening air penetrated the sweaty dampness of his buckskin shirt, and he shook like a whipped dog. "The wound isn't bad," he said haltingly, almost in apology. "I'm cold . . . plenty cold. Bring me my blanket."

Antelope Runs responded, jerking the rolled blanket from behind the saddle of the mare while Two Moons hurried over to examine the wound. By dark he could see little, only the oily slick of blood oozing from the base of the broken arrow. It was bad enough. He grunted once, and shaking his head, he said, "The bleeding must be stopped, my brother." Turning to Sound of the Wind, he told him to strike a fire for warmth. They would rest for a while and tend the wound of Man Called Tree. He ordered Antelope Runs to picket their own horses in the middle of the Cheyenne ponies and then find firewood.

Meanwhile, Ben quietly protested again. That much delay wasn't necessary. He only needed time to catch his breath, tie a bandage. "I can ride, by jingo," he said in gestures and broken words. "Don't worry about me. We can move on."

But Two Moons High was emphatic. "We rest! When the bleeding is stopped, we shall see." By his senior rank, he carried the pipe; he had made the decision. Soon afterward, by the light of the small fire, he took chokecherry root from his small parfleche, made gum and dust to put in the wound, and bound it. He left the arrow embedded. His opinion—the point was resting near the bone. Once back in the village, it could be properly removed by the tribal doctor, old Buffalo Horn, the highest-ranking medicine man who had strong medicine for such wounds. Two Moons felt his own medicine was not powerful enough to remove bullets or arrows. Nevertheless his field treatment was adequate, and the bleeding soon stopped.

The four men ate a small meal of dried fruit and antelope jerky. Ben had several hard biscuits, and he shared them. They finally lit one pipe and smoked, again recounting the fight at the crossing, each giving his own particular version. Ben began to feel somewhat better. His shirt was dry, his body warm, and he no longer perspired. That was a good sign. Replenishing the fire, the scouts dozed until near midnight when the heavens were brightest, then, remounting, they pulled their blankets about them, and under the light of a cold moon they rode slowly back toward the river bottom trail, pushing their new herd ahead of them.

Dawn came as slowly as the four scouts rode, with the heavy wing beat of an eagle; first the faint dusting of powder-gray, then the blossoming streaks of orchid, and finally the gold. And when the first full touch of *Masaka*'s hand cast frosty shadows in the bunch grass, the scouts paused again to rest, to prepare for the *aratsiwe,* the homecoming. They had kept charcoal from the night fire and each streaked his face, indicating that the party had killed the enemy. Sound of the Wind was dispatched as herald to advise the crier. Two hours after the rising sun, they heard drums pounding in the

valley ahead. Filled with elation, they raced their
horses through the village to the accompanying tremolo of the welcoming women. The village greeting was
enough to warm the heart of any returning brave, and
the long chill of the night was soon dissipated in the
fervor and excitement of the *arat-siwe*. Drum skins
reverberated over the chants, and as the celebration
fire grew bigger, an eagle-bone whistle pierced the air.
Young women danced, old women screamed, and dogs
sat on their haunches and howled. The blue smoke of
victory seeped through the rustling cottonwoods along
the Stillwater.

Ben Tree's exploits—killing one Blackfeet, dismounting another, counting coup on him and taking
his pony, and perhaps even saving the life of Sound of
the Wind—brought immediate accolades of honor, not
the least of which was swift attention and care. This,
he appreciated. In pain, but still refusing to complain,
Ben was too miserable to enjoy the kudos—the lengthy
orations—or to stay at the kill-dance and celebration.
His body ached. By now, stiffness had set into his hip.
His brothers assisted him to the third tipi of Two
Moons High's family, where he fell into a deep bed of
robes and slept fitfully, drums vibrating in his ears.

Later, women came to attend him: White Beaver,
wife of Two Moons; old Willow Sings, the young
brave's mother-in-law; and a younger sister of Two
Moons named Little Hoop. They brought broth made
of wild turnips, herbs, and prairie chicken, then fed
him elk liver to help replenish the blood he had lost.
This meat was rare, unseasoned, and not especially to
his liking, but he devoured it, leaving nothing to save
for his pouch. They washed the stain from his woolens
and brought warm water scented with herbs, and he
bathed as best he could. He washed away the smell of
horse, sweat, and blood, finally dressing anew in fresh
buckskin that the women had left him. They came

again to mind his fire until it was time for the medicine of Buffalo Horn.

As much as Ben dreaded the painful ordeal, he realized that he had to submit to the old man's medicine. It could not be otherwise. To offend the shaman would be bad medicine in itself, and a loss of face for the old Crow chief, who also was a renowned spiritual leader and seer. Ben had to rationalize: Of course, the arrow point had to come out. It might as well be now. He might not be as lucky as others. He remembered Gabe Bridger and *his* old hip wound, and how the old man had complained for years of the misery of an embedded arrowhead in his upper thigh. Gabe always had luck—his blood had not poisoned. And one day the Protestant missionary, Dr. Marcus Whitman, came along heading west, and he sliced the imbedded point out.

Ben felt a trickle of sweat on his temple. This Buffalo Horn, on the other hand, was certainly no Dr. Whitman. A troubled thought, there, yet the shaman's treatment could not possibly by any worse than that of Ben's father and brother, when they had pulled and tugged to set his broken leg bone. That had been pain, pure hell, without the benefit of spirits. He knew pain, and that much of it he would accept without outcry. He could do it. What he secretly feared, from witnessing the ugly experiences of other such unfortunates, was infection, blood poisoning, and a slow, miserable death. And there was that matter of his faith, somewhat shaky at the moment.

The old man finally came, a grizzled chief, a shaman of great power who remembered Beckwourth's days with the Crow long before. He had performed the wound ritual many times. Ben eyed Buffalo Horn suspiciously, for the Crow's ancient face was painted frightfully with gray clay. He wore a buffalo robe over his bent body and carried the tail of a bison decorated with red and white plumes. Chanting and dancing, he first dusted the floor, and after ordering that no dogs cross the front of the tipi to spoil his medicine, he dismissed everyone. Ben prepared himself for the worst. Buffalo Horn prayed and made another chant before removing the crusted bandage. The wounded thigh had swollen like a wet sponge, a fearful sight to Ben, but the medicine man quickly cleansed the damaged area with warm water. Then from his sacred medicine pouch he took out a sharp, hook-shaped awl. In one deft move, he traced it along the broken shaft to the point of the arrowhead. Tree wanted to scream. Moments later, the old man withdrew the awl and point simultaneously, blood flowing as freely as the cold sweat on Ben's brow, and a great dizziness swept over him. His stomach revolted, but by the time he had found his breath the medicine man was already lacing the puncture together with sinew. Soon Buffalo Horn began dusting the suture with a mixture of medicinals smelling strongly of camphor and the familiar chokecherry.

Ben's voice was hoarse. With sign and broken sentences, he told Buffalo Horn that his own vision had given him powerful medicine, too. In fact he had some in a small bottle, and he sure thought a dash of it might help his wound.

Without comment, the chief listened and continued to compress and work at the wounded hip. But Ben persisted, pointing to his parfleche, trying to convince the old man. Hidden there, he said, were two vials wrapped in wool cloth, one castoreum, the magic for trapping, the other a potion to purify the body, alcohol.

"Take some of that white water," Tree said. "Place it here." He nodded at the jagged edge of flesh.

Buffalo Horn pressed, tightening the stitch of sinew. Finally he muttered, "Ei, why should I do that?"

"By jingo," Tree groaned haltingly, "it will make your medicine even stronger. Look here, old man, you'll be honored among your people. Medicine, the white man's medicine, is strong." He placed two forked fingers to his forehead and moved them upward in a spiraling motion. "Medicine. It's good."

Unimpressed, wise in his many years, Buffalo Horn smiled faintly. "I am already honored by my people. You have much to learn, my son. The white man's medicine may be strong, but that doesn't always make it good. This, I have seen. Hear me, I am old. My eyes are dim, but I have learned."

"Ei," grunted Ben fatefully. Futility had clubbed him between the eyes. He fell back exhausted, discouraged.

"The earth is our mother," Buffalo Horn continued. "It is so. She gives us life, the healing of her plants. When we are wounded we go to Mother Earth and lay our wounded parts against her. We pray to the Spirit Father to guide us and help the healing. This is the way it has always been. Is that not enough, young brother?"

Ben emitted a sick sigh of frustration. He shifted in the robes and closed his salty eyes. Superstition would prevail. One more try: "Look, old wise one, sometimes faith can kill a man."

Buffalo Horn gave him a toothless grin. "Don't worry, you will heal. My medicine has removed lead balls. Ei, the white man believes our ways are strange. That is because he doesn't understand. We are 'savages' because our ways are not their ways. Listen, my son, I am not foolish. Hear me. Across the rivers I have heard legends, the legends of how their medicine has brought sickness and sorrow to our brothers. This is not my way."

Ben spoke and motioned. "Among all people there

are good and bad, my friend. Along with virtue, there is vice.''

Buffalo Horn understood what his young brother was saying and partially agreed. He began to apply the final compress, quickly binding it with leather strips. Finally: ''What you say is true—there are good men among your people. Ei, but do they bear a proportion to the bad? The white man has hungry eyes. I have seen this. He would feast upon all that he sees. I hear of those who come to profit, those who come into our land to sell whiskey. I hear of those who come to mark and divide the land created by the Great Spirit. I have seen the blackrobes, and the longknives, too. Trouble follows them like flies in the summer. Hear my warning and remember. I hear voices, more and more. My dreams have been bad. It is not good, my brother.''

Their eyes met and held. Ben said curiously, ''Tell me, what do your dreams say about me?''

The medicine priest reached out and touched Ben's damp forehead. There was a quality of tenderness, understanding, in the old man's voice. ''You will be well,'' he intoned. ''You will be strong, powerful, like a tree with many branches, and as each moon passes, you will speak like one of us. But it is better that you die young, because with each passing sun you will come to know death a thousand times. Ei, no more do I trust the white man's medicine. Someday, you will learn about what I speak.''

Buffalo Horn began a chant: ''Hey-yah, yah, yah, hey-yah, yah, yah.'' Then, bending low, and taking sign from the medicine wheel, he blew a mystical four times upon the bandage, picked up his sacred bundle, and left. Moments later, Tree hiked himself erect and looked around. He was alone. He quickly sneaked out his small bottle of alcohol, and lifting the bandage, saturated the suture with burning alcohol. Rolling on his bed in horrendous pain, he cursed. Hello, agony, and to hell with superstition!

Under his robes that night, he listened as the drums began to throb once more, a different sound, a different chant, an appeal to *Magah-hawathus*, the supreme one man. This was another occasion; for the hunter Crow needed guidance, the mysterious Spirit Chief's hand in the upcoming buffalo hunt. The hunters were leaving at dawn, most of the able men, many of their women. All afternoon, they had made their preparation. The tribe had found a herd to the west, near a place called the Gray Cliffs where the trees met the water.

Tree knew of this magnificent spot but he was not going to see it, nor would he take a place on the flank of hunters, waiting for the given sign to ride in close on the surround and make his kills. This hunt was a dead bird for him. He knew other things, too, disturbing in their consequences: that he probably would not be able to ride comfortably for weeks, that he was plain cached in, hobbled up like a lame pony. Blizzard winds would soon be sweeping the Powder and Wind rivers, drifting in the passages south. It was a worry he couldn't control. In the past, he had fought Arapaho and Pawnee raiders along the Platte, had supped with the Sioux north of Laramie, and had smoked many time with the Crow. But this was a new experience, one he had not counted on. He had never spent the long white months with Indians. For a time, his father and brother would wait for him at Fort Bridger, and he would not come. Until someone got a message through, their worry would become his.

As the night deepened the village noise lessened, subsiding to a quiet shuffling of moccasins, the unmistakable tread of the old women, the faithful ones, who were making the last rounds—grumbling, scolding dogs, banking fires, securing the stays at the tipis.

Since they owned the skin lodges, it was their manner and privilege to be quarrelsome and fussy. Order was maintained. Old Willow Sings was no exception. Returning to her place by the door, she began to prepare her sleeping robes. She spoke harshly to Little Hoop, who always slept nearby, and the young daughter of White Mouth (by his second wife) left. She returned shortly with a shinny stick, this to serve as Tree's cane. After she put it near his side, she attended the fire and went back to her own bed.

In continued distress, Ben tried to find comfort, repeatedly running his hand across his hip, nervously testing the heat around the bandaged area. It remained constant, the small fever there, but the ache slowly diminished. That was good, he thought. And there was no trace of bleeding. Watching the shadows of the fire play against the slope of the lodge, he began to rationalize again. After all, his situation was not so bad. Eventually he would mend, be well enough to work, to hunt, maybe even to trap, and until then he had good shelter and food. After the hunt there would be plenty of meat. Furthermore, counting the two horses he had brought from Fort Bridger, and his share from the raid, he now owned a total of eight, so he was not destitute. He still had about fifty dollars in gold coin in his pouch, too. Considering all, his plight might have been much worse. That arrow, for instance—had it hit several inches higher, likely it could have pierced his body plumb through and killed him.

Despite misfortune, he had some thanks to give. He would pray to God. And when able, he planned to share a little of his better luck with Buffalo Horn, presenting the superstitious old buzzard with two Cheyenne ponies for his medicine, however strong it might or might not prove to be.

October, 1856.

I was on a scouting party yesterday that turned into a small ruckus. We found buffalo to the east, but not herding like the Crow wanted. Heading to camp, we came on some Blackfeet raiders and captured 22 ponies. Made coup on three of their party and ended up bedding in the brush. Arrived back safely sore as billy hell, with an arrow in my rump. I'm patched up by an old chief called Buffalo Horn. He is a funny old man who told me off good on his line of thinking. I feel no worse than snake bite, but must forgo the big hunt. It's a bad deal for me. I'm cached here and might miss connections with Pa and Will. The word flies. They will know soon enough. Might be nigh three weeks before I can sit a saddle. My friend Two Moons High makes jokes—"Running man always gets caught in bottom." It's a sore joke this time. They have moved me into a big tipi and two squaws are looking to my ailing, White Mouth's kin. It's turning colder. There's early snow in the high Rock mts. and it looks like it's getting close to the valley. The fire feels good this night. B. Tree.

TWO

Once again dawn came cold and clear, gray mist on the river. Hoarfrost hugged the boughs, and tarnished autumn leaves hung motionless. Tree stirred at the first sounds of the morning. The village crier was now calling out the events of the new day, admonishing those who tarried in their tipis. Now it is dawn, the crier intoned, time to send off the bison hunters, time for others to gather wood, to build up the fires. He urged the sleepy Absaroke to brave the frigid water of the Stillwater and refresh their blood.

To Ben Tree, weary, stiff, too indisposed to move, the idea of a mountain bath in late October sounded like nothing more than an invitation to the chilblains. He cringed and shuddered beneath his robes. It was true—water thinned the blood. It healed the body. But in the short days, only a few hardy souls heeded the crier's chilly challenge. Like Ben, most of the villagers with less valor cleansed themselves when the opportunity afforded, but discreetly, within the warm confines of their lodges. Snug and comfortable, they stayed warm and listened to the brave ones outside screaming and sucking wind along the frosty banks.

By the time he hobbled outside on his stick, the hue and cry for the departing hunters had ended, and he discovered the village half-deserted, women ambling about, picking up the routine, children and dogs already at play. His hip terribly sore, he could not walk any great distance, so he kept close to the lodge, and when *Masaka* warmed the crisp earth he found more pleasant comfort on a buffalo robe, where he basked and dozed most of the day.

By the second morning, he felt only a small twitch of pain where the torn muscle had begun to knit. He ate well, too, thanks to his attending women. The disposition of the old one, Willow Sings, had warmed, and heartened Ben Tree. What little suspicion she once had had about caring for a white man seemed to have disappeared. She cooked and he praised her, bringing forth from her wrinkled face the smile of a picket fence. But she watched with raised brows when he traded smiles with Little Hoop, the daughter of Chief White Mouth. The young woman served Ben honey and flat cakes, and a bowl of stewed, dried fruit.

It was difficult to avoid the chief's daughter, particularly in such close confines, and to say that he hadn't noticed the girl would have been an outright lie. She had been in his sight before, right down to the very manner of her dress. She usually wore bleached buckskin. Her fancy dress of elkskin was beaded and fringed, a beautiful piece of clothing. He had seen this, too. In the summer she wore bright cloth of red and blue, and she was always somewhere close by, moving, flitting about like a butterfly. Now in her sixteenth winter, Little Hoop was slender as a red willow, and blessed with fine features. No doubt the young bucks watched her, too, and although Ben had already discovered that most Crow maidens were generous and loving, it was no great surprise that Little Hoop had neglected to take a husband or lover. After all, she was a daughter of White Mouth, a sister of Two Moons High, the member of an honored family. Though still young, she could afford to be selective, for her dowry would be expensive—only a few aspiring braves would be able to afford the rich gifts required for a permanent attachment.

As a guest, Ben Tree was not about to create any problems between himself and the family of White Mouth. He remained steadfast. Even though he suspected that she might play in the bushes, his discretionary reluctance prevailed—this, despite the surreptitious invitation lurking in her dark eyes.

On the second afternoon, Ben went to find his newly acquired ponies. He located them in a compound separate from the Crow herd, grazing on wild hay brought by the attending boys. For several days the horse guard would watch the Cheyenne ponies for signs of disease, distemper, or the strangles, anything of an infectious nature. To Ben the captured horses looked sound enough, fat in their bellies from the long summer range beyond the Greasy Grass. His brand, the mark of a forked tree, already had been painted on the flanks of six, including the one he had seized during the fight, a brown-and-white pinto gelding.

His mark was also on a young white stallion that he offhandedly judged to be no more than a three- or four-year-old. This particular pony immediately took his keen eye, and he had two of the boys single it out with a rawhide. The stallion came easily, its head handsomely high, ears pricked, an alert gray-eyed stare about it. Its nervous nose was covered with the first traces of winter hair. Obviously the horse had been broken to ride, for Ben quickly spotted the slight callus at the back of the pony's lower jaw.

Putting his staff aside, he came close to the horse.

With a critical eye he examined its body—the sturdy, well-proportioned flanks, up across its back to the lank but solid neck, down the withers to its trim fetlocks. Someone had taken good care of the young stud. It was a prize. It had all the marks of a chief's horse, one destined for a future. Even its hooves had been manicured and painted, as though readied for shodding, and for an Indian pony that seemed odd.

One of the boys said, "He's a good pony, plenty strong. What will you call him?"

Ben smiled and walked around the stallion. Looking down at the young boy, he gestured with open hands. "I don't know, friend. I suppose he *should* have a name, all right. What do *you* think?"

Admiration in his voice, the boy said, "This pony is white like snow. He will bring plenty of blankets."

Ben nodded. "Shall we call him Snow? How's that sound to you?"

With a small frown, the boy shook his head. "That alone isn't good enough. It's like the name of a girl. This man-pony is like a warrior, a war pony. See, how he looks? *Hai-yah,* he has the eye of a hawk, the way he watches us."

"Yes, you're right," Ben agreed. "Well, what do you think? Will he fly like a hawk?"

"I think he will be swift as the wind."

And for a moment, Tree pondered. Beyond finding a name, he was thinking ahead. He knew horse flesh, the blood of good stock. Bred to Sunday, his blue mare, this young stallion could father a handsome foal. He patted the neck of the horse, then squatted down beside the boy who held the lariat. Ben spoke slowly, hesitantly. "He is white. For that, we will call him Snow. And he is swift. For that, we will call him Hawk. His name will be Snow Hawk."

The boy smiled approvingly and nodded in assent. "Snow Hawk. *Hai-yah,* Snow Hawk! That is good."

Ben pointed to two of the other horses, both bays, and told the two youngsters to take them to the lodge of Buffalo Horn so that the medicine man would know that they were now his, a gift from Man Called Tree. He said to the boys, "The old man's medicine is strong, and he's seen the tracks of my moccasins this day. I'm well enough, all right . . . almost."

Another moon passed and the Indian summer lingered gloriously into early November, the Moon of the Falling Leaves. To the Bird People of White Mouth's village, the delay of Cold Maker was a blessed benevolence. Ben Tree wrote in his journal almost daily. These were good times for his brother Crow. Mother Earth had been bountiful, the Four Winds kind, enabling the villagers to make meat from sunrise until sunset. But Ben, still burdened by his handicap, found himself sitting by and glumly watching all the excitement.

The hunters hunted, and they killed. They burdened their sturdy pack ponies and travois with slain buffalo and robes. Women worked until dusk stretching and bundling hides and preparing meat, and nothing was wasted, neither bone nor sinew. By the morning sun, long strips of butchered buffalo were drying on the racks. Some of the meat was smoked, preserved, packed, and then there was the Crow staple, pemmican, made from the mash of berries and dried fruits, ingredients that the tribe had brought north with them. When the time of Ice-on-the-River came, the fresh meat could then be hung, suspended from the lodge pole tripods and kept indefinitely. Buffalo Horn predicted this would be soon, for he was making medicine daily and reading the omens. Winter was near.

The Crow, making haste, moved and worked around the crippled Man Called Tree. His idle existence displeased him. Unable to ride well, by day Ben jealously watched the hunters come and go, by night, heard their stories. He became restless. To alleviate boredom he began to walk, to exercise and test the mending muscles in his hip. Because he knew horses, he visited the compounds or walked to the distant pasture to single out and treat the lame ones, and because his eyes were as keen as a prairie hawk's, he occasionally joined the wolf lookouts on the camp perimeter, his senses alive for the unusual—movement on the horizon, a suspicious shadow in the brush, or the sudden turn of a rock, any of which might be a provisional death warning from Blackfeet or Piegan across the Yellowstone.

The eyes of Little Hoop were always following him, observing with the alert silence of an owl, and one morning as he was resting and making entries in his journal, she paused, once again fascinated by the tracks he always made on the paper. This was the morning he discarded the shinny stick. He gave it to her in front of the tipi where he sat writing. He was strong enough to travel, he explained. He wanted no more of the cane. And then he jokingly added that perhaps she might have need of the stick again for the girls' games.

She accepted his gentle jest, but without her usual retreat, the evasive eye. Instead, for the first time she tarried. Smiling back, she replied somewhat shyly, "Tree knows Little Hoop no longer plays the games of girls. His eyes tell me that I'm not a girl."

Mildly surprised, he set aside the journal. Her smart little reply disarmed him. Of coursed she was no longer a girl, nor had she been acting like one lately, either. She was flirtatious; she was intelligently alert, and oh, was she a pretty one! He would have to make a note of this in his journal, too. Most young Crow women were wise beyond their years. The early discipline of work, the strong unity of family, those enduring lifelong bonds, made it inevitable. Ben Tree had observed this. Girls were already little women by the time of their first menses. But had he been so obvious about Little Hoop? Had his own eyes been so revealing? Was his face a map of disclosure? "Ei," he finally admitted, talking slowly, choosing his words, "the reflection of the pool doesn't lie. It's like a mirror, a looking glass. But you are like leaves in the wind . . . everywhere. Where shall I look? Shall I become a blind man in your presence?"

Eyes averted, she shook her head. "No, I wouldn't like that." She pointed to the open leaves of his journal. "My brother, Two Moons High, speaks. He says you make the white man's tracks so you may remember the legends. Is this true?"

"Yes, he speaks the truth. I write so I can remember the Crow people and what they do."

She frowned, wagging her head again.

"Is this bad?" he asked. "Don't you understand?"

"I don't understand. My people remember. The wise men in the council, the chiefs and holy men, they know the legends. They don't forget. Is Tree so different, that he cannot remember things that pass? When our wise men speak, the people listen. It is so."

Ben broke into a wide grin. "I'm not wise," he answered. "Many things happen, so many that I'm likely to forget. I make this writing to remember everything. In my land, some people don't listen to the white chiefs. My people are many. Why, some don't even remember the law, and others are just plain crazy. Do you understand?"

"It's bad to forget. Will you show them the signs?"

"Maybe my people will read the signs," he smiled. "When I'm old and forgotten, maybe they will interpret the signs."

"What shall Man Called Tree tell them?" she asked, pointing again to the little journal. "Do you write the name of Little Hoop, too?"

Ben broke open the pages and thumbed through them. "I write about the land and the rivers, and about the goodness of your people. Yes, here is the name of White Mouth, and the name of Little Hoop. See, I write that Little Hoop is the sister of Two Moons High, son of a chief. I've written other things, too. See, here is a word . . . this one." He traced his finger across the page and underlined the letters for her.

Bending, she looked, but then sighed in despair. "I don't understand the writing. How can I know?"

He laughed and winked at her. "This word says 'pretty.' It's you."

Her dark eyes suddenly widened. Taken by surprise, Little Hoop jumped back and quickly looked away. "Coyote!" she whispered aside. "A coyote has tricked me! Man Called Tree writes it, but in three moons, he has not spoken it!" She picked up the shinny stick and walked hurriedly away, yet with a smile hidden on her dark face.

Ben laughed after her and called teasingly: "*Hai-yah, hopo,* my eyes! Didn't *they* tell you this, too?"

November, 1856

The old chief, Red Deer Comes, told me about this Stillwater Valley and the lay of the land hereabout. I cached my cane today. My hip is better but no steady riding. This afternoon I took a short hike five miles staying along the river. Kept my eyes peeled four sides. Plenty of game sign crossing the bottoms, tracks everywhere. I saw no man track. Like Gabe tells, there's still plenty of country north of the Black's fork where no white has made his mark, and there is room to breathe. This is a good place to remember, creeks and sloughs above almost a shout from camp. Good eating greens in the water. I saw signs of beaver all along the cottonwood. Also saw the tracks of a big bear, grizzly I suppose. The Crow call them white bear or silver bear, same as Sioux. The pine is plentiful above and thickets of cottonwood, willow, and alder in these bottoms, making for heavy cover. Marked out some set locations, likely mink and marten, maybe some plews when they come prime. I figure the fur is worth a try. I shall not become bored and fitful.

I took rest on a rise and mapped the tops of the Beartooth. Beautiful, the headwaters of the Yellowstone, sacred land to the Crow, and I'll allow about as close to the Almighty as one can get. These are the real Rock mts. High valleys up here, the ones old Gabe talks about, hot mineral springs and mud fountains. I would like to see these wonders. Looks like three days' ride from here and pass probably blocked with snow and deadfall.

My boys in the pony herd are sitting Snow Hawk regular now. This one is good stock, all right. When Sunday comes of heat, I'll breed her with the white. It's cold again tonight. My old squaw Willow Sings is sewing up a fancy otter hat. I suppose it's for me. I like these people, and I talk their tongue better every day. I like this land. Traded my pocket knife for a pair of winter mocs, all fur lining and up to my knees. I rounded up a few old traps. Little Hoop is watching me write. B. Tree.

Often, the solitude pleased Ben. When he went off alone, the Indians thought little of it, because he had done that on the Wind River during the summer encampment, ambling away on his blue mare, shoulders slumped, his lank frame at ease, but always with a sharp eye reaching ahead, taking full measure of the scrub pine, the juniper clumps, or the fuzzy haze dancing on a distant ridge. The children sometimes called him Man-Who-Rides-Alone. Wherever, whatever, he always found the environment compatible; the pinnacled canyons, the fiery buttes, flowered glens, or deep forests, or even the greasewood flats where the springs suddenly sank from sight and the thirsty dirt became gray powder under the press of a pony's hoof.

It didn't matter. Ben accepted the land, barren or fruitful, however little, however much it provided. Learn to live with it, his father warned. Fight it, and it will beat you every time. The high-country wilderness was no exception, yet certainly much less a hazard to a man who, indeed, was learning to live like an Indian, and who frequently thought like one. In his element, he found comfort. His blood ran both directions, intermingled, red and white, and he felt himself fortunate in that respect—breed, in his eyes a blessing. He took the best of both, would forsake neither.

Ben thought himself well enough, now, so one day he packed ten traps across his shoulder and cradled his rifle. His steady stride was as soft as a whitetail deer's. His direction was upriver. Following the game trails, the mossy ponds, he read the sign as readily as the written word: the parted cleft of a startled deer, a muskrat's silent eddy, dimpled slicks of feeding trout, and here, the splash of mottled feathers, a speck of blood, trailside death, the cat's deadly paw at work.

Frequently he stopped to place a trap, until he had moved upward to a point five miles above the village. He found a bank in the sun where the sand was warm. Here he rested and chewed on strips of jerky and an old biscuit he had stored in his pouch. The biscuit was flat, ancient, and hard, a remnant of rations from the scouting trip. In better times he would have discarded it, but now he relished it like rock candy. And it was just as hard.

At the village, he had only a meager ration of precious flour left from the small bag he'd packed at Fort Bridger. Coffee became scarce too, and now, hankering for a hot sip, he had to settle for cold water to wash down his frugal midday meal. A man must make do. He could wait it out. Before the winter set in someone would come along the Yellowstone trail with coffee and other staples. That gave him a thought. On his return trip to the village, he detoured to his previous day's route until he came to a clump of chokecherry. The trees were barren of fruit, the birds long since having come and gone. With his long knife, Ben hacked a section of trunk, stuffing selected small pieces of bark into his pouch. Without coffee, he could settle for less. Old Willow Sings would gladly brew hot chokecherry tea, for she had already taken him as a son.

Heading back, Ben found that the sun had brightened and warmed the afternoon. The heat penetrated his buckskin. He walked along the forest of trees by the river, those gaunt, spreading cottonwoods still heavy with withered leaves, hanging precariously, awaiting only the first wintery blasts to free them. Within the grove, he quietly came upon a small doe, its ears twitching with each halting, cautiously delicate tread. Its poise and beauty stayed his ready rifle, and for a moment they watched each other. Lest he frighten the gentle creature, he edged softly away to the side, making for the rim of warm-water sloughs about a mile above camp.

Nearing the ponds, the unexpected sound of women's voices brought him up short. Pausing, Ben heard the soft splashing, accompanied then by the unmistakable laugh of Little Hoop. Indeed, he thought, she is everywhere, like a nymph of the woods. With some surprise, and perhaps more curiosity, he pressed on, silently approaching the warm-water pools where he discovered three young Crow maidens up to their waists, gathering watercress and pulling free the buried tubers of the pond lily. Nearby, the mossy bank was covered with their harvest. A fourth girl, her shoulders blanketed against the early November chill, observed from the shore, occasionally poking and rearranging the stacks. Small wisps of steam rose from around the workers, where the warmer water met the cool air next to their partially submerged bodies.

Ben took another close look before indecision struck—whether to push boldly on and alert them to his presence, or skirt the group entirely and make it back to camp from another direction. Their buckskins and flannel shirts were rolled high above their hips, and in the glare of the afternoon sun their wet thighs and buttocks glistened like burnished copper. And despite his momentary indecisiveness, what he now glimpsed of Little Hoop was delightfully appealing, bringing a surprised hike to his brow. She was as smooth as a skinned sapling. Indeed, her young body made a lie of the long skin dresses that usually disguised her. Lithe and shapely, firm in her rear, she displayed none of the rotund posterior squatness that he had often seen among some Indian women.

Experiencing a tinge of amused guilt, Ben finally looked away, and stifled a chuckle. Admittedly, his present preoccupation left him slightly embarrassed. It was funny, yet it was not. Despite their occasional promiscuity, more often the Crow were extremely modest about their bodies, rarely exposing themselves in any manner. And he dared not offend them by a prank or jest, not without fear of ridiculing himself. He knew better. Sometimes, within a moment, their shame swiftly was converted into a harsh, cutting harangue, abusive enough to burn the ears of any young buck.

He had to make a move, a maneuver of some discretion, so after a moment of awkward deliberation he cupped his hands and broke into the staccato bark of a squirrel, warning enough to alert them. He waited.

When they had modestly lowered their dresses, he sighed and moved out from the shadows into the sunlight. He approached from the opposite side of the pond, keeping a safe distance between him and the gatherers. Affecting some degree of nonchalance, so he thought, he brought his left hand up smartly. This was a customary greeting. He began to pass.

Ordinarily, under different circumstances, Ben's gracious gesture, his innocent passing, might have worked, might have gotten him by with nothing more than a casual return greeting, perhaps several girlish giggles. But the presence of Little Hoop altered the situation. This was something out of the ordinary. There were no old women around, those ubiquitous guardians of social propriety. Little Hoop would have her way this day without any interference. He heard her calling. Obviously displeased with his continuing detachment, she cried out saucily, "*Hai-yah,* a coyote comes from hiding! What has he seen? Ei, I know! But look, he runs away!"

A rash of mocking laughter broke out, and the others quickly took up the taunt. They knew the ambitions of their sister. One called, "Tree is afraid! Yes, see him go! Man Called Tree is afraid of Little Hoop!"

They giggled in unison. When he bravely glanced back to smile and wave, indicating that he could share their jest with amusement instead of offense, they had turned their bodies around. His eyes bulged. They were wagging their bare bottoms at him! Their giggles followed as he disappeared into the brush. By jingo, he thought, those are spirited young women!

Buffalo Horn made medicine again. He consulted the omens. Meditating, the old man pointed his pocked nose to the wind and threw powder in the Four Great Directions. Eyes closed, lids heavy and fluttering, he sought out the spirits, and late in the Moon of Falling

Leaves, he made his prophecy. "Hear me, my brothers, winter is upon us! The storm is coming! Secure your lodges, bring the children close, look to your fires, store your fuel!" The crier carried his news, and the wind suddenly gusted for a night and a day. The wind was an omen in itself.

There were other signs, prophetic phenomena. Bunching nervously, the Crow pony herd grazed to the north, rumps to the wind, their tails tasseled and blowing like corn silk. Beyond the village perimeter, wolves howled. A sudden exodus of leafy missiles filled the sky, and overnight the trees became barren. On the second night, a southwesterly ripped through Chief White Mouth's sheltered camp, raking the tipi vents, shaking the lodge poles, sweeping the village floor broom-clean of debris. The next day a soft snow fell steadily, the west wind barely whispered, and Ben Tree found himself plodding through eight inches of white fluff to run his trap line. Buffalo Horn's new winter had arrived.

After this first storm, it turned cold for three days. The winds blew the snow from the lowlands, drifting it along the hummocks and brush. Tree had to tuck in the fur around his collar, and he pulled his fancy new otter headpiece close to his ears. A white-tipped tail feather from an eagle dipped jauntily from the hat that Willow Sings had so beautifully trimmed with ermine. He was entitled to wear feathers, and the hat pleased him. With his hunting ability, he repaid the old squaw almost daily.

Of course she tried to hide her affection, but a fine gleam was often in her eye. She carried scars of remembrance. This man was like a son: sons she had once had, and had lost. Tree's traps were seldom empty. He was a provider, a great hunter, bringing her rabbit from his snares, grouse that he clubbed, and she put the meat in her steaming pot. To an old woman the meat was tender, more palatable than that of the big game, for she had seen sixty winters and her teeth were almost gone. She used the rabbit fur to line moccasins and mittens. She worked hard. And when Willow Sings helped Ben flesh the fur-bearers, he often rewarded her with a fine pelt that she could later trade at one of the outposts. This was unselfish and good. Among the other squaws she boasted of his prowess, the strong medicine of his long rifle. By the mouth of Sweat in the Tipi he was riding again, and had slain wolf, bear, and elk. Willow Sings took the claws and the teeth and combined them with quill and bead to turn out decorative trim and finery. She was frugal and wasted nothing.

Likewise, admiration swelled from the other side of Willow Sings' tipi. Little Hoop smiled at Ben, often talked, and when the ancient eyes of Willow Sings nodded sleepily, she flirted with her own. She often preened her hair, combing until it hung like an ebony curtain, and it glittered by the light of the tipi fire. By day, she fastened it below the crown with a beaded band and it hung below her shoulders, coal-black against bleached buckskin and red wool. She scented herself. She was comely enough, her full, broad lips only slightly irregular to her small, straight nose. A chief's daughter, Little Hoop was innately proud, yet never outwardly snobbish. She was popular. Like Willow Sings, she beheld Tree with admiring eyes, but the perspective was not parental.

Precious time had ridden on the swift wing of the hawk since she had first seen him. Patience was a virtue she would not be able to claim forever. Restless, anxious, she was becoming obvious. She remembered him as she'd first noticed him in July—a rider, tall, bronzed, a single strip of leather holding back his long hair. Now she saw him in a different light, somewhat differently than he saw himself, or cared to admit—for to Little Hoop, he was more Indian than white. In August, the Moon of the Black Berries, she dreamed of him, and by September, when they had moved north, the song was in her. She had fallen in love, the dream became a voice, a part of her vision, and she told her sisters that someday she would carry the son of Man Called Tree in her belly. No one laughed. But they watched and waited with her, and Ben innocently, unwittingly, was becoming a part of a matrimonial plot, cleverly designed by Chief White Mouth himself, no less.

Fate, in the form of a Blackfeet arrow, had stopped Ben Tree, but it was no accident that he had been moved into the third tipi of White Mouth to recuperate. He suspected nothing. Because of the wound, the attention he needed, he had little reason to wonder. However, while the old crone, Willow Sings, was there by right and purpose, the presence of her young assistant was outright subterfuge. After Ben became well, Two Moons High stopped one night and suggested it would be wise to remain in the big lodge for a while longer. Tree's own lodge was too small. There was more comfort in the big family tipi. And after all, in the cold of winter there would always be fire and the helping hands of two women. Reasonable enough, Ben thought. His red brother was making good sense, and he himself had attained some stature in these new quarters. He enjoyed the responsibility. Two Moon's word had been almost prophetic—the winds of the first storm blew Ben's small vacant tipi far across the Stillwater hills.

On a subsequent night, he sat in the lodge of Two Moons High and heard the eldest brother of Little Hoop speak again. For the first time, the young scout began to read the hidden message.

"From the first sun until the last shadow, your tracks are many," Two Moons High began.

Ben grinned. Speaking slowly and making complementary sign, he explained that it had always been that way, even on the farm, even at the white man's school, and at the Tree stock corrals on the Big Sandy, the cabins at Laramie Creek. "I suppose work's a habit, now. Loafing like the stays-around-the-fort people isn't the way of my father. I hear-tell my mother was no different. It comes natural. I must earn my keep. I like it this way."

"When making meat is finished, a man must take rest," returned Two Moons. "You are with the ponies. You are in the forest, and sometimes you make wood like a squaw. Ho, this is crazy! A man should rest . . . see what is around him. Are you happy here?"

Smiling at his friend's bantering critique, Ben nodded. "I miss my family, but your people are good. I've found a second home."

Two Moons swept out his hands, cupped them, and pointed to Tree, saying, "Our village is your village. Our people are your people. My father honors your father, and we count you among us. It has always been that way."

"Thank you," Ben said. "This is good."

For a moment they were silent, staring into the flames of the night fire, sharing its warmth and listening to the small chatter of women and children in the leaping shadows behind them. Two Moons finally said, "My father speaks. He says you are welcome to stay with his village. He is old, but he remembers when he was a boy. He remembers men like Man Called Tree. They lived with the Absaroke many moon. They had many honors, and they became chiefs. They were happy."

"White Mouth is a great chief," Ben said. "He'll understand what I say. You're his oldest son. Someday, you'll take his place. That's his wish. It's the same way with my father. I honor him. My family is small, and your family is plenty. Hear me, I honor White Mouth, but you must tell him that in the first months of the green grass I'll return to my work . . . my other home. My father and brother will be looking for my tracks.''

Two Moons broke into a wry smile. "They have already read your tracks. Since the Moon of the Changing Season, the Blackfeet have known. The Lakota people know. Our scouts trade sign with passing friends . . . enemies of the Sioux and Blackfeet. They say word has come from the traders on the Mother River, the people of the fort. A white man who counts plenty coup is with the mountain Absaroke. Ei, he's like a wolf. He rides like the wind. He becomes a ghost in the mountains. His sign is Tree. It is so.''

"Is that so?" Ben replied. He coughed in affected modesty, but was not too surprised. Word traveled. The Blackfeet traded on the Missouri at Fort Benton. The Sioux came to Fort Union and Laramie. Traders listened to their gossip. The Indian telegraph was sometimes slow, but inevitably the stories, however exaggerated, always seemed to filter through, village to village, tribe to tribe, ultimately reaching the last outposts of civilization. Smiling back at Two Moons, he retorted, "I'm afraid the tail wags the wolf. My honors are small. The truth is, I'm nothing but a trail hand, a muleskinner at best.''

"The Sioux remember you," Two Moons said. "They say you counted coup on Pawnee and Arapaho, ei, the white man, too. They know you, and the other one who is made in your image.''

"My brother Will," answered Ben proudly. "Ei, we are like one.''

"My father, White Mouth, speaks," Two Moons continued. "He says the legends are true, and that you are a warrior. The others before you were warriors, and they became sons. The old chiefs were their fathers. They followed the buffalo trail. They went on the warpath with the Absaroke. They took our women for their wives. They were not greedy. They took nothing else except what they needed. They were happy.''

Staring into the fire, Ben nodded, his suspicion rising like the smoke above him. ''Yes,'' he said, ''I've heard these legends.''

Two Moons lit his small pipe with an ember and grunted once. ''My father wants to make you a son like the old chiefs.''

''I'm honored,'' was the nervous reply.

''White Mouth says it's strange that you know plenty about the ponies but so little about women.'' A small laugh escaped him. ''Ei, what could I say to my father? He knows that you're no *berdache* man-woman.''

Brows raised, Ben looked up. Hedging, he said, ''I'm afraid that I don't quite understand.'' But he did, and his feigned innocence was met with a blunt reply.

''My father is a good trader. To make you a son, he'll give a daughter, my sister, Little Hoop. It isn't his wish alone, that you must know. It's a family wish, and I also look upon this as good. She sleeps in your lodge. Why don't you make her your woman?''

What Benjamin Tree secretly feared in fantasy had suddenly become a reality. And if he had once wondered at the reluctance of the other young men to come courting, he wondered no longer, for undoubtedly White Mouth had passed the word: His daughter was meant to be Man Called Tree's woman. Stirring uncomfortably, Ben made a feeble attempt to belittle the proposal. ''She is the daughter of a chief,'' he tried. ''I'm without wealth or honor in your village. I won't shame her family. That would be against my medicine.''

Two Moons High began shaking his head. A wrinkle of amusement creased the corner's of his eyes. ''You are a fool, Tree. White Mouth has the cunning of Old Man Coyote. Little Hoop has spoken. Who do you think put her in the big tipí? Why are you in the big tipi? He makes bait for the trap. Once you mount her, you are caught. Now do you understand, my brother?''

Ben Tree swallowed once. Two Moons was brutally frank about it, and for a moment Tree found himself speechless.

Two Moons asked, ''Don't you think my sister is pretty? She boasts that you have written this in your book.''

''She's pretty,'' Ben finally admitted. ''Yes, I'll confess that I made a note of that. But what shall I do? Ei, a man like me! I'm not like the stays-around-the-fort people. Most of the year I'm riding the Great Medicine Road, down where the white man goes. How can I take this girl away from her people and her land? That would be bad. And I can't stay on here forever. Don't you see, my brother? It wouldn't be good medicine for a young woman like Little Hoop. Away from her people, she might become sad and unhappy.''

With a quick brush of dismissal, Two Moons High said, ''The Absaroke aren't like white women, my friend. They do not stand still. They ride and move. They have always ridden, moving and living where their men do. Our women make happiness. Hear me, if the Great Spirit had wanted the earth to stand still and our people to stay in one place, he would have made it so.''

''Yes,'' Ben protested softly, ''but Little Hoop is a chief's daughter. I have no great gifts to make to White Mouth, nothing to give to her eldest brother . . . a horse or two, a piece of gold. What honor is that?''

''To make Little Hoop happy, that makes White Mouth happy,'' Two Moons answered. ''You speak of honor? White Mouth doesn't forget his long friendship with your father. Your father is a man of his word, like the Absaroke. He never brought the yellow-eyes into our land. Now you have heard me and the voice of White Mouth, for whom I speak. Little Hoop is my sister, and I also give my permission. It would be wise to think on this.'' He smiled again and made a sweeping gesture to all that was within his own tipi. He added, ''The winter nights are long. It's not good to be alone, ei?''

Ben, sweat pebbling his brow, poked a stick at the hot coals and pondered. ''What about . . . what about love?'' he asked awkwardly. ''What if she doesn't love me?''

With a curt nod, Two Moons answered, ''She will learn.''

Lost in perplexed musings, Ben sighed. He felt the barbed shaft of fate lodged between his ribs. If he chose to stay in the camp of the Crow, he was a goner. But what choice did he have in the middle of winter? When he left the tipi, his brow was not only wet, it was hot, his stomach uneasy. Once outside, he sucked in the fine cut of the sharp night wind, its cold breath. By jingo, he needed the fresh air!

His talk with Two Moons High had been more than revealing—it had been downright disconcerting. The family had him cornered. They had all been in on the matrimonial ruse, right from the beginning. His trail had been blazed with the keen edge of a tomahawk, like a cunning ambush, with old White Mouth himself the chief perpetrator. Ben sighed. Well, there was no need to disguise his affection for Little Hoop any longer, and in a way that was good. But despite Two Moon's blunt assurances of a clear path ahead, Ben discovered that his emotions were racing madly in two directions.

On the one hand he experienced elation, the fulfillment of winter's desire, yet there was a current of underlying apprehension nagging at him. He was not satisfied with himself or his situation, this continual conflict of ideologies. His white blood bolted at the chief's calculated commitment, the cold tribal arrangement, made without any profession of love on the part of either Ben himself or Little Hoop. Ben recognized it, understood it, yet somehow abhorred it. With his white eyes he envisioned at least some courtship—some mutual understanding, the gradual, harmonious blending of two souls, not outright conquest. Such romantic nonsense would bring a guffaw from Two Moons High—mount the wench and be done with it! Ben cringed inside. Little Hoop deserved better. No savage, he would nurture love. He would try.

But he had never courted a woman. Not really. In his young life always the passing fancy, the bush affair, on the trail, at the forts. Romance had been fleeting, swift as the feathered shaft, and most often it had been fraught with the threat of discovery—the irate immigrant, the mover, the sodbuster pilgrim. Time had never been on his side, either, not on the Great Medicine Road. As the wagon ruts west deepened, the days became longer, and beyond the blue sage of Laramie his interest in gingham skirts and dusty bonnets often had been thoroughly diminished by fatigue. But this was not the Oregon Trail ordeal that he now found himself facing. Nor was it a passing fancy. It was the red man's stark reality.

Once in front of his lodge, he paused to peer up at the cold slice of moon, a silver sickle cutting through fleecy December clouds. Springtime seemed as distant as the silky clouds, and home a far piece. He shuddered once. He could not admit to loneliness, only its infrequent nibble. Confused, he poked his way through the tipi flap. Inside, the fire was low, banked with cottonwood. The tipi was invitingly warm. He became foxy. Without a sound, he moved to the side of Little Hoop's mound of robes. He squatted there, observing.

The firelight touched the smooth mold of her cheeks, and he saw the delicate flare of her nostrils, listened to the faint whisper of her breath. She was barely a young woman. He made no sound, but her eyes opened and she saw him, the shadow of concern on his face. When she started to speak, he quietly silenced her with the tip of his finger.

"Now, it will be soon," he whispered. And then, touching a finger to his own lips, Ben softly pressed it to hers in a kiss and left. In the faint light, he looked back and saw her bright smile. The small tear of happiness fleeing down her cheek escaped him.

December, 1856

At dawn, five of us rode to where the snow begins, about 12 miles back. We killed two young bull elk and a yearling, passing up six or seven cows. They are already with unborn calf and taboo. For the first time, I saw tracks of visitors above, near the point of my trap line. Three sets of ponies, probably Blackfeet looking for sign. My brothers became excited. We cached the pack horses and meat and followed these tracks for several miles until they made straight west going dead away.

Man Runs First, one of our party, says these Indians probably are scouts from a smaller camp. Sometimes they camp in the hills beyond the big river. I said nothing, believing it nonsense that anyone would be so foolish to try and count coup in this kind of contrary weather. This has since set me to wondering and I think on it, how close they came to my trap line, and if these are Blackfeet looking for me. From high ground the distances are as far as the eye can see, snowy mountains and small valleys. Our camp is about 15 miles upriver from the Yellowstone and is well sheltered and protected. The lookouts remain. I saw snowstorms in the Rock mts. It remained dry down below and we had sun, an unusual phenomenon. I wish brother Will could see this.

Little Hoop waited for me at the edge of camp. I handed her up on Sunday and we rode double amid much hollering. This is a custom of greeting sweethearts. I gave away most of my meat and sent a choice liver to Chief White Mouth. Found out the elk is part of old Buffalo Horn's vision, a sacred sort, and he will have none of the meat. We went to a party and feast at Two Moons High lodge tonight. The women sang and danced. We men gambled at hide-the-bone. I lost nothing. I write weary with an ache in my bones. From long hours, I suspect, but life is good. B. Tree

The small shelter of scrub pine suited him fine. Dismounting, he led Sunday into the sparse cover and, rifle in his lap, he waited. Although he had come almost a mile up the timbered valley, it was not until he turned west toward the rock buttes that he discovered someone was following him. Ben squinted for a minute before he made out the horse rounding the coulee bottom, heading along on the tracks of his blue mare. It took him less time to recognize the rider—Little Hoop on her small spotted gelding. Shawl thrown free, black hair flowing, she occasionally leaned to one side, looking for fresh sign in the damp sod and bunch grass.

Ben remained hidden. She was a foolish girl. The wolf lookouts should have stopped her, for she had no business riding out alone, following him. Even so, there was a touch of amusement curling the corners of his mouth. How he admired this lovely young woman! He had to admit it—she had spirit. She was persistent. Since declaring himself as her chosen one, she had taken to his heels like a camp pup. More often, she was a shadow in his mind. Love had nipped him. He proudly watched her steady approach, smiled as she paused to examine the sign again. His tracks abruptly cut off to the side. Her eyes followed them, and her surprised stare finally met him in the cover of trees where he rested on his haunches grinning down at her.

"Hopo!" he exclaimed softly. "Had you been the enemy, you would be dead. You're foolish to come here alone." But his pretense at admonishment had a gentle ring, a sound that told her he was not angry. She was not fooled in the least, for she also knew love.

"I'm not alone," she answered. "I see you, a man hiding like a rabbit. Come down, I have no fire weapon, only this bow." She laughed merrily and pulled her blanket close. Her eyes were direct now, no longer fleeting and evasive, misdirected as they once had been.

He walked to her, leading the mare. "Why did you come?" he asked. "How did you get by the guards?"

"I hurried to ride with you," Little Hoop said. "They knew you had not gone far." Affecting a haughty tilt to her chin, she made a pretense at offense. "Fools! They were like women, making bad jokes. I don't like them. They said I should take a rope to catch you, to keep you in the tipi." And she giggled, bringing a flush to his tanned face.

With a soft curse, Ben swung back into his saddle. Guiding his horse around her, he muttered, "I look at you, don't I? Ei, that's asking for enough trouble."

"I'm no trouble," she soothed. "I think you know that."

"So you want to ride? Well, we'll ride, all right. Look, the sun is high, and I've got work to do, so come along."

"Ei, Man-Who-Rides-Alone, you work too much!"

Ben clucked at his horse. With a slow grin, he muttered, "You've been talking to that lazy brother of yours again. He talks like a crazy dog."

"He is very brave," she said defensively.

"I didn't say he wasn't," Ben answered. He spat to the side of the small game trail. "Look here, woman, there's more to life than just fighting Blackfeet and Sioux and stealing those damn ponies all the time. If I was at my lodge on Laramie Creek I'd be working every day, whopping mules, breaking stock. Fact is, my pa wouldn't have it any other way. Why, he'd kick my bottom if I holed up all winter like a prairie dog. Work never hurt anyone. Can't make any money sitting around on your bottom. Like these furs . . . they're for the taking. Not much money anymore, but enough, and it's honest work."

"Too much money is bad," Little Hoop said flatly.

"Now, that's some notion! Whoever told you a thing like that?"

"My father speaks," she said.

"Ei, I should have known. He's always speaking."

"He's a wise man. He's a chief. When he has plenty, he gives away plenty. White Mouth is always happy. Wealth doesn't make a man big. That's what he says."

Ben grinned. "So I've heard tell."

"White Mouth says when the white man has plenty, he only wants more. That makes the white man unhappy, like the man who eats too much. He has a big pain in his belly."

Ben laughed heartily. "Your father is a wise man, all right. I won't be denying that. A man's no taller than his shadow. But you listen to me: An empty belly can make a man plenty unhappy, too."

"Are you happy?" she quipped, tilting her head prettily.

"My belly is full."

"Don't make bad jokes."

"Now, what makes you ask a question like that?"

he said, glancing back at her. "I make do. Sure, I'm happy. I'm no crazy dog, am I?"

"No, but Buffalo Horn says you have two faces. He says a man with two faces can never be happy. Only one face must be turned to the sun. A white man may become one of us, but an Indian may never become white. He says one day you will learn this. If you learn, you will live in our village forever."

Ben shook his head despairingly. "He's an old turkey buzzard. You listen to too many tongues. Look here, now, every man must make his own happiness wherever he goes. It doesn't matter. To be a man, to know that you're a man, that's the important thing, Indian or white." He smiled back at her, saying, "Sure, Buffalo Horn is right about one thing: The Great Spirit has set the mountains in my heart. But, you listen—I've already learned to live with two faces. It has to be. To deny either my father or mother would bring shame. See, look there, a bush! When you tear away its roots, you have nothing. There's nothing to grow, the soul is gone."

"I will ride in your shadow wherever you go," she said softly. "Will you have me always?"

"Yes, you'll be my sun," replied Ben. "Maybe you'll light my path." He smiled and asked, "Are *you* happy?"

Her face suddenly brightened. Her eyes became misty. "When I'm with you, my heart is filled with joy," she said in a small tremble. "Yes, as the brooks fill with water and the grass becomes green, I am happy. I feel like a girl first learning to sing, and I say to myself, this is love . . . you, my love."

Ben stared directly ahead at the fringe of spruce on the distant hill. They seemed to be dancing. "Then we're the same," he said. "That will make do for the both of us, ei, until the sun dies. Come on now, get along."

They went up the small ridge. She pulled abreast of him and they rode side by side, their legs occasionally touching. His mind constantly drifted, but he said nothing about his thoughts to Little Hoop. He loved her. He was happy, yet still somewhat confused. One thing—he wanted to prove Buffalo Horn wrong. He *was* content, certainly no less than he always had been, happy to be on the trail, the creeks, anywhere in the mountains, anywhere west of Laramie Creek. The shaman was talking smoke. What did a medicine chief know about his personal life? Ben found it most convenient to live with a double face. He could love the Absaroke, even establish citizenship, temporarily. He knew most of their beliefs and traditions and, with only slight reservation, practiced all the amenities. But forever? By jingo, he had feasted and smoked with the Sioux, too, and he was no less white, a *wasichu*. When necessary he had always reverted, had made the transition easily, falling from the complexities of one society into another, because he understood. He had learned early. But a man had commitments, Christian principles to follow, family traditions to uphold, some of which his red brothers just did not understand. He refused to believe that any change of circumstances could shape his destiny, medicine man or no. What more could one expect of him?

Soon they climbed another hill, farther west, before they reined south again—a most circuitous route to his trap line, Little Hoop opined. They were almost ten miles from the Crow village, she said. He only smiled. When they approached the crest of a third ridge, Ben suddenly dismounted and flipped his reins to her. Scrambling ahead in a crouch, he flattened himself in the rock and wind-blown snow at the very top. After a long look, he turned on his side and motioned, directing her to turn the horses downwind and join him.

Ben pointed. It took Little Hoop several moments

to locate the three figures far across the mountain. They were distant specks, almost a mile away, camouflaged in the brush on a bluff overlooking what Tree had named Willow Stink Creek because of the odiferous sludge along its many beaver dams. Almost a quarter of a mile beyond the trio were three horses, hidden in an aspen grove, a gray and two pintos.

Little Hoop stared silently. Perplexed, she looked up when she heard Ben chuckling. "Who are they?" she asked. "How did you know of this?"

"Damn fools!" he whispered, forgetting dialect. "They aren't friends, by jingo, that's for certain. Hell, they know me, for sure. Blackfeet. Some of your crazy dogs, I suspect, looking to get even with me. Been in the hills watching me for a couple of days, like as I didn't know. I've crossed their tracks twice." He turned to her and smiled. "I changed my pattern, and that's thrown them, has them wondering. They probably figure I'm going to come right up the bottom there, pulling my traps. I have three cached down there."

"But why didn't you speak to the Soldier's Lodge?" she asked incredulously. "They would come out and kill them."

"And make a fool of myself?" he huffed back. He nodded below. "Those devils melt away like summer snow. They want *me,* maybe alive. It's only by luck we see them now. A chance guess, not dead reckoning, not by a long shot. If I pulled some of your braves up here and there was nothing but grass, they'd likely laugh at me. Ei, they would call me a nervous, old woman."

Little Hoop peered between the rocks again. "They have come a long way for nothing. I'm happy. You are more coyote than I suspected. You have strong medicine."

"No," he said, rubbing her cheek. "We call it 'a

hunch,' like getting a certain feeling in your bones
. . . smelling out trouble.''

"Ei," she knowingly whispered, "the eagle sees
the leaf fall. The deer hears it, but the coyote smells
it.''

Ben turned and flopped on his back and laughed.
Little Hoop stared over at him curiously. "How can
you laugh?'' she hissed. "Are you crazy? They have
come all this way to coup you!''

"They aren't the first to try it, not by a long shot,''
Ben said. He suddenly reached out and touched the tip
of her nose, then kissed her lightly on the mouth. She
gasped, her eyes widening as though she had been bit-
ten by a small spark. Before she could speak he was
pulling her down to his lips again, taking her firmly
into his arms, and she eagerly moved into him. For
one precious moment, their bodies stiffened in warm
excitement. She tenderly caressed the side of his face,
longingly, lastingly, whispering, "Ei, I love you, but
you *are* crazy!''

"Like a coyote,'' Ben said with a smile, finally
kicking himself upright. With a sigh, he turned back
and peeked between the shelf. "What you say is true—
they have come a long way. Probably have a small
camp, three, maybe four hours, say, to the west. How
far to their big village, I wonder?''

Little Hoop shrugged and nestled warmly against
his shoulder. "I don't know,'' she said. "Does it matter?'' She tugged impatiently at his arm. "You make
me feel crazy inside. We should forget these men . . .
go find a warm place in the trees . . . lay together and
make ourselves one.''

"Yes,'' he noted, "your love tempts me, woman,
but these hills are no place for that, not right now.''

She kissed his cheek and stared out across the ravine
with him. "They are bad to spoil such a day. They
have many villages. Who knows? Plenty far. Across

the big river. In the winter, three days' ride. It is bad,
the wind, the snow. You must be very bad medicine
to them.''

He carefully checked the terrain to the right, tracing
a small finger ridge up to a point where it met the
opposite hill. Partially timbered, it was almost a mile
in width. From there, a small grassy slope extended
down to the hollow where the Blackfeet horses were
picketed. It was open country, perhaps a quarter mile
of it. He glanced at the position of the sun. By its
slant, he calculated it was about one o'clock—a little
more than four hours of daylight left.

Little Hoop touched his cheek with another kiss.
''What will we do?''

''My thoughts are in the sky,'' he said. ''For a fact,
as high as the geese fly. We can turn back. Or, if I can
get close enough, maybe I can wing a couple of those
birds. But I was thinking what a joke it would be if
those devils had to walk all the way home . . . get
their bottoms wet crossing the Yellowstone.''

''No,'' Little Hoop said, shaking her head. ''To
come this far, they must have more ponies, one or
two. The Blackfeet aren't fools. They are killers. My
people will tell you this.''

''We're all killers when we have to be.'' He laughed
lightly. ''No, they aren't fools, but I'll bet we could
make them look like it with a little fancy decoying.''

''Ei?''

''A trick,'' he explained. ''Fool them.'' Placing
both hands on her shoulders, he said, ''Now, listen to
me—what if I were to put you on Sunday, wearing my
otter, carrying my rifle, and you were to saunter down
this ridge a small piece? Say, like you're making for
the bottom . . . ?''

''I would be afraid,'' she whispered furtively. ''They
have guns!''

''My God,'' Ben exclaimed, ''from this distance

they couldn't hit you with a field cannon! Now listen to what I tell you. When you get halfway down, you turn real easy and ride back up here. By jingo, they won't know what's going on. By then, I can have those ponies of theirs busted loose and running. I can sneak back along that little spur right over there. They'll never know what happened. Why, we'll disappear like smoke in the wind.''

She shook her head and sighed. "What can I say? I worry. You try to make it sound like berry-picking.''

Tilting her chin, he said, "Don't worry, woman, there's no danger over here. When you see my sign, just ride out slowly. Go to the small rocks down there, no more. Ei, they'll be looking at you, not up above, not back my way.'' He removed his hat and fixed it upon her head, setting it at a rakish angle. He took away her red shawl. Handing her the rifle, he quickly departed, running for the distant trees.

Almost fifteen minutes passed before Ben found himself on the opposite hill at the edge of the open park. The cold air bit into the sweat of his buckskin. Wiping perspiration from his forehead, he looked around, checking out his surroundings. To his surprise, the slope of the hill was such that it obliterated the Blackfeet from his sight. This was more than he had expected. There was absolutely no way the Indians could see him from below, at least not until he reached the aspen. Ben waved at the point of rocks where Little Hoop was hiding. Moments later, he saw her appear on the blue mare. She was right on schedule. Checking his revolver again, he ran directly for the Blackfeet ponies in the aspen grove. When he was within forty yards of his target he stopped and began to walk slowly into the thicket, clucking gently, moving easily.

It was not until he had reached the first bridle that he made the decision—instead of chasing the horses, he would steal them! That seemed more logical, now. No less risky, it would be a real coup. Once through the aspen and heading back, he figured that the curve of the slope would protect him. He glanced across the far ravine again and watched Little Hoop. She was turning up the hill, back toward their rocky lookout.

Now he had to move fast, so he immediately untied the reins of the other two horses and began leading all three of them through the sodden leaves of the thicket. Halfway through he finally mounted, and at that instant a single shot exploded far behind and he heard a ball whizz harmlessly through the barren branches. The game was up. The shot sent him plunging madly ahead, hunkered flat, kicking wildly into his mount's belly. In a cold sweat he disappeared through the trees, out of sight, out of range, and when he finally topped the rise and glanced back, he saw three small figures running toward the aspen. Unable to resist the sudden urge, Ben turned and screamed a chilling war cry. God, what a feeling! The sensation was breathtaking, exuberant, and he laughed gloriously. After the long echo had died, a lone purple raven flew overhead, its guttural call creaking like a rusty axle in the still mountain air. Then, all was silent.

That night, the legend grew. There were more drums, and another impromptu celebration in the big lodge. Exhausted, Ben finally fell into his robes, only to awake in a fit of ague. The labor of the cold day had chilled him to the bone, and he trembled like a frost-bitten dog. Shaking uncontrollably, a feverish sweat danced across his brow. Little Hoop stirred across from him and finally crawled out of her own bed. She replenished the fire. By the flames, she watched and worried. Piling another heavy robe over his body, she then gave him some hot tea. Ben's hands trembled. All to little avail. She took a momentary look at the sleeping old woman, Willow Sings, then looked down at Ben, buried, searching for comfort in his fever. Without further deliberation, Little Hoop shed her flannel chemise and crawled naked into his shaking arms.

December 1856

I was down a few days with mt. fever but my luck has turned. I pulled my traps this day and took three beaver. Varmits made dinner out of one snared fox, probably wolf or coyote. Five of the Big Dogs went hunting for my Blackfeet friends. No luck, and I figured as much. I suppose they cleaned country and headed home, poor devils. Everyone is celebrating again. Little Hoop has moved to my side of the tipi and her father is toasting his friends as his part of the ceremony. We traded gifts. This business of taking a partner is almost like Christmas. I gave White Mouth the stud Snow Hawk and the three Blackfeet ponies. Today, he gave the ponies to Two Moons High, keeping the stud for himself, allowing his son the privilege of tending and riding the critter. I gave away two Blackfeet saddles and got four blankets back. Little Hoop has a new buckskin dress with a hundred elk teeth on it. It's a beautiful thing to behold but it rattles like a gourd. This woman is good. We'll be keeping each other. That's the way this love is. Pa and Will are going to like her. B. Tree.

THREE

March, 1857

Arrived on the Clarks Fork. Good head of water already coming down. Spring is early. There are ten in our party moving toward the Wind. We camped on a small creek about a mile up from the river. The village will follow in two days, our scouts leaving sign along the way. Some going all the way to Fort Union for spring trade, a very long ride. Brisk wind but sunny all day. I packed four ponies with pelts and hides and suspect I'll be getting a fair enough price at Bridger. Surprised to meet three Flathead heading west toward the Hell Gate. I ciphered their sign. The Indian country is quiet but there's big trouble down in the Utah territory. The word comes up through the Utes and Shoshoni—the "hairy face" are making war medicine, meaning the Mormons. I can only suspect its against the Federals, not so much the gentiles. They were raising Cain against each other last year. Little Hoop wants to wait for the village before we head on out. These farewells don't come easy. B. Tree.

The Crow village stopped for several nights of rest on the Big Horn, and amid the clutter of the moving camp Ben came upon Buffalo Horn sitting in front of his disassembled tipi. Several women were working in back of the shaman. Children raced and shouted nearby, dogs snapping at their heels. Yells rent the air as more horses and travois trundled by. Buffalo Horn, wrapped in vermillion, sat through it all, motionless, his eyes closed, stoic, seeking peace among chaos, only awaiting his shelter and the comfort of his robes.

Ben paused and looked down at the old man. "Ho!" he spoke in greeting.

Buffalo Horn made a slow motion, passing his hand in front of him. He said nothing. He saw nothing. He refused to acknowledge the confusion about him.

"The grass is green again under your moccasins," Man Called Tree said. "Are you well?"

The shaman finally spoke. "Ei, I've seen another winter. The earth is good." His eye lids were heavy, weighted down by contemplation and vision. "I feel your shadow. It's cold, Man Called Tree."

"You knew it was me?" Ben said inquisitively.

"Ei," the old chief returned, a small smile upon his lips. "I knew. Strange you should come."

"Strange?" Ben squatted down in front of the medicine man. "Why do I make you cold when you sit in the sun? Tell me that, wise one."

Buffalo Horn slowly opened his eyes, lids fluttering. "My dreams. My dreams, they have been bad."

Suppressing a smile, Ben replied, "Ah, your dreams again. Yes, I believe you. Your medicine is strong." He waited, knowing that Buffalo Horn would speak, that another incredible story was forthcoming.

"I saw many black geese flying, looking for food and water," the shaman finally began. His gnarled fingers traced a fluttering pattern of flight.

Ben Tree nodded, saying, "Ei, it's that time of year. Tell me."

"They made the sky dark with their bodies, and the noise of their cries sounded like a thousand coyotes. They came down and found tender grass by the river. They ate and rested, and their cries were no more."

"With full bellies, they were happy."

Frowning, Buffalo Horn waved off the young brave's levity. "I saw many, and among many there was a white one. His wing was bent. Three hunters came to kill him and eat his flesh. They changed themselves. They became animals. One became a fox, another a coyote, and the third, a wolf. Many times they tried to kill the white goose, but they could not. A bolt came from the sky, making the lame goose fly again, but the north wind touched him. He became a contrary. Ei, he flew backward far to the north where the land is cold. It was covered with snow. The water was ice. There was nothing left for him in the land, and the white goose disappeared beyond the mountains for eight winters." Grunting once, Buffalo Horn fell silent.

"That's all?"

"Ei."

Ben scratched his head and clucked his tongue. "By jingo, that's a strange one, all right. The goose just vanished, got lost?"

With another slow, passing gesture of his hand, Buffalo Horn agreed. He then pulled his blanket close. "When you came, I was cold. I knew it was you."

Ben, his curiosity piqued, asked, "What do you make of it, this wild goose dream? Take this white one, for instance. Is this supposed to be me? Is this what you figure?"

The old man stared impassively ahead. "You will be leaving."

Ben laughed uneasily. "Yes, how did you know that?"

Buffalo Horn merely shrugged.

"Yes, south a piece," continued Tree. "I'll be making tracks heading south for my own land."

"I would tell you not to go," advised Buffalo Horn. "Stay with the Absaroke, where there is peace and plenty. Stay and find peace. I have read the signs."

"But I can't do that, old friend. As much as I'd like to, I just can't do that. I have obligations . . . work. Understand?"

Moving his hand again, Buffalo Horn said flatly, "Then you will find no peace, my son. I see darkness among the white people, darkness for you. That is the dream. You will have no peace for eight winters. When you leave, the winter of content is done."

Ben studied the old man's wrinkled face intently. Here was an ancient warrior, a man who had seen a hundred warpaths, a man of honor and many visions. Wrinkles of wisdom hung heavy on his face. Ben Tree, as skeptical as he felt, found it difficult to turn his back on the old man, to ignore his words, to walk away without imparting some kind of understanding. This would be improper as well as impolite. Buffalo Horn's eyes had closed again. Ben finally said, "I hear you. I honor you. I'm without dreams myself, but I'll mind my medicine and do what I must. I can't choose sides. For a time I'll have to live by the white man's medicine, ei, and my own better judgment."

Sighing, Buffalo Horn waved his hand a final time. "Hear me, my brother—you are no longer a white man. Why do I say this? Because you have learned to think with your heart instead of your head. Your days of peace will be counted like tracks in the summer snow.'' His smile faded and his face reflected contentment again. He had spoken.

Ben gently touched the medicine man's blanketed arm once and left.

Ben had no need of his methodically kept journal, or the curious words of Buffalo Horn, to remind him. For all practical purposes, he knew the winter of content was over. The seasonal signs were everywhere. It was April. Geese were cackling on the high wing, gophers reborn and standing like sturdy picket pins in the warm sunshine, the air misty with the fragrant smell of fresh earth and new life. Ben made his tracks and they were south, toward home. Days later, near the Little Owl, he cut pussy willows and gave them to Little Hoop. Dark eyes widening, she was mystified, but then delighted when he told her it was a symbol of the white man's spring, a humble token of love and affection. She kissed him, expressing her own love. They held each other, watched and listened. The country was beautiful, its vastness staggering, and they were in love. They moved farther south, beyond the Wind. When the small party of Crow escorts finally left them at the Popo Agie, Ben Tree and his woman rode happily up the divide in a freshet, and on through scattered pine and melting drifts of corn snow. They finally came down into the desert rock late the next afternoon and made camp in fresh sage bloom and blossoming cottonwood along the Little Sandy.

On another day, they noticed a blue haze floating over the area where the Tree corrals stretched out beside the Big Sandy. It was smoke. Ben pointed and explained. It was too early in the season for whitetops, a mover's rest stop, and emigrants would be barely up the Platte by this time of the year. He doubted the camp could be any of his family, again for the same reason. Puzzled, he motioned to Little

Hoop and they rode on, slowly, cautiously, their small pack train twisting around the rocky foothill toward the swollen river below. Ten minutes later he spotted the small shelter cabin, smoke coming from the opening in its sod roof. Nearby were two tipis, Shoshoni lodges. There were five horses and fourteen long-eared Missouri mules in the corrals. Then, from the corner of his eye, Ben caught the unmistakable glint of a rifle barrel in the cottonwoods to his left. This was not hostile country; at least, it had never been unfriendly for the Tree family. Turning easily toward the movement, he brought his left hand shoulder-high, two fingers forked. But his right hand idled slowly to his hip, close to the protruding grip of his revolver.

Moments later, he heard a startled cry. "My God-a-mighty, it's Benji!" An older man, full-bearded, dressed in denim and buckskin and carrying a smoothbore, stepped out from behind the tree. "Benji, you rascal! Sure nuff, it's you! Why, I thought you got yourself lost and six feet under! By damn, get off that pony, boy, and shake the dust!"

"Hello, Ruben, you old mossback!" called Ben. "You get that turkey-buster off me and I'll be glad to sit a while!" It was the first white man that Ben Tree had seen in nine long months.

A hearty laugh echoed along the bottom. Ruben Russell, gaunt, grizzled, his tattered hat banded with snake skin, tucked his rifle under his shoulder and leaped forward to meet the approaching horses. From the other side of the trees three more persons suddenly emerged, a man and two squaws. They were followed by several small children.

"Hell!" Ruben yelled out. "I knew someone was coming!"

Ben smiled and dismounted. He turned and helped Little Hoop down. "I suppose if anyone would know, it'd be you, all right," he countered. "Looks like you were expecting someone else, someone like as not you didn't trust.''

Russell grabbed Tree's hand tightly and the two men took turns slapping each other on the back. Their arms locked and they rocked together, laughing. Tree finally said, ''Say, what's this all about, here? What you doing such a piece from Bridger?''

''Big trouble down there.'' Russell shook his head and spat a stream of tobacco. ''Bad things going on, Benji boy. Reg'lar burnings. Mormons made a ruckus down there. Wasn't but a spit-full of us on hand, y'see. They came riding in and told everyone to move out. They's taking over, claiming they bought the place. Government's disputing it. Got all our supplies out 'fore they burned half the place down. Yup, your pa's cabin, too. Ol' Gabe's the same, only he cached a year ago and wasn't around to see it. We came up here until the smoke clears. Holed up, for a fact. Some our folk headed on back to Fort Laramie to tell the troopers. Those rascals are gonna ruin our summer trade for sure, carrying on like this. No pilgrim's gonna trek through this neck of the woods when the word gets back to Mizzou, and the freighters'll have to pay double.''

Ben said, ''The Saints, again, ei? I heard some rumors up north about them.''

''Saints, hell! Reg'lar hellions!'' Russell spat again. ''Reckon ol' Brigham's riled up, those angels all toting arms. One of those fellers said the ol' man's sick'n tired of feudin' and the government's infernal meddlin'. Brigham ain't territorial governor no more . . . took it away from him. Ain't gonna be no trouble like they had in Illinois and Mizzou again, no sir, that's what they're saying. They broke the trails out here. They was the first to spread their blankets. Land's theirs, and they mean to run it. That's the gist of it. Yessir, to hell with the Federals.''

"Rebellion?" Ben said. "That's hard to believe."

"Secession," Russell answered. "They plans on keeping mos' everybody out, 'cept their own. Word from Zion is that ol' Brigham's taking over the country. He's gonna get his licks in. Anyone gets through from the east route, they'll be paying tariffs, mos' likely."

"By jingo, that's treason!" exclaimed Ben. "Why, President Buchanan isn't going to hold still for that, no more than blocking the trail to California!"

Russell gave Ben a funny look and said, "East and west, blocked both directions, Benji. This is a far piece from Washington. Blocked for certain, and your pa never came through with his train from Fort Hall. He ain't no sodbuster, but I ain't seen hide nor hair of him."

A spark of surprise hit Ben, a hint of fear. "Why, you must be joshing!" he said in quiet disbelief. "No word? Nothing?"

"Nary a word." Russell tried to brush it off. Feigning indifference, he said, "Course, knowing your pa, that don't cut much wood, anyhows. If they went choosing him, he'n Will likely holed up, or mebbe went back to Hall for the winter. Oh, they'll find a way of skirting around. Reckon he coulda taken the old Sublette cutoff north, if he took a notion. For riding, it'sa nigher route. Be back in Laramie by now."

"That's not like Pa," returned Ben, shaking his head doubtfully. "There are runners always coming and going, Ruben. Ei, even up in the Indian country. You would have heard . . . someone would have heard."

Russell shrugged. "Well, I'd not be fretting on it unduly. There's nary a word coming in of late. Jest have to sit on it a spell." And before Ben could pursue the matter any farther, Russell turned and addressed his Indian wife, White Crane, in Shoshoni. She and one of the older children immediately took the horses and led them toward the corrals. Russell grinned and pointed to Little Hoop. "Hey now, what's this? Is this what I'm thinking? Don't tell me you went and bought yourself a woman! Glory be, yahoo!"

Russell's sudden, explosive burst of enthusiasm momentarily broke Ben's perturbed, worrisome reflection on the whereabouts of his family. He answered simply, "Yes, Ruben, I suppose I did. This is my wife. Married since last winter."

"Well, God-a-mighty, Benji, if you don't take all! Is that all you got to say? Come sauntering in here minding nothing, stringing ponies, a load of pelts, and a woman to boot. Say, she's a purty thing, all right! Crow, I 'spect, those trappings she's wearing. What you call her?" He walked around Little Hoop once, inspecting her like a new piece of horse flesh. He bent down and took a hard look at Little Hoop's face. "Good teeth, too, by God!" he shouted.

"Little Hoop," Ben said. "her name is Little Hoop. She's a daughter of White Mouth."

"Well, I'll be damned! You don't say?" Russell grinned and slapped Tree on the shoulder. "By God, you went and married a blood-kin, didn't you? Jest like your ol' pap, a squaw man! Yup, fancy-like, too, a chief's daughter, mind you! Well, I 'spect you'll be finding out soon enough, Benji, yup, jest like the rest of us—ain't no finer women walking the earth, if you treat 'em right." He smiled at Little Hoop and started making sign, greeting her, making her welcome. "Yessir, Benji, we'll be having ourselves a celebration on this occasion, and I'm thinking you're plenty hungry."

"We'd be obliged, Ruben. We've been running short on rations the last couple of days. Almost meat-straight."

"Hell, we got plenty, for a fact!" Russell boasted. "Brought the whole larder with us—beans, fatback, flour, and all the fixins. Even fresh meat for pan gravy and biscuits.''

As they walked toward the cabin, Ben began relaying all of the conversation to his wife. This big man named Russell had worked for his father for four years. He was a post trader, now. Long before that he had trapped for Jim Bridger, the Blanket Chief. An old friend, Russell was a powerful hunter, a man who knew all the trails and traditions, and his wife was Shoshoni, like Bridger's—from the same village, in fact. These were his children. The other man in camp was George Denton, a blacksmith. His woman was Pretty Weasel, also Shoshoni. Little Hoop understood. She was happy to find others of her kind among the friends of her husband. And Ben tried to explain everything that Russell had just told him about the Mormon trouble; then, the fact that no word had come through on Thaddeus Tree, his father. These last words disturbed her.

First, she could not understand how white men could quarrel about their God and take the warpath because of it. It was beyond her Indian comprehension. She dismissed that quickly enough, but not the worry she detected in the eyes of her man, his concern for his father and brother. This was something new, something she had not seen before, and she was a part of him. Silently, she shared any new threat to their happiness, hoping as she did that some good could be read into the omens.

But they feasted. They talked long into the night, and the fire became translucent embers glimmering in the darkness of the sod hut. Outside, dogs barked and the coyotes yipped. The men discussed the trade and all that had transpired since Ben Tree's stay in the Indian country. They also made some hard decisions. Ruben Russell and his party decided to stay on the Big Sandy, at least until conditions normalized down below. Ultimately, they planned to return to Bridger. Their roots were already down. Tree agreed. The Saints could not possibly hold the old post, not for long. Russell bent his frontier ear to young Ben's tactical acumen, Ben allowing that the trading post was too remote and of no real strategic importance to the Mormons. The Saints would be hard pressed to keep it under constant surveillance. And once the word of hostilities arrived back in Omaha, the army would call out the troops. Regular troopers would come. The migration to Oregon and California country was too big, too important to be throttled by a band of religious fanatics, grievances notwithstanding. Frontiers were never meant to be stationary. No one had the right to impede progress along the Overland. No one . . .

Young Ben Tree suddenly checked himself. His voice trailed off, and once again he found himself pondering his inconsistent rationale. Unconsciously, he had made the transition again, red to white. His words had become domineering, selfish. He was now talking with the tongue of a selfish, discontented white man. Ashamed, he fell silent. He thought of Buffalo Horn, and the shaman's words became a small haunt: "those who came to mark and divide the land." Whose land? What frontier? These were questions Ben had begun to ponder. The wagon ruts of the migration were already deep, the Mormons, the Oregon sobbusters, the forty-niners. The ruts would become deeper, broader, far-reaching. The curious eyes of the white man, his penchant for the unknown, had always prevailed.

Ben began to understand some of his discomfort, and the dim light of his dilemma revealed a disturbing paradox. He had come westward, free, to what he considered a free and friendly country. Now he found himself living under the inevitable doom that his family had helped to create—civilization. Night embraced

him with uneasy arms. He could not understand why
his father had failed to pass some word down the trail.

But the affair on the Big Sandy was decided. Ben
and Little Hoop rested for three days. Ruben Russell
would bide his time, enjoy the sweet ripening of spring
and wait for the emigrants who always came, regard-
less of trail conditions. And he would return to
Bridger. Meantime, Ben Tree continued to worry. He
had several options. He could take the Sublette cutoff
west to Fort Hall, a risky trip at best, on the long
chance that his father and Will were in the area. Or he
could return to headquarters at Fort Laramie, sell his
pelts, and resume his labor and wait, if necessary.
And, he rationalized, if his father had indeed bypassed
Fort Bridger, the family would already be at home in
Independence. The people at Laramie could confirm
that they had passed through.

This latter option seemed far more logical, so, early
in May, he and Little Hoop packed supplies and trailed
east toward the North Platte. The route was as familiar
as the palm of Ben's hand. By the fourth morning they
were heading down the upper Sweetwater, generally
following the washed-out sign of the Fort Bridger ref-
ugees already ten days ahead of them.

Ben's casual slouch in the saddle, the lazy rhythm
that blended him into his horse, was the customary
mark of a trail rider. His body was at rest. Body, yes,
but never his eyes. Sharp and restless, they moved
constantly, warily reaching ahead, to the side, and frequently below. Experience had taught him. The red
blood in him had helped. He was forever watching for
the unexplained, unusual movement in the rocks or
brush, the stir of dust in a calm, or a configuration of
tracks moving in an irregular direction or manner.

For a while he did not mention to Little Hoop the
fresh sign they had just crossed, unshod prints, perhaps four or five sets heading northeast. Temporarily,

he let it pass. The country in that direction was protection in itself—flat for the most part, too sparse for hiding or ambush. But gradually it rolled up into foothills, grassy dunes, and rocky outcroppings. To the right of them was the Sweetwater, boisterous with spring runoff, its bottom interspersed with new greenery, mostly cottonwood and willow. The tracks, however, had told him something, and it disturbed him—almost as much as his own carelessness bothered him. Obviously, the party now in the foothills a mile or so away had spotted them first.

Only after another fifteen minutes had passed did Ben indicate that something was amiss. One shadow had been enough, that tiny, misplaced vertical on a horizontal horizon. Disguising his small worry, he smiled over at Little Hoop and said easily, "Would you be surprised if I told you that we have company? Yonder, there to the left, about a mile."

She stared straight ahead, and without alarm returned, "No. I already know it. Your head turns too much."

"Ei," he grinned. "Smart woman."

"Are they following us?"

"I'll wager on it," answered Ben. "They won't make fools of themselves, though . . . come riding down on us out here." Checking the time, he stared up at the sky, all curdled like a tumble of white marbles, a buttermilk sky. The sun was a bleary eye. "Plenty of time," he commented.

"Lakota?"

"I doubt it." He meaningfully touched his head once. Hatless, his long blondish hair was banded by leather again. "Those people know me. No, I suspect they're Cheyenne, maybe Arapaho."

Some concern finally crept into her voice. "You're not troubled? What are you thinking?"

"I know they're up there," he replied. "That's good

enough for now. We'll stay along the river trail for a piece . . . see what they're up to. That's what they'd expect us to do. I know how they think, and I don't want to spoil their fun, leastways, not right away. Let them watch us.''

Little Hoop frowned at him. "Coyote."

"Ei," Ben grunted. "A coyote with two heads."

"You're an Indian coyote."

"Well, yes, but I know how the white man thinks, too. Now, he'll take the easiest trail. He'll look for fresh water, a grove of firewood, a shelter of trees. He'll throw his blanket down by a big fire. He likes his comfort, and he'll go out of his way to find it. Now those devils up there know that, too . . . know right where we're headed. If they're up to testing us, they'll make it the safest way, picking their own ground, probably up high. They won't come riding down in this open country, not where I can dust them with a rifle.''

"You will make it plenty bad for them," she nodded with renewed confidence.

"If I get the chance," Ben answered. "But I suppose one of those braves up there has some sense in his breath feathers. At least, he *thinks* he knows what he's doing.''

Little Hoop asked, "And what will we do?"

"Well, I'm thinking on that, too," he smiled back. "I'll tell you one thing: We can't fool around and let it get dark on us. We'd have our hands full, then. No, we'll go on down the river a piece, woman, just keeping our distance. If they stay up there, I know what they'll be planning. It won't come off that way, not if I can help it. I'll be choosing the ground, not them. Fact is, it's about time we started teaching some of these fellows a hard lesson in manners.''

Little Hoop's eyes widened and her voice quickened. "You wouldn't try stealing ponies? Like the last time, the Blackfeet? Wasn't that lesson enough? Now you *are* the crazy dog!''

Ben admonished her teasingly, ''There's no one to blame for my stealing but those Absaroke brothers of yours. Damned if I'm not one of the best horse thieves this side of Laramie! Truth is, I'm getting so I sort of enjoy the challenge.''

''Ei, my lover is a fool!'' she whispered. ''You know this is different. Would you make me a widow so soon?''

Ben placated her by saying, ''Not a chance. No, you're too precious, my sun. Ei, I love you too much to make a fool out of myself. No ma'am, I won't go sticking my neck out when those devils have the upper hand, not with you along. On the other hand, I can't let them steal everything we have and decorate their war shirts with our hair, either.''

''But why do you frighten me? Your words . . . I never know when you make a joke. It's like a game. The enemy is out there, and you talk of love, my gentle man. You saw the Blackfeet that day. Ei, you laughed and kissed me. Would you laugh at death?''

''Not yours,'' he returned. ''Not by a damned sight.'' Man Called Tree nudged his horse ahead and rode on, as though he were checking the trail. Directly, he returned and nodded toward a far hill. ''See that rise yonder? The one with the notch in it? You keep your pretty eyes on that place. That's where they'll be sneaking across to keep ahead of us. Not much cover, but they don't need much. They'll cut it slicker than a whistle. Mark my word. Now, downriver a couple of miles is where the old wagon ruts take off. There's a couple of spots there no more than a hundred paces from the rocks up above. You understand?''

''Yes,'' Little Hoop nodded. ''They will hide and wait.''

''I'll bet a cracker on it. I know this stretch. Why,

we'd be like sitting ducks going through that place. It's ready-made for ambush.'' Ben looked over at her and grinned. ''We won't take that route, not this day.''

''You have another way?'' she asked hopefully.

''We don't have much choice,'' he said. ''And we can't outrun them, not the way we're packed.'' She followed his stare to the river. ''That's right,'' he continued. ''We'll put it between us. Soon as they cross that gap and disappear, we're cutting for the trees yonder and fording the river. They'll be out of sight for a while. Those are the Green Mountains way over there. We can trail the foothills if we have to . . . cut back down at Independence Rock. I've done worse.''

She gave him a doubtful look. The normally languid Sweetwater was turbulent, and even if they crossed, would not the enemy follow? She remembered . . . the Green Mountains, the Green River, a country that the Arapaho knew well. As they rode, Tree tried to allay her fear. True, the river was running high, but it was only dangerous along its hidden bars where the slit deepened into a quagmire. Above the bends, on the riffles, it was safe. There the water quickened, taking most of the spring sediment into the slower eddies below. Little Hoop nodded. Her man knew these things. But when Tree said that it was, indeed, probable that the Indians would follow, she threw out her hands in despair. Had he not already told her that they were unable to outrun them? Whatever was he thinking?

Ben calmly explained. ''By the time they come back to the point and start backtracking, we'll be two miles gone up the other side. You will, anyhow.'' He nodded toward the opposite shore. ''I'll just sit over there somewhere in some cover with my rifle and see if they have the nerve to come along. Maybe they won't, but if they do, by jingo, I'll show them what real bushwhacking is. They'll drop like flies in the frost if they try crossing behind us.''

And his guess was right—the Indians *were* headed for the rocks below. Shortly, Ben and Little Hoop detected only the faintest flash far away in the small shadows of brush near the gap crossing. Minutes later, he led their string of horses belly-deep through the river. After he had directed his wife to an area well away from the stream, Ben selected his own spot, a clump of driftwood and willow about ten paces from the water's edge. The sun was warm. He was thoroughly concealed, and had an unbroken range of approach two hundred yards each direction. Carefully checking the breech of his Maynard, Tree then placed four extra loads at the foot of the log. Satisfied, he settled back and relaxed. If they came they would be *below* him, positions reversed, and what a welcome he intended to give them!

The wait was longer than he'd anticipated. No matter, he knew better than to give it up, since Indians were so cunningly patient and he was certain they would come. Twenty minutes dragged by. Still no sight of any horses beyond the far trees.

Another five minutes had passed before he saw a horse and rider coming into the trees. Ben perked up. Easing his rifle butt onto his shoulder, he aimed out from between his blind. Moments later, the advance rider was joined by three more braves. Reining up at the edge of the trees, they paused, silently observing the distant bank. Curious, they were also cautious. Ben saw one of the men pointing to the small hills in back of him, the direction Little Hoop had taken. She was far out of sight, but the tracks of their stock in the new grass pointed the way like a signal beacon. No doubt about it now—the party was going to make the crossing and follow the tracks up the draw.

The first Indian into the ford rode a large gray. Ben saw a flutter of feathers trailing from his hair. He was an Arapaho brave with honors, and he came alone, not the way Ben had figured it, nor the way he wanted it. The others were safely hanging back. He cursed softly, suddenly struck by what he had almost forgotten—the Indian way. His own strategy went sailing down the swift Sweetwater currents. The four warriors were going to single-file it, far apart. For the moment he had only the one decent target, the advance rider. All he could do now was narrow the odds.

The brave came on, almost three-quarters of the way across the river before a second one rode out behind him. Ben held his fire, his quick eyes flashing from mount to mount, judging distance, his mind racing for decisions. Then, with three or four gigantic plunges, the big gray lead pony was on the bank below, no more than twenty feet away. When the horse wheeled, its warrior suddenly loomed above Ben. The brave stared directly down at the clump of downfall. In that moment, and in a blur of deadly swiftness, Ben Tree brought out his revolver instead of the rifle and fired. The impact of the ball tumbled the brave back across the rump of the startled pony. Rifle flying, the Arapaho rolled off and fell facedown in the mud and sand.

With bewildering speed, Ben then brought his Maynard into play. His next shot was forty yards across the water. The second rider toppled, bobbed once in the current, then disappeared in a swirl of murky water. His pony reared and splashed away to the far bank, and Tree hunkered back down behind his log, trying to reload. When he came up, the other two riders were fleeing away through the trees, poor targets at best. No chance, there. Straining his eyes, he tried to penetrate the shadows across the water; once, in the dim distance, he caught sight of a riderless horse loping upriver. He could only guess, a reasonable one, that the pony was following the two men who had escaped his ambush. Ben sighed in relief.

After a short wait, he moved out from his cover. The Arapaho on the bank was dead from a shot through the chest. Ben methodically began stripping away the dead man's small medicine pouch and skinning knife. He retrieved the fallen rifle, thus making himself a gun-snatcher of sorts. After rolling the body into the river, Ben clucked at the gray pony, coaxing him in. It took him only a short time to catch it, and with a shout and a kick he galloped away, following the trail of Little Hoop. His triumphant scream reverberated across the hills. She would know.

June, 1857

Fort Laramie. We put in two days getting the main cabin back in order. We'll be waiting here for a spell. Pa and Will haven't arrived, nor did they pass through. No one can figure this. It makes me worry, but I can only believe they must be north of the Salt desert, or on their way back. I cannot give in to despair. Plenty of people arriving. One company of troops, regulars and some old friends on hand. There's one camp of Oglala nearby. I'll smoke with them. Word is that troops are already headed this way from the States, guided by Gabe B. himself. Understand the Federals are under orders to take Salt Lake City.

I'll go down-country tomorrow and check on our stock—Wm. Banner and family been tending. More than forty head, he says, and most of them branded. Grass is excellent. Sunday is with foal so I turned her out to pasture and no more work. Little Hoop is pleased with the cabin and all these trimmings. She's plenty happy to be off the trail. In English she says ''I like.'' First time she ever bathed in a tin tub or slept in a feather bed. She's making like a woman with a new bonnet and ribbons. Supplies good and some women folk been dropping by to pay their respects to my bride. $400 cash for my pelts. Not bad considering bad state of fur market. B. Tree.

FOUR

Summer came behind mid-June deluges, the earth alive, wild mustard and daisy blooming, magpies nesting in the Laramie thickets. The adobe-walled outpost swelled by the week, with traders, immigrants, and fortune-seekers resting, cavorting, many biding time until Col. Albert Sidney Johnston's troops arrived. Hopes were high. The soldiers were downriver, not far, and the motley miscellany of frontier driftwood at Fort Laramie drank liquor, gambled, and waited expectantly.

Among the homespun brown, buckskin, and coarse, store-bought denim, nightly orations thundered under the warm skies outside the stockade. Bonfires roared with the sodbuster's optimism. Johnston's boys would put the Saints in their proper place, by God, right back in the vast Salt desert where they belonged! There were the usual condemnations, the ultimate black threats, because, for certain, the Mormons were going to pay for their marauding misadventures.

Bands of watchful Oglala Sioux came, looking for

whiskey and bad bargains. They smoked and drank,
too. They listened and went away amused over the
wasichus' anxiety and frustration. No roads, no boundaries, for the wild Oglala.

A few trains of eager immigrants, less vociferous,
less wary, paused among the clamor long enough to
recruit fresh stock, repair wagons, and replenish supplies. They moved out as soon as they could, weapons
at the ready, taking advantage of the balmy weather,
trusting their welfare to self-determination and the
trail-wise guides they had employed. Hostile Indians
and Saints be damned, it was Oregon and California
or bust.

Through it all Ben Tree toiled constantly, breaking
teams to the traces, trading and selling, though under
a continuing fret—Thaddeus and Will Tree were still
missing somewhere on the frontier, a year to the month
now. There had been no word, no sign, not even by
Indian telegraph from beyond the great Rock Mountains. A few traders trickled in from the wilderness.
Ben's inquiries were casual, emotionless, always the
cool front. No one read his mind, but to Little Hoop
his worry was apparent. She shared his love and she
read his eyes, the way they forever turned westward.
She also read the omens. They told her that by the
Month of the Black Berries she and her man would be
on the Great Medicine Road again. She began making
preparations.

Late one afternoon, while Ben was passing the mer-
cantile, another of the trail guides hailed him from the
shade of the wooden porch where men often gathered
to parley and smoke during the quiet part of the day.
This man was John "Domino" Dominguez, a wiry,
wrinkled Spaniard, somewhat of the mettle of Gabe
Bridger and a time-tested veteran of the mountains. He
had just come down the trail from Mormon country
after wintering at Fort Hall. Earlier, he had helped

scout for a wagon train headed to the Oregon territory. After that brief greeting, Ben asked Dominguez if he had heard anything about his father and Will.

Dominguez, with a deep frown, said, "This is what I wanted to see you about. No, I did not see them at Fort Hall. I only heard this bad news this morning, but I tell you, this Englishman Digby at the post remembers they went through, eh? He has all the news, who goes, who comes. This was a long time ago, even before I see you that day at South Pass. Ah, but when I saw you here, I say, ah, they must be back, maybe that you met them at the Big Sandy on their return, eh?"

"I didn't make it back from the Crow," Ben explained. "One thing and another, and I spent the whole damned winter with White Mouth's village."

Nodding, his clay pipe jumping as he talked, Dominguez said, "I see you still have your hair, eh? I think maybe Gabe has taught you well." His dark eyes narrowed into fine slits, and he went on. "About your father, it's like a puzzle, no? I think he knows these places too well to get lost, and has too many friends on the trail to find misfortune. So, what can I say? Many problems now—Indians, Mormons, banditos. Who knows a friend, anymore? I have nothing besides my horse, my rifle, and pack, and only three days ago I have to ride for my life up the North Platte. Arapahos, eh, and only the river and the night saves me and my hair." He shook his head sadly. "But, *Señor* Tree, he has big wagons, mules. This, I think, is very hard to lose, eh, not to see them along the way."

Ben Tree agreed with the scout. "That's what has me worried. They never get too far off the road with that kind of a rig."

"So what will you do, my friend?"

"Hit the trail, go looking," Ben replied. "At least as soon as things settle down over that way, maybe even take a ride over to Mormon country and see if they know anything.''

Dominguez gave him a dark, disapproving stare. ''Best to wait a little while, *amigo*. Yes, I think, until the army arrives. These hairy ones are angry with everyone, and will tell you nothing but to get out of their land. *'Mano,* they are worse than Indians, I tell you this.'' He smiled faintly. ''Only one difference, they don't take hair, eh?''

''How did you get through this mess?'' inquired Ben Tree.

Dominguez tapped his temple with the stem of his pipe. ''I slept two days, hiding, rode two nights, up high off the trail.''

Several days later, a mile to the southeast where the July heat danced atop a prairie knoll, three riders were sighted, two of them dressed in deep military blue. There were shouts of joy from around the fort and people came running from all directions. Johnston's scouts were arriving. There were cheers for the military, hurrahs and clapping when the long army train began to appear. Brigham Young would pay, now! The federals had arrived to march into Mormon land.

But it was the third man of the approaching trio that held Ben Tree's anxious interest. He was a special kind of breed. No blue cloth for him. Few others paid much attention to him in his drab frontier plainness, and many people at the fort could not even identify with him. He was slender, and he slumped in the saddle. The pony he rode wore a beaded Crow neckpiece. An older man, splinters of gray flecked his temples, and his eyes, hidden under the brimmed shadow of a faded cavalry hat, were squinted slits of dusty blue. His name was Jim ''Gabe'' Bridger, and he was wilderness legend, the frontier personified, thirty years of it. He never came with bugles of fanfare. That had been reserved for the troopers following behind. He simply shared a hello and several shakes from acquaintances before a young friend by the name of Ben Tree invited him to spend his blanket at the cabin.

By dusk, Bridger had heard most all of the news that had drifted downriver since his frontier departure almost two years before. He had gone home, then, back to civilization on the Little Santa Fe in Missouri. Now he was back again—the army had asked him to return, to lead the way at ten dollars a day, a very handsome wage. "Major Bridger," they called him. He joked with Ben about his title, more so about the tenderfeet behind him, the whippersnappers, the greenhorns, yet here he was guiding Johnston's troops to Salt Lake City.

It was not the money that had coaxed him back. Bridger freely admitted it. He could confess to Benji Tree, a young man made in his image thirty years later, a man he could now envy as well as admire. No, it was the call of the frontier, something strangely beautiful coursing his veins, swimming in his tired eyes, some lonely wilderness voice calling from the inside. Now nearing sixty, Bridger wanted that last refreshing glimpse before the great mirage disappeared under the grinding wheels and pulverized soil of ten thousand wagons. He wanted to taste the wilderness again before it vanished.

They feasted in the cabin—ham, greens, prairie peas, and corn bread. Gabe Bridger dipped and ate heartily. No field rations here; this was good, solid frontier fare, and he was delighted with Little Hoop, a woman of his kind, too. Bridger knew some Absaroke but he readily made sign, swiftly conversing with her, ignoring Ben's polite attempts to translate. Sign would make do, always had. There was no tribe on the plains that he could not parley with. He knew Little Hoop's father, White Mouth, knew the Crow intimately, had smoked with them many times ten, twenty, thirty years ago. He related stories of those days, the legends, the bad jokes, and they all fell into laughter.

But Jim Bridger was disheartened by the news of Thaddeus and Will's strange disappearance. Not surprised, but saddened. He was smart enough to disregard theories. The wilderness, no stranger to him, could beat a man to his knees and bring him to a prayerful death. Or it could caress him and sustain him. It had its unusual quirks. The wilderness was capable of swallowing men a hundred different ways, most often without a trace, and then, quite to the contrary, sometimes it often gave them up, miraculously alive.

But finally the present conflict surfaced, the reason for the veteran scout's presence: Mormons. Gabe Bridger quietly made his quaint postulate on the situation. Of course, he had no personal quarrel with these people. He was only along to do a job, to take the last measure of his own cup and the vanishing frontier. Realistically, the migration routes had to remain open, free from Mormon intervention. In his mind, there was no question about this. It was the only practical solution. It was a free country, was it not? If there were such things as priorities, who could put in a claim any better than Bridger? His blanket had gone down in the Wasatch long before Nauvoo and Sugar Creek, years before the westward vision of Joseph Smith, the fabled martyr. For a fact, he had greeted Brigham Young and his small, battered legion in '47, a bedraggled, weary, persecuted lot of Israelites fleeing from their Egypt. He knew all of their eccentricities, their legends, this lost tribe of Israel. Bridger counseled the Saints, took them into the great unknown and made it known. He knew Brigham, well enough. If Brigham was not Moses, he was the next thing to it. Zion had been established in the Salt desert basin ten years before. But it was Gabe Bridger, the true oracle of revelation, who had pointed the way, not the prophet, Brigham.

They were on Ben's small porch. Beyond, in a clearing, the celebrants were kindling the talking fires. The new troopers were at rest on the flats, and the squatters huddled around them. Bridger was speaking to Ben, continuing the dialogue.

"Fact is, it all boils down to religion. Always has. These are peculiar people, Benji, same as Injuns. Anyone who don't see eye-to-eye with what we gentiles allow is the gospel, is bound to be getting himself in a patch of nettles." He smiled over at Ben. "You had your schooling in Saint Louie, didn't you? Your pa's always making brag over it. Reckon you learnt something about the Revolution—folks a'breaking away."

"Yes, but the Saints asked for the Utah territory, wanted it made government territory . . . asked for it for their own protection and benefits. No one's disputing their religion out there. I don't begrudge any man his beliefs, but taking over the law . . ."

Bridger chuckled. "Ain't the way it's turning out, Benji. Way the folks in Washington sees it is that the church is taking to running the government. That's ol' man Brigham, course. Now, that ain't exactly the way the big paper reads, not like the government sees it. A man can't be governor and God at the same time. Hell, I knew all along this fussing was coming to no good, but right or wrong, the Saints are cutting their own throats fooling around with the routes, keeping the migration from going through. You're right on that. It's all a big mistake, and I'll allow they'll be finding it out soon as the army moves in."

"You think they'll make a fight of it?" Ben asked.

Bridger rubbed his grizzled chin and frowned. "Hell no, Benji. Agin four thousand troops? There's some fanatics, like I say, but they ain't gonna fiddle with the government, not for long, they ain't. They'll make a noise, sure enough, mebbe a little killing. If I know ol' Brigham, he's got one up his sleeve. He's a heap of stir but no biscuits. He'll turn around and make a cause of it, like always, but no big fight.'' Spitting across the porch for emphasis, he added, ''Knowing the ol' man, I'll wager on it.''

They were silent for a spell, watching the night fires spring up. Later someone struck a fiddle, and there was a clap and a shout, hoedown. Two young Indian women stopped by to talk with Little Hoop, and the three of them walked away to the side, fascinated by the evening furor. Bridger finally spoke up again. He was surprised to discover Benji at Fort Laramie, particularly with the trail over South Pass open. But then he understood the family situation, what had since developed, the missing kinfolk, and the brewing storm in the Utah territory. Understandable. But what did Benji have planned?

''Reckon you and that little woman plan on caching one of these days,'' Bridger said. ''Figure you got business out there somewhere. You're same as your pa, Benji, raring to go when the work is cut out.''

''Ei, business,'' Ben answered with a wry smile. ''Where does such a business start? I've been waiting, more or less hoping things'll take a turn for the better . . . some word on Pa and Will. I don't have any sign to follow, not a single thing, Gabe. I'm worried, plain worried, this Mormon thing and all.''

Bridger lit his pipe and puffed several times, then paused for a moment of calculation. He was a man who understood circumstances, who knew how to make ends meet. He knew character, the frontier mind and how it functioned. And young Ben Tree was his friend, his prodigy, and likewise his concern. ''I'll not be denying it, son,'' Bridger admitted, ''it don't augur well. Thinking on it, I reckon the best place to start would be Fort Hall . . . Shoshoni or Nez Percé country. They know your kin. Jim Digby might have some line on the Mormons up that way."

"It's been a year," interjected Ben. "A long year. John Dominguez just came back that way. Digby did see Pa and Will going the other way, west. That's it."

Bridger said softly, "Ain't good to let things chew on you too much, Benji. Riles the belly . . . bad medicine. Won't do you a lick of good." Pausing, he blew out a stream of blue smoke. "Now I was thinking, if you had a mind for it you might tie up with Colonel Johnston for a spell. You'll be heading west, anyways, I can tell that. Be obliged if you'd come along; that is, if there's nothing keeping you here. I'll be talking to the ol' man tonight. Scouting ain't bad, and my word cuts a path with him. You could hire on as far as my old post and push up to Fort Hall from there, check in with Digby."

Ben looked up quickly. "Are you joshing? Me? Scouting for these blue-jackets?"

Bridger shrugged and poked a thumb into his buckskin. "Lookit me, son. It's about all that's left out here. Why don't you think on it?"

Pondering, wondering, Ben said, "I don't know. Sure, I've had a notion, moving out. Chores are about cleaned up. I suppose . . ."

"Well, for certain, I could use your eyes," Bridger continued. "Mine ain't exactly what they used to be, fuzzy 'n' all. You come along. I could sure fix it with the Colonel if you're aiming to cache. Say, mebbe at five dollars a day and vittles."

Ben bent his brow, contemplating the surprising invitation. But the suggestion had merit. Because of his father and Will, he realized that a journey west was already in the offing. It had been on his mind for a long time. And he *did* know the trails, as well as anyone. Riding ahead of an army would relieve Little

Hoop, too, of her fear of another misadventure with hostiles. Ben finally said, "That's a fair wage, Gabe. I'll sleep on it . . . talk to Little Hoop."

"You do that." Smoke curled around Bridger's head. He chuckled. "These soldier boys ain't much for knowing the land, Benji, not like the post troopers here. Have to point 'em to the latrine, for a fact."

The night deepened. Bridger thought he might go now, perhaps report in with the Colonel and then find a place to throw down his bedding.

"I didn't know about your eyes," Ben probed. "Nothing serious, I hope?" He stood with the veteran scout by the steps.

"I have my poor days," Bridger confessed. "Oh, it's nothing to go talking up—jest between you'n me and the gate post, y'see. I figure this'll be the last of it for me, anyways. I can use a right knowledgeable hand on the point, though. You'd be handy, for certain. Reckon there's a passel of Sioux and Cheyenne up ahead. Like as not, this war party of the Colonel's might make for some fancy smoking and talking if any Injuns ride in."

"The land is peaceful enough," Ben said. "There's a few Arapaho picking on stragglers. I didn't spot any Sioux or Cheyenne my last trip in. They're usually no bother unless some greenhorn starts riling them by trespassing, or some other foolish notion. Dominguez got chased a few days ago. But the troopers here at the garrison seem to get on well enough. At least, they steer most of the pilgrims away from trouble. I don't know the mettle of your Federals, though. I hope your Colonel Johnston has more sense than some of these movers who keep sneaking up the wrong valleys. It's making some of my Indian friends up north nervous, if you know what I mean."

Bridger smiled sadly. "I know what you mean, Benji. That's high-feather talk, something only you'n me savvy. I read the omen, too. Country's a'changing, getting all cluttered up. For better or worse, I don't know. Depends on what you stand for. Might as well fess up: Like it or not, the pilgrims are here to stay, and there's a passel more on the way."

"I'm talking about the treaty lands they keep making tracks on."

"Too big to put a fence around, I 'spect," Bridger said, shaking his head. "I used to figure there was plenty of land out here for all. Sometimes it jest don't work out that way, treaty or no. Y'see, the Injun is a'changing, too. Used to make jokes about those movers, all their funny contraptions. Yep, scare 'em up plenty, take a few gifts and then go away bellylaughing at the yellow-eyes. Ain't laughing much now, cuz yellow-eyes ain't so scared anymore and the country ain't so infernal lonely like it used to be. Y'see, people only respect the land when it's wild . . . when it scares the hell out of 'em."

"By jingo, the squatters are beginning to scare the hell out of me," Ben said glumly.

Bridger nodded sympathetically, saying, "Hell, I know, Benji, I know. Why, when I was your age, I started riding out every time I heard the crack of an axe. Scared me, too. Damned if they didn't chase me all the way north of the Salt desert. Never heard a church bell for thirty years. Can't say that I missed all the preaching either. Always seemed like to me there was God-a-plenty for me in those big mountains. Yep, the big lonesome. Now, I hear tell the blackrobes are toting bells all the way to the Bitterroots, and I don't 'spect it's for the Flatheads alone. Settlers, I reckon." The mountain man hesitated, puffed several times, then continued with a chuckle of kind understanding. "Benji, looks like you'n me been caught on the horns of ol' man time, throwed into the scrub and resigned to picking thorns outta our asses. Boy, we jest ain't got much choice, either. When you stand still too long, everyone passes you by. First thing you know, you're last in line.''

"Yes," Ben grudgingly admitted, "it's damned if you do and damned if you don't. I'm finding that out. You know, Pa's been trading with the migration for ten years, doing his best, pulling pilgrims through dust and mud, fighting their battles, come Hell or high water. He always says when the water's running high, there's no shutting it off with a finger.'' The young scout stopped and sighed. He gave Bridger a pathetic look, a look of fateful resignation. "I suppose Pa's right—if we weren't taking the farmer's trade, someone else would be. It's a living. Never used to bother me too much, the busters. They kept on moving on. I don't know, now. I'm getting so I hate the looks of them anymore.''

"Yep," agreed Bridger, "jest like beggar lice—fetch one and y'get a dozen.'' He paused on the step and shook his head. "Hard to understand. Never content, mind you, always looking for a better rock pile, wanting the whole hog of it. It ain't all milk and honey out here. Course, you can't tell a greenhorn any different. They figure all of it's a free country, signed, sealed, and delivered by the U.S. government. And when there's gold about they'll pay you no mind, not 'till the day of reckoning—when a few neighbors start losing hair. Yep, and that's when there's all hell to pay.'' He raised his forked fingers in friendship. "You're a smart boy, Benji," he said. "You know how to read the sign . . . understand it, same as me. Only one thing: I don't think we're ever gonna find a way to make settling out here tolerable.''

Knocking out his pipe, Bridger was about to turn and head for the troop encampment when one of the young Oglala women who had been with Little Hoop suddenly ran up to the porch. Her words were breathless fragments, almost to the point of being meaningless. She began gesturing, making some frantic attempt to be understood. Bridger quickly picked up the drift of it. She was saying that some *wasichu* at one of the nearby fires had seized Little Hoop. They were shaming her, trying to make her dance up and down like the white men. It was bad, but only she and her friend had managed to escape and run away. By the time Bridger had turned around to translate, Ben already was reaching for the peg inside the cabin door. Buckling on his gun belt, he leaped the porch rail like a startled deer and ran for the new encampment. The mountain man was loping right behind him.

They soon came upon the boisterous scene at a camp directly outside the stockade gate, where the wagons of several whiskey drummers and muleskinners were drawn up under the trees. Bunched in a ragged circle around the fire, a dozen men were clapping and shouting in tune with a lone harmonica. In the middle, two of the party were stomping in jig-time, taking turns shoving Little Hoop back and forth between them. Pathetically, there was no escape for the Indian girl, and her young face read panic. Ben immediately seized a long bullwhip from one of the wagons and shoved his way into the ring. With his foot, he sent one grinning spectator sprawling. The circle suddenly broke rhythm. The harmonica stopped on a high note and wheezed off with a sour screech. Making a huge serpentine arc with the whip, Ben deftly curled it around one of the dancer's legs, bringing the man down like a smitten ox. Little Hoop staggered to the side and, sobbing in shame, disappeared into the darkness. Several angry shouts erupted, but before they had died Ben, in a continuing motion of fury, had snapped tension into the big whip, snaring his fallen victim. With a swift jerk and a great heave, he dragged the entwined man directly into the hot embers of the fire.

Screaming, flames licking up his trousers and shirt, the muleskinner rolled away into the dust, finally curled himself into a ball of agony. Two of his companions lunged forward and fell over him, frantically beating at the burning cloth. Moments later, only the crackling wood and intermittent gasps of pain from the stricken muleskinner were heard, but the air fairly crackled with tension. Aware that trouble had arrived, several men, less drunk, began melting away between the wagons. Three others, less convinced, moved sullenly toward Ben, but suddenly stopped when Jim Bridger came up behind the stranger with the whip. Respect temporarily prevailed, and for the moment it was a standoff.

Shaking a fist at Ben, one of the men angrily shouted, "What kind of ornery critter are you? We was only having a little fun with the squaw. By Gawd, you're spoiling for it!"

"Yessir!" another snarled. "Why, we oughtta take that whip to you right good and tan your goddamned hide. Lookit what you done to the man!"

Ben stared at them in white anger, the cords in his locked jaw nervously kneading. He obligingly threw the whip to the ground. "Try it," he challenged lowly. "I'll blow the fingers off of the first man who touches this whip. Which of you will it be?"

Toward the back, a drummer slowly began edging a rifle from the wagon seat.

Jim Bridger moved in and spoke calmly. "It's all over, boys. Let's be forgetting it." He glanced over at the man with the rifle. "Better cache that thing, son, real careful-like. You'll be making a sorry mistake. Like as not, you'll never get it to your shoulder. Come on, let's all ease off, now. We'll be going our own ways."

"It's yer word, Gabe," one put in, "but it ain't yer fight! That's a dirty, mean trick, this feller pulled! You saw it! Ain't yer place to go siding with trash like that!''

Several growls of assent went around the group, but no one made a direct move toward Tree. He coldly waited, testing each of them, hands loose at his sides, his eyes level and steady. No one pressed. Nodding at the man groaning to his side, Ben said, "If that friend of yours ever crosses my trail again, I'll kill him.'' With that, he turned on his heel and left.

Bridger patiently held up his hands. "All right, she's done with. Best to let bygones be bygones, boys. Jest a little mistake in judgment, that's all.''

"He burned ol' Bob!''

"Jest singed him a touch,'' Bridger allowed. "Why, he'll be good as new in a couple of days. Probably nothing more than a few scorched tail feathers.''

"We ain't forgettin', Gabe!'' another said. "The squaw came passing by a'lookin', three of 'em, by gawd. What's the harm in a little jiggin'? That cuss is a mean'un, coming uninvited. Trouble's his game, for sure.''

Bridger sighed. Peace had become his forte. But he was struck now by annoyance and ignorance, and his patience began to collapse. Shaking his head, he explained sarcastically, "Y'see, some of these Injun gals ain't never seen you *civilized* people before. . . . Just plumb curious to see how *gentlemen* act, I reckon. All the hullabaloo 'round here's bound to attract the savages. Now, if you'd pulled such a fool stunt on some brave's woman, one of those Oglala brothers, like as not you'd be a dead duck in the morning. Yep, and everyone 'round here would be fixing to fight Injuns, by crackee.''

"Haw!'' one of the men shouted derisively. "Over those stinking squaws? Now, that's a bull tale, Gabe! Who in the hell's gonna side with Injuns? What kinda bull you spreading this time?''

A round of uneasy laughter cut the night air.

Bridger said easily, "Well, son, the one you went dancing that way jest happens to be the wife of that feller. You're lucky in that respect. Least, the Sioux won't be down and cutting off your bag."

"A squaw man! Wal, Jesus Crise, Gabe! How's we to know such a thing like that! He oughtta be keeping her in his goddamned tent where she belongs."

"He'll get his dues," another promised bitterly. "Don't matter one whit."

"Mebbe," Bridger drawled back, "but I'd think on it. He's a mite more than a squaw man, if my word means a bean. He's a caution. Mind what I say, men, that feller is a caution."

"What you meaning by that?" one asked. "That ornery cuss ain't no better'n the rest of us, dammit!"

"Mebbe," Bridger repeated. "Tell you one thing— he's counted more coup than you got teeth. Why, if that young buck painted the foreleg of his pony, it'd look like a barber pole. Case you're interested, his name is Ben Tree. If you greenhorns ain't been this way, probably means no more than a cold bean and a dry hole. Ben Tree. You remember it."

"Drovers," one of them said. "I heard of the family, just drovers."

"One a killer," another put in. "Yeah, I heard that."

Jim Bridger spat in the fire. "You hear right, boys. Last fool that made a move on Benji Tree, caught a ball right between his eyes." He motioned toward the dark knolls beyond the wagon. "Feller's buried up there a piece. Fancied himself a hand with a pistol, I hear. Probably more brag. Name was Bullock, so says the marker." Bridger tipped his faded hat and turned away between the wagons. "Night, boys," he called back.

* * *

It was not "good night" for Benjamin Tree. Hurrying to the cabin, he found Little Hoop and one of the young Oglala maidens sitting together in the darkness on the porch stoop angrily making sign. Hands flashing, cutting the evening air like boning knives, they were both venting their anger on the vile, unmannerly *wasichu*. If Little Hoop had fled the bonfire scene in shame, it had taken only moments for the shame to turn into sheer outrage. Never had Ben seen his young wife so angry. Of course, his own emotions were as taut as a banjo string.

The Oglala girl thrust her chin outward and spat. *"Shunka witko!"* she cursed in Siouan.

"Hau, hau," Ben agreed grimly. He sat beside Little Hoop, put an arm around her, and said softly, *"Bi-itsi."* Good woman.

Little Hoop, her eyes two black slits of fury, forked her fingers and poked them toward the distant fire. *"Ictua wapaxaxiky!* I stick it in his eyes! He eats fish! If I had my knife, I would have cut his face! Ei, my man, I won't make this mistake again. These men of the wagons are plenty bad."

"Ei," Ben agreed once more. There was little use in trying to pacify the two women, but he added, "Some of these people don't understand our ways . . . what is proper and improper. They are filled with stinging water. I'm sorry. I should have been with you."

The Lakota girl, Red Robe Woman, made a series of wild flourishes. "Bad music! Bad dance! Who is so crazy to jump up and down like a clumsy bear and call it dance? Did you ever see a bear dance on two feet like that? *Eyah!*"

Ben Tree smiled faintly, then signed back to the women, "This man won't feel like dancing for one moon. It will pain him plenty to squat. He put out the fire with his bottom."

The two young women stared at Ben, then at each other, and finally Red Robe Woman giggled. Little Hoop giggled back. Even though it had been a humiliating incident, they saw some humor in this.

The Colonel marked a map west to move an army—not another caravan, but an army, a task most ponderous, prodigious, a challenge in logistics to the old campaigner, Albert Sidney Johnston. Once completed, he would be rewarded, promoted. The Black Hawk and Mexican wars had seen Johnston first, Shiloh was a shadowy future yet to claim him. But for now it was Brigham Young, and one thousand miles of tortuous Oregon trail still ahead. On the best maps, crude at best, it looked a sprawling S. The route was established, yet in some respects it was not. Depending upon various conditions along the way it often wandered, but the general direction sufficed: from Fort Laramie's adobe-and-stone walls, northwest along the North Platte to the vicinity of the Poison Spider; west to the Sweetwater and up to South Pass; then southwest across the Little Sandy and on down to Fort Bridger. This was a circuitous path, but indeed, by necessity, the way west. Not shown on the rough map were the wandering ruts of ten years' travel, the scattered debris of mistakes and failure, a winding trail of prairie dunes and bunch grass, desert rock and mountain boulder, and alkali sinks that bleached the skin and left one choking. Also uncharted were the lesser hazards—bad water, short grass, hostiles, and the west's deadliest wildlife trio: mosquitoes, buffalo gnats, and horseflies. And always the impressive night sounds of coyotes and wolves in prairie space. All most formidable, sometimes deadly, for the uninitiated and unprepared.

And there were troops to be fed, stock to be watered and tended, and supplies to be brought up. Yet Colonel Johnston had approached the gigantic task without delusion. Experience was on his side, and he had Jim Bridger. There was no easy way, but men like the Blanket Chief had the wisdom to make it less hazardous. He also had a young man named Ben Tree, a Bridger counterpart, yet thirty years his junior.

The army was bivouacked below the fort near the creek. By his journal, Ben thought this was a sight in itself, several hundred large squad tents and scores of wagons and field equipment spread over a half-mile of the Laramie countryside. In such a lonely but beautiful surround, the convoy's magnitude was staggering to the frontier eye of Ben Tree. In his mind's eye, he foresaw a mere punitive expedition against the Saints. Such a horde could be an ominous threat to the very west itself. Well, it wasn't a pretty sight by any stretch of the imagination, but he and Little Hoop had decided they would make the journey as far as Fort Bridger, and from that point take up the search for Thaddeus and Will Tree.

Ben moved along the encampment, down row after row of tents, following a young lieutenant. Colonel Johnston, flanked by several officers of lesser rank and the Laramie commandant, was seated at a small field table under the awning of the headquarter's tent. Ben's escort smartly saluted and stepped back. Ben stared directly into the Colonel's eyes and said, "My name is Ben Tree. I'm a friend of Jim Bridger. He said you'd be expecting me."

Johnston pressed at his immaculate beard with one hand, politely arose, and extended the other across the table. "Mr. Tree, yes. Yes, Major Bridger speaks highly of you. So do the troopers here. Welcome to our quarters, sir." He eased himself back into the chair, crossed his hands on the desk, and stared up at Ben. His speech was almost lazy, a mark of his southern sojourns. He first had been a Kentuckian, later, a

Texan. "Major Bridger is my chief scout for this expedition," he began. "I trust his word and his judgment. He tells me that your assistance would be most valuable to this army, its mission. He informs me that you know the land between here and Fort Hall as well as any man . . . excepting himself, of course."

Ben smiled along with the Colonel, acknowledging the point made. "I know the country," he said simply.

"Moreover," Johnston continued, "you have a good understanding of the native people west of here. They respect you, I'm told."

"I know the Sioux, the Crow, and some Shoshoni," he answered. "Gabe knows them, too." He grinned then. "I can't exactly speak for the Arapaho . . . that is, respecting me, sir. We've had our times. They *know* me, I'll allow."

"Yes, I understand," Johnston said. He drummed his forefingers together and contemplated Tree for a moment. "Mr. Tree, frankly I'm more concerned with the topography of the country than I am the resident population. While this can in no way be construed as an Indian expedition, and we intend no encroachment upon their treaty lands to the north, I do have the responsibility of my men and equipment, their safety and well-being. Besides your Indian knowledge, Major Bridger reports that you understand all of the peculiarities of this great region. Is that so?"

Ben nodded affirmatively. "I'm familiar with the land. I know the water holes . . . a few safe cutoffs. I know where the best grass is, if that's what you mean."

"Precisely," returned Johnston. "You understand our problem, moving a contingent of this size, hauling up supplies to feed my detachments. I presume you're also aware of the harassment possibilities by hostiles. I say 'possibilities,' because we have only one goal: the Utah territory . . . establishing order. I trust your engagement might prevent some senseless chasing in the hills, something that my men are neither equipped nor properly trained to undertake.'' He smiled. ''Major Bridger refers to them as 'tenderfeet.' ''

''Yes, sir, I understand.''

''Very well, Mr. Tree. If you're agreed, you will take orders from the Major or myself. Report directly to either of us.'' The Colonel scratched a crow point across a sheet of paper and handed it to Ben. ''This will authorize your pay and any supplemental supplies you might need. The quartermaster will take care of your necessities.''

''Thank you, Colonel. I'm agreed.'' Ben tipped his hand to his forehead and turned to leave.

''Mr. Tree . . . one moment.''

''Yes?''

''Ah, there may be a few stragglers,'' Johnson said hesitantly. ''Civilian parties for the most part, moving freight behind us. While we afford them some protection, generally speaking they are not our responsibility. To avoid any animosities or testing of your reputation, I would suggest you stay well in advance of our columns. I presume that your wife will accompany you. Understand, you're working for the army. Keep away from these laggards behind.''

A faint smile touched the corners of Ben's firm mouth. Obviously, the previous night's incident was already a matter of gossip in the big camp. Ben returned politely, ''I never mind another's business, Mr. Johnston, not when I can possibly avoid it. I can't say that I abide bad manners, though. Now, if those Taos lightning peddlers get lost in a westerly and go thirsting to death, I'm most happy to know they aren't my responsibility. I allow their whiskey's no better than their manners, and not fit for human consumption in the first place.''

''Your assumption is correct, Mr. Tree. Here at the Fort we have a brandy ration, the same as the troopers.

Civilian wares are not intended to be consumed by my men. What these scoundrels peddle to the savages, unfortunately, is not within my jurisdiction.''

With a continuing smile, Ben answered, ''In the eyes of the Great Spirit we're all human beings, Colonel. My mother taught me that. She was an Osage, not a savage.''

Johnston flushed slightly, then nodded politely. ''My apologies, Mr. Tree. Major Bridger didn't allude to your heritage, only your unique abilities on the frontier and in the wilderness. I wasn't aware of your blood. Your hair . . . its color . . .''

''No apologies necessary, sir.'' In parting, Ben once again touched his forehead. His long hair was the color of new hemp. Adjusting his headband, he said, ''I've never found it necessary to apologize for my origin. I'm also white. The measure of a man isn't his blood, Colonel, but his actions.''

''Precisely,'' agreed Johnston. ''Good day, sir. We appreciate your service and . . . for myself, this little lesson in propriety and understanding.''

FIVE

August, 1857

A day of news. One W. Thornton, a Missouri packer, came downriver today with nine in his party. News of the army is all across the Utah territory, and the Saints are pulling their horns in. Ft. Bridger is already back in business. Ruben and family doing fine. Thornton says one caravan is there, two ahead of us. He came up south of the basin and encountered no armed patrols. No news of Pa and Will and now I fear the worst. Our soldier boys made only nine miles of it today. Main party camped a mile up from the trail because of cropped grass. Only seven of us riding ahead now. Lt. Sampson took a fever yesterday. High country coming on and my woman sees the Wind range foothills far ahead. I know her thoughts are turning up the Yellowstone. Only personal business keeps me from trailing north again, away from this mess. A good rain would help settle the dust.

Little Hoop and I went half a mile up the creek for a bath. No-see-um gnats thick and we made short work of it. B. Tree.

They rested on a high, observatory knoll, the rich, pungent smell of crushed sage around them. Jim Bridger, head scout, dismounted and stretched. Lt. Samuel Carruthers, West Point '55, tipped his canteen and drank. Ben Tree's eyes followed the sun-beaten course below, down to the North Platte, a small ribbon of green creasing the broken plain. Several miles back were the advance columns of Colonel Johnston's plodding army. Tough going, all the way. Tree remembered his father's admonitions from those days long ago when the big rush was on, when they had first come out of Independence riding the trail to Fort Laramie. "Travel between grass and hay, Benji." That was reserved for the first leg, that lonesome, awesome prairie. But once beyond Laramie, where the mountains and plains finally intermingled, where shimmering summer heat scorched the meandering trail with the cherry touch of a branding iron, those age-old warnings meant little.

No less hazardous, this was a different country entirely. Johnston's army was moving through it slowly, laboriously, but moving. The route was firm enough, now. The deep, axle-licking mud that had once tested soul and patience on the lower Platte had been left far behind. Now search for the grass, search each cautious bend, and search the spectral hills beyond, always alert for omnipresent dangers. For the newcomer, mountain strangeness was always a heavy burden, and there were plenty of greenhorns and surly stragglers on this trip—thousands.

The ascent along the North Platte was gradual, but the scenic upheaval constant. For most it was a new kind of land, harsh in its contrasts, at times surprisingly beautiful, blessed by verdant bottoms, brushy benches, and distant ridges of jagged pine. Within an hour, what had been a pleasant trail of shady cotton-woods could easily give way to an agonizing twist between barren buttes and mirages of greasewood flats. Each day the air became thinner, drier, and wagon wheels often wailed in protest; delays were frequent and mandatory, this depressing to Ben Tree, who always had his anxious eyes to the western horizon. Wagon tongues, sapped of strength, became brittle, and under the strain of a grade splintered like ripe kindling. Always, time out for repair.

Temperatures turned into a delusory fraud. Dawn was brisk and biting. By midday, the morning's wraps had become burgeoning stains of sweat. Once shucked, clothes left them exposed to a burning sun that quickly made its mark. Little respite here, and Ben Tree rest-lessly pondered. Independence Rock was still ahead, and the winding Sweetwater, and the long, rolling plains nestling at the toe of a Wind range; ultimately, the gateway, South Pass.

The delays were discomforting to Ben, for he had made much better time of it on other trips. By himself, unfettered, he could easily have halved the journey. This foray already was fast becoming tedious, the goal too distant, and Fort Hall seeming as elusive as the next mirage. Impatience was rearing, becoming his enemy. Ben looked upon the creaking clamor below as some kind of white man's circus, a performing con-tingent of doughboys waging a battle against a relent-less environment, perhaps a far more formidable foe than the Saints might ever be. If the Mormons had passed through with a song, a prayer, and a cause, then Johnston's patriots would surely suffer the trip with a curse. In the end, someone would pay the price for the misery of the march. Brigham Young, the

troopers hoped. There were no Saints among Johnston's boys.

This was the ninth day, the day of encounter. From
the brow of the hill, the riders coming were only dim
specks on a far rim. Bridger already had picked up
Ben's steady stare. The breed's eyes were unfailingly
true. Lieutenant Carruthers probably brought his field
glasses into play, and abruptly spoke up.

"Five of them, Major. Indians, coming our way."
He handed the binoculars to Bridger. "What do you
make of it?"

The mountain man squinted into the aperture, using
only one side of the glasses in the fashion of a tele-
scope. After a moment of deliberation he said,
"Scouting party, mos' likely. Can't tell the breed. Way
we're stuck out up here like turkey necks, they see us.
They're coming head-on, aiming to parley."

Tree leaned forward on his big Arapaho gray and
took the glasses. Slowly drawing a focus, he grunted
once.

Bridger asked, "What do you think, Benji? I'm discounting Crow and Sioux."

"Cheyenne, by direction," Ben answered. "Little
Powder's due north." He handed the glasses back to
the young lieutenant. "I suppose we might as well ride
out and meet them . . . show our colors."

Sam Carruthers tucked nervously at his belt and
looked over at Jim Bridger. "Are they trustworthy,
Major?"

Smiling, Bridger clucked at his horse and moved
out. "Can't rightly say. One way of finding out,
though. Y'might rest easy on your holster. If they start
spreading out, that's when you hug the saddle. Ride
easy now, Samuel. Keep your eyes peeled on those two
bucks in the front."

They rode. Shortly, Bridger drew to a halt and threw
up his left hand. He held the position until the trotting

ponies coming toward him slowed to a walk and the lead rider extended the same sign of greeting. The ponies exchanged snorts and neighs. Hands folded, Ben sat easily to the side, but his eyes swiftly took measure of the five horsemen. They were Cheyenne, and Bridger began passing sign with the first brave up, a warrior with honors, three feathers dangling from his hair. The brave said they were from a hunting village to the north, toward Thunder Basin. Their chief was Black Bull, a great leader. News of the great white chief's army already had reached them and they had come to see for themselves, also to seek assurances. They knew the army's purpose, but they were apprehensive about outriders. The chief wanted no longknives on their lands while they were making meat. Bad medicine. The warrior pointed at Lieutenant Carruthers.

Carruthers, apprehensive himself, nudged closer to Bridger's mount. "What does he say, Major? Is he speaking about my presence here?"

Aside, Bridger mumbled, "He says you're welcome, long as you don't go chasing their curly cows. Most of the rest of it's hogwash. These bucks are jest looking us over, mebbe poking 'round for some Taos snake oil. Plain ol' scouts, that's all, nosin' 'round t'see if there's any easy pickings. No rank, to my notion."

Bridger turned back and responded, explaining to the Indians that the Great Medicine Road was wide in too many places, that grass was short along the main trail. Many people, traders and emigrants, were behind the army. His longknife leader could not account for them all, but there would be no trouble from the soldiers.

By now, there was little doubt that the Cheyenne knew Bridger. Even though the scout had not revealed his identity, the rapid exchange of words and gestures from the Indians in the rear indicated as much. They knew. The man speaking to them was the famous Blanket Chief of the Shoshoni, one who had counted coup before they were born. He was a mountain man, a white Indian.

Meantime, Ben Tree had curiously edged his pony to the side for a better look, his eyes cast upon a dingy white horse directly in back of the Cheyenne spokesman. There was something about that pony. . . . The horse's coat was faded by dust from the trail, but there could be no mistake about its identity—it was Snow Hawk! Originally a Cheyenne stud, stolen by the Blackfeet, raided again by the Crow, and now returned to the Cheyenne—thrice stolen. Ben eyed it closely again. His old paint marking on the flank had long since disappeared. No matter, those silver-gray eyes were the same, the thin nose and flared nostrils identical. By jingo, Ben mused, how had such a coup come about?

His continual glare made the Cheyenne rider nervous. He seemed a sturdy brave, with his sheathed rifle on Snow Hawk's shoulder and cradled lance brightly decorated with hair and breath feathers. Tree's curiosity melted into molten outrage when he spotted fresh scalp hair decorating the upper strip of the rawhide hackamore. A grim smile creased his face as he began backing his own pony away, but his angry eyes never left the Cheyenne atop Snow Hawk.

Addressing Bridger from the side, Ben said, "Ask him how that buck next to him got the white he's riding. Ask him!"

The tone of sudden irritation in his young companion's voice startled Bridger. Frowning, he reined around and stared at the horse. He saw nothing special about it. Grime and sweat hid its former beauty. "What's ailing you, Benji? You know this critter? You're acting all riled."

"Ei," Ben grunted, and that brief guttural word

brought an immediate snort from the brave under scrutiny. "I know that stud," Tree said flatly. "It used to be mine up north. Ask him where he got it."

Bridger's chariness was apparent, for he too had now spotted the decorative hair, and it was against his better judgment to press the matter.

"I'd rather not do that, Benji," he said, shaking his head. "Might go causing us a passel of trouble, upset the Colonel something fierce. Like as not, one of us might be getting ourselves dusted right here and now. Better ease off, son."

But the object of interest already had become too obvious. The continuing look of displeasure on Ben's face was enough, yet strangely misinterpreted. The Cheyenne leader glowed and spoke up, moving his hands again. "What does the young white scout want? What does he see?"

Ben himself moved in and gestured back. "Where was this white pony taken? How did it come about?"

Surprised at the unexpected dexterity of Tree's sign, the ranking brave hesitated. He glanced back at the stallion once, then nodded his head and smiled. He would be proud to tell the story. And quite unaware of Ben's relationship to the Crow village of White Mouth, the Cheyenne innocently began relating how coup had been counted during an early-summer raid east of the Wind River. They had taken eight Crow ponies, and a bitter fight had ensued.

"This brave is Iron Bow," he continued, motioning. "This pony once belonged to his brother, a chief. The Crow stole his ponies and killed two of his tribe. Iron Bow avenged this. He made coup on the Crow. One of his party was killed. That was bad. But we killed two of the enemy. Iron Bow was brave in battle and couped the rider of the white pony, a young chief. That is the story."

Ben Tree's stomach turned and blood rushed to his

head. The young Crow chief! It could only have been
Two Moons High, for only he would have had the privilege of riding Snow Hawk. This had been the will of
Chief White Mouth. Ben suddenly spat on the ground
at the hooves of the Cheyenne's horse. "That's a bad
story!" he replied in swift motions. 'The Blackfeet
first stole your ponies and killed, not the Absaroke.
This I know, for it was I who took this very stallion
from the Blackfeet on the Yellowstone during the Moon
of the Changing Season." Sharply reining his gray to
the side, he addressed the rider of Snow Hawk directly. "Dog! You made coup on the wrong man. You
have killed my brother!" With an angry flourish of
movement, he said, "His sister, the daughter of White
Mouth, is my wife!"

Immediately the other four Cheyenne backed away,
clear of this bizarre confrontation born of coincidence.
Bridger shouted and held up his hand, desperately trying to intervene. He motioned hurriedly to the Cheyenne leader again. This was not the time to spill
blood. "Speak to your brothers!" he pleaded. "You
have wisdom!"

Lieutenant Carruthers, shaken by the excited round
of talk and angry gestures, moved closer to the old
scout. "What's happening, Major? What's this all
about . . . this confusion?"

"For God's sake, sit easy, Samuel," Bridge cau-
tioned. "We're a long way from West Point, y'hear?
And don't go making any play for your sidearm. Seems
like there's bad blood over that consarned stud there
. . . some infernal killing between the Crow and these
bucks."

"What does that matter to the army?" Carruthers
said. "What does that have to do with us?"

"Benji's Crow kinfolk. . . ."

"You mean someone killed a friend of Mr. Tree's?"
Bridger nodded, trying to follow the meaning of the

conversation raging opposite him. The Cheyenne were arguing, but fortunately no one had reached for a weapon. "Looks like that buck on the white went and killed Benji's wife's brother, leastways he thinks so."

Carruthers suddenly paled. "Oh, my God!"

The talk abruptly ended. A decision had been reached. Iron Bow came forward, and in a gesture of challenge and contempt, firmly planted his lance in the ground in front of Ben. *"Wagh!"* he cried, and the shaft quivered violently. He spat into the dust.

Ben immediately seized the lance and angrily snapped it in half across the pommel of his saddle. Dashing the broken pieces to the ground, he then made sign. "At the first sun I'll come to kill you, sperm of a dog!"

Iron Bow bristled but replied stonily, *"Eyah!* I will see you dead, yellow hair!"

Jim Bridger passed another sign to the Indians and motioned to Carruthers. "Ride out easy, Lieutenant. We'll be caching. It's all over for now, by crackee. Let's get outta here."

Sam Carruthers glanced over his shoulder at the departing Cheyenne. "That last thing? What was that all about?"

"Means they'll be looking to kill tomorrow." The scout clucked his horse. "Somewhere in the hills back there, jest the two of 'em. Matter of honor . . . a challenge. Big shame; if they don't . . . dishonor."

Carruthers shuddered once. "Why, that's absolutely savage, Major! It's hideous! Over a dead Indian, a stolen horse . . . a misunderstanding? Mr. Tree is an educated man! How can he be a party to such savagery? I don't understand it!"

Bridger grinned wryly. "Didn't think you would understand," he drawled. "When we civilized whites get ourselves all riled, we fetch up a couple of fancy dueling pistols and do a little pacing. When a man kills, he kills, but I reckon we're a mite more civilized, eh, Samuel . . . the way we do things.''

Lieutenant Carruthers had no ready answer. Wiping at his forehead, he looked back to see if Ben Tree was coming. He was not. The young scout was heading up the hill, following the sun. Carruthers gave Bridger a questioning glance.

"Wants to be by himself," Bridger said. "That's the way it is with Injuns, Samuel. He'll be all ready in the morning, like a hungry cat, I'll wager."

"But . . . but what about his wife?"

"I'll be making medicine with her," Bridger replied. "We'll be keeping a fire at the end of that ridge way off yonder. If the medicine's good, that's where he'll come down tomorrow . . . with Iron Bow's scalp."

"My God!"

Alone, atop the very spine of the ridge, Ben's anger quickly subsided into grief and sorrow. For a long time, he meditated. For the love of his woman and her dead brother, he made prayers. For himself, he sought divine guidance, the blessings of God *and* the Great Spirit, the dual obligation of his spiritual belief. And then, for the ordeal at hand, he calmly collected his senses and brought all of his frontier acumen into calculated focus.

His emotions were running in a wide course. He had to channel them, direct them into practical meaning and usefulness. Little need to beat his chest in agony, or in bravery either. Mock bravery, a sham. In his mind, caution was the better part of it, bravado the ceremonial front whetted by the frenzied thumping of the big drums, the chant, the stomp. And he had no mystical medicine bundle, no sacrificial potion or bits of animal hair and bone to offer up from his pouch. His medicine had always been unfaltering courage tempered with common sense. Luck, in the form of charms, was only an outside chance in the game at hand and was contrary to his reasoning white mind. He knew danger, both instinctive and learned. It had never paralyzed him. He must make himself ready. Iron Bow would come, honor paramount, perhaps a fool too brave for discretion, perhaps only to lose his soul in the sun. Ben Tree scanned the surrounding terrain, fixing a mental imprint. Each hill, each gully, would determine the course of action, how he would attack. Herein, his coldly methodical preparation for bloodshed. Kill or be killed. Herein, the metamorphosis of a functional killer.

Under the cover of darkness and a hazy moon, he deserted the ridge and made his way down through a broken gully. Tethering the gray in the bottom to graze, he stared up at the breast of the adjacent hill. It was approximately two hundred paces. He already knew his direction, his manner of execution. He would mount this ridge and follow it north until it overlooked the knolls and gullies from whence he had come. The direction southwest was no longer of any strategic importance, not in his scheme of things. East was the imminent threat, as it would make him a moving target in the glare of a rising sun. And Iron Bow could not be *all* heroic fool in this deadly game of hunters. Like Ben, he would stalk and wait until the surrounding hills were narrowed down to one lonely corridor of death, a path of no retreat. If at all possible, the sun would be at his back when Iron Bow closed.

Ben had made his own decision at sundown: Move high and far to the north, well beyond Iron bow's point of entry. In no way could he permit the Cheyenne to come in behind or above him. That might prove disastrous. He wanted to make his stalk down-country, too, but unexpectedly, from the north, the direction Iron Bow would least suspect. Taking only his rifle and blanket, and one final draught from his canteen, he climbed the hill and moved northward. He had threaded his way through brush and rock for almost two miles before he stopped. Here was the place—a brimstone shelf, with a flat approach on top. He squinted across the gully to the hill below. Now, it was too dark to determine the distance with any degree of accuracy—two hundred yards, two-fifty. Adequate, he decided. He curled up in his blanket and dozed.

Shortly before dawn, Ben stirred, numbed by chill. Stars were dimming in a carmine sky, the early-morning air fresh, cold. He clasped his body and rubbed, bringing back the circulation, then edged slowly up over the ledge for a look due north. Was he above Iron Bow? Had he come far enough? For the most part the country to the north was open, the gray light of dawn barely penetrating the scattered patches of sage and buckbrush. The edge of the horizon was dusted with gold. Shooting time was close at hand. Moving any farther in that direction, he decided, would be a poor risk, now. The cover was relatively sparse. Better to stay high on the hill.

Easing back under the protection of the shelf, he carefully inspected his rifle and methodically thumbed the action of his revolver. He waited another ten minutes before slipping over the crag. In a low crouch, he sneaked into the brush and began working his way along the top of the hill, keeping the open flat below him. Ben calculated that the river was at least three miles south, but from his present vantage point it was completely out of sight. Iron Bow had plenty of room in which to work. Within an hour, the area would shrink dangerously to a measurement in yards—down the long barrels of rifles.

When the sun peaked the horizon, Ben dropped back into the rocks and waited, his eyes constantly frisking the first two hills paralleling the river. The first movement came with the full sun, a flash of dusky gray and tan. He quickly picked up the form, then eased back with a sigh—a large doe. Mule deer. A stiff-legged fawn soon followed. For a moment, he thought little about it. Then it hit him, the direction of the early-morning breeze. The doe was moving downwind, in no particular hurry, but alert. He watched closely as she stopped again to glance back over her rump. She was not feeding. She was making a decision, and her next move would be in his direction, across the small bottom, then up the hill adjacent from where she had come, the usual mule deer tactic, doubling back to the next draw, running uphill.

Ben curiously observed the two creatures. The fawn had come alongside, waiting for her mother's next instinctive move. The large doe hesitated, nosing the wind behind her, ears twitching. To Ben's surprise she refused to make the climb to his lower left, the side of his hill. Instead she bounded to the right, directly down the middle of the gully, fawn following, and disappeared into the thickets below. This was a revealing move—a spooked deer.

A foreboding suspicion of treachery suddenly struck Tree. He could only suspect, but he had the uneasy feeling that Iron Bow had arrived—with reinforcements. Someone was on *his* hill, or near it, someone opposite him. If so, that made his own position precarious, opening up the possibility that he had exposed himself to attack from two directions. His only recourse was to remain hidden. He could not creep out and get behind Iron Bow. If need be, he could turn his rock pile into a fortress, at least from three sides. Only from below was he vulnerable, and any approach from that direction seemed highly improbable now.

What Ben expected from the opposite hill directly materialized—at first only the shadow of a form, one that he could barely cover with his beaded front sight.

Drawing a breath, he waited. Another moment dragged by, another long breath, and at the peak of that instant, when he caught sight of bare shoulders again, he touched off his round. The explosion split the quiet morning air like a bolt of lightning. The echo rumbled and rolled three miles below, where Little Hoop suddenly gripped the arm of Jim Bridger and stared up in fright.

Without assessment, Ben began reloading. Time was precious, his position now dangerously marked. A small, telltale pall of black powder smoke hovered over his head. Hunkering low, he waited, heard only the morning cries of birds, saw nothing but the golden sky fully awakening above him. Five agonizing minutes stretched to ten. He finally poked his head around the rim of rock and looked down the breadth of his hill, visually picking at each brushy clump and rock until there was nothing more left to investigate. The hill dropped away.

He wet his lips and thought about it. Perhaps he had been wrong. Perhaps Iron Bow had been alone after all—if, indeed, that had been Iron Bow across the way. His eyes went back to the far point, traced the subtle slope of the rim down to the edge of brush. There it was—a partially hidden form, inert, motionless below the boughs. His shot had been true enough. The brave was either dead or mortally wounded.

The sun slowly climbed. Ben patiently waited another twenty minutes, surveying the hills of nothingness around him. Finally, the sharp *kuk-kuk-coo* call of a valley quail stirred him. Turning at the ready, he peered down the slope in back of him, his hammer cocked, his eyes at a deadly squint. Fifty yards away, sitting on the brimstone ledge, pipe in one hand and rifle in the other, calmly rested Jim Bridger. The scout waved nonchalantly and smiled.

"Nice morning, Benji," he called "Y'gonna spend

the rest of the day sittin' those rocks? Ain't much up here but varmits.'' He pointed with his pipe to the distant hill. ''That one seems dead, for sure, and your woman's waiting down yonder . . . plumb worried sick.''

Heaving a great sigh, Ben fell against the rocks, exhausted, relieved. He tried to laugh, to spring the last coil of tension in his taut body, but found he couldn't. Gathering his blanket and rifle, he stretched, closed his eyes, and offered up a silent prayer to the Supreme Being. The sun touched his face. It was eight o'clock, but it seemed as though the day already had spent itself. A fine rim of sweat circled the underside of his leather headband. God, and he had been so cold on the mountain! Turning, he saw Bridger approaching. ''Hell, Gabe,'' he finally called back, ''I thought there was another one up here! I didn't know!'' He felt foolish admitting miscalculation to a man like the Blanket Chief.

But Bridger understood. ''Like as not there was, until you dusted that feller over there. Thought I knew the sound of that long-Tom iron of yours.'' He stepped over the last boulders and came up. He took a canteen from his shoulder and tossed it to the young scout.

Ben drank, then asked, ''How's she taking it? Badly, I suppose.''

''Always do, don't they?'' Bridger placed a friendly hand on Tree's shoulder. ''Moaning half the night 'bout you and the brother. Went to sleep this morning on my shoulder. She'll come 'round when she sees you. I'd say that buck's hair might make her feel somewhat better. Tradition.''

''An eye for an eye,'' Ben said wearily, sadly. ''Not much compensation, only some small satisfaction. I'm sorry for her. I'm sorry for White Beaver, those little ones. By jingo, Gabe, it's a tough road.'' He wiped at his forehead again and stared across the gully. Death was over there. He felt no elation, barely satisfaction. "Well, it's done. It's over, but I'll swear there was another one of them up here."

"He'd a'made tracks, Benji," Bridger opined. "How did it come off?"

Ben began explaining what had happened, down to the unusual behavior of the frightened deer. The veteran scout listened with interest, drawing his own conclusions. A curious happenstance, he thought, perhaps worth another look. So, together, they inspected the remaining cover of the ridge for sign. They found none.

Bridger finally went on to the very end of the hill, a quarter of a mile farther, where he suddenly stopped and beckoned Tree with a shout and a wave. Ben made the distance in large leaps. He stared down to where Bridger was pointing. There, a surprising sight: the Cheyenne stud, picketed in a patch of weed and bramble. The horse was eyeing them, its head high and ears pricked, as usual.

"Well, I'll be damned!" murmured Ben. "Snow Hawk, you old devil! Look at that, Gabe! Look at that, will you!"

Bridger broke out in a smile. "Yep, there's your other varmint. Reckon that spooked muley deer didn't like the smell of that pony any more than she did the Injun, Benji." He nodded at his young friend, posing a thoughtful question. "Wonder if that critter rides double?"

Ben took off with a bound, shouting back, "He'll get used to it again!"

SIX

Time presided again. The sorrow and pain shared by Ben Tree and his wife over the death of Two Moons High soon relinquished itself to the routine toil of a great army on the move. At least, for Colonel Sidney Johnston, luck and fair weather prevailed, for on a good day his soldiers were now making fifteen miles of it. The advance scouting party was continuing to come and go, meeting regularly with him for conferences, charting the day's goal and how best to attain it. What Jim Bridger missed or inadvertently forgot, Ben Tree retrieved and managed. The two scouts worked as a team, practically and efficiently, but even so there were continuing incidents and foolish escapades that were out of their guiding hands. This was the trail west, and let no one forget it—as in the case of the small patrol lost in hostile country overnight while cutting poles for wagon repair. Ben, accompanied by several troopers, had brought the strays back to the comfort of the fold, tired and hungry, yet thankful—their scalps were still intact.

Still, an another occasion the consequences were less fortunate—a civilian freight unit lagging a full day behind, attacked by Indians at dawn, a bullwhacker shot and eight herd of stock stolen. Blaming Ben for their misfortune, (hadn't he provoked the Cheyenne?) the angry traders gathered reinforcements for a punitive expedition. Army be damned, they rode away in wild pursuit, a hardy band of muleskinners and bullwhackers, seeking blood, this despite repeated warnings along the way by the cagey veteran, Bridger. The nondescript lot quickly paid the price of inexperience and mountain foolhardiness. They were soundly thrashed and routed, half of their mounts shot out from under them, and they had to run for their very lives. By nightfall, under the cover of darkness, they straggled back to the rear echelon of the big military train, sore afoot and in bad humor.

The next morning, they rode ahead and complained to Johnston's aides. Worse luck, two of their companions had not made it back at all. Bridger was there, listening, smoking his pipe, shaking his head in disgust. They were not brave men at all, he told them. They were "fool jackasses," the mildest of frontier invective he could muster with the officers looking on. The mountain man reluctantly dispatched two Omaha scouts to investigate, knowing full well what they were most apt to discover.

The scouts returned late that afternoon, reporting that sign near the pierced bodies of the two "lost" muleskinners was not Cheyenne at all. The raiders had been Arapaho, and the Omaha scouts threw down two broken shafts to prove it. Ben was vindicated, yet with little consolation. One Bob Skinner, still wearing the red welts of the Laramie night fire on his rear, asserted that Bridger's young assistant was poor luck, anyhow—a bad breed, at that.

Mishaps notwithstanding, the army continued to

move. August passed into the first frosts of September, and the soldiers finally topped South Pass. By the time the Federals had reached Fort Bridger, the mountain air was full of both ugly rumor and autumn chill. Nevertheless Jim Bridger, understandably nostalgic, told Ben it was good to be back; the country looked the same. But it was not the same, and they both knew it. Times were.changing dramatically, and the countryside was, too.

The fort had filled in recent weeks with gathering Oregon country emigrants, some pitifully behind schedule. There were miners by the score, following the rumors of riches. Winter was coming on. Beyond that frightening prospect, these people were fearful of pushing on into a bristling, hostile land, with avenging Mormons and unpredictable Indians on the prowl. As if that weren't bad enough, the Paiute Indians were siding with the benevolent Saints. No mind, several California-bound trains and their herds had moved boldly ahead, making southwest toward the Old Spanish Trail, expecting little trouble from the few Mormon missions scattered along the way. The emigrants would make their own way.

There were traders at the fort, too, up from the south, dickering with the remaining emigrants and prospectors who impatiently waited until Johnston's patrols began to work the north route to Fort Hall. And Bridger's old friends, the Shoshoni, had arrived, led by the great Chief Washakie. The Shoshoni swarmed by the hundreds when the Blanket Chief Bridger finally made his appearance, and Chief Washakie, Johnston, and the mountain man sat down to talk and smoke. Amid the troubled air, a festive mood set in—for a while.

Two days went by. Not all was rumor. The entire land was restless and stirring. Most of the word, enriching to some, yet discomforting to others, came from Ruben Russell, who had already sold out a supply of hardware and was reduced to dealing in staples, blankets, cloth, and buckskin. His news extended beyond the Mormons, to the north and the vanishing wilderness. He talked and Ben Tree and Bridger listened, reading distress into the latest signs of progress. Most ominous: the gold fever that had struck the Oregon country, diverting many of the speculators into the northern wilderness. The profit-takers were already on hand, anxious to move, the best and worst of human elements, preparing for the assault, gathering like army rats, ready to brave any danger in hopes of finding yet another bonanza. Over the hills, the golden cup of plenty was waiting. Pitfalls, too; the dregs of adversity waiting for the unlucky. Some had already fallen. Gold strikes in the Colville fields, the traditional land of the Cayuse and Yakima, had touched off sporadic skirmishing between the miners and tribesmen. The Indians were on the warpath. Down the Columbia—a far piece, opined Bridger—troops were being mustered. But Russell, his chin whiskers jumping, marked a line much closer to home. Along the Hell Gate, a few isolated prospectors were poking dangerously east toward Gold Creek, where Francois "Benetesee" Finlay earlier had discovered some color. The Stuart brothers had made a strike in the same area. Distant rumblings came from that quarter, too, the Indian gateway to the buffalo grounds, the land of the Blackfeet, the hunting plains of many.

Ben frowned and glanced at Bridger. "My old friends," he commented. "Ei, there'll be trouble if any fool goes extending himself with the Blackfeet. They're a determined people, to my notion, just like the Sioux."

Russell retorted, "Hellfire, Benji, there's trouble already!" With a wave of his big hands, the old trader went on to say that he had even heard talk of plans to survey a wagon route from Fort Benton, running southwest across part of the bison range down to Hell Gate and onto Fort Walla Walla, every foot of it a perilous journey through wild country.

Ben listened in disbelief. The profiteers were courting disaster with such a venture. This was the land of the Crow, his brothers, the Bird People. The Shoshoni, Flathead, Blackfeet, and Nez Percé all hunted there, too. "Those are the hunting grounds," he finally said. "My brothers hunt there. Your brothers hunt there, too. It's their home when and where they spread their blankets. Unceded land, Ruben, sure, but it's no place for a *road*, by jingo! No, I can't believe it."

"Government's buying and bribing, jest like always," Russell said. "Yep, treaty-makers, getting passage for a trifle. The treaty says 'military posts and roads fer keeping the peace.' Military roads! That's the joker in the deck, y'see. Like as not, it'll be another Oregon road one of these days. Movers on the prowl, taking half our trade away down here."

Ben protested quietly, "There's paper on the Oregon country up that way, signed two years ago by Isaac Stevens."

Chuckling, Bridger intervened with a gentle jibe. "Benji, you know better. What the hell does that paper mean? Take a miner, now. Ain't no fool miner that can read a marker, less it's put there on a claim stick. And even that don't mean much to some of 'em. Like the trapper, a damned prospector'll take his chances in Hell for a scratch of color. If he's collared, he'll beg off or start hollering for the government, jest like the movers."

"For a fact," Russell put in. He paused to spit over the step. "Take yer Nez Percé, now. I hear tell they already got sourdoughs sneaking up the Salmon and Clearwater, and that's Injun land if ever I seen it, regular billy goat hills. Ah, but there's gold there fer the takin'. There's Governor Stevens' treaty fer ya! Y'spect those Injuns t'know what the paper really says? Can't read, y'know, and the agent's always talking two ways, one for hisself and one for the Injun. Yep, while the blackrobes preach gospel and peace, squatters and sourdoughs been sneaking north right and left.'' Russell grinned and gave Ben a friendly poke in the ribs. ''Leastways, some of those Flatheads in the Bitterroot got a belly-full. Hear tell the preachers up there moved themselves out. Plumb gave out. Settlers ain't much fer that religion either, I reckon.''

''What's this?'' Ben questioned in quiet surprise. ''You mean Father Ravalli's mission? The priests have given up?''

Russell nodded and spat again for emphasis. ''Hear ol' Saint Mary's been belly-up for a spell. Right there it is fer ya, plain as a wart on a toad, Benji. If an Injun can't understand the black book, how y'spect him to understand that treaty paper? Specially, all the fancy writing.''

Ben scoffed at his old friend. ''I'll allow there's more to the blackrobes moving out than meets the eye. For one thing, Chief Victor had that lower valley land taken away from him by Stevens. The tribe is north now, and I don't think the blackrobes went up the Bitterroot to convert squatters. Appears to me they've just lost most of their business, that's all. Ei, but I'll grant you one thing: That paper isn't worth a damn to the Indian nations.''

Russell grinned. ''Well now, depends whose side yer on.''

''You've already said it in so many words,'' Ben replied. ''The white man doesn't practice what he preaches. He never has. That's what our people are beginning to find out.''

"*Our* people?" Russell smiled again and nudged Bridger.

Ben Tree said, "It's a white man's government, Ruben, but we're not all fools. Sure as shooting, you should know. You married a Shoshoni, didn't you?"

Russell burst out in a sharp cackle and looked at Jim Bridger. "Now listen ta Benji preach, would ya! Like as *we* didn't know! Now, Benji boy, who in tarnation understands a savage? You jest tell me that. Like as not, only ones like us who's took up with 'em—squaw men. Lemme tell you, Benji, if you stay on out here you're gonna be bad medicine to some of these new white chiefs coming in. You're too smart, what they call one of them consarned "moralists.' Nothing worse than an educated Injun. Why, it's downright humiliating! How can you cheat 'em like that? Now, if I went learning White Crane how to mark my books, no telling what kinda fool cuss she'd be making outta me."

"A jackass," Bridger snorted.

Ben laughed with the two mountain men, but then added soberly, "Maybe I'll have the final joke on your white chiefs, my friends. Ei, they'll not be forgetting me. I don't look like any Indian they've ever seen."

"Well, he's sure right, there," Bridger said, puffing on his pipe and looking wisely at Russell. "Only one thing that'll go tipping his hand, eh, Rube?"

Ben glanced from one to the other. "Yes, and what's that?"

Bridger said solemnly, "Benji, I reckon you don't know it, but you've changed hats. No, you don't look like an Injun, but ever since you came down from Crow country, you been *talking* like one. Understand, boy, you can't have it both ways anymore."

Ben stared thoughtfully off into the distance, saw the white tops of the Shoshoni lodges, bright against the late-afternoon sun. He allowed that Jim Bridger was right. Not only was he talking like an Indian, but more and more he was *thinking* like one—with his heart.

September, 1857

Bad news is coming in, disturbing reports from down the California trail territory. A man named Chambers reported to Col. Johnston this morning that Mormons and Paiutes have ambushed a train out of Arkansas first week of month, killing over a hundred of the movers. Only some few children escaped death. This is a terrible occurrence if the report proves itself. Everyone is up in arms and the word here is now "shoot on sight." Johnston sent companies southwest and north. This place of ambush is called Mountain Meadows, beyond the Cedar settlement. The army will be moving out for the Ham's fork. Gabe tells me this is likely to be the wintering grounds and the best place to base for patrol work in the territory. I draw my last pay tomorrow. Little Hoop and I are anxious to be away from this confusion. Good riddance. We'll be leaving and trailing to Fort Hall to see about Pa and Will's disappearance. B. Tree.

For several days fragmentary reports of the Mormon affair at Mountain Meadows continued to trickle in, each fresh bit of information more damning to the Saints. Stunned and angry people at Fort Bridger were calling it a massacre of the most villainous nature, an incident unparalleled in the history of the young frontier. Soldiers and civilians alike were incensed, and the immigrants began combining forces for a safer journey. They armed to the teeth, exhausting the post's supplies of shot and powder. Meanwhile Ben Tree, listening to all the distressing news, began to have dark second thoughts and new suspicions about the mysterious disappearance of his own family. What chance would two gentile packers have against an angry band of avenging Saints?

Others at the fort sifted the news and tried to make decisions. An angry Chief Washakie began to express his wrath at the Paiute intervention. This was bad medicine. The Paiute participation also disturbed many of his Shoshoni chiefs and braves, and a council was finally called, with Jim Bridger speaking and telling the Indians all that he had heard. Ben and several officers joined the circle and listened to the mountain man's report. Bridger said that some of the immigrants of a wagon train had reportedly antagonized a number of Mormon missionaries along the southern route cutoff, creating bad feelings on both sides. A confrontation had been avoided by a truce, the misunderstanding apparently resolved. The immigrants had agreed to stow their weapons, and did so, only to be waylaid later by a Mormon militia and a large Paiute war party. This word set up angry growls among the Shoshoni. They called the Paiutes cowards. Bridger told them that the killing had been so devastating that only eighteen small children were spared. After stripping and mutilating the victims, the attackers tried to cover up the atrocity, dispersing the captured stock and equipment, and disposing of the bodies. The man named Chambers had accidentally discovered some of the shallow graves.

Bellicose and angry, the council adjourned. Shortly afterward, Chief Washakie, splendidly dressed in crimson robe and full feathers, asked to talk with Colonel Johnston. Accompanied by Bridger and his companions, he went to the headquarter tent of the army commander and offered to supply twelve hundred braves to use in the campaign against the Mormons. The Paiutes were merely dogs, and would be treated as such.

Surprised at the magnitude of the chief's offer, Johnston gave Bridger a questioning look. The scout nodded his silver thatch, saying, "He means it, Colonel. Reckon those Saints don't set too fancy with the Shoshoni, and the Paiutes, well, they're cricket-eaters, the lot of 'em."

"But what can I say?" Johnston sighed, with a helpless gesture. He stood and paced in back of the field desk. He didn't want to offend Washakie, but the chief's proposal was quite impossible. This wasn't any part of the army department's carefully prepared plans. "It's out of the question, Major," Johnston finally said. "It would be a serious mistake to involve the Shoshoni, and it's contrary to the military standards we have to maintain on this assignment. It's a gallant gesture, but acceptance of such a proposition might well precipitate another conflict. My God, I don't want the responsibility for another Indian war on my hands! One has been quite enough."

Chief Washakie spoke again to Bridger, using his hands for emphasis. The scout then turned back to Johnston. "He says his braves and your longknives will rub out the hairy-faces and dog Paiutes who've brought such misery to his friends of the white chief in Washington . . . before the snow flies."

Reluctantly, Johnston said, "Tell my friend that it will be best if the Shoshoni refrain from taking the warpath against the Paiute, that these Indians are receiving bad counsel from the Mormons. The Paiute will be punished, in due time. I want no more unnecessary bloodshed, not on the hands of the Shoshoni. They're our good friends, and shall remain so."

Bridger nodded once and began to translate. While Bridger was speaking, Johnston said aside to Tree, "Washakie must understand, Mr. Tree, that I appreciate his offer, but the consequences, the repercussions of launching his warriors against our adversaries might prove disastrous to all of us. This is contrary to policy, a hard thing for these people to understand."

"Washakie will try to understand, Colonel. He'll take your word on bringing the guilty to justice, only there might be some difference of opinion on how to go about it. I don't think his kind of justice is tempered with mercy.''

"Rub out the guilty . . . ?''

"Those were his words,'' Ben replied. "After this tragedy in the meadows, he damn well knows the Indian has no corner on brutality. It's a bad thing to die without striking a blow. He'd pay the bushwhackers back in kind, giving them no quarter.''

"And you agree, Mr. Tree?''

"Colonel,'' Ben said wearily, "I once saw a man hanged for stealing a crippled horse. And in Fifty-four, there was that stupid Grattan affair. I saw Indians and troopers killing each other just because some Sioux shot a sick cow lagging behind a mover's wagon. Now, in my mind, those are damn poor excuses for killing, but how do you justify mass murder?''

"Those responsible for this crime will be brought to justice,'' said Johnston. "What would you have us do, ride out on a blood bath?''

"Punishment should fit the crime,'' Ben answered. "I'll allow if that massacre had been a train of troopers, every Indian village in the area would be catching hell by now. Ah, but Indians, they're all alike, so what does it matter? That's the premise.''

Johnston softly protested, saying, "Oh, come now, Mr. Tree. The military is bound by law.''

"Only when it chooses,'' Ben parried. "To my notion, the law is too contrary, Colonel.''

Stroking his beard thoughtfully, Johnston admitted, "You have a point of discussion. You're a very engaging young man at times. While I might have some sympathy for your rather impetuous viewpoint, yes, and our obvious inequities under territorial and army law, rest assured that this barbaric matter will be pursued to the end—but in the proper military manner. Fortunately, or unfortunately, whichever pleases you, this is my direction and obligation. Right or wrong, my contention is that the Shoshoni, however courageous, would only add fuel to the fire, a fire that I've been assigned to put out as judiciously as possible.''

Jim Bridger had turned back to the conversation, once again addressing Johnston. He made a cordial gesture toward Chief Washakie. ''He says he repects your word, Colonel. The Shoshoni won't take to fighting unless you ask them. But he says if any of those Paiutes come up in this country, he won't take any help from you, either. Says his braves will kill 'em all.''

The commander smiled and raised his hand, acknowledging their friendship. Then to Bridger he said, ''My advice is that his village move on to the buffalo grounds and hunt in peace. This is the way it should be. Tell Washakie this is the way the great white chief in Washington would want it.''

The exchange was made and the brief meeting ended. No war for the Shoshoni. Instead, Washakie and his tribe would strike their tipis and head east at dawn to make meat on the buffalo grounds.

Others at the fort were planning to leave at sunrise, too. A few happy shouts floated across the grassy flats of the Black's Fork, and farewells passed around the campfires. These were the movers, newly organized, confidence restored, and fully prepared to trail northwest into Oregon country, far removed from Mormon hostiles.

Little Hoop, visiting her last with White Crane, watched some of the night's festivities from Ruben Russell's stoop. She, too, was happy. Her man's work for the longknives was done. Soon, she would be in the country of the Shoshoni and Nez Percé at Fort Hall. She knew about the Nez Percé, a good people from the Land of the Winding Waters. Tree had told her. These Indians were friends of the Absaroke, often meeting with them for good medicine at the hunting grounds near the Three Forks of the Mother River. And, with good omens, there was still time to make the trip to the Yellowstone before the deep snows came. That possibility was lurking in the depths of her young mind, the eventual return to her own village, taking back the scalp of Iron Bow, presenting the white stallion, Snow Hawk, to her great father. She had not mentioned it to her man, of course, but north was the direction of the *Echeta Casha,* and hope was blooming in her heart.

By the time she said her last good-bye, the night had deepened. Across the flat, the Shoshoni council would be ending. She made her way behind the fires of several groups of emigrants and quietly headed across the deserted field toward the trees where her husband had made their camp. It was not until she neared the small holding corrals below the fort that she detected the hurried, heavy steps behind her. When she turned to look, the dark form was already upon her, a man, lunging, catching her across the shoulders, roughly shoving her into the shadows of the equipment shed. Her short scream was muffled by a heavy hand. She sickened and fought to free herself of the stale odor of whiskey and tobacco. Pressed hard against the weathered boards, Little Hoop had only a brief moment to get a wild look at her assailant. She knew him, the unshaven face, and yellowed teeth: Bob Skinner had come to collect his due.

His voice was gruff and coarse. "You go shouting," he hissed, "and I'll whomp you good, Injun! You'n me gonna do some real jiggin', now." He laughed hoarsely. "You'll be none the worse for it, not a bit."

Little Hoop's eyes were two horrified discs of white. She understood nothing of what he was saying, nor could she come away from the rough hand raking her mouth. But she was ready to fight.

"That breed of yours'll never know, and knowing how it is with you squaws, you won't be talking about it." Laughing lowly against her struggling, he finally managed to fall over her. "My word agin yours, anyhow, and

I'll be long gone by sunup. Come on, now, little bird, goddamn you, better if I don't have to—''

His voice suddenly hung, sucking wind. Her one free arm had whipped out from behind, jerking a small knife from its beaded sheath. The slim blade flashed once as she buried it deeply into the muscle and bone of his shoulder. Skinner heaved up, gasping at the searing pain, and then, in a rage of uncontrollable anger, his big hands found her throat.

Later, he staggered away into the darkness, the frightened eyes of the young Shoshoni boys following his footsteps. They crept over from their hiding place in the shed and took one look at the crumpled maiden, then quickly leaped the corral fence and ran toward the camp of the scout called Tree.

Ben Tree found her there beside the shed, a small, lifeless bundle of buckskin. Before he touched her face, he knew. A great sob escaped him. Tears flooded his eyes. Taking her gently up, he moaned once in despair, now smitten by the deepest hurt he had experienced in his twenty-three years. Time flashed by in his billowing pain, instant recall in his welling eyes, every precious moment that they had joyously shared from the time of meeting. And God, it was gone! Gone! Mother Earth had left him barren as the winter desert, had torn away his very soul.

Ben stared up into the somber faces of the two young Shoshoni. Finding his voice, he finally managed to speak brokenly. But they did not understand. Lowering her body, he took the knife from her knotted hand and embedded it in the ground, marking a spot. He turned back to the boys. Making sign, Ben told them to say nothing, only to point the way the wounded man had fled. They made quick motions—the man was bleeding and plenty hurt. Ben disappeared.

Later, in the dark of the night, Ben Tree trailed northwest with his four horses. He was riding the Arapaho gray. Directly behind him came Sunday and the white stud packed with his belongings. The body of Little Hoop, wrapped in blankets and draped over the back of her sorrel gelding, brought up the rear. At dawn, in the distant hills overlooking the valley, he buried his Crow princess. With her, he also buried the last vestige of his white blood.

Barking dogs milling around the far corral fence had aroused the curiosity of one teamster. He peered out from the traces, down toward the deserted equipment shed where the new sun was touching its ragged gray roof. Pulling his coat close against the chill of the September morning, he slowly ambled across the field, straining his eyes until he made out the form, a motionless one, suspended like a crucified Christ from the poles next to the shed. Without approaching any farther, he turned on his heel and ran back to the wagons for help.

They came upon the monstrous scene, five of them, and for a quiet moment they stared in horror.

"He's dead, all right," one finally said. "Deader than a doornail, cut ear to ear and scalped clean." The man suddenly kicked out with his foot. "For God's sake, get these infernal dogs outta here!"

"Skinner's his name," said another. "I know him. Three or four of his party on the other side of the fort. Bad sight, boys. Better cut him down before the womenfolk start gathering."

"Jesus!" a strapping muleskinner exclaimed. He stepped back quickly. "Who would do something like this? Look at that, would you!"

"What's that, Luke?"

"Under there . . . hanging . . ." The man named Luke reeled away as though he were going to be sick.

"By the Lord, it looks like his . . . his tallywhacker . . . cut . . . stuck right in his mouth!"

Two of the men quickly cut the leather strips holding the body to the poles. It fell, horribly stiff, to the hard, frosty ground. A man dressed in brownspun stepped up and with a shove of his foot rolled the body over, face-down. "By the God, that's Indian work if ever I saw it!" he exclaimed.

"A foul deed!"

"Rightly," still another agreed. "How do you figger it?"

"He must have been a philanderer, this one, violating some Injun's woman. The wages of sin, men."

"Better call the law," Luke suggested.

"Law!" the man in brownspun cried. "What law? You know damned well there ain't law west of the Injun' territory, only the military over there, and I'll wager they'll be making no civilian their business, leastways not this one." He pointed across the flats toward a pink cloud of dust boiling up against the early sun. "Injuns are leaving. Anyone want to ride out and discuss this with them?"

"There's two thousand of those Shoshoni, my friend."

Silence.

The muleskinner finally spoke up. "I'll go tell Skinner's pardners. They can come and fetch him. He's a white man, boys. Least we can do is put him away proper."

BOOK
TWO

SEVEN

May, 1858

I arrived back at Fort Hall last night with a cache of hides and received the bad news from J. Digby. He reports word of two men killed north of here more than a year ago. A Frenchman, one Henri Bilodeau, brought in this depressing news. He and his Indian wife departed two days ago to rendez-vous with a Nez Percé hunting party. Digby says that Bilodeau marked the two graves in Pierre's Hole country. He also took two head of horses on the range, both branded Tree. I presume these to be Trace and Traveler and can now believe what I have feared for so long.

I'll be trailing north to find the Frenchman. Digby has tended Sunday and the new colt, a red and white paint of promise. We shod my Indian stock this afternoon, bad medicine for the stud, but the big gray and my lamented wife's pony made little trouble. One freight outfit in here, and supplies plentiful. Also one small train of Oregon movers who wintered below now camped here. Routes east and west all clear. These movers had to winter at Bridger and report that Johnston's army is heading into Salt Lake City. No reports of fighting, Saints withdrawing all directions. I mapped out some of the upper Snake creeks for Digby, all the way to the smoking rivers of the Yellowstone. From the far north there's a report of pox among the Blackfeet. Some deaths, and the runners suspect red measles. I have arranged to sell the Tree stock at Laramie for $4,000. Digby will take receipt. B. Tree

The man wore a black broadcloth cloak and matching, wide-brimmed hat. Under the cloak, his trousers bagged comically in Zouave fashion, the billowing bells partially obscuring the tops of his high leather riding boots. He appeared ready enough to attack the trail. Dress notwithstanding, the big problem was his frontier goal, or how best to attain it. The young Jesuit was temporarily stranded on the Overland Trail, looking for passage into the north country of the Flathead. Once again, he had come to the stoop of Fort Hall agent James Digby.

And for the second time, Digby was telling the priest that money was an irrelevance. "It isn't the money, Father Novello, not at all. As I said, it's a matter of convenience and some fortitude. That's up over the pass to Beaverhead country, on up to the Hell Gate. Few travel that way this early in the season. Few trust the wilderness, hostiles and drifters being what they are. I realize your bishop is no credit risk, but even so that's a trip of serious purpose, and you'll be lucky finding someone. It's certainly no lark."

Father Joseph Novello's dark eyes studied the agent for a moment. With a steady, determined voice, he finally said, "You know I have purpose, Mr. Digby. 'Go forth into the whole world and teach all things whatsoever I have commanded you.' And I have supplies to deliver, most urgent."

The Englishman shrugged offhandedly. "Then the good Lord might be more of assistance than I in getting you up there. That's over six hundred miles of wild country. No sacrilege intended, Father, but you can't make it alone on faith and a prayer."

"I understand," replied Father Novello. "I understand."

"Ah, but you have several choices," Digby continued in his crisp English accent. "Stay with the immigrant train and come back east from Walla Walla. It's a much safer route, Father. Or you can while your time . . . wait for someone who's stout enough to make the short route of it. That might be another month. Contrary weather, the high passes, snow . . ." He trailed off, shaking his head.

The priest remained undaunted. Reluctant to compromise, he said, "The trail doesn't fighten me, Mr. Digby. I've come this far, and time is precious." He looked across the grounds of the historic fort, where the deepening shadows of evening cut sharp silhouettes on the new grass. Beautiful, he thought. He had already put so many tedious miles behind him, the worst of it. Of course this was all God's country, the good and bad, and he could accept any of it. But his most worthy endeavor still lay far to north, up where Fathers De Smet, Mengarini, and Ravalli had been before him. His assignment: first, deliver his goods, then bring the worshiping flock back to St. Mary's, rescue the displaced Indians, heal them in body and soul. This was his faith, his duty. No, compromise was out of the question. Time, indeed, was precious. The sharp ring of the blacksmith's hammer floated up to him. He glanced back at Digby, saying, "What of the man the smithy mentioned? Tree, was it not?"

"Ben?"

"Yes, Mr. Ben Tree."

"I don't know. I didn't talk to Ben about your problem. The man has had a few bloody ones of his own. Stays to himself, he does."

"One of the best guides around, so the smithy advises me."

"That he is," acknowledged Digby. "Yes, Ben's heading north, but the lad most probably will turn east at the Three Forks, not west. That is, after he catches up with Bilodeau . . . a personal matter. But then, I can't say, either."

"Why east?"

"Rather a guess, Father. Ben Tree isn't that talkative. Like I said, stays pretty much to his blooming self these days . . . up in the hole most of the winter, living like a mountain man. Ah, I don't know. Hard to say what's on the lad's mind. No one trifles with him."

"Unusual, a quiet man," Novello said with a small smile. "I've met so few on the frontier."

"Well, sir, he has his troubles, you know—that affair of his father and brother, missing all this time and, no doubt, dead. Had to sell out the family business. I say *maybe* he'll turn east, depending on what news he gathers. I really don't know. That's where the Crow villages are. He lived with them. His wife was Crow."

"Was?"

"Died down at Fort Bridger last autumn," Digby explained. "Rumors . . . rumors are that she was done in. Ben never mentions it, but the word came up the trail. Indians know all these things. Ben Tree has somewhat of a reputation among the natives, don't you know. One of those coup-counters. Yes, I daresay I shouldn't want to cross with him in any manner. Some have, you know. A mistake, I'll tell you, a very bad mistake.''

"A renegade? Is that what you mean?''

"Oh, not at all, not in my opinion. He's a capable chap, he is, and a man of his word to those who know him. Yes, just like his father, but a mite bitter.''

"I'm sorry to hear about his wife,'' Novello said softly. "Perhaps I can help in some—''

"Tut tut,'' Digby cut in with a warning frown. "I wouldn't if I were you, Father. He's a rather unusual person, Ben is. And if you plan on trying to engage him, such an endeavor might well damage your chances. Don't play on pity. Begging your pardon, but he's not one for brotherly love, if you understand what I mean.''

"I don't understand.''

"A matter of circumstance, you might call it. I'd say he loathes sympathy. He's no bleeding heart, you know. Quite a lad—literate, too. Educated in the East, but prefers the West. Why, he's already seen the bloody best and worst of it; some say he's a gunman, and by my recollection he's no more than twenty-three or twenty-four years. Out here, one's contempt for civilization isn't so unusual. Personal freedom, you understand. With Ben, it seems to have become somewhat of a fetish of late.''

"Why, you make the man sound almost primitive . . . forsaken.''

"Well, it's a way of life that few seem to understand.''

Father Novello sighed. "But when one loses the Lord's way . . .''

Digby broke in with a chuckle. "The day Ben Tree loses *his* way has yet to be seen. He could make his way through these hills in the blackest of the good Lord's nights and never miss a step.''

"Then I must talk with him," Novello mused. "I must have his services."

Shaking his head doubtfully, the agent said, "Well, I'll be wishing you luck."

"Faith," Novello said, smiling. "Faith, Mr. Digby."

Digby shrugged. "Oh, I'll say this: If he's a mind for it, you'll not be finding yourself in better hands. But, Father, best not to go offering the lad *your* particular services. Just a reminder. His kind of mourning needs no comfort. Best keep your proposition strictly business."

Ever hopeful, and mindful of Digby's advice, the priest nodded and disappeared behind the agent's quarters.

Meantime, Ben Tree was reluctantly packing away a hide tipi in the loft of the post shed. He had finally decided to substitute its spacious comfort for the small army tent that he and Little Hoop had shared on the Johnston journey the year past. It was a hard decision. The larger Shoshoni tipi had served him well during the winter. He hated to part with it, and to his functional mind the little tent was a poor substitute. However, he was well aware of its practicality for the trail ahead of him. Pitching it, for instance, was a relatively simple task. It was speedy cover for the contrary high Rock Mountains' spring weather, shelter enough against the gusty rain and snow squalls.

In milder climes the robe of a bull, or simply a blanket or two had sufficed. Centipedes, fleas, and snakes sometimes had proved bothersome. And on occasion, without adequate cover, a bad turn of the weather had really taught him a hard lesson in trail discomfort. Hardy as he was, he allowed that the small tent would serve him better, and he was busy lashing it when the long shadow of Father Novello fell across the ground beside him.

Ben paused only briefly, managed to nod as the young priest introduced himself and began the dialogue of his present plight. Continuing with his work, Ben listened with a patient ear. But it did not take him long to make up his mind about the Jesuit's proposal—he had no interest in it.

His refusal was polite but blunt. "I'm sorry, padre, I can't help you."

For a moment Father Novello said nothing, only watched the quick, experienced hands of the strange man in front of him. The priest had no intention of making an exit, not just yet. Killer or not, this knowledgeable frontier guide was his last hope, his ticket through the wilderness, his gateway pass to the missions and settlements beyond. The Jesuit persisted. "But . . . but I understand that you're traveling this direction, up along the Great Divide. Couldn't you possi—"

"I don't exactly know my own plans," Ben cut in. "Understand, it's not the easiest trip, even for a man who can tolerate it. Ei, and the responsibility of a blackrobe . . . Well, I can't afford to take that chance . . . the delay. I'll be pushing hard."

"But I assure you, Mr. Tree, I would be no handicap. I'm quite accustomed to the trail. I'm an experienced horseman."

"You're heading for Flathead country," Ben said over his shoulder. "Not my direction. Your missions, what's left of them, are almost two hundred and fifty miles west of the Missouri headwaters. That's a conservative guess. Now, I may not know too much about the north country, but I'm acquainted with some of the Indians who live up that way."

"Mr. Digby says the Indians respect you."

Ben grunted and went on with his work.

"Isn't that true?" asked Novello.

"By jingo, I'm not talking about Flatheads or the

pierced-nose people. I'm talking about Blackfeet . . . Piegan.''

"Blackfeet? Why, the Blackfeet made peace with the government three years ago, Mr. Tree," Novello returned softly.

Turning, Ben grinned and nodded toward the north. "Padre, I'm not the government, and the Blackfeet didn't make peace with me. They want my hair." He stared at Novello for a moment, wondering at the priest's naiveté. "Another thing," Ben finally continued. "Governor Stevens' treaty doesn't mean a whit to me, no more than it does to some of those braves who've come to know the color of my hair. Once over those Rock Mountains, a man makes his own trail and takes his own chances, They didn't name that country the Hell Gate without reason. Ei, and I'll allow you'll see the day when Stevens' paper on the Oregon country goes up in smoke, and some of your missions as well.''

But Novello, not easily put aside, said confidently, "I'm prepared to take my chances. Perhaps I could find my own way west from the Tree Forks. If you will allow me to accompany you that far, once I strike the waters of the Hell Gate I can—''

"By jingo," Tree exclaimed, "the Hell Gate's a far piece across the Divide from the Three Forks!''

"But the trail from Fort Benton?" questioned Novello. "I hear that the route is being used . . . a new trail.''

Ben put his knee against the fold of the tent and began to secure it with a length of rope. "Maybe so, but it's Indian country most of the way up, too. Ei, Bannock below and Blackfeet above. Look here, padre, the fact that you're a man of the cloth makes no difference up there—providing you didn't go losing yourself in the first place. No, I'm sorry, but I'm just not interested in the job. No, Father, you'd be better off coming in from the western settlements, say Fort Walla Walla. Wagon freights making it now. If not, then there's a few Shoshoni around here who might be talked into taking you. Nez Percé may come this way later. Jim would know about this, I suppose.''

Novello said determinedly, "Mr. Tree, it will take me two or three months by Fort Walla Walla, a most inconvenient route.'' He stopped to stare across the grounds, then beyond to a few Shoshoni lodges. Shaking his head sadly, he said, "And the Shoshoni, it seems, are more interested in hunting buffalo. They show little interest in the work of our Holy Savior.''

With a wry smile, Ben agreed. "That's understandable. The soul has no stomach, and those people are hungry. You can't eat religion.''

Novello stood back and clasped his hands in front of him. He said firmly, "I'm prepared to pay a good wage: five dollars a day. I wish you would reconsider this most imperative matter.''

Ben laughed outright. "Money, is it? Do I look that destitute, padre? The way you're looking me over . . . Don't you know I'm not a poor man?''

"I'm sorry," Father Novello apologized. "I didn't mean to stare. Frontier dress intrigues me. I couldn't help but notice the beadwork on the front of your shirt—intricate, beautiful, certainly not destitute. I've never seen anything quite like it, the repeating design. May I ask, does it have any particular meaning?''

"All things have meaning," Ben answered, touching the trim. "This, only to myself and the one who made it.''

"The sun . . .''

"Ei, the sun, the coyote, and the tree.''

"It's beautiful.'' Curiosity piqued, but sensing something of a more personal nature, Novello politely made no further inquiry. He backed off. He had suddenly remembered James Digby's blunt advice. Discretion prevailed, and now it seemed as though the conversation were coming to an end, his quest fruitless. Yes, the priest thought, it must be finished politely. He extended his hand, saying, "Thank you, Mr. Tree. Thank you for your time."

Their eyes met with the clasp of their hands. Father Novello began to move away.

But something unexpectedly touched Ben Tree. Curiosity, shame, regret, he did not know, nor did he dwell upon it. "Wait a moment, padre!" he suddenly called.

The Jesuit turned and faced him again, his eyes a question mark. "Yes?"

In a weary tone Ben asked, "What makes you think those Flatheads up there are so anxious to see you? Tell me that, will you? You'd risk your own hide with the notion of saving a few souls? Ei, and most likely some souls that your brothers already gave up when they cached the first time. Now, that doesn't make much sense to me."

"I'm sorry," returned Novello, "I can't give you a simple answer regarding those unfortunate circumstances of the past. I shall only say that the Kingdom of God is open to any man whosoever shall receive Him. I have my duty ahead. I shan't waver."

"Are you a preacher?"

"I'm a pharmacist, a man of medicine by training, a missionary by choosing." He smiled up at the scout. "Yes, and a preacher, if you will."

With a grin Ben inquired, "And that makes you in such a godawful hurry? Salvation?"

For a moment, Father Novello's eyes sparked. He nodded, saying, "Yes, of course, that's part of it. Salvation, administering to the sick. Perhaps I should have been more explicit, Mr. Tree. Yes, perhaps I am in a 'godawful' hurry, as you put it. I *do* have three packs of medicinals, some already in danger of losing their beneficial properties by further prolonged journey in such inclement weather, an incidental matter.''

Ben kicked the tent aside and gave the blackrobe a questioning glance. "You mean you're packing medicines? Is that what you're telling me?''

"Yes, and I've tended them and sheltered them like flowers to get this far. They'll be received by the Indians at Saint Ignatius . . . Saint Mary's, if the mission is reopened and the settlers there want us. My duty is there, of course, but I also have the obligation of delivering my freight.''

"Three packs? For Indians?''

Father Novello smiled. "Why, yes, four when we left Independence. The emigrants along the way . . . they heard . . . needed . . . ''

Shaking his head in disbelief, Ben interrupted the priest. "Look here, your people back east must be stupid, padre, plain stupid. Why bother with the medicine if it doesn't preserve? My jingo, they should know enough about this country by now, and how long it takes to get through. They've been poking their long noses this way for more than ten years. They should know better. Serve them right if the whole lot of it spoils.''

"There were these unfortunate incidents," Father Novello patiently explained. "Both real and imagined. Yes, and the fear of the Mormon brigades. I've been on this journey for a year. Because of conditions and constant delays along the trail, I was among those forced to winter at Fort Bridger. So you see, it's more than a personal interest in expedience.'' He stopped and held out his hands. "And when I heard of the shorter route, naturally, my interest—''

"Yes," Ben said with a dismissive wave. "Yes, I see, but by jingo, why didn't you say you were carrying the stuff in the first place? You don't make sense at all, padre, no more than your chiefs.''

"I didn't intend to come seeking pity," he quietly answered. "Mr. Digby advised me against this. He told me that I should seek your hire only on a business basis."

"Digby, that cousin Jack!" exclaimed Ben. "Why, he knows better!"

"I do think he means well by you," interjected the priest. "He speaks very highly of you, your integrity." He stared hopefully at Ben Tree. "Then, you'll reconsider my proposition? I can pay."

Ben gloomily stared away, pondering the priest's words. In disgust he kicked a loose board, then laughed ironically. "Now this is some kettle of fish, padre, it sure is! No, I still can't imagine myself leading some poor blackrobe through prickly pear and sage, and God only knows what else, and then charging him for his suffering. Now, that *is* a joke!"

"If my robe is a source of embarrassment, Mr. Tree, I can seek help elsewhere."

"Oh, for God's sake, padre, don't go playing the bleeding heart! You're not going to get help anywhere else, and you damn well know it." He made an abrupt pass with his hand. "Look here, I'm not commanded by any man's station or purpose. Understand that. No, I want none of your money, either. The only constraint I've ever had out here is the conditions of nature and my own will. What you and that black cloth represent means nothing in particular to me one way or another. But that medicine might be another matter. Do you understand?"

"Yes, I think so."

"And right now," Ben continued, "my own free will is telling me, yes. Yes, I suppose I'm a little daft, but I'll guide you." Hesitating, he stared directly into the priest's eyes. "I'll take you along on one condition, and that's that you'll do what I tell you when we head into the mountains. Ei, *exactly* what I tell you.

And you must stay on the pace like a man. Now how does that strike you, padre?''

Father Novello took a deep breath of relief. Then, radiating sudden pleasure, he exclaimed, ''Yes, of course, I wouldn't dare have it any other way! And God bless you!''

''God bless the both of us,'' Ben said curtly. ''You be ready at dawn, right here with that stock all loaded and ready to move. I want no delays.''

''At dawn, Mr. Tree.''

Dismissing the priest with another flourish of his hand, Ben turned back to the shed loft. ''Now if you'll pardon me, I have some work of my own to do, and it isn't the work of the Lord.''

Dawn came with a sodden limp, gray rain, the new day bleak. Five mules were lined up near James Digby's quarters by the time Ben appeared with his own stock. He stared at the unexpected sight. Cloak pulled tightly about him, the Jesuit sat atop a long-eared gray. Another mule carried the priest's belongings. The remaining three packed his medicines. The drizzle was light but steady, and filmy mists shrouded the neighboring mountains. Leading Snow Hawk, Ben came up close, stopped in front of Father Novello, and scrutinized him once more, wondering at his crazy choice for a riding companion into Indian country.

Novello spoke first, a note of cheer in his voice. ''Good morning, sir!''

Ben merely nodded, and with a grunt turned away from the curious sight. He walked down the line of Novello's mules, inspecting each one for soundness and proper packing. Satisfied, he came back and looked up at the priest for the third time.

''It's *not* a good morning,'' Ben finally said, nodding toward the distant hills. ''Likely to rain all day. You think that's good?''

"The rain doesn't dampen my spirits, Mr. Tree! I've been waiting for this moment for five days. I'll not be depressed."

Ben grunted again. "Before this day is out, padre, the rain will have damned well dampened your bottom. I'll vouch for that."

"A spring shower," replied the priest, undaunted. He stared up at the dark heavens. "Perhaps it will clear and we'll ride in fresh sunshine. I'm optimistic."

"Signs don't point to clearing." Skepticism rode Ben's words. "Wind is down, and those clouds are hanging, not on the rise." Sniffing the damp air again, he settled his poncho about him, then wiped off his saddle. "Ei, the weather is as contrary as that critter you're riding. Thought you said you were a horseman?" He swung up and glanced over at the priest. "That's a jackass mule."

Novello smiled back at him. "Do you find my mount objectionable, too? The animal already has borne the burden of my body halfway across the continent. I've found no reason to complain. Jericho has been most dependable."

"Jericho?"

"His name, sir."

Ben snorted contemptuously. "That figures. A contrary name for a contrary animal."

"But, I think not."

"Mules are contrary," Ben countered flatly. "I've been breaking stock like that most of my life. I know mules for what they are. One of those damn critters broke my leg, once. I wouldn't ride one of those jackasses across a plowed field."

"There are men who have done with less," answered Novello. "King Solomon, King David. And yes, our Holy Savior came astride a lowly ass, without benefit of saddle or accouterment."

Brushing away the priest's gentle rebuff with a wave

of his hand, as if it were a gnat, Ben chuckled. "I'd say you're atop close company, then. The mule is just one stop removed from the ass, padre, Jericho or not. Ei, and if we have to do any fancy running on this trip, I'll allow you won't be coming in like a king. You'll likely be a damn poor second on that nag." Ben reined around in front of the cabin, where a smiling James Digby was standing framed in the light of the doorway. Grinning back at the Englishman, he touched his hand once to his otter hat. "I know what you're thinking, Jim, but don't say it."

"Best of the morning, gentlemen!" Digby called.

"I'll be seeing you before the snow," Ben said. "If not, don't worry on it. Take care of my two horses, ei?"

"That I will," Digby returned. "And godspeed. Keep your powder dry, Ben. Good-bye to you, Father, and good luck."

Father Joseph Novello, ever grateful, made the sign of the Cross and pointed Jericho north.

For a day the two young men rode steadily upriver, ultimately passed the falls of the Snake, and began to search for a crossing. Even though the country was relatively new to Tree, the repeated stories he had heard of it were not. Gabe Bridger, among others, had broken the trails, and the Shoshoni, Flathead, and Nez Percé often passed in this direction. Remembering these tales, he knew that he had to strike due north, cross the big river, and make for the Camas. On the other side of the pass he would come down on the Red Rock and, finally, the Beaverhead.

He was thinking ahead, not about the welfare of Father Novello. With any luck at all, he could catch up with Henri Bilodeau and his party before the Nez Percé hunting rendezvous. That was his only reason for the journey: to locate the Frenchman and get all of the details on the two white men he had buried in the

Pierre's Hole country. Rain or not, and priest included, he intended to get the most out of each day.

By dusk the misty rain had spent itself, but the air was cool and moist, without sun, heralding a colder night. A few miles beyond the river ford they finally made camp, drying themselves in front of a leaping fire of cottonwood. At this point, Ben had little concern about attracting raiders or drifters. This was not a place of habitat. Too barren. To the east were the broad, rolling Snake River plains, a semi-arid region for the most part, yet greening now from the spring rains. It was a country one usually hurried through, particularly when the hot winds of summer curled the land dry again. Beyond the Camas to the north the slope was gradual, leading to the high mountain plains before finally climbing up the timbered ridges of the Great Divide. Ben had no fear of this country, only of what it might offer in the way of a dreadful confirmation and details from the trapper-drifter, Bilodeau. He went to his bedroll thinking on it again. If indeed his father and brother had been done in, by whom, and why? He tossed fitfully.

Visions of Little Hoop also crossed his mind. Since the tragedy at Bridger his dreams were usually bad, his slumber filled with missteps and false starts. Islanded in the sodden plain, cottonwoods barely rustling, the night cold, a weary Ben Tree finally managed to sleep, for a change, a deep sleep. Only asleep was he free from his usual inner torment and outcry, released from the visions of what his life once had been. Nearby, Father Novello fingered his beads. He intoned a prayer and new words for a new companion he did not quite know or understand.

The crack of the new fire awoke Ben. The rich aroma of fresh coffee and damp sage bloom stirred him. It was barely light, and he was mildly surprised to find Father Novello already at an assortment of tasks. Ben

Tree was pleased. The tax of the priest's strange new companionship suddenly began to ebb, and he thought to himself that perhaps the padre might make a dependable partner for the trail after all.

After a quick breakfast they struck the small camp, and it was only as they prepared to ride that Father Novello's continuing curiosity was piqued again. The empty horse that Ben was trailing—why? Ben had packed the Arapaho gray, but once again, strangely, he was trailing the sorrel pony. It remained barren, except for the beautifully beaded halter and neck piece. Novello's tactful inquiry didn't take Ben by surprise. More than once he had sensed the priest's interest.

"Sentimental reasons, Joseph," he explained without turning. "That's my wife's horse. You probably guessed as much, didn't you?"

"I only assumed. I wondered . . . wondered if I dared ask without offending you."

"Fear begets ignorance," Ben replied. "It's this way: I like to think she's riding along with me, just like it used to be. You find that strange? Something that might strain your clerical intelligence? Some folks think I'm touched. You know, crazy. That's good. It keeps the curious away from me. Only an Indian would understand something like this. It's spiritual."

With hesitancy, Father Novello replied, "No, I don't find it strange at all."

Ben gave him a sidelong glance. "What do you know about women, padre?"

"Very little," Novello replied. "I do know something of compassion. I think this a gesture of compassion. It's a touching thought. I must confess, Mr. Digby did mention your wife's passing. I dared not intrude on your personal life, but I must say in all honesty, your outward bearing, Mr. Tree, is no indication of the gentle sensitivity of your soul."

"Soul?" Ben Tree smiled grimly as he slipped the

hackamore on Snow Hawk. "Soul, you say? Thanks, padre. But I'm sure there's a few that would take issue with that."

"Thoughtlessly."

"And my so-called outward bearing, as you put it, does hide more than meets the eye. Yes, this pony means something to me, all right. When Little Hoop died, I had two choices: kill the beautiful critter and send it with her, or ask the Great Spirit to let her ride with me. I chose the latter."

"You have strong faith."

"Yes, stronger than most white men."

Father Novello looked at him curiously. "Indeed?"

Mounting the stud, Ben said aside, "I'm Indian, a breed. I suppose Jim and that big British mouth of his neglected to tell you that."

"I'm afraid he didn't . . . and, well, I find this hard to believe."

"Believe it, Joseph, I'm an Indian—Osage by blood, Crow by family. In the eyes of some, that makes me a savage." He laughed lightly, trying to disguise a touch of scorn. "Ironic, isn't it, that you came to a soulless savage to show you the way?"

"But Mr. Digby implied that you were a Christian. And you look . . ."

Ben clucked the stallion ahead. Adjusting his hat, he said, "Most of the damned fools riding these hills claim to be Christians, when in plain fact they're a disgrace to the Lord and the land—hypocrites, the lot of them. They only know Jesus Christ by name. I don't claim to be a Christian, not anymore. And I can't help it that I have blond hair. That's some of my pa's doing. He was a white man, a good one."

Father Novello said, "The gift of faith is not easily retained. Perhaps you have reason to feel bitter. I can only say that the gates of our Lord's kingdom are always open to the sanctified and repentant. God is merciful.''

''Ei,'' grunted Ben, ''that's where we differ some, padre. I'm one for justice, not mercy. I don't forgive sinners. I kill them.'' He reached around and touched the wisp of scalp hair on his bridle. ''Take this one here, Joseph, a stinking whiskey drummer, a killer. I'll wager the gates he found weren't pearly. The devil take him and all of his likes.''

Father Novello shuddered and quickly crossed himself. He managed to say in a quiet voice: ''Be not overcome with evil, but overcome evil with good.''

''Beautiful words, padre, beautiful,'' retorted Ben. ''But this is the frontier, or the last of it. Don't be forgetting it, either. Scripture can't buy it, and law can't make it. You go trying to play the good Samaritan out here, and it'll likely get you one hell of a hole in the back. That much, I know.''

''There *is* good, my friend.''

Ben sniffed indifferently at his words and retaliated. ''Now see here, I'm no oracle, but I suggest you try and remember something: Just because you're wearing a robe and riding an ass and spouting holy parables, don't get the fool notion this is the road to Jerusalem. You hear me?''

The priest smiled wanly. ''I'll try to remember that, brother Ben.''

EIGHT

High on the Divide, Ben Tree stopped amid the pine forest. Scattered in between the last remaining drifts of corn snow were glades of yellow and blue buttercup, and the white-plumed spears of new bear grass. This was the high country, the air thin and crisp, permeated everywhere by the perfumes of fertility. The long valley below was a carpet of brilliant green. To the north and east, the spectral spines of the Rock Mountains shoved their snowy peaks into great rafts of billowing clouds. It was truly a majestic land. Ben turned and beckoned Father Novello to come up and bear witness to the inspiring sight.

The young priest quickly dismounted. Once on the crest, he breathed deeply. He, too was elated and refreshed. Feasting on the beauty of the distant perimeters, he finally said, "Yes, this is God's country, Ben, the magnificent work of the creator. The glory of nature is God."

"The work of the Great Spirit," quietly corrected Tree.

"As you will," returned Novello, smiling back at him. "The land is beautiful, yes, a magnificent wilderness."

"Only a wilderness to some," Ben said. "Not to me, Joseph. Here, you'll find everything is tame and bountiful, not wild. And if this is God's country, as you say, then the ground is sacred. Why does man disgrace it? This is what it's all about, isn't it?"

Once again, feeling a sudden, deep empathy for his companion's idealism, Father Novello thoughtfully nodded. Indeed, one could not help but be struck by the spectacular vastness and beauty of the scene, the continual roll and upheaval of verdant land in every direction. For a moment he shared Ben Tree's feeling, but his thoughts soon gave way to realistic misgivings. In time, as time had gone before them, the land would relinquish itself to inevitable change, and this beautiful scene of primitive dress would bare the blight and scars of still another moving civilization, the voice of nature stilled. The priest finally said, "Time doesn't stand still, my friend. People have to move with it, the good and the bad. I fear this has been our historic heritage of tragedy."

"Sometimes the whole of life is tragedy," Ben replied. "A few more passing suns will see us here no more, only the legends. Maybe that's best, at least for one like me."

"Perhaps the people will profit by the legends, brother Ben. I'm hopeful."

Ben Tree shook his head doubtfully. "No, I don't think so. It hasn't worked out that way. There are some places never meant for the white man. I believe now that he comes only to confront and conquer. Once upon a time this was all the Indian's land, and his faith, his religion, the burial grounds of his fathers, ei, a part of his own being. Hear me, Joseph: I curse myself every day for the pilgrims that I've guided along the trails down below. Never again.''

"Ah, but Ben, if you think this great land should be a no-people place, what meaning is there?'' Father Novello sadly clucked his tongue. "What of it? No eye to see the beauty, no mind or body to love the land.''

"There are those who love the land,'' Ben returned. "I only disclaim those who come to profit by it. And you're right: Time holds for no one. But I'll tell you this: In my small way, I aim to delay time as long as I can, padre. Day and night cannot dwell together.'' He turned then and pointed down the winding ridges of evergreen. In the valley below, small splinters of silver were reflected from the meandering creeks and waterways. "There's our direction, at least for another day or two: the valley.''

"That certainly seems the best of it,'' Novello opined.

Squinting against the sun, Ben said, "Ei, don't let the beauty down there deceive you, padre. We'll stay to the hills above it for a time. Safer that way. When a mountain's better traveling than a valley, that's when you've reached the worst of it. We'd be easy pickings. No profit in letting trouble get on top of you.''

"What do you mean?''

"My brothers still watch these valley passes, Joseph, and they have reason to be jealous. Like I said, they have claim on the land . . . the use of it.''

Father Novello nodded. It was an argument he could not contest. He wandered to the side, where he found several purple trilliums flowering in the cool shade of the damp earth. He plucked one, offering it up to his companion for identification. "It has the delicate look of a lily,'' he said. "What is it?''

Ben took it and momentarily reflected, held the flower close and smelled. "A mountain lily, a trillium, found only in the high country. It was my woman's favorite. The sign of an early summer, a good one.''

Moving in a crouch, Novello began to examine the flora around them, varied and profuse. Struck by enthusiasm, he suddenly turned to Tree. "Ben, I would like to know *all* the indigenous plants! Look at them . . . everywhere! Do you think you could help me?" He carefully pressed the trillium into a paper he produced from his cloak. "Why, I can make notes . . . their properties and values. Think of it! The country abounds in plants that I've never seen before. What do you say? Will you help me?"

"Like a medicine man?" Ben broke into a grin. "Are you serious?"

"Why, of course! You certainly must know most of the flora, the edibles, the herbs, those of true medicinal worth. Think of it: Once gathered, the information on these species would be invaluable."

"But I'm not an expert, padre; far from it."

"You've lived on the frontier most of your life!"

"I only know what my brothers have taught me," Ben explained. "I've learned only to live in an honorable alliance with the earth, using what it provides. Ei, the medicines, too, but I'm not an authority. Only the Little People who live in the trees are the true authorities. . . ."

"The Little People?"

Ben Tree smiled. "This is what an old man told me . . . an old man by the name of Buffalo Horn, a man who may have saved my life, once. Ei, the Little People in the trees. Only a few privileged ever see them, sometimes in visions. These mysterious little fellows have great powers . . . control all of the medicines that come from Mother Earth. They know them all, every herb, tree, grass, and plant." He grinned over at Novello. "Perhaps you should seek out one of the Little People . . . have a good chat with him—or her.

I only know a small part of the good, just enough to keep from starving to death.''

Yet Ben agreed to help Father Novello, and when he began to explain some of what he knew, he surprised even himself. He had learned well. There were over a score of edible tubers and roots on the frontier, and a dozen plants alone for the making of meal and flour. In season, wild fruits grew in profusion. He knew most of them. At least ten were used for making sweet jellies and jams. Ben said he would be happy to mark these trees and vines along the way. But the medicinal plants were of more interest to the priest, and he pressed his friend for more information. As best he could, Ben tried to oblige him. Among the herbs and barks, he quickly spelled out those the Indian used for poultices, styptics, tonics, and antiseptics. He knew where many of them were found and how some were prepared. When the opportunity arose, they took samples. Father Novello rode along, listening with interest and surprise.

"Oh, but with all our spiritual beliefs, the Little People and all, we're really savages, padre," Ben dryly commented. And before the priest could reply, he pointed ahead. "Why, even that old sage has medicinal qualities . . . makes for some good."

"Camphor," Novello said knowingly. "Poultices."

"Good for cooling the mouth on the trail, too," Ben said, grinning across at Father Novello. "I'll allow it's not all that palatable, though. As much as I respect my brothers, sometimes I have to draw the line. Fact is, padre, that stuff tastes like hell."

Toward evening, Ben moved from the slopes of the ridge and began to follow the creek. He found a suitable campsite on a small knoll several hundred yards from the water. He also found the sign of the party ahead of them, a mixture of tracks, shod and unshod stock—undoubtedly Bilodeau and his six Nez Percé hunters. The young scout calculated that he would overtake them by the following day.

Later, as he sipped black coffee, he observed the priest carefully unrolling a small bundle. Novello finally withdrew three joints of slender bamboo, unlike anything the frontiersman had ever seen, not even in Uncle Jediah's hardware store in St. Louis. Jointed together, the rod was as thin as a bullwhip, and sounded much like one when Novello flexed it once or twice in the air. The priest had his eye turned to the nearby creek, where the dimpled slicks clearly told him something.

Ben curiously continued to watch, and directly the Jesuit explained. "My angling rod, Ben. The newest thing from the Continent for taking trout." He nodded toward the water. "From what I observe, the brook there contains trout."

"Infernal mosquitoes, too," Ben warned. "I didn't realize you were a fisherman. You surprise me, padre, you and that thing you call a fishing pole."

"Really, is it so strange to you?" His glance was from the side, the hidden smile. "Several of the disciples were fishermen. Our Savior was a fishermen, too—of a sort. Oh, I shan't be long, not unless the mosquitoes become too offensive."

"Ei, and like the Lord's disciples, I'll wager you'll catch those darters easier with a net."

Father Novello laughed. "Have *some* faith in me, Ben." He whipped the rod once. "See here, the tension of a trout strike is absorbed by the rod's flexibility; a minimum of stress, you understand. Allow the trout to take line when it dives away. Retrieve when it tires. Relatively a simple matter, once you gain the knack." He stepped away and started down the knoll.

"Nonsense," Tree muttered. "You'll be needing some bait instead of faith, won't you?"

"I'll use a mosquito . . . an artificial one, of course."

"Of course," Ben Tree sighed, shaking his head.

He stared at the priest for a moment, once again amused, but also somewhat perplexed by this unusual blackrobe who kept his face pruned as slick as an Indian, who seemingly would rather collect specimens or catch fish than read the Bible. And surprisingly, the wispy rod did not break. The two men broke bread at dawn with hot coffee and fresh pan-fried trout. Ben complimented him for saving their supply of bacon. This pleased Father Novello, who from behind a sheepish smile, finally had to admit that perhaps it was a bit more than a matter of frugality. He *had* fished for a purpose—it was Friday, a meatless day for him.

Ben had been within sight of the Bilodeau party for fifteen minutes before two of the Nez Percé riders up ahead broke away and circled back to investigate. Five minutes later, the two groups met on a sagebrush flat not more than a half-mile from where Blacktail Creek empties into the Beaverhead River. The sun was almost directly overhead and the day was warming. Ben's eyes quickly took in the sweating horses. Within a moment, he felt his heart go faint. There, daubed in Indian paint, was his father's old mount, Traveler. His breath faltered and he stared sadly back at the priest.

"Padre," he finally said, "there's Traveler over there, my pa's pony—the bay that young woman is sitting. I don't see Will's, but there's not a doubt about this one. It's old Traveler, all decked out with a braided mane. Pa never would have parted with that horse. I suppose you know what this means."

Indeed, it was the fateful confirmation. The priest nodded. "I'm sorry, Ben," he said softly. "I fear you may be right."

"Can't say that I'm surprised," Ben sighed. "Digby

had it right. They were gone too long." He blinked once or twice and tried to set his trembling jaw.

Novello asked quietly, "What about the Frenchman? Do you suspect . . ."

"No, padre, not a man who would bring in the news himself. No, it doesn't figure, but we'll talk. Ei, we'll talk on it. Here comes the tallest one of them. He's the chief of this bunch."

One of the Indians proudly rode up and motioned to a grove of trees near the river bottom. Ben acknowledged his signal, and a short time later they had all dismounted under the shade of the cottonwoods. There were actually ten in the Nez Percé party: Henri Bilodeau and his Indian wife, six Nez Percé braves, and two of their wives. Obviously, the slender young warrior who had directed Tree and Father Novello to the grove was the leader. He immediately called for tobacco. Blankets were soon spread for the circle.

While the Indians curiously eyed the priest, wondering at his presence, Bilodeau, with his hand extended, approached Ben Tree and introduced himself. The exchange of greetings quickly made the rounds and the Frenchman said, "I knew it must be you, Ben Tree. At first, I did not know who these dead men were, eh? Monsieur Digby tells me . . . the two missing freighters. *Oui*, and now you come."

"Then, it's true . . . ?"

"*Oui*, I found them," Bilodeau said, making a helpless gesture. "They had nothing. All was taken. But now I know. You have the same look of the young one, a brother. I knew you were Ben Tree and they, your family."

A cold sweat had broken out across Ben's brow. Feeling weak in his knees, he sat limply on the blanket and looked across at Bilodeau. "I heard about the two horses," he said. "I see one yonder. I knew the worst when I saw it. It belongs to my father."

"*Oui,* I caught two horses down-country, a day after I found these two men." He stopped to sigh. "It's all very sad. I'm sorry, Ben Tree."

The fearful apprehension that Ben had lived with for two years now surfaced in his trembling voice. He faltered, waited, searching the silent faces around him. They knew why he had come, and he sensed their sympathy, their understanding. He finally asked, "How did it happen? How did they die?"

Bilodeau moved a hand toward his back. "Foof! Like that, Ben Tree, shot in the back. They had nothing, not even their belts. *Pi c'est tout! That's all!"*

"Bushwhackers," muttered Ben. Trying to steady his voice, he studied the Frenchman for a moment. Bilodeau was still shaking his head, hands thrust upright and forward in an empty gesture. Ben then asked, "Mormons?"

"No, no, Ben Tree, I do not think so." Making a quick motion around the top of his head, the trapper said, "Ka-poof! Both of them, their tops gone. Indian? I do not know, Ben Tree. I only guess."

Nearby, Father Novello whispered to himself and made the sign of the cross.

From the back of the circle came a woman's voice: "*Eeh, shoyapee!"*

Ben Turned quickly and stared up at her, the same Nez Percé woman who had been riding Traveler, one of the prettiest maidens he had ever seen. "What does she say?" he asked, glancing back at the trapper.

"My wife, Rainbow," Bilodeau explained with a tired and trying smile. "She says *shoyapee.* White man. Hah, she thinks a white man killed them. *Shoyapee cultis,* no good white man, she says. But she is only a girl."

"*Tukug!"* Rainbow exclaimed again. You are right!

"*Oui,* but that does not explain the scalps," Bilodeau replied, looking back at Tree with another flourish of his hands. "I do not think these Mormons would mutilate your—"

"They had Paiutes with them at Mountain Meadows," Ben broke in. "The movers were cut to pieces."

Several of the Nez Percé suddenly began to talk among themselves, until their leader raised his hand and demanded silence. Turning, he addressed young Rainbow. Another brief exchange ensued. Henri Bilodeau looked over at Tree, explaining. This man now speaking to the circle was Gray Hawk, a son of Red Grizzly Bear, a ranking chief in the Salmon River country far to the west.

When the young brave had finished, Ben immediately began passing sign with him. The exchange was rapid, back and forth for several minutes without a sound being heard. Everyone in the circle understood the language of motion except Father Novello. Fascinated, his dark eyes darted from sequence to sequence.

Directly, Gray Hawk spoke out again. Passing his hands flat out in front of him, he said, *"Sepekuse!"* So let it be.

Nodding, Ben pressed two fingers to his mouth and pointed his thumb, first to himself, and then to the Nez Percé brave. "We are brothers." The pipe began to make the rounds, each man taking a puff before moving it to the next.

Father Novello sensed that the group had arrived at some kind of conclusion. He eased close to Tree. "What have you learned, my friend?" he whispered. "Is it over, this disagreement?"

Turning to the priest's ear, Ben said, "No disagreement, padre, only a difference of opinion. Seems a few things came up that Henri didn't calculate. You have to understand: A couple of bodies in the mountains out here never means too much until someone starts asking questions. Only natural.''

Meantime, Bilodeau shrugged and spoke up. "I only did what I had to, Ben Tree. *Et pais voilà*. But that's it. I buried them. I saw no tracks, only those of the stock. *Oui*, the scalps? What can one assume?''

"Ei," Ben finally replied. "I understand, and no matter, now. There's Jethro Collins to think about. It could be . . .''

"And who is this man Collins? the priest asked.

Ben addressed Novello again, catching him up on the conversation. The Nez Percé, he explained, thought it highly unlikely that any Indian had committed the crime. It made no sense. For example, the horses had been set free, even their saddles intact. Only the bridles were missing. That seemed too suspicious to the Nez Percé, for Indians always placed high value on good saddles and stock. Only the pack mules were missing. Most likely, Ben continued, Indians would have retrieved the two horses, a customary reward when counting coup.

"But . . . the bodies . . . scalped?'' Novello questioned. "Why?''

"Well, Gray Hawk there says maybe someone wanted to make it look like an Indian job. It's an old trick. I'm sort of in accord with that calculation, Joseph. These boys are ruling out the Shoshoni. You see, Pa knew the Shoshoni too damned well. Ei, they were his friends. Blackfeet? Not likely, down below the pass that time of year. Bannock? Maybe, but the shape they're in, poor devils, they'd have taken the ponies and everything insight.''

"That leaves the Mormons,'' Novello said. "And this fellow Collins you mentioned.''

"Henri took care of the Mormons. None riding the

country above Fort Hall, as far as he knew. Some of the regulars from Hall said the same thing. Appears those angels were on the south trails.''

''*Oui*, that's true,'' interjected the trapper. ''No Mormons.''

''That leaves us with Rainbow there,'' Ben said, pointing his chin toward the young squaw. ''A few days before Henri came back to camp, she says she saw three men trailing northeast, same direction Pa always took for the cutoff. They weren't Indians. They were drifters. One of them had a gimp arm, like a bear had chewed on it.''

''Aha!'' exclaimed the priest. ''Renegades, perhaps.''

''Yes, except another had red whiskers. That could be Jethro Collins, and Jethro's no renegade, if that's who it was. He's worked for us off and on for five years. Fact is, he came into Hall with Pa last trip.'' Ben rubbed his blond hair back and adjusted his headband. ''Hard to figure, Father Joseph, but by jingo, I'll wager on the woman's intuition—*shoyapee*, not Indians.''

Father Novello stared over his shoulder at the pretty girl. She nodded emphatically again, then moved away. When he turned back, Ben was getting to his feet. The young mountain man smiled down at Novello, a tired, expended smile. He touched the priest gently on the shoulder, then walked away toward the river.

Near a silent eddy where the water was slick and green, he stopped. The sun was a hot swirl of crimson, blinding him as he looked upward. He stared vacantly, wondering what was happening to his life. Along with his family it was slowly disintegrating, shredding away like discarded prairie linen, from the far reaches of the Crow nation, westward to the land of the Shoshoni. No solace here: his brothers, his wife, his kin, all gone. He was quite alone by the river. He thought of the old shaman, Buffalo Horn. He began to pray, eyes open to the brilliant sun.

"Hear me, O Great Spirit! Hear me in my sadness! Hear me in my anger! My soul is gone, and I am sick at heart! Take care of me! Take care of me that I may not find coldness in the earth until my vengeance has been done, and in the name of my people, I promise you vengeance!"

June, 1858

There is no doubt, Henri Bilodeau has confirmed deaths of my father and brother. I am heartsick. I have prayed. I now have but one direction, north to deliver Fr. J. Novello to the Flathead. I will search from there. No white man has come this way lately or passed through Hall. I'll set myself to the task, for I know that no man can ride this country and escape me. We will travel with the Nez Percé for a few days until the rendezvous. I told Rainbow she could keep Pa's horse. They said Tracer went lame and they turned him to good pasture in the Hole. There is now more comfort in our number since we have come into Blackfeet country. Saw some sign this afternoon from other Indians unknown. B. Tree.

Accompanied by Gray Hawk and an often silent, brooding Ben Tree, Father Novello rode near the advance of the small Nez Percé party. They moved northeast. The country wasn't new to Gray Hawk, the handsome eldest son Red Grizzly Bear, the nephew of Chief White Bird. He had been to the buffalo grounds twice before. He knew the trails between the belted pine ridges down to the brushy green bottoms, a heartening and fortunate happenstance for the wide-eyed Jesuit, who swayed from side to side on the gray mule beside the young chief. Father Novello, who had come out of the Diocese of St. Louis and was familiar with the flora of the Missouri bottoms, continued to radiate excitement as each fresh landscape unfolded before him. This was all extraordinarily new. Despite his curious strangeness to the Indians, his animated gestures brought forth smiles of pleasure from the party.

He was like a child on a new pony. The land around him was alive. Here, the sight of eagles soaring the high currents; herds of nervous pronghorns testing the wind, their white rumps fluffed in alarm; or the proud posturing of prairie chickens preening on the strutting grounds. And the plants and shrubs! The blossoming spring foliage was exquisite in its fresh beauty, the variety remarkable, seemingly infinite. The blackrobe was eager to learn. One by one, each species was identified by either Tree or Gray Hawk. If they happened to falter in their knowledge, someone in the group ultimately came to the rescue. The priest devoured the aggregate knowledge like ambrosia, making copious notes and drawings. This was his element, his calling.

The pace had grown more leisurely now, the Indians seemingly in no particular hurry. The slower pace did not bother Father Novello. He knew his destination was close at hand, his cargo safely intact. He was enjoying all of what he saw, witnessing the beauty of new life everywhere, even among tumbled moraine where the tender shoots of ubiquitous thistle sprouted in strange harmony with ancient, lichenous rock. Once, Ben plucked and shaved the new blooms, and the three riders chewed the tender stalks like candy sticks. No thirsty ride, here. Father Novello marveled and remembered. This was far removed from last summer's dusty desert trek, his blistering encounter with sand and sage, tepid sinks, the stench of ancient buffalo wallows and fouled water. Here, his mule's tracks were often obscured by blue stem and bunch grass, and water sparkled in every canyon. Oh, Lord this was creation!

As the priest's excitement mounted, his red friends' curiosity in his mission seemed to lessen, more so after Ben had revealed the contents in Novello's packs. Even so, the Indians politely set themselves apart from the Jesuit. Not that they distrusted him personally. It was his God. His God confused them. They maintained a discreet distance simply because some of their Nez Percé brothers to the west, the treaty Indians, were being taught under another denomination, Protestant. Gray Hawk said this was good enough for those foolish Indians who wanted it, who believed it, the white man's word of God.

Father Novello remained suspect. He was another breed, different, a man similar to those who lived among the Flathead, "Catholic." Gray Hawk knew about the Flathead. He said that some already had lost enchantment with the little black book and its teachers. In some instances, biblical comprehension was secondary. The Indians had become skeptical about the strong battle medicine of the Cross, the value of its protection in their continuing skirmishes with the Blackfeet. And the drums went on beating.

They continued to ride, Gray Hawk passing sign with Ben again about the white man's religion. Father Novello gravely followed the translations. Too many tongues, Gray Hawk gestured. Very bad. Why did the white men always quarrel over their God? This was strange. He had thought on the dilemma many times, he said. The son of a great chief, his travels had taken him to both sides of the mountains. He knew the Protestant church as well as the Catholic mission. Yes, and he had heard about the Mormons, too. They had yet another book, one of their own. Somewhat puzzled, he recognized the good each denomination sought to do for his people, yet he chose to remain proudly aloof and skeptical. Too many books, too many words. What did he need from the missionaries?

With patient restraint, the priest continued to watch. Unlike the white man, Gray Hawk said he was not confused about his own religion. He was at peace with his own God, *Hunyewat*, always had been. But what of these different blackrobes, their wagging tongues? They told too many different stories about their holy book. They fought battles with words, and competed against each other for souls. Yes, souls! How could he tell what was right or wrong when the white man continually argued over dogma?

"You talk to the Great Spirit," Gray Hawk said, making sign. "You pray that we might see as you do, when you yourselves are blind, always quarreling about the light that guides you. How is this?"

Ben Tree, slightly amused by his friend's empirical logic, tactfully altered part of his translation to the priest. Even though the padre was a gentle, well-meaning person, Ben could not resist the temptation to bait him on occasion. It had become part of the game on the journey, a friendly jousting of words.

Father Novello caught the scout's smile. "What is the chief saying now?" he eagerly asked. "What does he say?"

"He says he can't understand you people, Joseph. And, of course, it goes without saying, the feeling's mutual. He seems to think that if his people had nothing, the whites wouldn't go bothering with them. And he says this business of saving souls throws him, just like that jackass Jericho is going to throw you one of these days. Ei, and he knows where his soul is going—*Ahkunkenikoo*, the land above, he calls it. So he says what can you give him that he doesn't already have?"

"Ben, the church is not mercenary!" Novello said in a deploring tone. "You know that! Tell him that the holy church has only *one* interest in all people. Its work is primarily spiritual, not material. We come in peace and salvation. And I daresay, Ben, there is a more heavenly realm than the Happy Hunting Grounds. My goodness, can you explain this to him without arousing his anger? I sense we're creating a misunderstanding here.''

Ben laughed and turned back to Gray Hawk. The Nez Percé listened with interest and smiled himself. He was enjoying the banter. After another short parley, Ben looked over at Novello. "Like I figured, Gray Hawk's not impressed," the scout said. "He's not interested in talking about your book anymore today. But by jingo, he likes you . . . says you're different from the others, taking stock in everything to eat along the way. He says that's better than praying all the time and turning into a beggar like some of your brothers. When winter comes, you won't go starving to death.'' And with a continuing grin Ben added, "Want me to tell him that you're a damn good fisherman, too?''

"Perish the thought!'' Father Novello exclaimed with a wave of his hand. "Tell the man I respect his word, even though our opinions may differ. Wish him well on the hunt, and let the matter drop for now.''

Ben relayed the words.

Gray Hawk nodded and returned sign, adding, *"Uakos tiokan.''*

Ben Tree looked at the priest and translated again. "He says you aren't too handsome on that ugly mule, but you're *uakos tiokan.* From what I make of that, he means you're as big as a giant. And that's about the best compliment you'll be getting out of this chief.''

From beneath a small, dark blush, Novello said softly, "I'm flattered, Ben. God bless him.''

Later that same afternoon Ben pointed his nose toward a distant hill, where two figures were silhouetted against the lowering sun. The scout motioned to Novello. The Nez Percé hunting village was nearby.

These were wolf lookouts on the far ridge. Ben told the priest that the rendezvous was now at hand, and Gray Hawk, making a long outcry, suddenly galloped his Appaloosa forward. Like a fading mirage, the lookouts immediately melted from sight. They would alert the village, Tree explained to Novello. And it was only a short time later that the advancing group did sight the Nez Percé camp, forty or more brightly painted lodges spread out across a partially timbered bench near this new river, which Ben learned was now called the Jefferson Fork of the Missouri.

Sounds of activity began to float out across the grassland. It suddenly and fondly reminded Ben of the happiness of his brother Crow. How they loved the homecoming! Ei, it had always warmed his soul, too, the noisy outcry, the heavy beat of the Nez Percé drums. Excited cries of awaiting relatives and friends filled the air. Lines were forming. Ben described the activity to the priest. After the initial greeting, the newcomers would distribute gifts and specialties ordered from Fort Hall. There would be feasts among the tipis, family reunions. Then, in another day or two, on to the *Moosmoos illahee,* the buffalo country, for the hunting of bulls.

Once again, Father Novello was fascinated. The joyful celebration that followed that first night was like a summer carnival: the dancing, the singing, the great spectacle of a true native encampment in the wild. So unlike some of those scenes he had seen behind the backdrop of the Oregon Trail forts: the Indians beating their chests, drunkenly boasting of their conquests, the Shoshoni ranting about the fires, berating the Sioux, swearing revenge for some ancient incident. These Nez Percé braves seemed so handsomely lithe and agile, so dignified in their regalia. And there were the chiefs, magisterial and commanding around the circle, gravely listening to the monotony of the medicine songs and propitiating the spirits for a successful hunt. There were women, too, some of the prettiest that he had ever seen among the tribes, *palojami*, the fair ones, bedecked in beads and finery, shell necklaces swinging from their slender brown necks.

Indeed these were splendid, friendly, freedom-loving people, and the young Jesuit was enjoying their fraternity—to the extent of his inhibited capacity. This could have very well been the frontier's Eden. But alas, he knew better. Despite his many admirations, the wonderment in his dark, roving eyes, unfortunately these people were imbued with superstitions and practices abhorrent to the civilized mind. They were without religious direction. They idolized everything about them, the sun, the moon, the winds, and the earth, yes, and their *Ahkunkenekoo* and *Hunyewat*. Too much, too much. Indeed they were noble and proud, but, God forbid, they were savages; knowledgeable savages, perhaps, but it still saddened Father Novello that the Protestants across the mountains had done so little for the souls of these people. Even so, the easy rhythms of their life, their quaint customs, and the primal beauty in which they lived, all had begun to etch unforgettable patterns in the canyons of his Jesuit mind. Ben Tree's cynical words suddenly came back to him: What *could* he give them that they didn't already have?

NINE

The trapper Bilodeau and his attractive wife, Rainbow, were trading a few last words with Father Novello. Nearby, Gray Hawk and Ben Tree conversed, surrounded by the remnants of the small party that had traveled the Beaverhead together. The scout and the priest were leaving. *Taz alago,* Gray Hawk finally told Ben, good-bye. And the young chief reminded Man Called Tree that he was always welcome in his village on the *Tahmonmah,* the River of the Great Salmon. He recognized Ben as a true brother, one who brought medicine to the Flathead, a warrior, a follower of the sun. He was good medicine. Ben accepted with honor the name that his new friends gave him: *Pootoosway,* Medicine Tree. Allowing that this was a good omen, the scout told Gray Hawk and his brothers that he would travel where the trails led him, but that before too many passing suns he would return to smoke with them again. Ben wished the Nez Percé good hunting, then made one last sign to them, a note of foreboding, like the sound of *hattia tinukin,* the death wind. He was deeply troubled. He told them that the spirits of his father and brother were restless for vengeance.

"When you meet the *shoyapee*," Ben said, "tell them that I'm up here, ei? Hunting for the killers of my family. They will come to know Ben Tree."

And so the two travelers, each with separate missions, left the Nez Percé, following the Jefferson for a day until it swung south away from the part of the Great Divide that closed them off from a valley the Indians called Deer Lodge. Before the Deer Lodge, Ben would have to climb another pass. Beyond that, the waters of the Hell Gate rose on the west side. But now a great mass of rock stood before them. Nature's trails were up there, over the mountains, ancient paths of migrating animals winding up through the canyons, rimming the boulder-strewn cirques. Other Indians had followed these precipitous routes, too. The sign and well-trodden trails easily directed Ben. On the second day, they were near the summit. It was cold and raining. When the downpour became incessant they made camp under a protective shelf of granite, built a fire, and settled down for the rest of the afternoon. They made some conversation and took to their personal chores. Ben began catching up on his journal notes while the priest sorted his growing collection of specimens. Under the fire's reflection against the rock, they bedded down and slept warm and dry. When they awoke, a skiff of snow covered the highlands, and the hills around them were obscured by drifting clouds.

The priest was alarmed at the whims of nature, its diversity on the high Divide. Such peculiar weather, and this was far from good. But lo, the sun broke through, and by the time the two men had threaded their way to the bottom the air was warm again, the grass green and succulent. Ben let the hungry stock graze. Father Novello, ever the naturalist, once again busied himself searching out new plants on the foothill slopes. From white to green, God's hand seemed to be everywhere. This was the Land of the Shining Mountains, Ben told Novello, a very good land. In complete accord, they continued to move through it, northwest toward the Hell Gate River. They were making good time, and a day later, at a point where the Little Blackfoot swept into the main Hell Gate and coursed west, Ben stopped to take another bearing.

It was late afternoon. By his calculation, the east-west trail linking the Missouri River posts with the Walla Walla settlements was directly across from them. The river was running high, and he thought about searching for a suitable ford. But no matter. He elected to stay on the south side of the valley, well back from the swift stream, at least until the thick forests ahead forced him down. Ben explained this to the priest— that they would continue to travel the high ground, where the visibility was less restricted. The trail opposite them on the other side of the river was new. He trusted nothing to chance in unfamiliar country. Most often, he said, the roughest trail proved the safest. Father Novello nodded in understanding. He had no reason to argue that point with his mountain man guide. They had come a long way together without incident.

The following day, atop another rise, Ben paused again to check the terrain ahead, to mark his next directional point. But by habit, he surveyed everything around him. It was off to his right, far across the river, perhaps a half-mile to their rear and well below them— a string of animals filing across a small clearing. Without moving, he nodded to Father Novello, saying, "Padre, sit steady, now. There's some activity back of us . . . across the river." As soon as the distant figures had disappeared into the trees, the scout motioned ahead. "I think we'd better ease down to some cover and wait a piece."

"Indians?" questioned the priest. "Your old friends, the Blackfeet?"

"I don't know, but we'll be finding out soon enough."

From their shady point in the pines, the two men silently observed the approaching animals. Ben finally counted horsemen—seven riders, trailing fifteen mules and four extra horses. It was not an Indian party. From what he could make out, the men were packers. That mildly surprised him. Obviously they had made the long trip west from either Fort Benton or Fort Union, along the newly proposed freight line that Ruben Russell had first told him about a year back, a time when the mountains were chilled by rumor, a time when Brigham Young's avenging angels were on the prowl. It now appeared that this northern route into the Oregon country was no longer rumor. It was fact. Somewhere to the east the army engineers were on the job, mapping a new wagon road; this much was certain, for Indians had seen the longknife surveyors at work. Apparently a few hardy travelers already had taken up the challenge, convinced that the government's work was enough assurance to trim the edge of danger from the mountainous trail, a rugged pathway once used only by migrating hunters.

Ben smiled to himself at such flimsy conjecture. There were those who would disagree that there had been any lessening of danger along this trail, and he was one of them. It had always been the Indian's route, and they could be every bit as contrary as the high Rock Mountain weather, particularly if movers and prospectors started invading the traditional hunting grounds. Ben had witnessed the age-old pattern before. Surveyors first, wagonmasters next, and inevitably the squatters, and then the troopers who usually followed to try to keep the peace. And that was always bad medicine for the Indian.

Father Novello, taking note of the scout's stony silence, said, "They must be merchants, Ben. Wherever are they coming from, way up here? Fort Benton?"

"They're merchants, all right," Ben returned tightly, his eyes narrowing into two flinty slits. Only now had he noticed the peculiar packs on the mules. His ire swiftly built to hate. He knew a whiskey train when he saw one. "Coming from the upper Missouri, I reckon, and armed to the teeth." With a deep frown, he glanced over at the priest. "Look, padre, we won't be joining them, if that's what you're thinking. They're not my kind of partners for a trail ride. Ei, and I don't think they'd exactly appreciate your company, either, not from what they're packing."

Puzzled, Father Novello said hesitantly, "I don't know exactly what you mean. And from this distance, how do you know? If they are merchants going our way . . . ?"

"Merchants, hell!" Ben exclaimed bitterly. "Joseph, to your notions, those buzzards are selling sin. And you're supposed to be fighting it—in your own special way." He nodded back down at the passing train. "See those packs? The way they're shaped to fit the critters? Tin tubs, Joseph, most of them probably full of raw whiskey, allowing what they've been diluting and selling the Indians along the way. Now if you want to go shaking hands with the devil's disciples, I'll take you down there right now. As for me, I'd just as soon peel their hides."

"Well, indeed!" Novello leaned forward and stared at the pack train. "Whiskey salesmen! I'm sorry, I wouldn't have known. You're very observant, brother Ben."

Ben's face turned grim. "By jingo, I damned well have reason to be!" He looked sternly at Novello. "No, you'll find no souls to save down there. They're drummers, the lot of them, scum of the frontier, debauching the Indian with raw alcohol they call 'whiskey.' Allowing that pure stuff might peddle for nigh on to a dollar or more a gallon, I suppose they're carting a small fortune. Ei, by the time they water it down.''

Father Novello tutted sadly, wagged his head despairingly. "God forbid.''

"Going your direction, too,'' Ben commented sagely. "Probably to Hell Gate and Fort Owen . . . a few grubstakers and Indians along the way. Plenty of firewater in those tubs, padre, Taos lightning and demon run, enough alcohol to pickle a man's brains.''

"Yes, I understand,'' the priest replied. Unconsciously, his hand wandered to the neck of his robe. A few words of Latin escaped him.

Ben reined around and headed back up through the pines. "Don't be saying any forgiving words for them, Joseph,'' he said over his shoulder. "Those boys are already spoken for. By jingo, I sure wouldn't want you to go wasting your time trying to bail them out. They're not worth the price of a drink in Hell.''

Novello said quietly, "Our Holy Savior would disagree.''

"Your Holy Savior! Yes, the miracle man.'' Ben spat to the side and grunted. "Now if he's good enough to turn water into wine, I suppose you *can* work on that proposition with those cussed scamps. No reason why the good Lord can't reverse the process, is there, ei, turn that rotgut into water? That, for certain, would be a miracle.''

Father Novello momentarily grimaced, then looked to the heavens. But he understood. How could one possibly engage such an embittered young man, a man so burdened by adversity, one whose whimsy often bordered on outright blasphemy? From someone else, such irreverent musings would have brought from the Father a gasp of mortification, a bowed head, an askance prayer for forgiveness. But this was Ben Tree, no one's man. And had not a whiskey drummer killed his wife? "Ben," the priest implored, "I'm sure you would be surprised at the power of prayer, the peace it may bring one."

"There's very little that surprises me anymore, padre, especially your continued concern for my soul."

"Indeed?"

"Indeed," retorted Ben with a sly smile. "And as for this matter of peace . . . well, that's not exactly what I'm looking for." Then, forking two fingers in a sign of friendship, he added, "Now, see here, Joseph, I've come to look upon you as my friend, but right now I can't chant any canticles of praise to your God. You'll just have to forgive me, but it's not in me. All I need is some proper direction, so let's quit worrying about my soul."

"Direction?"

"Yes, direction. This country is big, but not big enough to hide the renegades, the likes of those drummers down there. It'll take me a little longer, but I suppose I'll have to find my own way, catching up and striking down the wicked. I've made my vows. Sooner or later, I'll mark my own days of atonement."

"And perhaps become a renegade yourself?"

"In the name of justice, call me what you will."

Father Novello wagged his head sadly. "Ben, you are too much of a civilized man to destroy yourself—your life. Really, you must put yourself at peace, sometime."

"Live and let live? No, I'm an Indian, Joseph."

"A human being, Ben, a valued life."

"But what is life, padre?" Ben asked. "It's so damned fleeting, passes so swiftly. Ei, like a small shadow fleeing across the grass, losing itself in the sunset. Does it matter that much?" He clucked his horse ahead. "We don't die, we only change worlds,

and by the word of another holy man I have five De-
cembers left. There's *my* peace.''

''But . . . but do you believe that? Really, Ben!''

''Buffalo horn's medicine is strong. My way isn't
crooked, padre. It *is* the way of old.''

''I will pray for you.''

Ben Tree said nothing.

Near midnight, he quietly threw back his robe and
slipped on his buckskin breeches. For a moment, he listened to the easy breathing of Father Novello. A slight
feeling of guilt touched him as he stared down at his blackrobe brother, yet he knew this deception was necessary.
Ben finally sneaked from the small tent, taking with him
only his gun belt and skinning knife, his high-topped
moccasins, and a blanket to drape over his bare shoulders.

He chose the Arapaho gray, led it quietly for a short
distance, then hopped on bareback and made directly
for the river, fording it easily. The night ride along the
foothills on the other side took him no more than
twenty minutes, a much shorter trip than he had anticipated. When he caught the faint whiff of smoke in the
chill night air, he knew that he had ridden as close as
he dared. Tying the gray to an alder trunk, Ben took
off at a trot toward the camp of the whiskey-packers,
his nimble tread falling like a cat's paw.

The sight he soon came upon was somewhat less
daunting than he had expected. Only one guard was
about, sitting near the night fire of the camp, propped
up comfortably against a saddle thrown over a huge
log, and from the looks of his drooping head he was
dozing—another lucky break. The man was heavy, his
jowls relaxed and hanging. Ben's quick eyes took in
the rest of the peaceful scene. Directly behind the lone
sentry were the packs and a few more saddles, while
in the shadows nearby the rest of the party had bedded
down under buffalo robes. Everything seemed in or-

der. Smiling, his plan already formulated, Ben backed away on his belly. These drummers would think twice before ever trailing the Hell Gate again.

The horses and mules were picketed a short distance behind the sleeping men, and without disturbing their grazing Ben swiftly cut the lead ropes to the picket pins and removed the hobbles from the bell mare. The stock was now free to stray, even bolt, if the night suddenly ended in complete chaos. The red in Ben wanted to strike fear, to destroy, to make this an efficiently destructive job, but admittedly the odds were not the best, seven to one. If the drummers even so much as caught him on the prowl, he knew they would kill him without question. The first obstacle was dangerous enough: the nearby guard, nodding by the fire, a ready rifle in his lap. Somehow the fat fellow must be dispatched silently, without outcry, for this was the only possible way that Ben could gain a clear path to the whiskey tubs. And even then, beyond disposing of the guard, there was great risk: the line of sleeping men only fifteen feet away from the huge pile of packs. These packers, like any others on the trail, always slept with their weapons at hand.

Flattened in the shadows, Ben briefly pondered the situation. He finally drew a long breath and pulled out his skinning knife again, idling its blade against his thumb. It was his only chance, the only way—slit the fat man's throat. Simple enough, he thought. Or was it? He had dispatched Bob Skinner, his wife's killer, in like manner. Ei, but Skinner had been wounded and drunk, easy prey, his death's labor no more than a slight gurgle. Yet in retrospect, Skinner's demise had been much too easy, much too painless for a woman-killer. Ben's eyes came up in narrowed slits, and he moved forward on his elbows like a hungry lizard on the stalk. By jingo, these men were not a damned bit better than Bob Skinner; peddlers of death and misery, they deserved no less a fate.

Ben grimaced. If Father Novello were not along it would be such an easy job, one to be relished, picking them off one or two at a time from the bluffs, shooting holes into the tubs, making a deadly game of it for a few days, right down to the last maddened man. Oh, how he would have enjoyed that! Yes, seven coups— seven carcasses for the wolves and varmits to devour.

But now! And his knife suddenly leaped forward, carving flesh and vein, the force of the swift slash cleanly halving the fat man's gullet. Before his victim could topple, Ben quickly seized the back of his collar, gently righted him in repose, and replaced his hat. Except for death's quiver and the oily slick oozing down into his bib, the man might as well have been sleeping, no one would have known the difference.

Without a trace of emotion, Ben backed away and faded into the shadows of the stored packs. His hands were quick, frisking the bindings, searching out the plugs, and within moments he had one spout flowing freely. Another tin tub followed, but the pile seemed endless, as time was precious. He brought his knife into play, quietly needling its sharp nose into half a dozen more. At that point, the incessant puddling suddenly seemed deafening, and Ben thought he could do no more damage than he already had without arousing the camp.

In a crouch, he took off through the trees, paying no mind to the small trickle of alcohol inching its way toward the dying flames of the night fire. This had not been part of his plan, nor had he given any thought to such a scheme until he was well away and mounting the gray horse. At that instant, he happened to notice a strange glow in the darkness behind him. Flanking his pony, Ben rode to a higher point where he turned and stared down at the conflagration.

There was no doubt as to what had happened. He heard frantic shouts in the night air. From his far perch all he could see was a huge, bright fire. No, this was no great puzzle. Nevertheless, he was chagrined that he had not planned it this way in the first place. But it was something that he would not forget, a mental note for the future, how well raw whiskey burns. Before he reined around, he heard the sound of heavy hooves pounding below, the faint tinkle of a bell, the ungainly gait of escaping mules. The stock had bolted. He smiled and nudged his gray back toward the high camp. Ei, indeed, the packers would think hard on it before trying the Hell Gate again, and these men, without mounts and supplies, might well perish before reaching civilization.

The next morning, Ben kept the winding river in sight, usually about a half-mile to the north, and for the first hour he frequently stopped to scout the distant flats and ridges on both sides. This had been his usual procedure all the way up from Fort Hall, and Father Novello was more than content to bear it. Certainly there was nothing irregular in it, or so the priest thought. Progress had been safe and steady under Ben Tree's careful hand. True, they were some distance from their destination, but they were getting close. By Ben's best estimate, the Hell Gate settlement was now only three days' ride to the west. From there on, either north to St. Ignatius or south to St. Mary's and John Owen's trading post, the hazards of the trail would abruptly come to an end, and so would the continued scouting.

To the priest the journey had been extraordinary, and he felt he owed Ben a deep debt of gratitude. Each day he had been expressing his appreciation to the scout. Each night he had been giving thanks to Almighty God and praying for the young man's soul. Father Novello elected to believe that Ben's masterful execution of the dangerous route, free from attack or mishap, had a certain touch of divine guidance about it. The Jesuit could hardly believe that his guide had any resemblance to the ruthless renegade and loner once described to him by the Englishman, James Digby. The young priest had purposely avoided staring at the scalp hair decorating his friend's bridle. God forbid, those barbaric momentos of revenge! Along with his constrained religious comments, Father Novello tried to dwell on the more spiritual aspects of the scout: the touching spectacle of the riderless sorrel pony; his companion's reverence for the shining mountains, the benevolence and sanctity of Mother Earth; his frank acceptance of a Supreme Being, and admission that perhaps there *might* be some unity between God and the Great Spirit. Whatever the conversation or casual incident of the day, it had been a blessed trip, and Ben Tree had made a profound impression upon him. And he continued to pray for the man night and day.

For Father Novello, the new day had barely begun. He was drinking in the purity of the early-morning air, maintaining his usual alertness for any new plant life, when Ben's raised hand brought them to a halt. The scout was pointing off to the right, across the river, and although a surprise to Novello, it was a sight that Ben ultimately had expected, at least in some bizarre manner. The priest strained his eyes, but even then couldn't quite make out the shapes. It appeared to be another small party moving west.

"Well, Joseph," Ben finally said, "now, what do you make of that little parade?"

For a moment Father Novello continued to stare, perplexed, wondering. He finally counted three distinct figures. They were afoot. Unusual, he thought. "Why, I can't say," he answered. "From this distance, Ben, it might as well be a mirage. I'm always amazed at the range of your vision. I would have never—"

"Movement," grinned Tree. "Knowing when and where to look, unusual verticles on the horizon." He swept his hand forward to say that they should proceed. "Probably hunters, padre."

The priest faltered. "Hunters? But we've seen so little game along this stretch. Don't you find it rather unusual? They seem to be without mounts, too."

"Deer in the bottoms," Ben replied offhandedly. "Probably tied up their ponies to make a stalk."

Novello nodded. That seemed entirely logical, but for some reason it did not quite ring true, and Ben Tree obviously was not the least bit excited about sighting the strangers. "Do you think they're Indians?"

"Well, that's possible, Joseph, but I doubt it. Can't say that I've seen Indians bunched up like that, not hunting deer."

Father Novello suddenly exclaimed, "Look there, Ben! They see us! Why, they seem to be waving . . . hats! I think they're white men, waving at us!"

"By jingo, it sure looks that way, doesn't it?" Ben lifted his hand and casually waved back. He also kept his pony moving west, apparently with no intention of making a cursory investigation. He already knew who the men were. "You might as well give them a nod, padre," he added, "because that's all they're going to get this day. Come on, let's keep moving."

"But . . . but, I don't understand," the priest answered. He was still pointing at the distant figures. "It certainly appears to me that they're hailing us. Look there, my good man! Do you suppose they're in some kind of distress, need assistance?"

Ben chuckled and nodded affirmatively. "If they have no mounts, I'd say you're as right as rain." He glanced back at Novello. "Take another close look.

See those splinters they're carrying? Now they may not have horses, but they damn well have rifles, don't they? And I'm allowing they know how to use them, too. Don't be foolish, padre. My guess is they'd go through Hell and high water to get our ponies. Ei, even old Jericho there." He grinned at the priest. "And that's being about as hard up as one can get."

Squinting at the men, Father Novello mused, "It seems so strange, if what you say is true . . . that people can possess such savage inclinations. It's so hard to believe, Ben. I wonder if we shouldn't . . . ?"

"Believe it," said Ben flatly. "A man's horse is his life, up in this country."

The priest fell into another thoughtful quandary. It was beyond his comprehension, how little importance his friend attached to the obvious plight of these beckoning men. Now the drummers were in desperate flight, running toward the river bank, waving frantically. Father Novello persisted, exclaiming, "Ben, they're definitely not Indians! See the manner of dress!" And another light suddenly flickered to assumption. "Do you suppose those vile whiskey salesmen we saw dispossessed these poor men? Perhaps they were attacked . . . robbed."

"They didn't get their rifles, did they?" quipped Tree without another glance. "And that's a fact." He grunted once and gave the priest a pathetic look back across the rump of his horse. "Joseph, I can see the goodness of your heart is eating away at you. You aren't going to be satisfied until we see what this ruckus is all about, are you? You sure as hell don't intend to give me any peace. That's what you want me to have, peace, but you aren't going to give it to me, are you?"

"The good Samaritan?"

"I know that old story, Joseph."

"Don't you believe we should at least make inquiry?"

Ben smiled wearily. "Look here, just because some priest passed the Samaritan by is no reason *you* should go feeling guilty about it the rest of your life. I'm allowing it sure wasn't anything of your doing."

"Ben . . ."

Ben helplessly succumbed. "Well, hold on a piece. I'll see if I can find out what this is all about. Looks like you'll be making a sinner out of me unless I don't." With an exasperated sigh, he glanced back at Novello. "And when I go down there, I'll allow I'll be making a fool out of you. Well, so be it, if that's what you want, a fool you will be."

"Bless you," the priest murmured. "I shall play the fool if I have to."

Ben kicked Snow Hawk into a gallop toward the river, no doubt in his own mind as to the circumstances surrounding the men's plight. He knew what to expect, but this time he was determined to prove a point to the padre. Sizing up the immediate situation, his guess was that three of the drummers had gone upriver and three down, searching for their panicked stock. He reflected briefly and laughed to himself. Why, the way those spooked critters had been snorting and charging through the bottoms, by now most likely they were already kicking up their heels on the buffalo grounds! He stopped purposely several hundred yards from the river and dismounted. Giving the stud a sound pat on the rump, he watched it trot back up the hill toward the pack string. Then, checking the breech of his Maynard, Ben decided to walk only to within hailing range. No use making a good target of himself. He reasoned that he had already disappointed the men by not riding down with the padre and the entire string. He was not that foolish. At fifty yards, the stranded packers could easily put a couple of balls into them and make off with everything.

Near a stand of protective chokecherry, Ben addressed the group by cupping his hand and calling out. One of the men began shouting back, stating their plight: They had been attacked by renegades. They needed grub, one called, yes, and a horse or two. Another man held up his hand. Money! They would gladly pay. They had cash. Ben chuckled when one of them agreed to ford the river to make payment and take delivery.

"Can't do it!" Ben finally called back. "Only have enough to make it through ourselves! Can't spare any stock, either—full packs!"

"Then let us trail with you, mister!" the man holding the money cried. "Have pity! We're flat busted, and goners if the Injuns come back!"

"Indians, you say?"

"Hell, yes! These hills are full of 'em!" he said. "Let us throw in with you! It's a fair deal for all of us!"

Ben waved them off. "Sorry, boys, looks like you'll have to hoof it! We have nothing to spare!" He turned to the side, taking another quick bearing. As his eye cornered, his instinct told him it was time to scramble. Two puffs of smoke suddenly clouded the air across the far bank, but he had already leaped clear. He dived headlong into the chokecherry, and by the time a third report rent the air he was completely flat. Ben badly wanted to get a shot in himself; however, when he jumped up to fire, the men were nothing but darting shadows in the downfall and willow thickets. Bad luck, poor targets; no reason to waste powder busting twigs.

Cursing, he bellied off back up the hill, fighting the brambles all the way. He finally rolled over into a small gully and inched away to safety on his back. By God! he cursed again, what must I do to prove a point to this crazy blackrobe? Growling, he brushed angrily at another nettle patch. Rose thorns raked his buckskin and picked at the side of his face. Out of range, disgusted and bedraggled, he reached the top of the gully only to stare up into the shocked face of Father Novello.

"Are you hurt?" the priest asked in a flustered, concerned rush. "Those men . . . evil . . . terrible . . ."

"Damned poor shots."

"Why, they could have killed you!"

"Well now, isn't *that* some notion!" Ben hawked and spat dust. "Hope you're satisfied, Joseph, dammit!" He gave the priest a hopeless stare. "Now, what if they'd got a lucky one in? Figure you could say a few words over my pile of rocks?"

"I'm sorry," Novello apologized. He began nervously dusting the scout's tunic. "Truly sorry, Ben. God forgive me. I feel terrible about this. I had no idea. . . ."

"Well, *I* did," Ben huffed, wiping off his rifle. "But you had to go and intimidate me, didn't you?"

Father Novello came up with an empty gesture of complete defeat and humiliation.

Ben spat again and wiped his mouth. "Well, if it'll make you feel any better, those scamps are part of the pack outfit we saw yesterday. I had a hunch."

"The whiskey salesmen?" the priest whispered. "Why, whatever happened to them?"

"Said they got raided," Ben answered innocently. "Seems like some savages did your Lord one better . . . went and turned their whiskey into fire instead of water. Burned up their camp and riled them like a nest of hornets."

Novello's face lit up. "Ah!" he exclaimed quietly but triumphantly. He made a motion with his hand, forefinger upward. " 'Vengeance is mine, saith the Lord. I will repay.' Do you see, Ben? Now, *there's* your justice! Don't you see?"

"Bushwah! 'Let justice roll down like waters, and righteousness like a mighty stream,' that's the word of Amos. This time, the stream was of whiskey, ei?"

"I beg your pardon?"

Brushing away the last burrs from his breeches, Ben gazed hard into Novello's dark eyes. Finally: "Now look here, Joseph, they said *Indians* riled them up, not the Lord, dammit!"

"Indians, indeed? But . . . but where?"

"Yes, Indians, and don't go arguing the point, or I might have to make a fool out of you *twice* this day!" Grunting once, Ben trudged back up the sunny slope, the priest trotting behind him like a heeling dog.

"But I'm afraid I don't understand," Father Novello said.

"Just as well," Ben answered. "Might set you to fretting all over again."

TEN

June, 1858

We should sight the Hell Gate post by sometime
tomorrow. Some sign of traffic on the trail now.
Ruben Russell told it straight. The white man is
making his customary tracks, and up here the wilderness is also ending. We met two white men,
one A. Gardipee and Thomas Black. They are
heading upriver to F. Finlay's old prospect. Some
claims staked on this place called Gold Creek by
the Bros. Stuarts. J. Stuart is the one I met last
year in Ft. Hall, a good man. Gardipee says he
and friend pulled stakes on the Colville diggings
to west. The Yakima Indians are still raising Cain
with the grubstakers over that way.

These men were no help on information I seek
on Pa and Will. They say many strangers around,
and one small village of Flathead camped north
of Hell Gate. This latter news pleased Fr. Novello, who plans to meet them forthright. I warned

Gardipee about drummers on the trail. Fr. Novello spoke to them of Indians! Of course I was not at liberty to dispute this false information. I did tell them that we ourselves had not met Indians since the headwaters. Since I was the guilty party, and in fairness to the Indians, this was the best I could do. B. Tree

He had made only a brief inspection from the distance, but it certainly seemed adequate. Ben Tree was not impressed with Hell Gate. "It sure doesn't look like much, padre," he said. "I don't know who in tarnation named this neck of the woods, but maybe the handle fits."

"Forgive the name, Ben; by whatever name, it's civilization!" Father Novello returned happily. "Our people are down there, friends, perhaps even fresh news from the west coast. I'm delighted! We've come through! We've arrived! Think of the miles between here and Saint Louis!" He sighed and soberly crossed himself. "Few others have had this privilege; yes, and to endure so little. May I offer grace . . . congratulations?"

"I don't know, Joseph," Ben said with a tired smile. "Maybe you'd better hold off until we ride in. Looks like a regular hog wallow to me." He clucked the gray ahead, down over a grassy knoll. "Yes, I'll allow it's our people down there, all right. Hell Gate, ei? Well, no one else but the devil himself could make a mess like that. By jingo, padre, I was little better than a boy the first time I saw Fort Bridger. Let me tell you, it sure looked better than this pigsty."

Yet the blackrobe's assumption was correct—it *was* civilization, if only the barest beginning of one. Hell Gate was the primitive frontier—raw, crude, robust, nothing more than a half-dozen or so nondescript log structures set among a haphazard array of lodge-pole corrals. It was new and dirty, a conglomeration of discards, building debris, and horse manure. It was midpoint on the new north trail. The trade had come, with it the speculators, frontier hucksters, propectors, a few tradesmen and settlers, most of them willing to gamble on the future of the Five Valleys country, which in time would become known as Missoula. The signs were good. The wagon road was coming, the neighboring Flathead were peaceful. The rolling, unceded land was fertile and spacious, the winters here relatively mild. Excellent cattle country, a man named Fred Burr had already brought the first stock through. A few courageous pioneers were even beginning to turn the rich soil near the river bottom, and nearby a sawmill was under construction.

Another two days to the north, the Jesuit would find sanctuary among the Flathead and Salish at the mission of St. Ignatius. He had brought the medicines, but his vision was now reaching out for other goals. Beyond St. Ignatius, perhaps another task, God willing: bringing back worship to St. Mary's, in the place named Bitterroot Valley. Father Novello was happy with his assignment. Gardipee told them of a small Flathead village only a few miles north. These Indians could take him the rest of the way.

But for Ben, Hell Gate was the end of the pack trip, the finish, and this was a continuing, disturbing thought to the priest. Although the arrival had creased his swarthy face with elation, he still found it impossible to disguise his concern for Ben Tree, given the fateful, violent course his young companion had charted for himself. Novello contemplated the thought of parting company, and it was a sad one. Somehow he felt that he had failed, that his prayers for Ben's salvation were going unanswered, were drifting away somewhere in the mists of limbo.

Yet there was still hope in his voice. He had not

given up on his guide. "And what will you do now, Ben?" he asked. "Where will you go?"

Ben vaguely shook his head. He had thoughts, too, however fugitive. They wandered like his mind. he had no idea where the whirlwind of destiny would carry him, relied only on his reason and his will to survive the wind. His premonitions were growing more frequent, becoming stronger. He had good medicine—his dreams were no longer such nightmares. He sensed that the Great Spirit was watching over him. Native instinct and frontier acumen were guiding him, and in his dark mission he had found some light, sensed some direction. "Can't rightly say, padre," he finally said. "Nose around some, maybe ride south to this Major Owen's place for a look. It all depends. I'd suppose you might call it hunting—hunting of a sort. Ei, I'm off to a hunt. My nose is itching."

The priest said soberly, "Then, you haven't changed your mind? Haven't given up on this terrible vendetta?"

"Barely begun."

Father Novello sighed regretfully. "Ben, what can it possibly gain you? I was hoping . . ."

"No chance, Joseph. I'm committed."

"Ah, but you have so little information, such meager evidence, only a word! It seems so futile . . . this vast land." The priest tutted sadly. "And after almost two years. Oh, Ben!"

"Information?" Ben questioned. "My pa's mules are around this country somewhere. Ei, three men, one with red whiskers, another a cripple. Somewhere, they passed. I don't need any more of a lead than that."

"But how do you know these are the guilty men? You have only the word of the Indian woman, her intuition . . . or yours."

"In time, Joseph, in time. The omens say so."

Then Novello nodded at the sorrel pony behind them, still fully saddled, still decorated for a woman. His heart saddened, for he had never gotten accustomed to the pitiful sight of the riderless horse. "Your people, the Crow," he said. "What of them, now? What do your omens say about honoring them? Have you forgotten so soon?"

"No, I haven't forgotten. They're my people. I know where they'll be in the Moon of the Changing Seasons. No, sir, I haven't forgotten, but I don't plan on frittering away the rest of this summer, not after I've come this far. Only a damned fool would do that, turn back now."

"And if you lose? Find nothing?"

"I'll come back, Joseph, again and again. What do I have left to lose? I have nothing, nothing but my own kind of faith. And this is the time of the white man's work. The weather is warm, the days long. When the snows come, he makes few tracks in this country. It's too damned cold." He looked across at the blackrobe. "Do you know what makes the wolf a good hunter? He's relentless . . . never gives up. He has an instinct for singling out fear . . . and he always has his nose to the wind."

"A pity, brother Ben. I fear the devil is reaching out to shake your hand. Nothing will dissuade you?"

"I'm afraid not." Ben smiled again. "Ei, not even the devil himself."

The priest made a small gesture, a sign of peace. "So be it," he said. They rode a distance in silence. Then: "How can I express my thanks, my gratitude for what you have done? Words up here, why, they seem so paltry, so insignificant; this space . . . infinity. You have shared an experience with me that I shall never forget, never in my life. Yes, by the grace of God and Ben Tree."

"Those are kind words," Ben said with a grin. "I

don't expect I'll be forgetting it, either. I'll say this, you're a caution, you are—and old Jericho there, that flop-eared critter of yours. I'll allow you've had someone besides me on your side, to keep your bottom in the saddle this far.''

''I had hoped to prove myself the trail hand you desired,'' the priest said. ''As I recall, you were quite pointed about that when we left Fort Hall. You growled like a mongrel—nay, more like a bear with a stomachache. Yes, I dearly hoped to prove myself.''

''You tried to make me out as a wicked man. I didn't appreciate that, Joseph.''

''I had hoped on other matters, too.''

''You've done well, padre. You are first a man. I'll make a note of that in my journal. I'll speak well of you, my friend . . . always.''

''Thank you, Ben.''

''I have probed *you,* too,'' Ben continued, a twinkle coming into his narrowed, dark blue eyes. ''I know your heart, the good in you. I can't blame you . . . that you don't understand my ways.''

Father Novello reflected a moment. ''No, you have given me insight into another kind of sanctity, a feel for the earth. I appreciate that, Ben. But on other matters, those that I mentioned . . . Oh, you must know that you've been a part of my prayers! Every man must find the right path, the way to eternal peace.''

Ben nodded. ''If my path seems crooked to you and your God, it's only because the white man has made it so. But I don't consider myself among the wicked, only among the misjudged.''

Father Novello stared skyward. He closed his eyes, saying, ''I'm not a judge, brother Ben. I'm your friend. Ah, the questions you pose, so difficult to answer at times . . . I know that you cannot be all wrong, given the faith of your convictions. That much of you I do understand, but this I know too: only by forgiving will you find peace with yourself.''

"I have nothing to forgive, padre," replied Tree. "And I won't be turning my cheek to any man, red or white. I never have."

And so they rode in. Several men, curiously observant, watched them pass, a strange pack outfit: a blackrobe and a mountain man, calmly chatting as they entered from the east. It was an unusually small train to be bringing in supplies. Only after Ben Tree and Father Novello had reined up at the small shed and corral that served as a livery stable did the news of their arrival filter though the tiny settlement. Several interested persons wandered over to John Gibbon's blacksmith's shed, where Ben was busy unloading the packs. They were curious about the freight, any new freight. Someone was always looking to buy wares, anticipating an arrival of fresh merchandise, but in this case few tarried after learning the packs contained nothing more than medicine for the blackrobe's mission.

One man wearing buckskin paused long enough to inquire about traffic along the east trail to Fort Benton. Several pack strings were expected within the week. What were the signs along the route? Had the army started to build the wagon road? Any hostiles about? The scout had little to answer. Father Novello supplied most of the answers, explaining that he and his guide had traveled from the south, Fort Hall, not the east. They'd seen few white men, only one group of packers along the river, men who apparently had lost their entire train to hostile Indians. They were afoot when last seen. With a disturbed frown, the inquisitive man scurried away toward the far building that housed the post store and saloon.

Ben Tree, ever observant, paused to watch him disappear. Slipping the cinch on the Arapaho gray, he smiled over at the priest. "I don't think your news set too well with that fellow, padre, not the way he cached."

"Yes, he did seem in a hurry."

"Likely as not, someone around here was expecting those whiskey drummers."

"A pity," Father Novello said in mock sorrow.

Nearby, John Gibbons, the blacksmith, suddenly looked up. "Didn't you parley with the packers? See who they were?"

"Parley, indeed!" exclaimed Novello. "They were vile men."

And Ben casually explained, "Only from a distance. Fact is, they took a shot at me. Figure they were looking to our horses. That's the long and short of it."

Gibbons expressed surprise. "Is that so? Why, that's an odd one, it sure is!"

"Why?" asked the priest. "Is it possible you might know them?"

"Maybe yes and maybe no. Don't sound right, but it could be one of Moran's outfits. He's been looking for a string in here nigh on a week now. Only a guess, understand."

Ben thought for a moment. Moran? It wasn't a name that he recognized. He hoisted a saddle up over one of the new stalls. "Moran . . . Moran . . . ?"

"Jim Moran. He's been running the trail regular."

"Ei, never heard of him, but by jingo, if it's his crew, he's wasting his time on bad luck." Ben Tree wiped the dust from the gray's flank and pointed to his brand. "Ever see a mark like this, Mr. Gibbons?"

The blacksmith bent down and examined the brand, what appeared to be a double arrow, two sets of points on a single shaft. He immediately nodded. "Why sure, I've seen it. Yep, out of Missouri. That's a mule brand, a Tree. You're damned tootin' I've seen it. Good stock."

The scout patted the gray pony on the rump, running him into the corral at the back with the rest of the stock. Ben grinned at Gibbons. "Figured anyone in your line west of Independence would recognize it."

"Never saw it on a horse before, no Injun pony like that one."

"Not likely you ever will, unless an Indian owns it. That's my mark, Mr. Gibbons." Tree nodded at Father Novello. "You've met the padre, there. My name is Ben Tree."

A spark of nervous recognition suddenly seemed to have been struck from the blacksmith. Gibbons' head bobbed several times. "Tree . . . Ben Tree . . . Laramie. Yep, I've heard tell . . ." He trailed off, then resumed in a stutter. "R-reckon that's the family b-brand . . . m-mules and such. Why . . . why, I shoulda known, Mr. Tree." Obviously perplexed and flustered, Gibbons stared curiously at Father Joseph Novello, confused by these strange comrades standing in front of him, one man a killer, one a priest. His flushed face reflected it.

The blacksmith's befuddled state amused Novello. "Another old happenstance?" the priest quietly asked.

"Oh, no!" Gibbons returned defensively. "No, not at all!" Composure regained, he said in a rush, "Up here, a man's business is his own. Yep. Best that way. Your business is none of mine; 'less it's stock, of course."

Nodding, Ben said, "Well, in your business I suppose you see most of the traffic going through here, someone always looking to get a critter shod and fed. Seems to be a regular way-point, now."

"I see my share, Mr. Tree. I do."

"Yes, I allowed that. I was wondering if you recall seeing any mules up this way . . . mules with that particular iron on their rumps, say in the last year or so.''

John Gibbons shook his head slowly, doubtfully. ''Can't say that I have, not offhand. Y'see, I ain't been here all that long . . . six months, maybe seven.'' He pointed to the pole rafters, then made a flourish around the small shed. ''Ain't even finished, waiting for lumber from the mill. But I'd a'noticed anything of late, a brand like that. Yep.'' His eyes wandered back to the priest, then fell on Ben again. ''Someone make off with some of your stock? Is that what you're meaning, stealing?''

''They could have strayed . . . been rounded up. I don't know.''

The blacksmith whistled softly. ''More'n a year back, y'say? Hell's fire, that's a far piece! Too far for me, understand. I'm afraid I can't help you, Mr. Tree. I'm sorry, plumb sorry.''

''No matter, I'm obliged.'' Ben's tone was softly polite. He looked toward the corral. ''If you can get at it, I'd appreciate you tending the left rear shoe on the white stud. He's peaceful enough.''

''My pleasure,'' Gibbons said. Then, on a second thought, he held up a callused hand. ''Now, hold on a minute, I just happened to think. There's a chance . . . yep, I recollect there's a breed . . . a horse trader hereabouts, name of Tin Cup—Tin Cup Joe. Now, *he* might be helping you about those strays. Reckon he knows these parts as well as any man, nigh on two years, maybe more. Yep, if he's a'mind to parley, y'might look him up.'' Gibbons pointed toward the post. ''Comes regular of evenings. Likes to play the monte bank over there.'' Gibbons gave the priest a crooked, apologetic smile. ''Less you're a squaw man, ain't nothing much else to do in Hell Gate, 'cept play cards and get snakebit.''

Ben Tree thanked the blacksmith and turned away to find a campsite for the night.

Father Novello complemented Gibbon's wry grin with a nod toward the departing scout. "I assure you, Mr. Gibbons, my partner hasn't come this great distance for drink or gaming. We'll both be gone of this place by tomorrow. The mission is expecting me, and I rather suspect Mr. Tree will return to the purity of the mountains—not that I blame him."

"I understand," returned Gibbons. "Reckon I know just what you mean." Then aside, in a hushed voice to the priest: "But I don't think I'd like wearing the boots of the thief that made off with those mules, Father, no siree, not with that young fellow around. Heard tell that wherever he goes, trouble's bound to follow. That's the gospel. And you, sir! Plumb dangerous, trailing with a man like that. Begging your pardon, but that's the story. Didn't you know? Why, even the Injuns know him!"

Father Novello gave the smithy a reassuring pat on the shoulder. "My good man, I doubt that *anyone* really knows Ben Tree. I daresay the tales out here sometimes grow to great proportions. Let me say this, Mr. Gibbons: I'm forever indebted to him and his kindness. My many days with that man will be among the fondest in my memories, I can assure you of that."

On that note the priest quietly left, and sometime later, after he and Ben had made camp near the back of the blacksmith's property, five Flathead braves and a lone white man appeared on the scene. They came with greetings from Chief Victor. They had already received news of the Jesuit's arrival. Even the mission blackrobes to the north knew he was on the trail and nearing his destination. While this somewhat mystified the priest, it was a common occurrence to Ben. Strangely, the Indians always seemed to know. He had been a part of the phenomenon several times. News of significance had an uncanny way of traveling through Indian country, and in Ben Tree's time he himself had often sensed the presence of the known but unseen. To anyone who had lived among the Indians; this was no surprise. Ben's present surprise was of another sort—the man accompanying the Flathead visitors, the trader, Tin Cup Joe, who had come because he spoke Salish, a Flathead tongue. He was there to translate, to arrange Father Novello's journey to St. Ignatius.

Only after the Indians had talked with the priest did Ben Tree make a casual inquiry about the stray mules. Tin Cup listened, his Indian friends solemnly seated to either side of him. A lone feather decorated his faded gray hat, a headpiece that had seen many suns. A sweat stain had seeped in and settled above its beaded band. Placing the colorful hat in his lap, he struck a thoughtful pose. In broken English Tin Cup Joe reflected, saying that he thought he could help the frontier scout. He explained that in the early days before the settlement, only a few men had passed through the Five Valleys. Tin Cup Joe had seen some, others the Indians had told him about—strangers without status, drifters, most of them bedraggled and broke. Some were dangerous renegades; enemies of the Indians, and unwelcome, they never stayed long. A few owned mules and Indian ponies. But that was before Tin Cup began trading and selling stock. He had paid little attention to brands in those days. No one had. He knew nothing about the missing mules. But strangers! Now, they were a different matter. They always came under close scrutiny, especially those without purpose, and Tin Cup Joe remembered, and so did his brothers.

For a moment, Tin Cup and the Indians traded words. Across from them, Tree and the priest were exchanging anxious glances. After several nods, the Indians fell silent. It had been decided. Tin Cup Joe began relating what they had recalled, including some of what he himself remembered. To Ben Tree, the breed's information immediately took on ominous significance. Indeed, three men had passed through the Five Valleys, to the best of the Indian's recollection, late in the fall of 1856. They'd had mules. The men were coming up from the Bitterroot Valley, from the small trading fort operated by Major Owen. They had traded some of their stock there and had bought supplies. They only could have come across the mountains from the south, the country of the Shoshoni and Bannock. A few Flathead had made sign with these men in the Bitterroot, before directing them to the Clark Fork of the Columbia and on toward the Oregon Territory settlements.

At the time Tin Cup Joe had not seen any of these men, but they had returned a year later. That trip, he saw them. According to the Indians, they were the same three who had passed through the year before. Two trailed south and one stayed at Hell Gate. In fact he was still there, a packer named James Moran. He might know something about the mules. No one knew the names of his two companions, but one of them was a small man, a man with a broken wing, a withered left arm. No one had seen him since.

Ben Tree's flickering senses flamed upward like a prairie fire. By the light, his mind's eye took focus: what the Nez Percé woman, Rainbow, had seen; the time coincidence; the same number of men, one a rider with a crippled arm. Everything seemed to fit, everything except the brands on the stock, and in time he could ride to Fort Owen and trace the mules. Far from solid evidence, still it was a foundation, a link, perhaps more than coincidence. His own keen mountain intuition told him that. And he now had one of the suspects located—James Moran—someone who might talk and give him a firm lead. Eyes flashing, he glanced at Father Novello, and, as if their minds were one, they both came up with the same question: Did one of the three riders have a red beard? They stared at Tin Cup Joe, waiting. He puckered thoughtfully. Rubbing at his outthrust chin, he finally said no.

At first, the man called James Moran considered running, but it was too late to run, and his calculating frontier sense told him it was also quite useless. So, with little alternative, he waited for the inevitable—a meeting with Ben Tree. The day had begun badly for Moran, with news of the shattered pack string that he had financed. He accepted that loss resignedly, because he had no choice. It was one of those hazards any packer had to accept, a gamble any man took when backing a frontier enterprise, particularly in hostile country.

But Moran did not know his luck would appreciably worsen, not until the first ugly hint of it came up from the blacksmith shop, word that the stranger accompanying the blackrobe was some notorious frontiersman whom the Indians called Tree. That bit of news struck a sour chord for Moran. He knew young Ben Tree, a fact of which others in the outpost were not aware. On the surface, the packer tried to take the news calmly. He disguised his dread with a jolt of his own raw whiskey, meantime hatching a plan to make himself scarce, sick if need be, *anything* until Ben Tree rode out the next day. A sweat fringed his balding head. He had to stay low, out of the young man's sight. He could not afford to tip his hand. Only alone was his secret safe. So Moran retired to his cabin and bolted the door, harboring high hopes that trouble would not come knocking.

But Tin Cup Joe came knocking, instead. And the news that the breed brought collapsed Moran's ruse like a bear atop a rotten log. Tin Cup told the packer that Ben Tree had just left him and the Indians. The notorious breed wanted to discuss some vague matter about mules and Moran's old cronies, the two strangers who once rode with him, and that left Moran in a deeper fret, for this was the worst of any possible news. By dusk, he was numb. Those mules! He knew better; at the time he had told the others to leave the pack stock behind, and now he was unable to come up with a good story of his own, an alibi that would take him off the griddle. He raked his brain, but his excuses came up more rank than a buffalo wallow.

What kind of a tale would a man like Ben Tree believe? The man was no greenhorn, no gullible fool from the east. Worse yet, there was no escape from encounter, not even in the dark. Ironic. As big and lonely as the country seemed, where could one hide from a mountain man, especially one who was more Indian than white? James Moran scratched hard for courage, knew he had but one chance, an outside one. He himself had survived in the Big Lonely. He had made it for many years. He would do what he had to: face up to his past and hope for the best. He carefully checked his pistol and went back to the post saloon to wait. His friends were there. Moran saw some measure of safety in numbers. All he needed to do was get in one good shot and he would be in the clear.

About an hour after he had seated himself at the plank table where the monte bank was in progress, Ben Tree and Father Novello came in the front of the post. It was dim and warm inside. A few flickering lanterns were casting yellowish hues across the rough-hewn log wall. The lighting was adequate for present purposes, to see a deck of cards and the tin whiskey cups on the rustic table. To James Moran, the surroundings were familiar. He had already chosen his strategic spot.

The heavy odor of tobacco smoke, the low tones of

men at play, steered Ben and the priest toward the game. Five persons were in the back, four seated by the lone table. The atmosphere seemed congenial, the talk quiet and friendly. There was absolutely no hint of impending violence, nothing remotely to suggest it. Everyone present knew Ben Tree was at the post. Everyone knew why—or thought they did. He had come as a guide for the blackrobe. If the fact that he had inquired about some stray stock disturbed anyone it did not surface, not even on the ruddy face of James Moran. The packer was present as usual, casually watching the cards, a drink in front of him. He had had several. Tin Cup Joe's earlier message to him about a parley had been delivered, no insinuation or threat involved, so by all appearances it was just another one of those routine evenings at Hell Gate.

Ben Tree and the priest had entered quietly, almost without notice, until they approached the fringe of yellow light. Only then did their movement garner some attention. A voice came out of the shadows to their left. Tree tried to adjust his eyes to the darkness. It was John Gibbons speaking.

"Well, there, Mr. Tree!" Gibbons called out merrily. "Evening to you, and welcome! Looks like you went and decided to take some of our pleasure, anyhow!"

Nothing more was said. Before Tree could even reply, or walk into the ring of light, the man called James Moran leaped to his feet, upsetting the table and lantern. In that instant, a billow of fire and smoke belched from his weapon. The dumbfounded men around him fell away in an avalanche of confusion, scrambling for safety. Moran's shot went awry of the mark, the ball creasing Ben Tree's left cheek, tearing away a tiny piece of his earlobe. But before Moran could thumb his hammer for a second round, Tree's Navy six roared once, and the ball was true. It slammed into Moran's body with a heavy thud. Under the impact the packer flew backward against the log wall, where he collapsed in deathly convulsions. Ben's single shot had caught him in the middle of the breast.

The first person over the fallen man was Father Novello. No one at the table knew that Ben had been hit, or for that matter realized that Moran had drawn his revolver first—only John Gibbons, the blacksmith, had seen it all, including the quickness of Ben Tree. The others had their backs to the post entryway.

"Why, he tried to kill you!" Gibbons exclaimed lowly. "Gawd a'mighty, he upped and tried to kill you! Why? Why in the hell would he do something like this?"

Ben wiped at the sting cutting through his wounded cheek. His hand came away bloody from the ragged edge of his dripping ear. "Ei, he marked me. Another step and he would have done the job, all right."

The other three men, including Tin Cup Joe, came slowly up from the floor. Speechless, they were unable to muster a sound. They heard Father Novello, though. They listened. His low monotone of prayer cut the silence for them. The priest finally crossed himself and stood aside. His swarthy face was ashen. "God take his soul," he said aloud.

Tin Cup Joe whispered brokenly, "He's kilt? Dat crazee Moran? But why? Why he do such a theeng?"

"Bring me some light," Ben said, motioning to Gibbons.

"You're wounded, Ben," Father Novello said.

"A scratch, no matter. Please bring a light."

The blacksmith grabbed a lantern from a nearby wall peg. They bent over the prostrate form of James Moran, Ben moving the flare close to his face.

Father Novello asked quietly, "Do you know this man?" He quickly tore a piece from his robe and handed it to his bleeding friend.

A long pause ensued. "Ei, I know him . . . once a good man," Ben finally said. He compressed the cloth hard against his wounded cheek and ear. "I had a broken leg the last time I saw him."

"You know ol' Jim?" John Gibbons said with surprise. "Why, I thought . . . You said you never heard of him! That's what you said."

"His name isn't Moran," came the stony answer. Ben gave Father Novello a quick look, then nodded back at the body. "That's Jethro Collins, padre. All clean-shaven, he is. Used to have red whiskers. Knew my Pa all his life . . . Will and me since we were sixteen. By jingo, he was a friend, a *good* friend, mind you. Can't understand why . . ."

Gibbons stuttered. "A . . . a f-friend?"

"God forgive him," Father Novello intoned.

Ben Tree took another look at the fallen man. Then, without rancor, he said, "I'll allow it wasn't all of Jethro's doing, not by a long shot, poor devil. Someone got to him, somehow." Holding the cloth to his bleeding cheek, he quietly excused himself and disappeared into the darkness.

The blacksmith and another man hoisted the body up onto the uprighted table. Shaking his head in exasperation, Gibbons turned back to Father Novello. "I don't understand this. It don't make a lick of sense, Father, not one lick. And trying something like that on that Ben Tree! Hardly flinched, he did! Like a rattler strike, by gawd!"

Tin Cup Joe brought a blanket. Father Joseph Novello covered the body of Jethro Collins.

BOOK
THREE

ELEVEN

October, 1858

There was a celebration in my honor and homecoming. I must confess that I wept. My Crow
brothers look upon me as a warrior and tell me
that I will become a chief. They know by the messages of the wind what I have done, the coup I
have counted on my enemies and the enemy of
the Absaroke. They know of my sadness in the
loss of my wife, Little Hoop. I told them how
once in my joy and well-being I failed to heed the
prophecy of Buffalo Horn. I told them how I became an Absaroke and what I must do now to live.
The Absaroke are kind. I'll remain for the hunt. They
want me to stay on here but know that I cannot. I
now trust in the Great Spirit to help me find my way.
I have three eagle feathers. B. Tree.

During the Moon of the Changing seasons, Ben Tree
trailed west, away from the Stillwater village of the

Bird People. The vowed return to his adopted home had not dispelled the sadness within him. But, keeping a promise to himself and the spirits of his wife and her brother, he had gone back, had made honorable amends to his relatives. The stallion, Snow Hawk, and the sorrel of Little Hoop were in the hands of Chief White Mouth. The scalps of Iron Bow and Bob Skinner had been burned in ceremony. It was the Indian way—leave no death unavenged. Ben had hunted with the Crow once again, he killed seven buffalo, and had eaten liver and roasted hump and rib. He had sat with the braves and chiefs in the soldier's lodge, a place of honor and prestige. Yet he was deeply unhappy.

It could never be as it had been, those early days in the village by the Stillwater: the medicine songs, the war songs, the love songs, his happy woman riding beside him through juniper and sage, those mountain meadows of fragrant lupine and buttercup. Burdened by sorrowful reflection, his peace was gone; familiar faces, too—Buffalo Horn, the ancient holy man, dead, buried on the Yellowstone, his prophecy yet unfulfilled. The old woman, Willow Sings, had died only that spring, and White Mouth himself was ailing, perhaps in his last winter. Two Moons High and Tree's own beloved Little Hoop were beyond *Nah-Pit-Sei*, the Bear's Tooth, the great mountain, and the white man's shadow was getting longer in the beautiful valley below.

For Ben Tree, both bitter and sad, it was a time to be moving on, south to the post on the Snake. It had been almost six months since he'd left Fort Hall, the memorable trip north guiding the good Jesuit, Father Novello. From there the trails had been elusive, the summer long, yet he had gone on, searching for men, across the far mountains to the west, down into the Walla Walla, the Willamette, and Yakima country.

The trip had not been easy. After Hell Gate, both

his name and word of his deadly mission preceded him. While the white man respected him, they also feared him, most often avoided him. The squatters came to recognize the famous scout, his quiet demeanor, his long blond hair, the Indian garb he always wore, and the unmistakable scar of a bullet wound on his left cheek. He was a subject of conversation, his very presence bringing apprehension, a pox. In due time the two remaining killers, fearful of the shadow lurking behind them, had lost themselves in civilization, the safest place to hide from a hunter who had come to abhor it. Ben returned from the journey with only a name: Jack Gresham, a drifter who had a crippled arm. And the frightened Gresham, he learned, never spread his blanket too long in one place.

Moving south toward the Snake, Ben continued to listen to the talk at the campfires where he often stopped. With diligence and cunning he watched the trails, but heard no further report of Gresham that fall. By early November he was back at Fort Hall, where he found James Digby in good spirits and the post business prospering from the brisk trade between Fort Bridger and Fort Boise. The southern part of the territory was safe again, at least free of the Mormon brigades. Brigham Young's abortive rebellion had been thoroughly quashed by the Federal army, or the presence of it. The Saints wisely had refused to contest Colonel Johnston's strength. There had been no fighting, not so much as a skirmish with the troopers. Governor Young had been deposed from office, and a new staff of territorial officials appointed by President Buchanan. Ben also learned that Johnston's army was being dispersed. His friend Jim Bridger had been seen in Fort Bridger in September. Tour of duty completed, the old mountain man was once again en route to his Missouri home in Little Santa Fe. He had seen his beloved land for the last time.

James Digby, enthusiastic about the flourishing trade and reports of new gold strikes to the northwest, encouraged Ben to help operate a new wagon freight enterprise along the Overland Trail. The route between Fort Hall and Fort Boise, then on up to the Mormon settlement at Fort Lemhi on the Salmon, seemed lucrative enough, but the scout politely declined to lend a personal hand. However, to please his longtime friend, Ben contributed considerable cash to the venture. He invested, and that was the extent of it. He knew all about the California rush, what the movers and squatters had done to the trails, eventually would do to the land.

Those were his white days, long ago. Now the red in him was disturbed. Dismayed by the increasing traffic, he wanted no personal involvement in helping populate any land so perilously close to the Indian territories. This was against his medicine. Besides, he had other work in mind, more in keeping with his mode of life. Even though the fur market had gone stale, he would live alone and trap, at least during the winter months. Only a temporary existence. The currents of his mind still ran deep with vengeance for men like Jack Gresham, who made their gruesome profit in a lawless land. Like the predator, these men always returned to their prey: the luckless, the foolish, the unsuspecting. There lay Ben's real work—the human hunt.

Arriving at Fort Hall, tired and weary, he had taken comfort in one of Digby's small cabins, where he tried to sleep in a bed again. For a night or two it worked, but he soon found it impossible to relax. His mind, like a constant sledge, pounded when he loafed. Idle time was his enemy, and his conscience rebelled, uprooting visions of the past, a future unresolved. Impatience goaded him. With each passing sun the earth seemed to be growing colder, and he often chilled, fearful that precious time would run out before he could fully complete his mission of justice. Despite Buffalo Horn's prophecy, what Ben really feared was his own death; untimely, premature death. Once a source of humor, the old shaman's revelation had now become a never-ending haunt, a foreboding dream, one that could easily misfire, perhaps result in his own premature demise. His time was half-gone. And if one could believe the prophecy, two of Buffalo Horn's dream men already had tried to kill him, one leaving death's errant stroke like a burning warning across his cheek. It had been that close.

Because of his fearful reputation, Ben Tree's own existence had become precarious. He knew it. Fate was a shrouded rider, a black shadow, always lurking behind some distant ridge, ready to gallop out and put an end to his avenging quest. No man was ever exempt in the mountains, and the frontier already had fattened itself into ugly proportions, with hairy new faces filled with eagerness and challenge and, yes wickedness. Invariably, in the name of honor and glory, there was one fool out there destined to test him, perhaps to come away lucky.

Ben forced himself to work. He was a worried man, and he was a lonely man. He had to occupy himself until the leaden skies brought the first heavy snows, until the cold edge of winter primed the fur. So he began to break the young gelding out of Sunday and Snow Hawk; long hours of tedious work, but his hand was gentle and kind. Pleased by the painted beauty and spirit of the horse, he finally named it War Paint. The pony had the fine head of its mother and the sturdy, well-proportioned frame of the Cheyenne stud. Within a week, he had it greenbroke. Within three weeks, the pony was coming at his call and fondly nuzzling his collar.

Each dusk, he deserted the corrals and took on other

chores, sentimental and secret. He labored on two slabs of pine that he had already rough-cut to size. These were the markers for the graves of his father and brother, and the work was personal, done within the privacy of his cabin. It was not the work of an Indian. This was Christian, white work. Once smoothed and polished, Ben scribed the names and dates, and one afternoon before he was ready to leave for the snow country above old Fort Henry, he stopped by the blacksmith shop and burned in the letters with a branding iron. Still later, on another afternoon, on a brushy knoll where the north wind whipped the withered sage and tumbleweed, he broke frozen ground over two rocky mounds and pounded the signs home. This was the last of his Christian endeavor. After embedding a sprig of mountain holly on each of the graves, he spread out his arms to the Great Spirit. Instead of a prayer, he sang the death chant of the Crow.

Ben Tree trapped until mid-December that winter, and by his journal, took forty-four beaver and an assortment of other marketable furs: marten, muskrat, mink, fox, and bobcat. He also shot four wolves and one wolverine that had plundered his trap line. Shortly after Christmas, he was back at the Fort Hall cabin. Other friends had arrived, too. Henri Bilodeau and his wife had come in a week before him, forced out of the hills by heavy snow and Rainbow's pregnancy, the latter to no avail. In February, Rainbow's child was stillborn. A late winter rain had set in, and during the incessant downpour, Ben Tree and the Frenchman buried the infant in a plot in back of the post. James Digby was there too, to deliver a prayer, and Ben, suddenly consumed by compassion and grief, turned away from the tiny grave and wept.

Later he went to Bilodeau's small cabin to see Rainbow, not knowing what he could possibly say or do.

In a meeting of eyes, she spoke only one word, *Poo-toosway*—Medicine Tree, the honored name the Nez Percé had given him that summer on the Beaverhead. The rest was written in her dark eyes, the mirror of her Indian soul. And the anguish that Ben read therein would stay with him the rest of his life.

Winter finally eased its selfish grip and spring broke out, gloriously benevolent. Restlessly, Ben Tree watched the great land's velvety transformation. Near his small cabin, the first crocus split Mother Earth's warming crust, and in the lowlands the red willows suddenly broke out in a fresh pox of fur. For a moment he sadly reflected remembering how near the Little Owl he had cut pussy willows for Little Hoop, a white man's humble gesture of affection. And he had been a white man. And in love. Few cares in those golden days. And ultimately, like the land he now loved so much, he too had been transformed. But that much of it was good—to be Indian.

The old familiar signs of spring stirred in Ben, the desire to move, to breathe deeply, to ride. It was time to travel. So before the first buds had dropped, Ben and Henri Bilodeau struck east to Fort Boise to buy Appaloosa stock for summer trade. By early June the two men were back at the post, trailing in a herd of ponies. Once fattened, shod, and clipped, the horses would sell at a premium price to the Oregon-bound pioneers.

Although the omens had not revealed it, some of Ben's old friends began reappearing on the early-summer scene. Strangely, they became part of his destiny. He just missed seeing the first one, the young Nez Percé chief, Gray Hawk, who had come and gone while Tree and the Frenchman were on the trail back from Fort Boise. But Gray Hawk left his startling news with Rainbow, in the form of a golden belt buckle that had once belonged to Thaddeus Tree. Ben was momentarily stunned at the unexpected sight, until the young woman explained. She began talking, making sign, her husband translating, relating how Gray Hawk, trading for trinkets at Fort Lemhi, had noticed the emblem of a tree carefully tooled into the face of this particular buckle. He had immediately recognized the sign, the same brand that *Pootoosway* carried on his ponies. The Nez Percé chief had pressed for more information. Strangely, the white man who originally traded the buckle had passed north only a few days before, one of a group of three, and his left arm was lame.

If Ben Tree had ever had the slightest doubt about Jack Gresham's complicity in the murders, it ceased to exist at that moment. Dark thoughts were instantly reborn. Picking out phrases, Ben listened gravely, waiting for Bilodeau to interpret details. Despite Gray Hawk's effort to follow and perhaps trap the three men in Nez Percé country, the trio had turned east, crossing a range of the Rockies into the land of the Big Hole, a long hunting valley bordering the Beaverhead. Rainbow said that the Indians knew these three men were drifters, *cultis,* no good, but they now carried the tools of prospectors. They were after gold, or pretended to be.

What Rainbow had relayed was heartening, heady enough news for Ben, but more important, it gave him a new trail to follow. Within a day, he was packed and ready to go. Even so, it was not some trip of chance, a hasty journey taken without calculation. Before departure, Ben carefully checked all of the options with Bilodeau. The Frenchman, a veteran of the land, knew the rugged terrain to the north, well up into the heart of the Blackfeet nation. Ben finally came up with several conclusions as to Gresham's destination. His quarry was heading toward the new diggings on the

American Fork by way of the Deer Lodge, or else making east to one of the new prospecting valleys along the Missouri headwaters. Either way, the scout felt confident about cutting the men's tracks, most likely bisecting them in the upper Big Hole. Once cut, it would be a matter of his own patience, how well he could keep himself cool and collected.

For once, Ben had plenty of time. Summer was nigh, the time of the white man, so Ben foresaw no complications. He tied the three eagle feathers behind his leather headband. Gresham was his man.

June, 1859

I'm well down the Beaverhead by the forks this night. Camped near an old site once visited with Fr. J. Novello and Nez Percé. As was true the last time, mosquitoes still here in great numbers. I'll be heading east toward the Passamari. This morning I met four Shoshoni hunters packing elk and antelope. They told me of an altercation between three whites and some Bannock over one of their women. The white men had to move on. I'm allowing this is the Gresham party. I traversed the Big Hole crossing from the Grasshopper and found old sign this same direction, shod stock with mules. They are ahead of me two days, maybe three. B. Tree.

It was sundown, the burnished touch of *Masaka* on the horizon, a haze of purple fringing the timbered ridges. Ben was atop a knoll of high sage, looking east toward the Madison fork of the Missouri. He had followed the Passamari almost to its headwaters, picking up signs along the way and passing several abandoned camps and numerous scars in the creek bed where men had ineptly probed for color. He was now certain that he was nearing his goal. The tracks had led him up through a small canyon and a small grassy pass, and had ended down below near a thicket of aspen. A camp was there. He saw the horses, the mules, peacefully grazing, saw the curl of smoke from a new fire, the three men huddled around it, preparing their evening meal. Ben's keen eyes reached out beyond, across the distant river, up the breadth of the long valley, now misty with the dusk of eventide, then back to the gray figures below. These foolish men were hopelessly trapped. Within the long heave of the Great Divide, such a ready haven for one like himself, there was no place for these men to hide, no escape.

That first night, he let them know that he was above them. They heard his distant, haunting chant. For the next three days he followed them like a spirit, making his presence known in a most frightening manner. By day, he often appeared on a far hill, his Crow war whoop shattering the quiet calm of the sunny draws and meadows. When they managed to find a sheltered rest, a random shot always moved them on. When they foolishly came to meet him, he mysteriously disappeared. By night, they split for safety, two on guard, one in nervous sleep. At any time Ben Tree could have killed them, one by one, from ambush, but he had no intention of making it that easy. This was to be an ordeal, an agonizing, mortifying experience, a wilderness encounter never to be forgotten.

By the third night the three harassed men were haggard, and once they pitifully called out for a parley. They had finally recognized him, as he had thought they would. They knew why he had come—Jack Gresham was there. Ignoring their pleas, Ben kept to the hills above them, often out of sight, but his frequent, chilling outcries made them aware of his presence, aware, that, although unseen, he was still there. On the fourth morning he rode the perimeter and found them again, camped near the river in the flat land of willows, slough grass, and hummock. This was a poor campsite at best, for mosquitoes hummed there in billowing clouds. From a distant clump of brush, he came in close to observe. In an hour, he saw only two men, and despite the accuracy of his roving eye he found no sign of the third, or any hint of a possible ruse. The lame-armed Gresham had disappeared. This disappointing circumstance took most of the zest out of his harrowing play, for now he had to change tactics. He quietly threaded his way through some willows and directly walked in on the two remaining men. But even expecting him, they offered no resistance. Helplessly raising their hands, the two men showed him they were unarmed, their rifles at rest, and they pleaded mercy. If they were cowards, they certainly were not fools. Ben Tree stopped at the edge of the small clearing, twenty paces from them.

"Don't shoot!" one called. "Don't shoot, we're clean!"

He partially allayed their fear. "Lower your hands," he told them. "I've come to parley."

One man sighed mightily. His shoulders slumped and he sat down across from the charred logs of the night fire. "Thank the Lord," he muttered. "Man, you been giving us a terrible fit, right terrible."

Ben stood at the very edge of the willows. "Where's Gresham?" he asked, staring at the man still standing.

The stranger, his bloodshot eyes wide, shrugged. "Cached last night. Down the river, I reckon. Said he was taking to the river. He's cleared out."

"He cached, damned well!" the other broke in. "Told him if he didn't, we'd kill him ourselves! Y'see, it wasn't none of our doing, mister. Hell, we didn't know ol' Jack was bad luck till he upped and told us two days ago. Fessed up, he did, and that's the truth of it, I'll swear on it. We're clean, Ben Tree, harming no man and not aiming to, either. *He's* your bait, and he's cleaned country.''

Ben nodded, then asked calmly, ''How long have you known this Gresham?'

The two prospectors exchanged glances. ''Lashed up with him last fall, west of the mountains,'' the one standing said. ''We's up from Carson City, y'see, and he tells me and Jake that he knows the country . . . where the best scads is.'' He stared back at Tree. ''What's your game, anyhow? We ain't trifling, just looking for a stake, a little pay dirt, that's all. Why you dogging us like this? It ain't lawful, making misery out of us this way.''

''Lawful?'' Ben smothered a scornful laugh. ''You'd speak of the law where there is none? What do you white men know of my law?''

''But we ain't broke *any* law!''

''My game is with Gresham,'' Ben finally said, his smile at an end. He studied the two frightened men for a moment. Obviously they were quite useless, poor dupes, worth no more than information. If at any time they had foolishly agreed to stand with Jack Gresham, they certainly had no stomach left for the endeavor, not anymore. He spoke again: ''This man, did he have a friend when you met him? Across the mountains?''

''Hell, no,'' Jake mumbled. ''We staked him. He was dead broke, down and out By God, we never knew he went and had a falling out with the likes of you, not till he fessed it.''

''I only know his name,'' Ben said. ''I don't know the man, personally.''

Jake looked up in surprise. ''Why, he told us he crossed you real personal, that's what! Crossed you. That's what got in our craw. Yes, sir, and we told him to git. We didn't want no part of his tomfoolery.''

Spitting at the dead fire, the other man cursed. ''The

dirty biscuit-eater did us in . . . put one over on us. Can't you see that? We ain't bulling.''

Measuring them both, Ben finally said, "You are fools, both of you. You should know the man is a murderer, a bushwhacker. Hear me: By my hand, he's as good as dead, river or no. And don't speak to me about law. Up here, the law is what I choose to make it. You remember this . . . tell it to anyone else who happens to come this way.''

Jake's eyes widened. "But we didn't know anything about him killing, and that's the gospel, Tree. And lookee here, what have we done? My God, what you aiming to do to us? Just a little dust, and we'll be caching, just enough for a stake. Can't you take our word on it?''

"Don't be busting us!'' the other pleaded. "Give us a chance!''

"I'll do nothing,'' Ben answered, backing toward the willows. He pointed his chin toward the west. "But I'd advise you to stay out of this valley. The buffalo come here. Get over the hill, there, beyond the Passamari. Keep out of this land. Tell your friends.''

"Don't seem like a fair shake,'' Jake protested. "It's open country, Tree.''

With a flinty stare, Tree spoke. "A fool's tongue is long enough to cut his throat, stranger. Take my word for it. Don't stay here.''

Jake gulped once. Visibly shaken, he said, "If that's the way you want it, we'll be going. Like I said, we ain't looking for trouble.''

Passing the edge of his hand across his throat, Ben said, "Yes, that's the way I want it. If you pass this way again, by jingo, I'll have my brothers kill you and make a feast of your livers.''

Back in the brush, Ben mounted Sunday and galloped up the hill. When he looked down, the two men were busily packing their stock. Once again, temptation got the best of him. Throwing back his head, he suddenly emitted one final horrendous scream. And he felt better for it.

Later that day, Ben found sign of Gresham's horse in the river bottom. The other men had not lied, and he laughed outright, contemptuously, staring down at the erratic, wandering tracks. Any novice could have followed the sign of Gresham. It was written in panic. And for a time, the mountain man's pursuit was almost effortless in the sandy lowland. But by late afternoon Gresham's trail suddenly took a hazardous course, a perilous path down through a boulder-strewn canyon where the Madison roared into white-water rapids. Ben backed off. The route was little more than a game path, unfit for stock. And it was ideal ambush country. Instead he rode up the ridge to high ground, to a point where he could follow the river's winding course below. From there he charted his own circuitous route, well above and away from the river, up to the rolling hills, the high benches of pine and juniper. Once on top he could make the journey around the gorge's spine in less time, in less danger and his visibility was excellent. Somewhere in the steep valley below, Jack Gresham would be forced to bed down for the night, trapped by darkness in the river's rocky neck.

Ben's assessment was unerring. Shortly after dawn, he cut back to the edge of the cliffs and began riding the rim, occasionally peering over the side. By the time the first rays of the sun were penetrating the deep waterway, he spotted his quarry far below, bent over a small fire near the riverbank. Chilled by the canyon's brisk morning air, Gresham was boiling coffee. Ben picketed his horses and made it down the slope by foot, without dislodging a single rock. Within ten minutes he was behind Gresham, squatting silently on a granite boulder, his drawn pistol aimed squarely at the man's back. In his other hand, he held his father's gold buckle.

Unlike his two companions, Gresham was fully armed. A revolver was strapped to his waist, a rifle rested against a rock by the fire. When he turned to face the small derisive laugh behind him, he found himself staring into a shiny barrel only fifteen feet away. Gresham had never seen Ben Tree before in his life. What he now saw was an apparition, a ghost from the past; the resemblance to the twin, Will Tree, was horrible, striking. And Gresham saw the gold belt buckle dangling from a strip of leather held in Tree's other hand. He paled and forced his words.

"So . . . so, it's you. . . ."

"Yes, I've come."

"You . . . you don't look like no Injun . . . not like I expected. I knew *someday* . . ." His voice trailed off. He turned to the fire. "Coffee?"

"I wouldn't be moving," Ben warned.

Gresham froze, came away easy, and stared back at Tree over the rim of his tin cup. "Y'don't have to keep pointing that thing at me. No need, son. I'm not figgering on pulling down on you, no way."

"That would be foolish," Ben quietly agreed.

"Don't much matter one way or another, does it? Hell, my ol' life is short and full of blisters, anyhow. What chance . . . ?"

"You'll talk. Ei, then we'll see."

Gresham smiled faintly. "Talk? Well, that's something! You're a queer one, all right. Hear-tell Collins never had the chance to talk. That's the word. Kilt dead. Too bad. He wasn't a bad sort, y'know." He sipped his coffee.

"He had more chance than my kin had," Ben replied. "I suppose you'd know about that. This buckle, how did you come by it?"

Gresham shrugged once. "Look, son, what can I be

telling you that y'don't already know? You already done and gone made yourself judge and jury. I'm not one for begging, never was. . . ."

Ben clicked back the hammer on the Navy Colt. "If I break your right arm, you'll have two broken wings. If I break a leg, you'll have only one to stand on. Tell me about it. You only have but a minute."

"The Injun way. That it?"

"Not in the back, not the way you bushwhacked my pa and brother."

"That wasn't like me and ol' Jethro Collins allowed it'd be," Gresham said. "Not the way we was planning, hear? It . . . it just happened. They got on to us, and Boone says there's no other way, not with Red Collins along. They knew Jethro, and that was bad for us all."

"Boone? The other one?"

Gresham looked at Ben curiously. "Y'don't know him? Ol' Booney?"

Ben shook his head.

Gresham suddenly laughed. "Well now, that's some kettle of fish! He sure as hell knows you! Why, he thought you had him sure over in the Walla Walla last summer! He saw you, knew who you were, and he cached at night."

"Tell me about him," Tree said.

"Booney?" Gresham shrugged once and swirled his coffee. "Ain't much to tell. 'Booney,' he calls hisself. That's right, and I don't know where he's lit, now. Boone, that's all of it I know. Mean enough, sure-shot desperado, and a ringtailed rounder when there's gold around."

"My pa's string. Tell me about it."

"We got nigh on three thousand. Yep, got on to it drinking it up with Red Collins; the job, y'understand, him working for your pa. He wasn't planning on no killing, though, not ol' Red. But we wuz spotted, see . . . that ol' man of yours, eyes like a hawk, and—''

Gresham never finished. The canyon suddenly roared from the pistol shot. Ben's ball smashed into the crippled man's good arm, spinning him backward into the sand. A lone scream followed, and the eerie echo died with a moan. It was all over in one sudden, excruciating moment; Gresham sprawled out in a faint, and Ben Tree coming away with a chunk of bloody hair and flesh dangling from his fist. Jack Gresham had been scalped alive.

TWELVE

Journal entry. June 1859

Jack Gresham's confession confirmed my original belief—Jethro Collins, a trusted friend all of those years, was connived into that robbery, and I truly believe he thought there would be no killing. Fate plays a strange hand. This fellow Boone is a puzzle to me. I have a strong suspicion that he must be wanted by someone else besides me. The puzzle is that he uses only the one name, Boone. He always seems to be on the run, never spreading his blanket in one place too long. The puzzle does not end here. I have no idea what this man looks like. But I now have his name. This, I truly believe, will be enough. I must remember the most valued virtue of all—patience. B. Tree

By the journal, old friends continued to appear on the wavering horizon that summer, enemies too, strange reunions in the offing. And by Ben's reckoning, it was once again the time of the white men. They were coming to mark the land, to chart a new route north, seeking a junction with the road that Lieutenant John Mullan was cutting southwest from Fort Benton. Captain William Raynalds was heading the small part of engineers and surveyors, and Jim Bridger, out of retirement for the second time in three years, had elected to take them into the great Rock Mountains to the Madison Valley. By heart, the country belonged to Bridger, if any white man could emotionally claim it; in his time, he had worn it like buckskin. Back again, the Blanket Chief was retracing the long tracks he had made in the Big Lonely thirty years before, when he had first fondly used the land and later returned it without a scar.

By midsummer, Bridger had led Raynalds through the rich bloom of Pierre's Hole. They followed the winding Snake tributaries up to the western slopes of the Rock Mountains and breached a timbered plateau. Then the mountain man took them north across the divide, mapping to the left. They bypassed the dense pine jungles of the Yellowstone and the hot waters of Colter's Hell, and soon they were coming down, heading toward the Madison arm of the Missouri. It was a broad valley below, interspersed with grassy hills, where to each side yawning canyons were spewing icy waters, turbulent creeks that had never known a name. It was the high country of long winters, frozen lakes, and windblown snowdrifts. Magnificently cold and pure, the trappers had used it, civilization had scorned it, but winter or summer, it was a sanctuary to men like Ben Tree.

This was a summer day in 1859, and Captain Raynalds was speaking. "What do you make of it, Mr. Bridger?" He put his binoculars aside and looked questioningly at the veteran guide.

Bridger's tired and oft-tested eyes made another

passing sweep of the rocky ridge. Quite a piece, up there. The lone figure on horseback was almost a mile above them, motionless, nothing more than a distant silhouette, like a painted picture on the blue skyline. By its serene stillness it could have been a painting, something born from an artist's brush. But it was no picture. Bridger had viewed similar landscapes many times. "Injun', mos' likely," he finally replied. Chewing on his pipe thoughtfully, he continued, "Ain't coming down. Highlining it, safe up there, and keeping his eye peeled on us."

"Curious cusses, aren't they?" said Raynalds.

"Always are, up this far. See one, a dozen you don't, when they take a contrary. Bluecoats ain't welcome company."

Raynalds moved his mount up behind Bridger. "Then you assume there are more? Some hiding up there? Others in the vicinity?"

"Didn't say that, and I reckon not. That un's been with us, say, mebbe two hours. I'd say he's single, right enough, up there for a reason."

"Two hours?" Raynalds reined up and stared curiously at the far ridge again. "But you never mentioned it."

"No mind to, Captain, only when there's hostiles." He chuckled and winked over at the young officer. "Take a piece of gold for every one of those braves I've seen, 'nother for ones I ain't, and I'd likely buy the queen's jewels. That 'un up there is thinking hard on something."

Peering upward, Raynalds suddenly said, "He's gone! He's ridden on . . . disappeared into thin air!"

Bridger grinned. "No, sir, he's still there, backside of the hill. Mos' likely coming down." The mountain man pointed up ahead. "That draw yonder, mebbe a half-mile. See it, Captain? He'll come out there, one side or another. Back the other way, she's all cliff.

Trail gets littler and littler, till it runs right up a white rock.''

''A white rock?''

''Kee-rect; whiter'n a billy goat's whiskers.''

Slightly bewildered, Raynalds nodded. Jim Bridger, in his unique way, always seemed to know about these mountain phenomena. Little use to question him. Further discourse often proved to be an exercise in futility. ''Of course,'' Raynalds finally agreed. ''And what do you suggest? Ignore him? Or shall we mount a guard and ride up to meet him?''

The scout shook his head. ''Meet him? Not to my notion. He'd skitter a straight coattail. No, sir, if he's a mind, he'll come into camp toward evening to smoke with us.''

''Whatever you say, Major.''

And so, as though affirming James Bridger's uncanny insight, near sundown a rider in the personage of Ben Tree quietly appeared on the fringe of camp. A brief flurry of excitement followed. Several startled soldiers instinctively leaned toward their rifles. They had merely turned and he was mysteriously there, as though born of the ground. They gawked uneasily. This unusual specimen of a man in decorated buckskin, obviously white yet so much Indian, was staring down at them from atop a painted pony. He was masculine and leathery. A scar shot across the bronzed cheek of his hawklike face, and three eagle feathers hung at the back of his long hair. Yet what the soldiers noticed most of all was the braided hackamore on the beautiful pony—and the scalp locks dangling to each side of it. One of them seemed to be fresh.

With a hesitant wave, one of the guards finally spoke up. ''Hullo, mister. What's your business?''

Ben Tree steadied War Paint and let the other two horses come about. Dismounting, he said, ''An old friend of mine is with you . . . Gabe Bridger by name. That's my business, just a friendly chat with him.''

At that point a lieutenant stepped forward. Protocol prevailed. ''This is the command of Captain William Raynalds,'' the officer announced smartly. ''Identify yourself, sir, and I'll take you to Mr. Raynalds.''

Ben looked across the small camp, peanut in size compared to the Johnston expedition. He gave the trooper a tired smile. ''Tree . . . they call me Tree, young man. Just tell Gabe, that's all.''

''Tree . . . ? Ben Tree? Ben Tree, sir?'' The lieutenant's eyes widened. A few whispers of surprise passed among the soldiers looking on, but the officer rallied and straightened. ''I'll call Captain Raynalds.''

''Hold on there!'' Ben called easily. ''I didn't come to see your captain. Gabe Bridger's my man, and if you're obliged, I think I can find him myself.''

Toward the back a knot of men stirred uneasily, and in the confusion a low chuckle came from the side. Bridger armed his way into the ring, his face wrinkled with a small smile. ''Benji, Benji!'' he said, ambling forward. ''Might a'knowed, and crazy I didn't, that ridge-runner up there this afternoon. Heard you wuz north some point raising hell. Why, Benji, you devil, you're looking like a lean hound for a long race!'' He seized Ben's hand and gave it a hearty pump. ''How in the hell are you?''

''I'm fine, Gabe,'' Ben returned. ''Not poorly, but fine. My eyes didn't lie . . . the way you sit that pony, I knew. I've been up there, watching you poke along. Ei, I'm fine, fit for a race. You name it.''

Bridger spoke aside to the officer. ''Hear that? Said he's fine. He's an ol' friend on the long side, Lieutenant. Tell those soldier boys over there to stand easy, hear? And you step aside. We'll be smoking a spell. We sure will. Come on, Benji, come on.''

They walked slowly toward the front of the camp,

making animated gestures, laughing, slapping each other on the backs. All eyes followed. Raynalds and another officer soon joined the two men. They smoked and talked, only briefly, then the last of the mountain men deserted the officers and went off by themselves to eat and make good medicine.

There was very little news from Ben that Bridger had not already ciphered. The old scout, by bits and pieces, had been closely following the misfortunes of his young friend. Reports were always filtering in along the frontier. Indians frequently passed sign with the mountain man. The Shoshoni had sadly related the story of Little Hoop. Bridger had heard that yarn, a tragedy of the worst kind. And the death of Bob Skinner, fast becoming a legend, had been told with relish and great acting among the tribes. Of course, no one but Ben Tree could have been responsible for such ghastly retribution. Horrible, but God, how cunning, how strong, the act of a true avenging warrior, committed in the midst of a great longknife encampment!

Jethro Collins' demise at Hell Gate also quickly spread across the trails. In this instance, a simple shooting had become a gun duel, Ben Tree again legendary as the fast hand. But the folks back at Laramie had known that for a long time. Understandably, at least a half-dozen unexplainable incidents had been attributed to Ben Tree, the great *Pootoosway,* the renegade breed, and even the government at Fort Walla Walla had received complaints from a few frightened packers. Like a ghost rider, he appeared on every trail, or was always riding the next hill. Myth, legend, reality, whatever, the tales continued to fatten like swine on summer corn.

Tree's quick elevation to notoriety was no surprise to Bridger. Bridger was an old hand at ciphering stories. He always interpreted change and circumstances for what they were worth. Ben Tree, for instance, was a special case, and the mountain man's sympathy was fully weighted to the young breed now sitting across the fire from him.

"Benji," Bridger said in a low but deliberate voice, "it's only the short haul of it you're making. Aw, not that I'm blaming you, like hunting this feller Boone. You been cluttered with trouble, a fact. But there's a whole passel of creatures and critters coming in here now, good and bad. Time's a short wick. The law's a'comin' to corral this territory, for certain. Troopers . . . these consarned trails to the gold country, only a part of it. Damnation, ain't no way t'stop this migration. It's against human nature, and can't be done."

"Maybe so, Gabe," answered Ben, "but I'll not be moved, not by just any damn white man. And I don't like these new trails coming so close. Neither do my brothers."

"Like it or not, it's for certain. And lemme tell you, your head's a'blossoming for a grave, carrying on this way. It's bad, son. Someone's going to cache you in and I don't like that, not for you. You boys and your pa always been kinda special t'me."

Kind words from a kind man, and Ben gravely nodded. "Every man makes the journey. Ei, death is written on the face of every man. Hell, I'm not afraid of that, Gabe. I just need time to finish my commitment . . . justice, in the name of my family." He looked into the flames and sighed. "Fact is, I don't want to be around when my people finally see the fire on the mountain. One of these days, they'll have to fess up. They'll have to fight. The land will burn, ei, and my people will fall like flies in the frost. I don't want to see either one of these things happen. What little I can do in the meantime . . ."

Bridger clicked his tongue. "Benji, if the Federals go putting a price on your head, 'mos likely you won't be 'round to see the fighting. You'll miss out on everything.''

''Miss out?'' Ben returned a weary smile. ''I sure as hell haven't missed much so far, have I? You think the Federals scare me? By jingo, I've been kicked by a mule; worse yet, one of my own. I've been shot in the ass by Blackfeet . . . in the head by a white man. The Blackfeet, Arapaho, and Cheyenne are looking for my hair, not to mention a few miserable drifters who want me deeper in Hell than a pigeon can fly in a week. Federals? What difference does it make? And I'm an Indian, a breed at that.''

Grinning, Bridger said, ''You're a regular coyote, that's what! Yep, Injun, for a fact . . . an educated one, I recall. Told you once, didn't I? No one likes a smart Injun.''

They talked long into the purple night, each knowing it might be their last parley. But they also both knew, like the velvety shades surrounding them, that civilization's shroud of darkness was slowly descending, and no man's hands were strong enough to stay the curtain's rope.

September, 1859

Colder today, some wind from the north, and this hot spell is broken. I put the run on some whiskey drummers early this morning. Fire by accident. Ha! I crossed the Hell Gate, camped this night on upper Little Blackfoot. Times and matters have terribly changed since my first visit through with Fr. Novello. It's sad enough. I also saw signs of a wagon wheel today, the tracks of many mules, probably down from Ft. Benton where the whiskey comes from. A man named John Grant passed, looking to settle along the Deer Lodge. Indian wife, bless her. We ate together and talked of the country. I told him of a place near the Deer Lodge. I'll pass over the Divide tomorrow and strike for Crow country to hunt. No news of Boone out of the Missouri River settlements. South routes via Ft. Hall my only hope before winter. Heard yesterday that J. Bridger and survey party headed south. No matter, his heart is here. I'll miss him, a loved one. B. Tree.

Ben caught a glimpse of them and had a hunch trouble was at hand. Without a second look, he immediately lit out for the jack pine jungles. With screaming war whoops the Indians followed, and Ben took his horses up a creek for another mile before finding enough rock to hide his tracks. Luckily, the tactic slowed them. And dusk helped. He finally lost his pursuers in the darkness. He still had his hair, but he went without a hot meal that night, and found little comfort sleeping in the rocks. Well before dawn he was out of his blanket, backtracking on foot, just to make certain. He located their camp just as the sun came up, and hunkered behind a clump of juniper to glass the enemy.

True enough, they were Blackfeet, seven of them, young and old, including one scarred veteran that he immediately recognized—that ruined cheekbone, the warrior he so long ago had dumped on the banks of the Yellowstone. Old Broken Bone, as Ben jokingly had come to call him. This one never gave up. Broken Bone was back once more for another try at revenge. The humiliation of the Yellowstone River coup had continued to swell like a boil, had festered into one burning obsession: to recapture his tribal honor.

This was not the first time Ben's old enemy had been close enough to claim him. The warrior's periodic quest had become a continuing story among Indians roaming the *Echeta Casha*. Ben was aware of it. Anytime he trailed the north country between the Three

Forks and the Yellowstone he was fair game in this personal contest, for there were no rules or treaty exemptions in the vendetta. The Blackfeet's true name was Walking Bear, a leader, a chief with wounded pride, pride that had been bent, wrinkled, and warped by revenge. His honor had been badly damaged a second time when the young White Crow outsmarted him one winter below the Beartooth Mountains, thwarting an ambush and stealing three ponies. Still another time, only recently, Walking Bear had missed confronting Ben by only a day or two. The scout had managed to reach sanctuary high atop the Divide, and Walking Bear and his men found only what *Pootoosway* had left behind: a miserable white man with bad arms, and so dishonored by scalping that they took unexpected pity and left him a few scraps of food. But by the time the chief scouted the Madison, his quarry had disappeared in the rocks. It was an old story. Later, the Blackfeet saw the Blanket Chief and a party of longknives exploring the river, and they reluctantly returned home.

Ben Tree wasted little time sizing up the small camp. His present situation was perilous. These were Indians, not white men, and for the present the odds were definitely against him. In a way the Blackfeet had him trapped in the basin, and any attempt at playing games with them would be sheer folly.

Edging away on his belly, he hotfooted it back to his rock ledge on the other side of the hill. He quickly herded the three horses into a small, rocky ravine high above him, and dumped a load of brush into the neck of the gully. Wedging himself in between the boulders below, he then prepared to hole up and spend the day. The Indians were shutting him off to the east and north. Not good. If they blocked the valley too many days, he would be hard pressed to make it back to the Absaroke on the Stillwater the usual way. Obviously

Walking Bear had learned something about his travel-ing habits, his frequent treks into the land of the Crow, discerning enough of a pattern to intercept him this time.

The big rocks around him were cold, the early-morning sun weak, and for a while Ben suffered from a nervous chill. He knew that he was in serious trou-ble. But as he shivered he watched the fringe of pine below, the spot where the Blackfeet most likely would appear. Two hours passed. He failed to detect any un-usual movements, saw nothing but a few rock rabbits and pine squirrels. A ray of sun finally penetrated his hole, and he momentarily dozed. Near midday, he saw two braves moving through the edge of the timber be-low. Directly they stopped and stood silently for sev-eral minutes, scrutinizing his rocky slope.

Ben hunkered lower and, eye to a crack, carefully fingered his pistol again. Barely breathing, he waited. The call of a magpie drifted up through the bottom, but the ring of it was false. One of the braves directly below him cupped his hand and made answering call. Moments later, the two Indians disappeared. Sighing softly, Ben rested back, letting the sun stream over his face. He napped for an hour.

Only a fool would have claimed victory. Ben knew better. True, this day was his, but he knew Broken Bone had not given up on him. He finally emerged from his hole when the sun was low, and like an old coyote, sat up and took a calculating look before mov-ing too far. Safe enough. Then, in the first long shad-ows of evening, he made his way down in the direction of the Blackfeet camp. He saw no smoke. Moving closer, he found only the ashes of their morning fire. He tested the charred wood. Cold. Attempting to con-fuse him, his friends had moved, but only to another location for the night.

Instead of circling the ridge back to his hideout, Ben

worked up the hill to its highest point. It was nearly dark by the time he had climbed to the top limbs of an ancient pine. Scanning the country below, he finally made out a tiny wisp of smoke near a meadow three, maybe four miles to his right, and toward the main valley. Ah, his old enemy, Walking Bear, was smart. The chief had set up camp right in the middle of the best and only practical way down. Making a quick but careful survey of the terrain, Ben saw only one hope left: to come down the ridge to the left, well above the Blackfeet. But to do it by night would be a tricky feat at best. Once in the valley, he could clean country in a hurry. By dawn, Ben figured he would have six hours on his side, and old Broken Bone would never catch up.

It never quite came off that way, at least not the way Ben had planned. He had not allowed that Walking Bear would split up his small band, dividing it to cover all possible escape routes from the slope, both sides and the middle. Ben forgot that Walking Bear had some knowledge of human nature and desire. Walking Bear knew that Man Called Tree was possessed with dogged, cunning determination, that he would find some clever way to try to escape the Blackfeet trap. And that was precisely the mind of Ben—in some cunning way, he had to get down from the mountain, back to the benchland, where he could make faster tracks.

The route left to him was the worst, and in the darkness, doubly hazardous. Downfall littered the few game trails leading to the level of the ridge, immense thickets of scrub pine and spruce to either side. The noise from one stumble or dislodged rock could easily alert the Indians below, perhaps completely blow his ruse. That was the worst of possibilities, but he had to make his play. He had no other choice, and another day on the mountain seemed a worse chance than the one he was now taking.

Ben started down slowly. He stopped at the small creek and briefly watered the thirsty horses. From there he let the Arapaho gray have its head, and rode side-hill, away from the direction of the enemy camp at the bottom of the basin. Once atop the ridge, he unexpectedly got lucky: The trail partially cleared. The moon was up, too. By midnight, the pace had quickened and Ben was making better time. Through the moonlit trees, the bottom finally came into sight, and suddenly with it, the ominous smell of smoke. It took Ben only a second to realize what had happened. He had blundered into a second camp.

No turning back, not now. Amid a clatter of hooves, he pulled up the horses and quickly jerked the lead ropes free. It was time to cache, make a run for it. At that point, he heard excited shouts directly below. A warning stillness followed, which meant only one thing: Someone was poised and waiting, all positioned to meet him at the trailhead beyond the trees. But he was too smart to meet them head-on in front of their awaiting barrels. Pulling his revolver, he reined sharply to the left, away from the trail, and dug into the flanks of the gray. Ben went plunging through the last remaining pines and out into the open, a galloping horse to either side of him. A shot came from his right, no more than twenty yards away. Instinctively, he turned and fired back, seeing by the firelight two moving forms there, leaping for mounts. Hanging low, he then wheeled right and put two more shots away, thought he saw a tumble, a falling body. Yet, in that moment, his eye caught a second flash from the camp, and he heard the sickening thud below him. The Arapaho gray suddenly went out from under him.

Ben spilled in the dust and weeds. Luckily, he came up on his knees, his pistol still clutched tightly in his hand. A shadow loomed up. He thumbed back for a fourth shot at the onrushing form, took quick aim, and fired. A hit. The figure melted away in slow motion, two steps to the side, knees to the ground, then collapsed. That was all, not another sound or movement. Ben cautiously hunkered, then stood up and listened, heard the beat of his heart and his own frightened horses running in the distance. It was all over. A few yards away, his gray was helplessly down, floundering, its foreleg smashed. He came over it, cursing mournfully. There was absolutely nothing that he could do. Blinking tears, he took deliberate aim and touched off his fifth round, and for one agonizing moment, that one hurt him most of all. The faithful pony shuddered once and died.

Sucking wind, Ben came away and stared into the quiet darkness around him. Disaster was there, too. The Indian nearest him lay motionless in the moonlight. Poking a foot at the body, he finally rolled it over, hoping that at least one of the two stricken Blackfeet might be old Broken Bone. But this dead man was not the old chief. It was not even a man. Bad medicine, it was one of the young ones, a mere boy, perhaps sixteen. And, once again, Ben cursed.

The single shot from the boy's rifle expended, he had charged with only a skinning knife, and the horrible price of his honor was written in blood oozing from a young chest barren of hair. Ben came away slowly, a catch in his throat. He ached with remorse, and felt terribly ill. The enemy, true, but these were *Indians*. These were *his* kind of people. Sheathing his own knife, he walked away. There would be no scalps this night.

He found the second Blackfeet body near the trees beneath a spotted pony; an older brave, shot in the head. Ben captured the horse and led it up to his dead gray. It took only a minute to change saddles and pull away his rifle scabbard. He shook out the extra blanket, went back and covered the body of the young boy.

Then, mounting the Blackfeet pony, he rode off into the night. From *Pootoosway,* no resounding war cry, only a lonely whistle. And it was a beckoning call for Sunday and War Paint, his other two ponies, running the cool plain somewhere ahead of him.

THIRTEEN

Time was passing quickly, time and events, two more years in the turbulent life of Ben Tree. He was twenty-nine, and among the Indians, a Crow chief. He was moderately wealthy. He had ridden with his brothers across the Clarks Fork and Big Horn, along the Tongue, and had lived in the villages along the Stillwater. Now a frontier legend, his transformation was complete. Man Called Tree was a full-bonnet, a leader among the Absaroke, a big voice in the circle, a counter of many coups, and his reputation continued to mushroom. The Blackfeet, Sioux, and Cheyenne angrily made his sign in their councils. Many moons ago, they remembered him along the North Platte, a brave white one. They knew him better now. He was still brave, but he had become as clever as a coyote, bold as a wolf, and he wore paint, the red streak of a tree sign daubed across the bridge of his nose and onto his cheeks. Riding like a whirlwind on a fleet painted pony, he plundered only the choice herds, accumulating the wealth of over one hundred head. He had fast become the epitome of a horse bandit, and the neighboring tribes cursed his cunning thievery at every turn of the pipe.

But if they denounced him, they also admired and respected him. First, he was a man, unafraid, and he was truly Indian. He had honor. He spoke out without shame or fear. His wrath for the depradations of the white man constantly unfurled like a war banner. His repeated words of warning about the white man's continuing incursions into their lands made strong medicine, and he refused to be intimidated by treaties and new promises. He frowned upon appeasement, and with few exceptions, even refused to spread his blanket with the white man.

Many suns had passed. Civilization had seen little of Ben Tree, something entirely of his own choosing. He had found comfort among the Bird People, some temporary peace. Man Called Tree had purposely shunned the new mainstream west, the burgeoning outposts, especially the robust placer camps despoiling the mountain creek bottoms to the west. Like his friend Bridger, he was always moving away from the threatening sound of the axe, the hammer, and saw. Even so he had a constant eye to the horizon, his ear open to the messages of the wind. He kept in touch. And despite his defection from civilizations complexities and disasters, the migration had not forgotten him. Tall tales about his exploits persisted. He was out here, and the man called *Pootoosway* still struck fear in the Big Lonely. With reason. Ben had become the infamous scourge of the northern routes, the avenging outrider. His constant eye glinted with hatred and contempt for interlopers.

Word of Ben Tree's unique determent methods always managed to get back to the outposts and mining camps. He still watched the Yellowstone Trail and occasionally raised havoc with pack trains. Like a phantom, he played on ignorance, superstition, and fright. And to the uninitiated, he was truly an unknown ingredient, like the mysterious potions of a medicine pouch. No one ever knew his mind or mood at any given time, or whether he was white or red. Only the whiskey trade could definitely count on his burning wrath. His hatred in that direction had been explicitly demonstrated, more than once. And it continued to be. The unexpected and awesome sight of his forked sign blazed into a lonely trailside tree always stood out like a provisional death warning to the drummers: "Keep out. Don't intrude upon the hunting grounds." Only the hardiest, most heavily armed trains dared take up his challenge, and even these pack outfits were not entirely exempt from his harassment. His smoke was on the crimson horizon. The high ridges of the eagle belonged to him, and sometimes a single shot was more than enough to give the drummers sleepless nights, a reminder that the renegade breed was still up there above them somewhere.

And his frightful presence rubbed off. Packers in general came to dread the more isolated reaches of the wilderness military roads. Prospectors skirted the land entirely. Always the watchful shadow of vengeance on the distant skyline, threatening, disturbing, omnipresent. They saw him, or thought they did. He was on the Mullan Road. Someone saw him on the Beaverhead Trail. He was everywhere, and anything that moved was suspect. Bleary-eyed men became edgy and quarrelsome; remote travel became a harrowing, haunting experience, especially when any rumor drifted up the trail that Ben Tree rode the high country of the Shining Mountains. He was like a hungry kite, a butcher bird, waiting only the chance to pick them apart upon a trailside thorn. There were few doubters, anymore. Stark evidence: Jack Gresham, badly warped and scarred, only the remnants of a man, had managed to survive his grisly ordeal on the Madison. One look at his gaunt face and bent body could make a firm believer out of the few skeptics who had not gotten the word. And no man was foolish enough to claim the name of Boone. Ben Tree was cold-blooded reality.

October, 1862

My message of last summer to J. Digby went through. Received return word this very morning on business and related matters. Some considerable amount of funds awaiting me from freight operation. H. Bilodeau has been ill. From Ft. Union, more news up from Missouri. War between states is spreading and the secession seems accomplished. Digby reports on a man called Boone Helm in Oregon Tr., wanted for murder. I'll follow this information. I packed buffalo hides and corraled 25 horses to trade at Bridger. Will move tomorrow. I had planned to make this trip earlier but tribal circumstances have kept me. These are my people. I can't interpret my dreams, but Ten Sleeps makes medicine for me. He says the omens are good. I'll travel in safety. He says the snow and the white man's greed will cover my tracks. Eight braves will accompany me, probably beyond S. Pass. Should make Bridger in three weeks—Ft. Hall later, and see about friend Digby's news. Weather turning brisk. B. Tree.

Long Hair on the Ponies, the Indian's summer, the Moon of the Changing Seasons, the traditional hunt—this was the time of the red man, when all the land was harmoniously his, and the tracks of the white man became faint. A snowy hint covered the highlands, a subtle warning to the traders and movers still braving the wandering ruts of the Oregon Trail. Winter was coming, frontier winter, time for the hairy faces to clean country, desert the trails, and lay in a supply of wood. And in increasing numbers they were deserting the frosty land, wisely heeding the threat of winter's first hardy clout. Man Called Tree found only a few stragglers in between the way points. He took his Indian party away from the last laboring caravans and mule trains, soon fell in with a band of moving Shoshoni near the Big Sandy. Before pushing on, he smoked a final pipe with his departing Crow brothers. He promised to return to the Yellowstone during the Moon of the Greening Grass. They knew he would.

Moving on to the Blacks Fork, he traded briefly at Fort Bridger. His visit was without incident, and it was short. One good look at the conditions there and he wanted out. There was no reason to tarry at Bridger, not anymore. Memories of bad medicine haunted him, and the old outpost had changed drastically. Imbued with gold fever, Bridger was a distasteful haven of motley humanity, milling strangers everywhere, new faces, new trade, the disorganized clutter of drovers, teamsters, packers, and prospectors, most of them attracted west by strikes above Lewiston and north on the American Fork and the Grasshopper. Fortunately few persons recognized Ben, only two or three of the old drifters. Most of the fur trade residents had long since fled, finding new opportunities to the west. His longtime friend, Ruben Russell, in pursuit of solitude, had left the year before, striking out for California at the invitation of Jim Clyman, another retired mountain man.

Partially disguised, Ben cautiously avoided the Bridger crowd, avoiding trouble, aware that his very presence now invited it. He donned his old trail hat, wore boots, and did his trading and buying quietly and quickly. Yet, out of respect and friendship, he did pass a few words with several acquaintances; nothing more, and lest he be followed he left the big camp by darkness, unnoticed. Man Called Tree did make one final stop before clearing the range—at the grave of Little Hoop, where he planted an evergreen and decorated the weathered mound of rocks with a string of new beads. Somewhere beyond the great mountain he knew his beautiful wife was smiling.

He moved on, carefully choosing his own direction, often shunning the now-hazardous overland, riding by night, circumventing the dangers that the heavy gold traffic had spawned. He was a high-rider, traversing the rolling slopes in safety, and the highland was as beautiful as ever. It had not changed. But the breed of people down below, the lawless profiteers, the bushwhackers, the road agents and high-mountain drifters, their growing presence had made the trail west an ugly experience for the foolish, the wayward, and unprepared.

When Ben finally came into Fort Hall, trailing six sound ponies and toting a considerable sum of cash, he had some reason for satisfaction. He had safely made the journey alone, something that few others would have even dared under such deteriorating conditions. But then, one could expect such a risky endeavor from a man like Ben Tree—that was the rather caustic opinion of James Digby.

From his office window, the wealthy trader had just observed his notorious partner's casual entry into the wild chaos of the booming outpost. Conditions at the post were strikingly similar to those down at Bridger, crowded, bustling, swelling, and rough. Fort Hall was filled with new people, men of every type and description, boomers, drifters, Indians, and always, the speculators. It was a frontier town, and a friend was a friend only as long as he proved it somehow; he might be shot at the drop of a hat if events proved otherwise.

Digby wasted no time in donning a coat and hat and

intercepting his partner at the livery stable. The Englishman was a concerned man, and although his greeting was hearty, friendly, and without rancor, it was short-lived. Quickly guiding Ben into the shadows of the big barn, Digby suddenly became somber. With a note of alarm, accompanied by a sweeping gesture toward the busy street outside, Digby said, "Good Lord, man, I had no idea you'd come riding in here in the middle of the day, presenting yourself to every blooming chap and his brother! Are you forgetting who you are? Someone's likely to kill you!"

Ben brushed away the friendly reprimand with a pass of his hand. Motioning for the attendant to take care of the horses, and glancing around, he began to check out the surroundings. Several strangers nearby were engaged in quiet discussion, too busy to pay him any notice. He was just another stranger in buckskin, one of many. Like the men in the street, they were occupied discussing the latest news of gold, the want of it, and as Ten Sleeps had prophesied, their personal anxieties covered his tracks. Besides, his transformation to a white man always had come easily, if only rarely. Shouldering his parfleche and rifle, Ben smiled down at the short Englishman. "I've been doing enough riding by night," he said. "Ei, just getting in here with my skin and money. Now, are you trying to tell me that someone here has a claim on me?"

"Ben, times have changed! The country has gone wild. And you . . ."

"The boomers are *making* it wild, Jim. That doesn't mean that I've changed."

"What!" exclaimed Digby. His hand went to the side of his head. "Whatever are you saying? Why, you're a man of reputation, and you know it! Everyone has heard of your play on the packers . . . Jethro, and that horrible Gresham affair."

"My side of it?" Ben asked quietly.

"No matter whose side, Ben. You're a renegade. You'll not be safe roaming the street, not here."

Ben smiled wanly. "By jingo, I haven't changed a whit. I'm still a man of principle." Nodding toward the crowd, he said, "Why, I'll wager there's not one soul out there who even knows me by sight. I hardly got a nod down at Bridger, except from a few of the old codgers. Ei, everyone's too damned busy talking the great war and counting their pokes to pay me any mind."

"That's a wager I'll not be taking." Digby said with a frown. "There's always an old face in any crowd. And look here, you'll jolly well not be passing for any miner or sodbuster in those frontier skins. And those bloody horses . . . Indian as the day is long!" He tutted and shook his head. "Damnation, man, there's every sort of chap coming in here, some of them armed to the teeth, road agents, gunmen. No telling when one of them will try to tack your hide on the post wall if they find out you've come down out of that bloody forest of yours."

Ben chuckled again, and gave Digby a sound pat on the shoulder. "You've only yourself to blame, then, my friend. It was your message that brought me."

"I expected a little more discretion!" protested Digby. "Yes, some exercise of your intelligence. I always believed that was one of your strong points. But now . . . ?"

And Ben said reassuringly, "Don't worry, I'll not be staying." He pointed his chin to the street again. "They aren't my kind of people. I don't plan on making any medicine out there. They'll see no more of me than I will of them. Besides, I've already done my trading. I'll hear your news on this fellow Boone Helm and I'll cache, no one the wiser."

Arm in arm, they headed for Digby's quarters, Tree's collar high, his brimmed hat tilted down over the bridge of his nose, his face hidden in shadow. He walked with the same soft tread he'd always had. His talk was the same, studied, deliberate, directly to the point. The only thing new about him was his gun belt. He wore it a little lower, on his mid-thigh, fastened with a strip of leather, only a few inches above the easy swing of his hand. And they talked in private, Ben with a deepening frown as he stared down at the congestion below: wagons, stock, freight, a stage bound for Corrine and Salt Lake City. And the people, always the hairy-faced people, and more on the horizon. As Digby had so caustically commented, it was a far cry from the old fur-trading days when the British had controlled the post. A golden flight of snow flakes suddenly burst from a thin, wispy cloud. Signs of winter. Down below, the stage began moving out, rattling away under the bleary eye of a late-autumn sun. And Ben knew that he, too, would have to be moving on soon, before the time of the blowing snows, before civilization destroyed him and before the tracks of Boone got any colder.

Digby was reading aloud from a newspaper clipping, now yellowed, that he had diligently cut out and saved. Ben Tree listened, drawing fateful conclusions. A man named Dutch Fred had been murdered in a Florence saloon, and the gunman, a killer known as Boone Helm, a man with many black marks on his record, had escaped, riding away hard to the north into Nez Percé country. Ben, his mind racing, finally took the item and read it himself, to make it indelible in his mind. This was his man, no doubt, the same renegade who had ridden with Gresham and Collins. It was a solid lead, yet a difficult one to follow. Law had come to the Oregon territory, parts of it, anyway. The government also had a claim on Boone Helm. Territorial officers were on the trail, and by now they were well ahead of Ben Tree. Even so, Ben thought that the chase was rightfully his, always had been.

Setting the clipping aside, he said to Digby, "I've waited too long to be put off."

"Can we be sure? This one might be him?"

"The name fits, even the area. Ei, and my *wyakin* tells me," Ben replied. "I'll take a gamble. I believe it's him."

"Understand," Digby pointed out, "the authorities have a legal right, lad. They have a paper on the man . . . evidence, witnesses; by this account, enough to hang him."

"But the first right is mine," interjected Ben firmly. "A moral right. If they've shut him off from the settlements, he'll have only one place to go—the hills. The hills. Ei, and that's all I have left."

"A slim chance, I'd say," Digby observed. "And you'll soon have weather. It's a poor time for such an adventure; a risk, even for one like you."

Ben shrugged. True, he thought, the weather might prove a hindrance. But he had always survived. Like Bridger, the mountains knew him, and winter had never stopped a mountain man. "Weather?" he finally asked. "You know my ways, Jim."

Digby nodded with a condescending sigh. "Ah, yes, I suppose I do. You're certainly the last of your kind, my boy. Damned if you aren't. A pity. Sad in a way." He took a bottle of French brandy from the cabinet. Setting up the glasses, he poured, then held one aloft to examine the clarity of the product.

Ben said stonily, "Pity isn't for me."

"Circumstances, lad," explained the trader. "Let's call it circumstances, then . . . the life you've chosen. For naught, I fear."

"The life of an Indian, or a renegade?"

Digby grunted once and sniffed at his glass. "Either way, Ben. Disaster, chaos for those who can't adapt.

Don't you understand? A gold rush is on! In Forty-nine they passed on, but this is *here,* right in our back-yard. How does one stop such madness? It knows no boundaries, recognizes no treaties. Squatters coming in from every direction, and our benevolent govern-ment, or what's left of it, always looking the other way. The Nez Percé are fighting the encroachment, right on their own reservation, mind you. And now, over in the Boise basin, the Bannock and Shoshoni.''

Ben stared gloomily into his glass, remembering, cursing to himself. Fools, no one had listened to the warning winds! His people had too soon forgotten the miserable trials of the Eastern tribes. He said bitterly, sarcastically, ''The word of the white man. Why must these treaty-makers be so damned consistent? The Ya-kima, the Cayuse . . . now, the Nez Percé and our people here. They should have killed that traitor Ste-vens when they had the chance, that unscrupulous bas-tard and his treaty of deceit. His words were crooked, Jim, his paper worthless to the Indians. The loop-holes!''

''The good governor probably was only doing what he was told to do, Ben. A pity, indeed.''

Ben said derisively, ''I'll allow the Union army is no better for his services. Ei, he's done his damage out here.''

Tutting, Digby replied, ''I'm afraid his services have ended once and for all. Don't fret about Governor Ste-vens. He shan't be back. He's finished, he is. The Confederates got him. There's a report in the Salt Lake City paper, a week back. Governor Stevens was killed at the Battle of Chantilly.''

Unperturbed by the news, Ben simply shrugged. ''Too little, too late. There are always others of his kind in the woods. Dogs follow dogs.'' He stopped to give Digby a perplexed look. ''And you question the life that I've chosen! How can I live with myself in any other way? Jim, I've grown ashamed of my father's people!''

Nodding, Digby said, ''Yes, yes, of course, I know how you must feel, but listen to me, lad. With reason, you've made your point up north. Well and good, while it lasted. But, my Lord, you can't ride herd on the whole territory, not now! Oh, you'll have your victories, making misery for a few culprits here and there, but in the long run it's futility. The wilderness is gone! You know it! The tragedy of nature out here is bound to the very tragedy of man. Our days are numbered, men like us. Shame or not, we're small people, Ben, small and insignificant.''

''Have I done that badly? And all for nothing?''

Digby gave him a grim smile. ''Not at all. Every knight has his day. You've frightened the hell out of the bloody lot of them. A dangerous game, I must say, but I fear it's over. The flood had come, the deluge. It's a lost cause, the frontier.''

''Yes, but for a white man, you're doing well,'' said Ben. ''You drink imported brandy, live a secure life, taking your full measure from the Bostons.'' He suddenly balked, surprised at his snide, self-serving criticism. This man was his friend and partner in business. It was a niggardly comment, and he abruptly recanted. ''I'm sorry. That's not fair, is it? I should talk. In a sense I'm not a poor man, either. I'm taking my share, however regretfully.''

''Money?'' With a wave of his hand, Digby laughed. ''Oh, come now!'' he exclaimed. ''Do you think I'm offended? Money is the least of it in our game. Certainly I've done well, and you, too. Ah, but this money never has meant anything to you . . . never will. I know that much of you. Why, you could jolly well make a fortune if you so desired, your father could have, too, had he only lived to witness this saga, the economic bonanza, the good and bad of it. No, I'm not talking about material values, lad, and neither are you. We're talking about what once was, and what can never be again: the land, the character of men, yes, and freedom to live, begrudging no man his lawful rights. We're talking about freedom and dignity, yes, against impossible odds. Time has caught up with us, Ben. Time and the confounded Yankee government.''

Ben's face was long. Familiar words here, he thought. Digby and Bridger, two of a kind. Only the semantics were different. ''Time and the government,'' he muttered. ''Neither is a friend of mine. I've been fighting both for seven years and I'm getting tired, Jim. By jingo, I'm getting tired.''

''Then we shan't drink to the bloody Union,'' Digby countered with a snort. ''It's already in pieces, and entirely too derelict to the territory of late.''

''Such a frightful *pity*,'' mimicked Tree in a mincing English accent, and with a wry smile. ''Bring back the British.''

Holding forth his glass, Digby said, ''Yes, that's a treasonable toast. Cheers, for old time's sake. God save the Queen!'' He drank heartily and smacked his lips. He put the glass aside, and resting back in his chair, stared across at his renegade partner. ''And what *will* you do? Just what are your immediate plans? Tell me.''

The scout pulled a money pouch from under his belt and slid it across the table. ''Put this to work,'' he said. ''There's twelve hundred there. I'll not be needing that much where I'm going. I have enough, ei, and some dry powder. I'll do some visiting . . . leave in the morning.'' He grinned then, saying, ''By jingo, I reckon neither one of us will get a lick of rest as long as I camp here.''

''Oh, dash it all!'' Digby sputtered. ''You know you're welcome! But don't condemn common sense. News travels. You know as well as I do that there's a hundred of those bounders out there right now, and I'd say you'd probably frighten the wits out of most, until some stupid chap comes along and drinks himself into a state of bravado. Idiots!'' Digby reached for his half-empty glass. ''Stay here for the night . . . supper. I insist. There's room, and it's been a long time, Ben, too long. And you should have an accounting of your funds. We've done well, you know.''

Ben expressed his thanks and accepted the kind offer of Digby's hospitality. But the funds were irrelevant. However there were other matters. He had the stock to check, perhaps replenish a few incidentals, the usual minor chores. Digby quickly quashed those notions, saying he would have one of the hired men take care of Ben's needs. Safe and simple, and Ben Tree agreed. After all, he was thoroughly tired from the long trail, tired and dirty. A hot bath, a good night's sleep would suit him fine. That left only Henri Bilodeau on Ben's mind, so he spoke up, making a casual inquiry.

''How's Henri feeling, now?''

Digby suddenly looked up, then deliberately downed the last of his drink. His fingers began drumming the empty glass.

Ben probed curiously, uneasily, ''His illness . . . you mentioned . . . ?''

''Bilodeau is dead,'' Digby finally said. He stared away, talking to the wall. ''Dead and buried three weeks ago yesterday . . . his stomach burning. Infection, we suspect. Rejected his victuals . . . wasted away to nothing, poor chap.''

Quietly shocked, Ben slowly repeated the words. ''*Dead* . . . ? Bilodeau is dead?'' Digby quickly poured them each another shot of brandy, and Tree drenched the swelling dryness in his throat. ''By God, it can't be!'' he said in a stunned voice. ''Nothing . . . nothing could be done?''

''Nothing,'' the trader continued. ''It soon became a hopeless case, Ben. His innards, some confounded disorder, so the doctor said. Tried everything in his bag. That's the nut of it.''

Eyes blurred, Ben went back to the window and stared out at the fuzzy scene; a miserable world, at best. "A damned shame . . . a good man.''

"Yes, in his prime, I'd say. A fine chap.''

After a moment of silent contemplation, Ben asked, "What about Rainbow?''

"Rather a sad case of it, you know. Ritual. Cut her hair, that sort of thing. She'll be leaving, of course, when her people come by. I sent word that way.'' Digby paused and drew a breath. "Oh, it's not all bad, my boy. The man left her a child. . . .''

Mildly surprised, Ben looked up. "I didn't know.''

"Yes, and a few funds, enough to get by on . . . the cabin. I'd say that's more than most of the squaws get out of it these days. And she's young enough to catch on again, a little over a score. I'd not by worrying on it.''

"I'll look in on the woman,'' Ben said quietly. "Ei, and the child.''

"She'd jolly well like that.'' The Englishman turned around and faced his friend. "The boy, he's near two years, now. This may interest you: They gave the little breed a Christian name.''

Ben, his mind once again crippled by grief, sadly attempted a smile. "That happens, sometimes. What name?''

And trying to make the best out of a poor situation, Digby replied rather proudly, "They call the lad Benjamin One Feather—Benji, for short. Makes one think that Bilodeau had someone . . . something on his mind, almost premonition. Benjamin One Feather. Unusual, what?''

By habit she always barred the door, but she quickly unbarred it when she had peered through the tiny window. It was dark, yet when she turned, her face was illuminated with joy, and for a sparkling moment or two Rainbow was happy again. Only when *Pootoosway* passed the signs of regret, a few broken words of condolence, did her dark eyes lower with sadness. And Ben Tree had seen that tragic look before, one rainy afternoon a few years when they'd buried her first child. His words became little stumbling blocks of awkwardness, but she understood. Directly, Rainbow took him to the side. Holding the lantern, she beckoned for the young chief to look. The boy was there, asleep in a bundle of blankets, and as though Ben Tree had not heard the news, she proudly pointed, saying, "Ben-jah-meen." The "One Feather" part of it came in sign.

"Kaiziyeuyeu." Thank you, was Man Called Tree's reply. "It is good. I'm honored." And it *was* good, and he felt a sudden glow of happiness suffuse his bronzed face. For a moment, it washed away his grief for the young woman and her dead man.

They sat by the hearth and watched the small fire. Rainbow was embarrassed. She knew he was a chief, a leader of men, honored, respected, even feared. Stories about the great Medicine Tree had come down the big river, the *Seloselo wejanwais*. Rainbow knew most of the legends and she felt small in his presence, tried to cover her short hair with a bandanna, quietly apologized for her drabness. He politely passed over it. He understood, and soon she was reading his rapid gestures, interjecting words and sign of her own, asking questions, nodding with renewed spirit as he unfolded the past and present. When he told her that he was leaving for the north country in the morning, her face fell again. She knew why *Pootoosway* was going. There was really only one reason that he had come down from the villages of the Crow: to kill another white man. Ever since she had first known him, he had been obsessed by the hunt. And, like Digby, Rainbow expressed her fear, but shyly, without sermon or lecture. She dared not trespass on his *simiakia*, his inner pride. After all, no one could really stop him. A true warrior always followed his destiny, whatever the consequences.

Ben quickly sensed her disappointment, for her lonely predicament already had disturbed him, the deep longing he knew that she had for her own people on the Salmon, especially since the loss of her husband. And Fort Hall was no longer the safe haven it once had been. Bad medicine, she was dangerously alone. Had he not lost his own wife under less trying conditions? And with winter closing in, who knew when a few passing Nez Percé would stop by? A week? A month? Brothers or not, they were damned unpredictable Indians. He was reading her thoughts, once again drawing some conclusions.

"You will ride with me," he said finally, making motion. "I'll take you to the *Tahmonmah* before the snows. It's on my way to Florence. It will be no bother. Do you understand?"

Trying to control her emotions, Rainbow nodded slowly, politely. Inside, she was glowing with joy. "Yes, I can be ready . . . two ponies." She motioned around the small room. "I will not take the past, only what I need."

"*Sepekuse,*" spoke Tree. So be it. "My *wyakin* tells me that we'd better get out of this place. It's not good for either of us, anymore. Ei, your people will be happy to see you and your son." He headed for the door.

With her left hand Rainbow gestured upward, fingers spread, and with her right she made a forked, spiraling motion from her forehead. The Medicine Tree. "And you, *Pootoosway*, my people will be happy to see you. They will celebrate. I will dance for you."

Ben Tree left. He felt much better than when he had arrived.

October, 1862

We fared well this day, good trailing and the weather moderate. Camped several miles north of the Boise settlement. I rode in single to buy staples, bacon and preserved goods. I saw only strangers and some soldiers who have been posted to keep peace. We'll strike north up Swamp creek toward the Seven Devil mts. east side and cross over. Saw plenty of tracks toward Boise basin diggings due east but met no travelers such as witnessed on Snake River route. Benjamin One Feather rode most of this day with me. Has the croup but is of good mettle. Rainbow pointed out several old landmarks. Her spirits are better. Anticipation, I allow. She has both spirit and beauty. Bagged three rabbits with my new shotgun. Had a feast of stew tonight with dumplings, turnips and tuber. B. Tree.

And so the small procession, three riders and six ponies, rode up the valley unmolested, heading for the rift separating the Salmon River mountains from the Seven Devils. The movers and military avoided this particular route. It was an Indian passage, high-country, well away from the big river crossing and distant Blue Mountains that had become so familiar to the booming Oregon trail trade. But the Nez Percé knew the old way; the Shoshoni and Bannock, too. For years they had used it, both in war and trade, whenever mood or circumstances dictated. By his journal, and weather permitting, Ben Tree was planning to enter the Nez Percé reservation from the south, coming across this traditional pathway down into the Little Salmon River valley. By his reckoning it was much shorter, and this suited his purpose. It narrowed the gap between him and the man called Boone Helm. And it was a safe route, far from the inquisitive eyes of the white man. The veteran mountain man had not allowed for unexpected delays, not with the pass coming into sight. He simply could not afford to waste time. The last link in the chain was directly ahead of him.

But there *were* delays. Two days above Fort Boise, Benjamin One Feather's cough worsened and he came down with a fever. At the same time, the elements of nature finally took a contrary course. A warm wind began to blow through the mountains from the northwest. This usually meant rain. Ben anxiously kept his eyes on the western ridges, watching the warning signs, the scudding clouds bunching, gathering until they finally buried the distant peaks. In his concern for the boy, he made his decision. They had to hole up, and quickly. Seeking a protected campsite, he pointed his painted horse toward the shelter of a nearby timbered canyon, then followed a creek until it opened into a small grassy meadow bounded by tamarack and spruce, free from the wind now slapping the hills around them.

It was an ideal location: adequate forage, water, and fuel, all readily at hand. Camp went up in a hurry. While the horses grazed, Ben and Rainbow separated the travois, rigged poles, and in a short time had erected their small Shoshoni tipi. Moments later, the first heavy drops of rain began pelting the hides. Within their snug shelter, and beside a crackling fire, Rainbow prepared a poultice. They fed Benjamin One Feather hot soup, wrapped his chest and throat, and bundled him into a bedroll, hopeful the fever would break by morning.

Shortly after dawn Ben was up, replenishing the fire. Outside, the rain had lessened. The morning was misty with a fine drizzle, but surprisingly the air was warm, somewhat easing his apprehension about bucking snow in the higher elevations. After he had tended the stock he circled the meadow, sizing up his new surroundings. And for the first time he noticed a slight discoloring in the small creek. The water was roiled. The rain had not been that heavy. Discounting that, his second thought was of beaver, but one look up the stream changed his mind about that, too. No impoundments in sight, no willow or aspen groves. Curious, he leaped the creek and went to the far edge of the meadow, where he immediately came upon a trail, a path only recently used. It led up the sodden canyon. It meant only one thing: prospects! Without further deliberation or inspection, he hurried back to the tipi.

He found Rainbow already busy, heating up another poultice. She spoke, making sign and a few words. Her son was better, at least his fever seemed to be breaking. Ben felt Benjamin One Feather's damp forehead and nodded in agreement. It seemed so. The boy was on the mend. And then he told her about the dirty creek, his suspicion of neighbors close by, probably only a short distance up the canyon. He wanted to investigate. Rainbow's eyes already were wide with alarm. This was bad, frightening. She had heard terrible stories coming from over the mountains, of how the white man was claiming the springs and streams, how her people were being cheated and robbed, even on their own land. And killed, too.

"We must leave!" she said in an anxious whisper and flurry of sign. "We must find another camp in the valley!"

Ben Tree shook his head. Her suggestion left him cold, for he abhorred the thought of any white man moving him from the land. It was against his medicine. Yet he did have the woman and child to consider. But he balked, his red blood protesting. "No, not yet, woman. First, I'll see who these men are . . . how far." He pointed to Benjamin One Feather and signed to her. "He must rest another day."

Their conversation was abruptly cut short by the whinny of a horse, an answering call, and then the sound of hooves thumping against the damp sod. Springing into action, Ben said, "*Hai-yah,* our friends have already arrived! Stay here, close by the opening." After buckling on his gun belt, he placed a loaded rifle in her hand. "Do what you must." And he stepped outside, only to find himself looking up into the barrel hole of a long rifle. A whiskered man seated on a black horse was staring down at him. He was dressed in a long canvas coat, the battered brim of his hat turned down to shed the rain. Another rider was coming up behind him, his boots kicking into the flanks of a laboring mule.

Brandishing his rifle, the stranger spoke first. "Smelled your smoke, Injun. Dead giveaway. You're not welcome here, see? Time to vamoose. Understand?" He motioned with the rifle, pointing back down the canyon. "Go! You go! Vamoose! Get the hell out of here, 'fore you smell up the place."

At that point the second stranger arrived and shouted excitedly, "Hey, lookee, Buck, there's a couple of real nice ponies over here!" He reined back and carefully scrutinized the man in buckskin. "Well, lookee what we got here! Say, you tell him he's messing on our claim? Camping here this way, trifling."

"I told him," the man called Buck said. Addressing Tree again, he said, "Who's in the hut? Who you got in there with you? Better trot 'em out so we can have a look, eh? In there . . . savvy?"

Finally Ben Tree said coldly, "I don't like you aiming that rifle at me, mister. Can't say that I like your manners, either."

"Well, I'll be hornswoggled!" the miner exclaimed. "You're a goddamned squaw man! Man alive, you are! Why, I took you for one of them stinking Snakes. Been on the prowl all summer 'round here, and shucks, you're no heathen at all, only look it." He leaned closer. "Yeah, your hair . . . eyes. Hell, I shoulda known."

"But he's jumping our claim, Buck," the other growled.

"Yep, that's the truth. What the hell you doing here, squaw man?"

Ben Tree took another careful look at the weapon hovering over him. He measured the entire situation in seconds. The rifle was cocked, the stranger's thumb on the hammer, not the trigger. He said, "I stopped here because of a sick boy. I didn't know anything about your claim—if that's what you're doing here. I thought this was Indian country."

"Ain't no more," quipped the second man. "It's done been ceded, that's what. It's anybody's that takes a notion. You're on our land, right and proper." He looked eagerly across at Buck. "Want me to roust that tipi?"

"Not so hasty," Buck said. He nodded at the Shoshoni lodge. "What's ailing the boy, the sick one?"

Ben Tree, his eyes still on the rifle, smiled and lied, "Think he's taken a case of the pox. He's all broken out in spots."

The man backed his pony several steps. "The pox! The pox, you say!"

"Take a look, if you want," Ben said casually.

"Hell, no!" shouted Buck. "Nobody's looking, see? And you better be making tracks, squaw man, in a helluva hurry! We don't want no pox 'round here! Just clear out, fast-like, hear me? We'll give you ten minutes to pull them goddamned poles and git." And then, aside to his companion, he said, "Go ahead, Rafe, cut out a couple of those fat critters. Hell, we'll count 'em for last night's rent.'' With a sardonic smile he added, ''Now, don't you go fussin', squaw man. Claim-jumpin' is agin the law, and that's the going rate for using our—''

An unexpected explosion ended the sentence. Ben Tree's revolver had erupted with deadly swiftness, and before the rearing black horse could have thrown Buck's body, still another split-second shot raked the stillness of the rainy morning air. Smacked in the stomach, the other man called Rafe also toppled over in the wet grass. Thumbing back his hammer. Ben leaped over Buck's limp body and looked down on Rafe, who was doubled in pain, madly clutching his belly.

The miner's mud-streaked face turned up in agony, and with a stuttering groan he muttered, ''J-jesus, man . . . you . . . you shot me . . . m-me and ol' Buck. Why? Why'd you have to . . . to do a thing like that? Help me. . . .''

''What choice did you give me, white man?''

''Jesus, can't you help me? Who are . . . ?''

Ben said coldly, ''Ben Tree. My brothers call me Medicine Tree.''

''Ben . . . Ben Tree.'' Biting his lip in pain, Rafe groaned and coughed. ''Yeah . . . heard once. Ben Tree . . . Injun Tree, a bad 'un . . . no help . . .''

''Ei, I'll help you,'' Ben replied. His third ball blew a hole in the man's temple.''

After Ben had fired his first rounds, Rainbow, struck with fright, had bolted from the tipi, rifle at the ready. But she saw Tree safely standing, strong as a bull elk, and in that last brief moment she witnessed the final exchange of words between *Pootoosway* and the fallen *shoyapee*. At the end, her trembling fear suddenly collapsed into tearful relief. When he finally came back toward the tipi she flew into his arms, sobbing violently against his chest, and for a time Ben held her protectively, tenderly, trying to shut out the violence around them, the deathly remains of it. Little avail in this. He knew that violence was there, always had been, so it seemed, lurking behind him for seven years like a shrouded specter. His eyes burned. The acrid smell of powder filled the air. The violence of death would not leave him be, even when he was not seeking it.

Taking Rainbow up into his arms, he carried her into the tipi. In a moment of disaster they had come to a mutual understanding, binding the loving need they had come to feel for each other. They both knew it, what was happening. He placed her next to Benjamin, and touching her with a kiss, he motioned, "Stay here. Take care of the boy. There may be others up above, and I have work to do." With that he turned and left, and she blinked away a tear.

There were no other prospectors about, but it took him almost three hours to complete the cleanup task. Remorseless, yet strangely with some compassion, he took the bodies back into the canyon, where he buried them. It seemed only fitting. Compassion? Necessity? Whatever, it was certainly more than they would have done for him, he felt sure of that. Later he returned to the miner's small camp, a log lean-to, crude but sturdy. After stowing the placer rocker, shovels, and the men's saddles, Ben set fire to the entire store. His destruction was complete. But it had not been in his mind to hide anything; quite the contrary. On the slick trunk of a nearby spruce, he defiantly hacked out his sign of warning. And when he returned to the meadow, he released the mule and black mare. The horses would stray far and winter well in the lush basin bottoms, at least until some wandering Indian could claim them on open range. And so, it was done.

By late afternoon, the sky was clearing. The sun finally broke through, dissipating the silver mists, and the day lived. But the mountain meadow had lost its enchantment. Blood had been spilled, olive blades of autumn grass spattered, mottled, red to brown. Spirits of the dead were there, not a fit place for a man and a woman now reaching out for each other. Ben packed the horses and moved closer to the main valley, well away from the scene of the unfortunate encounter. This made Rainbow happy. And the boy, Benjamin One Feather, was recuperating, his fever ending. Ben hopefully thought they could resume the journey the next day.

They did not. Love had been born. There was no strangeness in love, and so they stayed another two days in the quiet beauty of the upper basin. While the boy slept, Rainbow and Ben Tree found new love, each fulfilling the other's desire, for now it had come to pass. They had seen one another many times before. In their hearts, that latent love had finally been consummated.

She told him that he had no woman, no wife. Likewise, he replied, she had no man, no husband.

"Inepne hanisa," Man Called Tree said. I take you for a wife.

"Hama hanisa," Rainbow returned quietly. I take you for a husband.

And in their land, in their time, they needed nothing more.

FOURTEEN

November, 1862

The last of White Bird's village on the Salmon
returned this day. They have hides and meat from
the Missouri grounds. Another big celebration tonight. We erected our new lodge yesterday, one
more suited to our household. I'll be returning the
favors of our first days here and will give a feast
for friends. I feel rich with love, and the tongue
of my brothers now comes easily. Some news
from down below, not too good. The reports come
in from the Clearwater of more trouble. Miners
and squatters. One Elias Pierce is heading a
movement to legalize claims on the rivers of the
Nez Percé. There is talk of a new treaty in the
wind to sell the intruders access to the gold country. Sadly the villages here are not unified under
Old Chief Lawyer, and my brothers are finding
little or no redress for these continuing violations.
Gold and whiskey are the foul spots again. On

other matters pressing, I have made inquiries again among a few neighboring whites. A report that B. Helm has been arrested. I'll ride into the Lewiston settlement to seek information. B. Tree.

They sat in the sunshine in front of the new tipi. Ben's old acquaintance, Gray Hawk, was speaking, repeating the same concern voiced earlier by James Digby: Tree was a marked man in the villages of the white man.

"There are many yellow eyes in Lewiston," Gray Hawk warned. "Already it's a place of trouble and danger. Even the whites are fighting among themselves over their gold and their women. They rob and cheat one another. They quarrel over the civil war of the Great White Father. We don't go to this village, this place of dishonor. Only the treaty Indians go there, the ones who follow the drunken ways of the *shoya-pee*."

Ben, speaking slowly and gesturing, tried to reassure him. His planned visit to Lewiston was out of necessity, only a matter of inquiry. "I won't be staying long, my friend."

"For one like you to even visit this town is bad medicine," admonished Gray Hawk. "The people have ears. Even the reservation agents know about you. The man called Anderson already had heard of your arrival among our people. He's worried."

Ben smiled, understanding the implication. No, he had not come to meddle in the affairs of the Nez Percé; not that he would refuse any invitation to speak for them. He had already voiced his opinion to his closest friends: The Nez Percé were being misled about the aims of the government. In his opinion, any new treaty would only further reduce their traditional rights and take away more of their land. Ben knew that his friends needed belligerent leadership, men who would rally them in their fight against new concessions to the whites. But he was in no position to intervene unless asked. These were not his people, nor was this his land. Tree answered: "The white man only has words against me. These days, his words are meaningless. And what are these agents afraid of? They have the minds of gabbling women. I haven't come here to speak for the Nez Percé, only to spread my blanket for a time, ei, and to look for a bad white man, a *cultis*."

The young chief said, "The agents fear your words, *Pootoosway*. Only yesterday, this man sent a message to Chief White Bird asking about your visit. The agent is worried. He says a dog has pissed on his tipi. Bad medicine. By the day, his troubles multiply like horse-flies. His friends will talk against you in the councils of their people."

Somewhat surprised, the scout looked over at Gray Hawk and made a helpless gesture. This agent, one J. W. Anderson, was no more than another name to him, a piece of talk, and in the same conversations Ben had heard of another white leader, Calvin Hale, the Superintendent of Indian Affairs for the territory. Even though he had not met either of them, he recognized their type and the power they might wield. He had heard of some of the rascals that preceded them: the Cains, the Gearys, the Hutchins, and traitors like the late Governor Isaac Stevens, all of them hard-pressed to justify the boom in illegal land exploitation. Most had been pretenders of righteousness while espousing crooked words. While on the surface they repeatedly professed concern for the Nez Percé, they did little to protect them. They were appointed and replaced with regularity, their lawful duties thoroughly undermined by political whim and pressure from both territorial and federal officials. To Ben Tree, it was an old story, and a bitter one.

Not all of the Nez Percé were blind. Ben knew that.

Chief White Bird and his Wallowa neighbor to the west, Joseph, both were skeptical of the commissioners and their intentions. They were also openly critical of the injustices being heaped upon the tribes bordering the Salmon and Clearwater rivers. So were other chiefs. But none of them had asked Ben Tree to speak out. And Chief White Bird had said nothing to him about Anderson's recent message of concern regarding his presence in the camp. Exasperated, Ben finally asked, "And what will White Bird say, that I'm a trouble-maker, a breed? Will he ask me to leave this land?"

Gray Hawk shook his head. "No, my friend, you know better. He will say you are a friend. I'm only telling you this to remind you—you are known. What you are to these white men is only opinion, a mask. We know you by your heart. This isn't opinion. It's truth."

"Ei," Ben said, "By my name I'm known, but I'm not readily recognized, not up in this country. I've not been here for three years!"

"There are those who remember," intoned the Nez Percé. "Don't be misled."

With understanding, Ben smiled at Gray Hawk. He tried to make light of it. "Look, I don't go looking for trouble. You don't expect that I'll go riding into town wearing paint and yelling out my name, do you? I'll comb my hair. I'll hide under my drover's hat, just like a white man. No one will know me."

Gray Hawk brushed the jest aside, saying, "Among our people, there are those who admire you. With pride, they point and call your name. Isn't that enough to condemn you?"

"It is," Ben admitted. "But I'll have to take my chances. I haven't come this far for nothing."

"You've gained yourself a wife," Gray Hawk reminded. "A woman of beauty. And you say for *nothing*? You're a man of education. Think!"

The pointed observation struck home, yet it was not a

new thought to Ben. *"Tukung,"* he agreed. You are right. The concession came quickly and with reason, for it was true, something that had been in his laboring mind: Rainbow had suddenly given him renewed perspective, a brighter outlook on his gray life, a vision no longer predicated solely on vengeance. Even so the avenging desire, though dulled and blunted, was still there, embedded too deeply to be so easily withdrawn.

Oh, he had thought about Rainbow. Certainly, any woman who had enough love for two men was worth living for. In loneliness, Rainbow gave him sustenance. Like a mountain spring, torrents of affection spilled from her heart, filling the terrible emptiness that had swallowed him on that once cold September plain of Fort Bridger. But, likewise, he had come along to pick up Rainbow's own broken pieces at Fort Hall. They were lovers of a kind. Love lasts; love alone endures. Of course, he had to survive. More so, now. And that required outright intelligence and discretion, rather than sheer bravado and cunning. Here a dilemma, a puzzle of honor. Beset by love, sick of death, he still saw no honorable escape from his sacred vow. Boone Helm had plagued his battered mind too long. Ben was unable to forgive what he could never forget.

Almost apologetically, he looked over at Gray Hawk. "You know my cause," he said. "So does my wife. Both of you were once a part of it, over near Pierre's Hole."

"Eeh, I know," the Indian nodded. "I remember, and I only come now to warn you not to pursue it foolishly. A heart must have a soul. Take care of your woman and her child. The omens are clear. Hear me, there is little time left for happiness in this land, not for our people, not for men like you."

Ben reached across and took Gray Hawk by the shoulder. His smile was deep with friendship and kind understanding. "I hear your words, brother," he said. "I

respect them. I promise you this: My tread will fall easy.
I'll do nothing foolish, believe me."

And a day later, Ben Tree did ride into the new town of
Lewiston, but cautiously. Indeed Gray Hawk had spoken
the truth, for confusion reigned here; it was a place of
madness and disorder even worse than Fort Hall. Wagons
and stock lined the single muddy street. Along the hitch-
ing posts, bony-ribbed mules rubbed sides with fat Indian
ponies, and along the saloon stoops bearded miners,
packers, and businessmen traded conversation, merchandise, and money. Gold was the common denominator.
Humanity of every conceivable description known to the
frontier had gathered to reap the harvest of nuggets and
dust coming from the rich beds along the Oro Fino bar
and other diggings. Ben, as he had presumed, passed
safely along without drawing so much as a second look.
There were dozens of strangers just like him.

His new inquiries were casual. A stop at each livery
stable, a visit to several saloons. He thoroughly gleaned
the best of the news, and discovered that a summer of
violence had preceded him. But in the wake of the latest
killing, some semblance of law and order had been established in the town. Law officers had been appointed to
keep the peace, and after the shooting of Patrick Ford, a
prominent saloon operator, most of the outlaw element,
had quickly dispersed, heading for less vulnerable country. Among the missing, by the journal notes of Ben Tree,
were names new to him yet destined to make a blacker
mark across the mountains along the Grasshopper at a
thriving new settlement called Bannack—names like
Henry Plummer, Jack Cleveland, Billy Bunton, and Ned
Ray, and he entered them all in his journal. Another of
the territorial outlaws, one Boone Helm, had been captured in Canada and returned to the prison at Pendleton.
But there was some confusion over the legal status of his
impending trial.

That item of garbled conversation struck Ben Tree like a double-bladed axe. So the report of Helm's arrest was true! On the one hand, Ben felt cheated. Helm was *his* meat, but true to Digby's prediction the law had won out, ending the chase. The law's headstart had been insurmountable. Yet, on the other hand, a strange feeling of relief swept through Ben. Was this truly the end of his quest? Had he shaken hands with death for the last time? And what of the superstitious prophecy of the old shaman, Buffalo Horn? Had it finally been fulfilled, prematurely?

Ben Tree pondered the implications of these questions as he walked back to his horse. No, it all seemed too simple. Premonitions stirred within him. It was not over, not yet, not until the hangman in Pendleton had his day, and that disquieting thought sent Ben to the marshal's office, a stop that he had not planned or particularly welcomed.

The office he found was rough, still ripe with the piney smell of freshly-cut floor planking. A young man reading beside the pot-bellied stove quietly looked up when Ben closed the door behind him. He was a deputy, and he looked no more than twenty.

He spoke first. "Hullo. What's your business, mister?" Resting back in the chair, he put the paper aside and stared at the stranger in buckskin.

Nodding briefly, Ben touched his hand to his faded hat. His lone spur rattled against the hardness of the new floor. "Information," he finally said. He quickly surveyed the office, its rustic trappings; the bare necessitites, hardly a jail. "Information about a man your people have over in Pendleton, known hereabouts as 'Helm.' You know about the case?"

"Helm . . . Boone Helm," the deputy said. Scratching his ribs, he frowned once and grunted in disgust. "Yeah, I know about the case. Shot a fellow down in Florence. That's the story, anyhow. Whole thing smells worse than a chicken roost. What about him? He a friend of yours?"

"No friend," Ben smiled grimly. "An acquaintance, very distant."

"Just as well," the young officer commented. "He can't count many friends around this neck of the woods. Rounders, maybe, and the marshal's been putting the run on most of them. Helm won't be showing his face here again, mister. Likely end up in a box if he does. Hired killer, from all reports, and probably on the run by now."

Slightly puzzled, Ben said, "Wait a minute. . . . You say 'probably on the run.' I don't understand. I thought he was being held for trial."

The deputy stared up curiously. "Trial? Hell, there'll be no trial, not the way she looks now. How come you're asking, mister?"

Feeling a sudden tug of uneasiness, Ben said, "Well, I understood the law has him for murder. He's in prison, isn't he?"

"You heard right," was the answer. "He *was* in prison. Trouble is, the judge over there couldn't find no witnesses to that Florence killing. Four of 'em, mind you. Yep, four witnesses, at the time. One dead since, and the others taking off for she-bangs unknown. Laying low, is the rumor; scared to do any peaching."

Momentarily stunned, Ben asked firmly, "Do you mean to tell me they're letting the scallywag off free? By jingo, is that what you're saying?"

"Looks that way. They sure don't have much of a case without those witnesses, do they? And no dead man is going to peach on him." The deputy finally stood and faced the scout. "Say, what's your interest, anyhow? You know something about this Helm fellow? Evidence, maybe?"

"Only that he's a killer," Ben retorted.

"Well, if you've got some evidence . . . something the law . . ."

"Bad luck, there," Ben said. "You might say I have a matter to settle with the man; an old score, personal."

"Grudge, is that it?"

"I plan on seeing him hang."

"Well, it sure won't be happening, mister. Likely, he's out of the country already. Got a notice here two days ago. It's here, somewhere." The officer went to the desk and rummaged through a pile of papers, finally sorted one out and handed it to Ben. "Short of it is, he's going free. Like I tell you, no trial. Folks figure someone paid off those witnesses, or scared the hell out of them. Yessir. Probably the same one that paid Helm to shoot old Fred; leastways, that's the rumor." Turning back to the desk, he fished out a small poster. "Here he is. Pretty good drawing of old man Helm . . . made a few years back in California. Not much good, now."

Ben took the poster, studied the face closely. Boone Helm, the killer; broad nose, mustache, firm jaw, heavy brows. The mountain man scowled, and a slight flex jerked across the line of his jaw. Angry, disturbed, he felt thwarted, tricked by fate. What kind of law would let a man like this go free? He finally said quietly, "These other men, the roadsters who were here—they were his friends?"

"All out of the same deck, mister. Crooked as snakes."

"And where do you suppose they've cached? Any ideas?"

The youth shrugged, then stared suspiciously at Ben. "Where there's gold around, I guess. You know, easy pickings. Over the mountains, maybe. Like I said, old Helm would be a fool to show his face around here again. Has more enemies than friends, now."

"Yes," Ben nodded. "I'll wager you're right on that." He held out the poster. "You need this thing?"

"Naw, not much use here. Reckon you can have it."

"Thanks," returned Ben. "Thanks for your help. I appreciate it."

"Not at all." The young officer followed him to the door, a curious wrinkle still creasing his face. Finally: "Hold on, mister. Say, what's your name, anyway? What's your call on this Helm? You on bounty? Is that it? Bounty-hunting?"

Ben hesitated at the door. Smiling back, he said, "My name is Tree, son. No bounty, but maybe I'll just go looking for our old friend, anyhow—for old time's sake. Thanks again."

"Tree?" The small light of recognition suddenly glowed, and the deputy's jaw went slack. "*Ben* Tree? That one? From Laramie?"

With a nod, Ben replied, "Yes, I used to live in Laramie, say, maybe seven years back. Why? Do you have a call on me?"

Hesitantly, brokenly, the shocked lawman said, "Why . . . why, no, not that I know of . . . no legal papers, that is. It's just that you sort of took me by surprise, Mr. Tree. You . . ."

"Surprise?" Tucking the folded poster into his lone coat pocket, Ben said, "Surprise wasn't my intention. I'm sorry."

"Aw, you know, coming in here like this, all the stories and whatnot. And . . . well, you don't seem like . . . like what I heard."

Ben tipped his hat once more. "Yes, I understand," and he walked out into the gray afternoon.

The deputy called. "Pardon me, Mr. Tree . . . Understand, nothing personal, but I don't think the marshal will want you settling here too long . . . if you know what I mean . . . the townfolk and all."

Ben reined away. "He'll not have to worry, hear? You tell your marshal that. Tell him I just passed through, and best of luck to you, son."

Without another glance back, Ben Tree walked his horse down the street. He spent that evening at the reservation headquarters in Lapwai, much to the consternation of the

Indian agent, Anderson, who, wondering at the excitement below his post, dispatched a boy to investigate. The great Ben Tree had arrived, he was told, and was visiting with the treaty Indians. And to Anderson that was cause for worry, because everyone knew the disposition of Ben Tree, the infamous hero who constantly mocked, harassed, and embarrassed all territorial authority. The agent immediately, but reluctantly, made plans to meet his controversial guest first thing in the morning. He had to discuss the purpose of Tree's visit, find out what the renegade was up to.

Immaterial, to no avail—by dawn, the man that the Nez Percé called Medicine Tree had already departed. And by dusk Ben was back in White Bird's village on the Salmon, facing a hard decision of his own, though unaware of the nervous sweat that he'd left behind on the brow of the Indian agent.

No doubt about the joy in Man Called Tree's return to the village. Gone only two days, it was as though he had returned from the dead. Rainbow held back a tear of happiness. Ben felt the same way. He was as happy as his wife, unusually happy, because for the first time in years he had reality to come home to—a wife, an adopted son, and people of his own kind. Yet he had returned with a problem, a challenge. He was so close to Boone Helm, the trail so fresh. He badly wanted to strike while the iron was hot.

He rationalized, fought with himself, but no, it was too much to expect, to attack the mountains again, to take up another wintry search. Not that he wasn't up to the task. Not at all. He was wolf enough. Yet these friendly Nez Percé had overwhelmed him, and most of all, Rainbow, her beauty, her affection, her soul. Love and comfort finally smothered him. And, true, he was getting tired, fatigued by the endless hunt, the mental plague of it, the metallic whir of avenging wings inside his angry mind. Ben Tree succumbed. He would spread his blanket until the Moon of the Greening Grass. Boone Helm's time would come later.

He saw beauty, dazzling contrasts in the great valleys of the winding waters; quiet eddies of ice, splashes of silver, gray; a burnished hill, a purple horizon; barren brambles and withered berry; pine, accenting snowy ridges with caps of evergreen. Blue smoke came from the Nez Percé lodges, and frost rimmed the ponies' nostrils. *Pootoosway*, a hunter of men, saw winter, weathered it, followed the cleft hoof, became a hunter of game. A lone shot in a timbered basin has a sonorously perilous ring, and tracks there, man to beast, most always tell a fateful story, ultimately, written in crimson in the snow. Ben Tree tracked and made his kills, claiming bull elk, deer, and the highly prized ram, generously gifting most of the game to the less fortunate, the unlucky. No one went without meat.

By night, he often smoked in the tipis, listened to the old legends, the gossip, and always the bitter quarrels of troubled times. Some loved their land too much, others not enough. There were councils, concerned discussions over the threat of another revised Nez Percé treaty, a proposed parley with the Indian commissioners in the spring. Ben heard the wise chiefs speak: Looking Glass, Eagle from the Light, Big Thunder, Young Joseph, and White Bird. These headed the anti-treaty faction. They were Ben's own kind of men, men who sorely remembered the bad faith of the white man, the broken treaties of the past, annuities never paid, promises never kept, violations never corrected. The village heads continued to upbraid the old chief named Lawyer, and his followers, charging that the pro-white policies they had pursued had brought the tribe to its present troublesome crisis. Pointing the finger of blame at old Lawyer, they told him they wanted to keep their land, all of it, that they had been intimidated and defrauded too many times. It must end now, with the illegal miners, or bad times were surely ahead.

But Lawyer was not moved. He turned the other cheek, telling the anti-treaty chiefs that they had no respect for the laws of God or the American government, that they were bad leaders, and that they could all profit by the sale of useless land. Fighting was out of the question. The Nez Percé were a peaceful people, Lawyer said. It was too late for war. And he was a Christian. He had spoken.

Ben Tree helplessly listened as the bitter controversy slowly widened the tribal breach. He knew from the experience of the neighboring Lakota and Cheyenne that, without confederation and unity, the Nez Percé would ultimately suffer. At times when Ben retired to his own tipi he was bitterly disappointed, disillusioned, and sad. He confessed to Rainbow that he had a longing for his own adopted people, the Crow, that he missed the great freedom of the *Echeta Casha*. Here, along the Salmon, the omens were too bad. He saw little hope for the Nez Percé. Coercion was an accepted fact.

Ben's journal notes revealed that. He envisioned old Lawyer as a Judas chief, afraid to fight for his rights yet powerful enough to sell away the souls of his people and bring unhappiness to the land. Eventually, the inevitable would come—disaster. Ben Tree did not want his woman and child to be a part of it.

April, 1863

Decided tonight—Rainbow and the boy will go with our party to the Missouri hunt. She is tired of winter and eager to travel again. I suspect it rubs off, the troubles hereabouts. We both have heavy hearts. This will be yet another tragedy. I put new shoes on the horses this morning and took Benji for a ride. The hills are greening, good grass in the bottoms. Heard the treaty council is set for next month in

Lapwai. The deck is stacked against the Nez Percé. Activity down that way, some troops but few whites passing here. Just as well, the miserable times they have wrought. Rain again tonight, but only a drizzle. B. Tree.

In winter one merely existed, but spring was a renaissance. Behind April the warm rains came, melting the mountain pack. The land was reborn, the trilliums bloomed. Many of the younger Indians in White Bird's village climbed the sunny slopes in search of *kouse*, turning the moist earth, filling their baskets with the nutritious root. While Rainbow joined the diggers in the traditional harvest, Ben prepared for the trek east, mending equipment, stowing supplies of staples that he had packed up from Lewiston.

In his disenchanted mind he was planning for a long journey, likely one of no return, not back to Nez Percé country. The changing times frightened him, the pallor of civilization. He feared for his family as well as his own existence, and needed to get away. Caught up in the middle of James Digby's "deluge," the offscourings of the frontier, the avarice and misanthropy of the new West, Ben Tree was no longer his free self. His lonely mission had lost its sting, but if he had to concede defeat, he could never admit that it had been for nothing. He had made his wilderness fight, his avenging contribution to the honorable cause, the lost cause that Jim Bridger and Ruben Russell so long ago had predicted. And he had made a good fight of it. But now he had to accept the fateful prophecy of his predecessors as *fait accompli*—the wilderness *was* disappearing, his people doomed, slowly going down before tin tubs and crooked tongues.

The last tragic scenes were yet to be written. The only recourse for a man unable to adapt was release— escape from the greed, rancor, and sickening burdens of this new, unfathomable world. Yet Ben wondered if even this was possible. If the Nez Percé were unable to find freedom and dignity within the boundaries of their own reservation, where could a renegade possibly find it? Perhaps nowhere, and never. One thing—he was still a man, a warrior. If he could not escape the deluge, then he would have the satisfaction of taking a few more *cultis* white souls down into the bottomless pit with him.

They were buffalo hunters. Led by Gray Hawk from White Bird's village, and Ollokot, Joseph's young brother from the Wallowa, the Nez Percé band plodded through the wasting drifts and came down into the spring warmth of the Bitterroot Valley. Including the women and children they numbered sixty-two, and with their trailing herd of ponies these migrating Indians presented a truly formidable sight to a few of the ogling settlers along the way. Stopping at Fort Owen for two days of rest and trading, the hunting party then moved on to the Hell Gate passage and followed the river up past the small American Fork settlement. Few people there. Most had forsaken the Gold Creek diggings, moving south to the rich placers of Bannack and Alder Gulch.

Ben Tree, helping scout for the Indians, also had been making his usual inquiries along the route, still carefully noting each bit of information in his journal. For instance, at Granville Stuart's store in American Fork, some passing news from brother James Stuart struck a familiar chord. Two men from Clearwater country had stayed at the Stuart place the preceding fall, one of them identified as Henry Plummer, a name that Ben quickly found listed in his journal notes. Plummer was a killer, one of several rousted from Lewiston. The name of the other man, Charley Reeves, meant nothing, not at the time. But they were headed for the Grasshopper placers at Bannack. Coincidental? Meaningful? Perhaps too early to ascertain, but Ben Tree nevertheless made another entry about it. At the same time he reflected on what the young deputy in Lewiston had told him: Men like Plummer and Boone Helm always showed their hand where the pickings were easy. They were outlaws.

The Indians had moved on, planning on camping for the night below Johnny Grant's cabin on the Little Blackfoot; here again, coincidence, yet not so strange on the frontier. Ben rode ahead, up to the big cabin, but before he dismounted he knew: This man greeting him, Grant, and his Indian wife, were the same two that he had met on the river four years before. On that occasion they had smoked together, had shared a meager trail-side meal, and Ben had told Grant about this land with good grass. Now both Tree and Grant were staring at each other, remembering. Coming forward, Ben quickly introduced himself and began to explain his presence. He was traveling with Indians, Nez Percé hunters who were coming up behind him.

"Ben Tree," Grant said. "Yes, I remember you. Your scar, it healed well. Come and sit, Mr. Tree. You see, I listened to what you told me."

Ben, extending a hand, replied, "A long time has passed." He motioned to the cabin, the small log barn, the corrals. "You found the place, I see, away from the people. It's good. You've done well, Mr. Grant."

The rancher smiled and gave the scout's hand a firm shake. "Didn't know you then, all the talk. Some of it later, I heard. Folks telling me I was lucky, coming away with my scalp. Never saw it that way, myself. You were a stranger like myself. Always prided myself in knowing people, getting on, and your word was true."

"Thank you," said Ben politely. "Maybe you'll be

counted among those who understand something about this land and its people."

"By God, I should! My wife is Injun, you know."

"So is mine," smiled the scout.

So, returning the small favor of the lonesome trail, Johnny Grant entertained the chiefs and their squaws that night. And after supper he talked at length with Ben Tree about the changing scene; more important, the latest reports coming up from Bannack and the new diggings at Alder gulch. Tree listened with interest, hearing dark stories reminiscent of other times: ambush, robbery, murder, the inevitable aftermath of any gold strike. And the incident at Yankee Flat: two Bannock Indians having been killed by white drifters after an altercation over a squaw. The men responsible for firing into the Indian camp had been tried by a miner's court. They were banished from the area— manslaughter instead of murder—and one Charley Reeves was among the killers who went free.

That brought Ben's eyes up. "Reeves?" he said in quiet surprise. The name was a fresh entry in his journal. "Why, that's the same fellow trailing with that outlaw Plummer. . . . Stopped at Stuart's place last fall."

"Henry Plummer?" Johnny Grant leaned forward and repeated the name. "Henry Plummer, did you say?"

"The same," asserted Ben. "Plummer is one of those roadsters out of Lewiston. He pulled stakes when the law started setting down. He's killed a few men in his time. Plummer and Reeves were through here together."

"Well, if that don't cut all!" exclaimed Grant. "By damn, this Plummer fellow is the new sheriff of Bannack district! Now, what do you make of that fact? He's the *sheriff*, by damn!"

The scout stared back at him. "Are you level?"

"It's the gospel, so help me! Elected maybe ten . . . twelve days ago!"

Grant's news seemed most incredible. Henry Plummer was no lawman. He was a known renegade as far west as Nevada City in California. Shaking his head in disbelief, Ben finally said, "The miners are bigger fools than I thought; nothing above their ears, electing a man like him. Why, hell, Plummer's in cahoots with the devil, that's for certain. Doesn't make a lick of sense, Mr. Grant, not at all."

Johnny Grant's ruddy face wrinkled thoughtfully, and with a disturbed grunt he said, "By damned, it don't rightly figure when you study on it. Brings to mind last winter. . . . This fellow Plummer has a ruckus down there, a falling out with some friend. Well, he ups and shoots him dead. Self-defense, they said. Now, there's something else to chew on, ain't it? Shooting your friend? Makes a fellow wonder. Can't say that the townfolk don't know the man, not after a killing like that, but they've sure as hell gone and hired him. They sure have."

"Birds of a feather," answered Ben stoically. "Jack Cleveland. Likely Plummer had to shut him up."

"Cleveland? You know about him, too?"

"Only by name. Another one of the rowdy Lewiston bunch that ran the Clearwater. I have the word on all of them, and it's fact."

"That's some kettle of fish, by crackee, it sure is."

"Appears to me they're settling down on the Grasshopper like a plague. I'll allow that explains all the outlaw trouble along the trails. Hell, a dog can't change his spots. Someone ought to give those innocent people down there a clue about who they're dealing with. Maybe I'll get some word down to Digby, and he can handle it from that end." Ben stopped and reflected for a moment. Cursing softly, he said, "By God, John, keep your ears open. I'll wager that's where Helm is, too, down there somewhere living high on the hog, taking his sinful wages from others. That's his fashion.''

Grant stirred uneasily. Boone Helm's name again. He knew all about Helm, at least why Ben Tree wanted him—not a pleasant thought. He said, ''I reckon everyone in this neck of woods has heard that Boone story. Saw that poor fellow Gresham, once, couple years back.'' Grant stopped to shudder. ''Can't recall Boone's name crossing the trail here, though. Course, I don't expect he'd go advertising it, either, but I'll keep the gate open. Uh . . . just how long you been following him?''

''Too long,'' Ben grimly replied. ''Each day the trail gets longer; other worries, considerations . . .'' He motioned outside. ''Hard to stay on the track, with family.''

The sturdy rancher nodded. He had met Rainbow and the boy, Benjamin One Feather. ''Yes, I know how it is,'' Grant said. ''It's like sometimes when I look out that window in the morning, I thank God I'm still here, you know . . . can't seem to keep up. Then, I see that good woman of mine . . . those little ones, and . . .''

Staring thoughtfully into his empty hands, Ben said, ''Yes, it's strange. Sometimes the very life of a man can be a woman.''

''Will you be going . . . down to Bannack?''

Ben answered, ''In due time . . . when I have to. Maybe after the hunting, after the Yellowstone . . . the eighth winter . . . December. Yes, I'll have to come back. It is the legend.''

The eighth December? Although Johnny Grant stared curiously, wondering about the cryptic remark, the veteran scout made no move to elaborate. Grant finally said, ''Well, I'll sure try to keep you posted, case I hear anything coming up the trail. And I can pass the word along for you on that feller Plummer.''

In late June the Nez Percé party was camped at a second location south of the Big Belt Mountains, the hunters ranging out to the north and east. The times had been happy, the hunt good, with numerous big bulls and a few fat yearlings having been slaughtered. The Nez Percé drying racks were heavily draped with meat, and many shaggy hides, all scraped clean, were being cured in great piles. While the man called *Pootoosway* had taken his usual measure of good luck on the nearby plains, he also had forayed far across the ridges to make contact with other hunters, roaming bands of Shoshoni and Flathead. He sent messages by them to Father Novello and James Digby, perhaps the only two faithful ties that he had left with white civilization. To the Englishman, he specifically noted his suspicion of the lawmen in Bannack. He also rode into some Assiniboin friends from the northern Montana territory, reminding them to tell his Crow brothers of his whereabouts, that he planned to meet them once again on the Stillwater in the fall. And during all this time Ben rode happily free, far from civilization. He had not spotted the tracks of the *shoyapee* in a month.

But he had come upon other contesting sign. Once, when alone, he'd accidentally crossed a group of wandering Blackfeet. Luckily they passed ahead of him. Out of curiosity Ben followed his old adversaries along a ridge for several miles, simply to find out if he still retained the spirit of youth, the challenge of adventure. And undetected, he watched them move off in the distance toward the Musselshell country. Then, alone in the blooming sage, Ben had laughed outright. Oh, how he wanted to make his outcry, his scream of defiance, to let them know that he was still up there, that he was till the same old coyote! And indeed he *was* a coyote, although admittedly a somewhat tamer one than in the days of old. Even so, he had lost none of his cunning.

Ultimately, joy dissolved as the Nez Percé hunt finally came to an end. Lamentations accompanied the farewell. These were Rainbow's people now preparing to make tracks for their home in the west. Ben's concern was for his wife, her deep feeling for the tribe and her home across the mountains. Ben's course (as she well knew) would be to the east, toward the solitude and beauty of the lower Beartooth, where he envisioned a summer of peace. They finally talked about the departure. The nagging worry that he had shouldered about taking her away suddenly dissolved into thankful relief. Rainbow was far more woman than he had suspected.

Speaking in a low, straightforward manner, Rainbow answered him, saying that she had only a few misgivings about leaving, that her true home would always be with her man, wherever he chose it to be. Besides, except for the past winter on the *Tahmonmah*, had she not been away since she was sixteen? Four of those years with Bilodeau. *Pootoosway* was now her man, her happiness, her life. She loved him more with each passing sun. He was also a great chief. Among her people his voice had been distant, only a small rumble. They had not heard him, his wisdom only a whisper in the pines. But among the Absaroke his voice was like thunder rolling on the mountain, big medicine. And she was his wife, a position of honor that she was eager to accept. The Absaroke would become her people, too. And the child that she now carried inside her would be born in their village. That would be a great honor, too—to everyone. Oh yes, she had concern for her own people, their well-being in the troubled days ahead. But, *sepekuse;* let it be.

* * *

And so it was. They moved to summer sanctuary in the Beartooth, this time at the upper end of a long meadow. A shelf of high ground thrust out like a stage, and behind it was a backdrop of living green, a towering curtain of pine. They set their brightly painted tipi on the bench, its great crimson streaks of the Tree sign facing *Masaka,* the sun. It was seclusion, a camp in the shadow of *Nah-Pit-Sei,* the bear's tooth, magnificent high country, flowered glades, deep grass, and crystal springs. The glory of nature was not shallow beauty here. Ben Tree called this land "Eden." Unable to translate the word, he told Rainbow it was like *Ahkunkenekoo,* the Nez Percé land above, the land beyond. His pretty wife understood the meaning, the spiritual similarity, and she smiled knowingly. She knew his dreams had been bad. She prayed for his peace and comfort. They made the mountain their home for six weeks, listening to the quietness of nature and finding its heart.

This was also a country of good bounty, one that Ben looked upon with nostalgic reverence and respect. In his time with the Bird People he had traveled many of its game trails, the soft, meandering paths of needled pine, and as a hunter. Here he found plenty of deer and elk. The Stillwater bottoms knew him, too, the creeks, the ponds, the sloughs, the forks where he had once trapped so long ago that first winter. Memories were down below, where he had long ago heard the beat of the Absaroke drums, had become a true brother, had felt the warmth of the ceremonial robes— a young brave, his manhood proven. And lest he not forget, a woman's love, a first, like a shimmering mirage, beyond touch, yet always there. Understandably the spirits of the dead, Little Hoop, the many others, even the ancient shaman, Buffalo Horn, all had become a reverent part of this hallowed, beloved land. The bits and pieces of Ben's own enigmatic life, those

irreparable fragments, were scattered here with the
souls of these people.

Even so, the benevolence of the Great Spirit prevailed. Ben had not been forsaken. He always returned
to the origin of his haunting prophecy. The Great Spirit
had always guided him back safely, time and again,
ultimately had even revived love from the depths of
his embittered soul. And with Rainbow, the symphony
reborn, Ben Tree had found renewed happiness in the
land of the Beartooth. For a time, for the sake of a
woman, he tried to forget the last hunted man, Boone
Helm.

So they roamed the sunny slopes together, like happy
children, searching out the fresh edibles, the roots and
tubers. It was the Moon of the Blackberries, and they
found the bushes heavy with fruit, trees in the bottom
laden with plum and chokecherry. They took joy in
the picking and preserving of their rich harvest and
the traditional preparation of pemmican. The warm
afternoons often saw them bathing as a family, basking
in the sun alongside the creek that coursed their private
meadow. Naked and bronzed, Benjamin One Feather
was a squirming tadpole in the shallows, and Rainbow, her belly beautifully rounded, was now in her
fifth month. And there were those moments of never-
ending wonderment when Ben's callused hand, gently
placed atop her glossy mound, felt the small rustlings
of life within. He glowed, and her eyes, adoring him,
were dark pools of pleasure, mirroring a mutual love
story.

They shared the marvelous high country until the
Moon of the Changing Seasons, until it was time to
move to the warmer cover of the Stillwater bottoms.
When the leaves began to turn, Ben's periodic early-
morning forays down the adjacent ridge became more
frequent and longer. He had found a precipitous out-
cropping of rock for his lookout. Taking up his bin-

oculars, he repeatedly scanned the distant flats until one day he saw it: smoke, the meaningful sign that he had been seeking. His Crow brothers were returning from the Big Horns. Old friends would be there, bringing him news, fresh supplies. So, the next morning, the small family struck summer camp and rode down into the protection of the mountain Crow's winter village. Not unexpectedly. Word of Medicine Tree's reappearance on the buffalo grounds that spring had already traveled the Yellowstone, up the Big Horn and Powder. Beyond South Pass, Shoshoni runners, who had crossed trails with James Digby, delivered to passing Crow a message pouch directed to Tree. His presence in the Stillwater was known, his arrival in the village anticipated. When he and Rainbow finally appeared inside the perimeter, the Bird people set up a tremendous welcoming tremolo. A wave of women and children joyfully rushed out to touch hands with the new arrivals. To Ben it was heartwarming, to Rainbow acceptance, a new life.

In short time, friends came with gifts. They brought news and gossip, both of the past and the present. Curious to see Man Called Tree's new wife, a chorus of women quickly gathered. The tipi went up and her home was made. During the brief furor, Sound of the Wind arrived to present Ben with a tally on the pony herd that he had managed for the young chief during his absence. It was good. Tree's wealth in horse flesh had multiplied. And ultimately, the message pouch from James Digby was delivered.

Amid the excitement Ben put it aside, waited until that night so he could share the letter with Rainbow. By the light of the tipi fire he finally opened it and read, translating for his woman. First there was the congratulation on their marriage, then news of the business at Fort Hall. The freight line was prospering with additional traffic to the northern mining settle-

ments, specifically the new ones at Alder gulch—
Virginia and Nevada cities. Hundreds of people were
pouring into the area, and there was even rumor of the
creating of another new territory, to be called Idaho, em-
bracing all of the mountain valleys within the Shoshoni
and Nez Percé country. Obviously the gold strikes had
proved to be more than a flash in the pan, bad news to
Ben.

And trouble had come to the Nez Percé, themselves.
Face darkening, Ben read on, speaking out each line to
Rainbow. The new treaty had been signed. Old Chief
Lawyer and his followers had bowed to the treaty com-
mission's demands: For a small sum, the reservation had
been disastrously reduced to one-fourth of its original size.

Ben abruptly stopped translating. He stared disbeliev-
ingly at the Englishman's bold scrawl, trying to interpret
the unfolding catastrophe. True, he had expected *some*
treaty exploitation, but this was of the very worst sort.
The news seemed incredible, and he finally pronounced
bitterly to his wife, "They have robbed your people! For
a trifle, the treaty-makers have stolen them blind!"

Rainbow looked up at him from beside the fire. But her
man was staring at the paper with a bewildered look, as
though he had been stunned by a rock. She finally inquired, "Chief Lawyer, he has sold the lands of the others, too? White Bird?"

With deepening frown, Ben once again read the last
damaging paragraphs. No mistake; Ben had been clear
enough, detailing all that he had learned. "Looks that
way," Ben said disgustedly. "The old fool has given up
all of the Salmon and Clearwater mining country . . . for
fifty thousand dollars; ei, and that's a pittance."

"That is plenty of money," Rainbow said innocently.
"You think it's not enough? Is that it?"

"Robbery!" he exclaimed. "The miners have already
taken out three million from those diggings! Ei, and

they've done it all outside the law. No, my woman, this money is no more than a token."

"White Bird's land?" Rainbow asked again. She shook her head, "No, *Pootoosway,* White Bird would never sell the bones of his father."

"Ei, White Bird's land. And from Jim's word here, even the Wallowa, Joseph's land. Your people told him that neither one of these chiefs signed the paper. Old Lawyer took it on his own to sign for them. Why, that's like selling ponies that don't belong to you . . . bad medicine. Makes for nothing but trouble and fighting. I've seen it before, woman."

Sensing the dire implication, she said, "My people do not like war."

"Their war is already lost," Ben returned flatly. "They've lost it on paper. They're done for, finished."

Rainbow closed her dark eyes and shuddered. She wanted to cry out for her people. She reached for the strength of her man, took his hand and sighed. *"Sepek-use,"* she said sadly. "You, alone, are like a light in the darkness. Hear me, my husband, you must tell the wise men of the Absaroke never to sell the bones of their people, never to make bad medicine for our children. When the land is gone . . ."

Another lost cause, Ben reflected, hopelessly, unmercifully buried by the deluge. As Rainbow's voice grew choked with emotion, Ben blinked and read the last of the letter, searching each line for a shred of positive information of another sort: some revealing clue that the Englishman might have uncovered regarding the movements of Boone Helm. And what he had hoped for, albeit dreaded as well, suddenly loomed up in the final two paragraphs.

Your information on H. Plummer seems most valid. The man has a bad record. We have alerted our stage people and others of influence. Of strange coincidence,

one Sam Bunton came through only recently. This chap
is a drunk and braggart, obviously renounced of late by
his confederates. Billy Bunton, the one you mention, is
his brother, all from Clearwater. S. Bunton confirms a
rogue named Helm is in the Bannack district, of this
writing. Crime is prevalent up that way and we've lost
some on the express.

I should caution you, friend Ben: Bunton reports these
bounders are fully aware of your investigations in Lewiston and elsewhere. Outlaws one and all, they have
pooled resources to put a price on your head for these
impeachments. This is the word of the drunk, Bunton,
but cause enough for diligence. I deem it unnecessary
to impart any further warning. Shall I see you this
spring?

Yours truly, J. Digby, Esq.

Ben did not have to read the letter a second time.
He had already sorely absorbed all of its disastrous
facts and sickening implications. Once was enough to
envision all of the potential calamities in the offing,
including the resumption of his own selfish quest. He
had located Helm again. He kissed Rainbow on the
forehead, but purposely avoided translating the final
revealing paragraphs that Digby had so fatefully
scribed. The Nez Percé news had been pox enough.
Touching the tip of the dread letter to an ember, *Pootoosway* watched the small flame slowly burn its way
across the land.

FIFTEEN

December, 1863

This morning we experienced the joy and good
fortune of being blessed with another son. Rainbow is happy. She is well for the birth, sleeping
soundly tonight with the new one. I must confess
that my apprehension is at an end. My prayers to
the Great Spirit were answered. She and the child
are both hardy. Before dawn when she began her
convulsions the moon was white, the beginning
of a full moon. She liked this. It was a good omen.
She named our son White Moon. There is new
snow, little enough for good tracks, but the air is
fresh. We met Shoshoni scouts on the main river
trail Tuesday, moving west with packers. I sent
word to J. Grant on the Deer Lodge to keep the
latch string out. It seems I have finally caught up
with time. B. Tree

Man Called Tree was restlessly consulting the omens. He had not forgotten, for by the prophecy of Buffalo Horn it was now the eighth December. He also listened to the words of Ten Sleeps, who on three consecutive nights made strong medicine from his sacred bundle. On the fourth morning, a cold wind blew in from the northeast. The shaman came again, his face blackened, one hand painted red, and he spoke to Ben, telling him to go without delay, to follow the wind.

In a low monotone he said, "I have had dreams of a big storm. The sky was black with anger. I saw many riders, many ponies, all riding away. They were soon covered by the darkness of a terrible storm. I watched, and I saw the sun come back to the plains. The ponies were there, feeding. They were alone. It was so, they had riders no more. Hear me, Man Called Tree, it is for you to go before the storm. It is for you to fear it."

Ten Sleeps shuffled back to his tipi and disappeared. Ben pondered. Old men were wise. In a way, the message seemed clear; Ten Sleeps was only confirming the old prophecy of Buffalo Horn—the time had come. That was important. Ben knew the direction, the country ahead, the purpose of his trip. A storm? Perhaps, but he had weathered many storms in his day. More to the point: trouble? What part of his life had been without storm and trouble? Whatever, nothing would deter him from the mission, not now, not with the end in sight. Yet for some reason, he felt uneasy. Something else about the medicine chief mildly disturbed him, something more than his words. Ben tried to dismiss it, but Rainbow had seen it too—the paint of Ten Sleeps, the black and red of it, the ceremonial mask of death, the hand of blood. And the sight alarmed her.

"Those are the signs of a crazy dog," she said apprehensively, "a warrior who searches for death." She stared fearfully away, aware that Ben already had made his decision to leave. "I know you must go. I don't like it . . . what may happen. It was so long ago, this trouble."

"I'm not a crazy dog," he said reassuringly.

"They hunt you like a crazy dog, don't they?"

"A few," Ben admitted. "But you know me as a human being." He took her hand, caressed it. "You know that I'm not foolish. Don't be afraid. We've come too far together."

Her eyes came back to him, two large pools of sadness. "What is in your heart, my man? Is there no love?"

Hesitantly, considerately, he answered, "Love? Ei, love for you . . . and our children. I think you know that."

"Death?"

"Certainly, not death, not anymore." Ben shrugged and said thoughtfully, "I suppose once I didn't care much about living. In a way, maybe I became a crazy dog and didn't know it. Those were bad days. Death? I've always known death. But I'm not afraid of it, only of the misery it brings to others."

Rainbow's soft eyes lit up. "Eeh, then you understand?"

"Yes, I understand," was the gentle, reasoning reply. "I know misery. I know other things, too." And in kind admonishment he said, "Hear me, the souls of my kin are restless. You remember. You were the first to point the way. How *can* I forget? In misery, I've seen little of justice. This isn't something I want to do. Do *you* understand? Ei, my pretty one, you should know about justice after what the *shoyapee* have done to your people."

Rainbow pressed his hand to her cheek. "In my selfishness, my happiness, I don't care to understand. I cover my eyes. And I'm not ashamed. Eeh, I love you. How can I not be afraid? I say to myself, what is honor to a dead warrior, but grief to his widow and children? I want *you,* not honor. I know it's not my place to say such selfish things, but—''

Ben hushed her with a kiss, saying, ''Years ago, I made my vow. You know that.''

''You could never disgrace me by forgetting the prophecy of the ancient one, Buffalo Horn,'' she whispered back. ''Is the wise one's medicine so strong, to leave you without a soul?''

Ben sighed, reflecting on still another time long ago, another man, one dressed in black, another mission, one of medicine and lost souls. ''Woman,'' he said, ''I remember asking myself that same question. Yes, once, many moons ago. I wasn't an Indian then. I was a white man who loved my red brothers. Hear me, I remember Buffalo Horn. I thought he was a superstitious old fool. I laughed inside at this man, his paint, his bundle of magic, his crazy talk. Yes, I laughed, showing my ignorance. And he healed me. He healed my wounds. I denied his words, too, and his vision. Ei, and they came back to haunt me, to rob me of everything that I loved and honored. A strange old man, strong medicine. Superstition? I don't know, my woman. I wonder now at his wisdom and what has come to pass in this great land.''

Ben took Rainbow close, cradled her head against his shoulder. ''Oh, how I love you and your place beside me! Yes, speak freely, but trust me. Trust me and the hand of the Great Spirit. In the name of justice, I've survived. And now you . . . you and the children. Only a crazy dog would carelessly throw away the last scraps of his life.''

By his journal notes, Ben Tree's last trail ride west was without immediate consequence, probably somewhat of a surprise after he had lent an ear to the foreboding words of Ten Sleeps. He rode toward the Divide

safely surrounded by friends. For two days Ben had
the company of his brother Crow, finally leaving the
fifteen Big Dog society braves in the Gallatin foothills
on December 23. Later he crossed the Divide in ten
inches of snow, ultimately came down to Johnny
Grant's cabin on the Little Blackfoot sometime after
Christmas. It was a cold land, but unlike the old days,
it wasn't dormant. Traffic was on the Mullan Road:
wagons, horses, mules, and people, more people,
lured and sustained by the attending gold fields. The
trackless days of the red man were gone forever.

Ben talked long into the night with Grant, and by
the rancher's account the angry citizens in the neighboring Bannack district were finally stirring with vengeance. They had armed themselves for a fight with
the lawless element roaming their streets and valley
trails. But among the ugly reports of violence, Grant
had heard nothing of Boone Helm. However another
roadster, George Ives, had been hanged in Virginia
City only four days back. More important, there were
strong rumors coming up the trail that a secret citi-
zen's committee was being formed to ferret out outlaws terrorizing the district. This news had taken on
ominous but meaningful tones.

Grant shot a long, dark look at Ben Tree. "Vigilantes, I reckon you'd call them. When something like
this gets started, no telling where it'll end—or whose
name they're gonna pin on the list. They sorta go
crazy, pick on anybody they take a notion against,
anybody who has caused trouble. Know what I mean?
It don't bode well."

Ben's brows furrowed, and in that instant he saw Ten
Sleeps' storm clouds gathering. He also understood
Grant's insinuation. "I understand," he finally said.
"Any suggestions?"

"Not my proper place to go telling a man his business," replied Grant. "You know how some of these crazy miners and merchants are."

"You're a friend. Say your piece."

Rubbing his chin whiskers thoughtfully, Grant said, "Well, I'd not chance getting messed up in it, that's what. I'd hightail it back across the mountains. No fussin' over there in your country."

Ben shook his head. "As much as I hate the settlements, I can't do that. I came here with a purpose."

"Figured as much," Grant said dolefully. "But you asked." Then, almost regretfully: "Well, if you're fixing to ride down Bannack way, it just might be wise to go a little easy, that's all. Some folks hereabouts have long memories, and they have no notion that you helped get all the ruckus started with that news on Plummer and his bunch. You know how 'tis, why, they're apt to bring down trouble on most anyone. And with vigilantes, if that's what's going on . . . well, it ain't exactly no trial. More like loaded dice."

Ben forced a smile. "Yes, but I'll allow bad law is a damn sight better than what the white fools have: no law at all." He looked over at the rancher. "What about our friendly Plummer?"

Grant shrugged. "Haven't heard that much of it, but it seems like you ain't the only one knowing about him and that Clearwater bunch. Oh, there's been some talk on the man, both good and bad. Hard to figure. He has friends in the territory. Dangerous business, Ben. Have to mind who you're talking with. Yep, hard to say about a man like him."

"Friends of *his* kind," commented Ben dryly. "I've heard this from Digby. It's a loose operation. Jim says Plummer's done little to protect the stages on the Hall route. They've been fair game for a blind man. That has a bad smell, I'd say."

"Well, if Plummer's been taking under the table, it ain't been proved, not that I've heard, and there's always some of his old sidekicks coming through, hanging out and drinking it up down the line at Cottonwood. They're a talking lot; some bull, but they know about you, I reckon. They know your name, and don't consider you a friend.''

''I've heard that, too.''

''That's something else to think on, I'd say. Sorta like looking into a double-barrel shotgun: vigilantes on one side of you, and those roadsters on the other. Bad times, Ben, bad times. You could get yourself caught right in the middle.''

Ben stared gloomily, silently, out the window at the new snow. ''The land has gone sour,'' he finally pronounced.

''Depends on whose side you're on, these days . . . where a man casts his lot.''

''Ei, I made my choice a long time ago, friend.'' Grant's two brown-eyed children were hugging his legs. Ben cradled them in his arms, and then with his forefinger he drew the picture of a tipi into the frosty sweat of the windowpane. He traced two little children playing alongside. The tots smiled joyfully. *''Sepekuse,''* Ben said. So be it. He felt terribly lonely.

At the insistence of Grant he stayed on at the ranch for another three days, helping out, hauling hay and poles, and resting his own horses. He played with the children, and he watched an occasional rider come and go; paused long enough to catch the news filtering up from Bannack and Alder gulch. Reports of the new Vigilance Committee were no longer rumor—they were startling fact. Ben learned that the secret lawmen already had been in action, fully asserting their self-proclaimed territorial authority, riding far from their homes. They had come as close as nearby Cottonwood, searching for two of their wanted men, and Cottonwood was no more than a two-hour ride down the Deer Lodge Valley from Grant's cabin. The two outlaws, George Brown and Erastus Yeager, captured later on the Beaverhead, had been taken away to the Laurin ranch west of Alder a gulch where, in Grant's opinion, they probably would be hanged. Stark days ahead, averred the stocky rancher, Hell to pay.

The Indian in Ben Tree smiled as he saddled up. White men killing white men; Ten Sleeps' mysterious riders smothered by stormy darkness, then riderless. He thought that this must be part of the shaman's dream. Probably coincidence, but the parallel was strikingly familiar—and Ten Sleeps had warned him to avoid the storm. With a troubled mind, Ben headed out on the painted pony, trailing his pack on a black-and-white pinto.

Later that afternoon he rode down the rutted, frozen street of Cottonwood, with no mind to tarry too long. The wind was kicking up a skiff of snow and he had miles to make toward the lower Big Hole River. Grant had told him of several of the new ranches along the way, the Evans or Clark spreads where he could always find overnight shelter, perhaps escape a wintry camp-out. Weather permitting, Ben had figured on a good three-day ride to Beaverhead Junction, a place where old memories lurked. Years past, he had first met the Nez Percé there; Henri Bilodeau and Rainbow; had once heard brother Joseph call the spacious land, "God's country." Time, indeed, had not stood still, and the people had moved with it. This was Father Novello's "historic tragedy," written in the raped gulches and creek bottoms of the Grasshopper and Passamari, the gluttony for gold; contingent miseries for most, riches for a bare few. God's country? Ben blanched, thinking of the past. What few memories could he yet cherish?

And this was Cottonwood, a dingy outpost on the border of frontier civilization, a point between points on a cold, unfriendly plain. He wanted only hot coffee, a shot of brandy, some warmth under his belt to send him on his way, and he had shed his shaggy coat and mittens at the door. The place was called Cooke's saloon. It was logs and rough-hewn planking, dimly lit. At least it was warm.

Ben shunned company. He stood alone at the bar, well away from the faro game at the end of the long room, where by his quick eyes he saw four or five men; nearby, two young Indian women squatting against the wall next to the blazing hearth. He casually passed only a word or two with the barkeep—the weather, his direction, nothing more. Yet, after several isolated moments, he sensed it: the sudden discomfort, the curious eyes at his back. The women had stared, giggled once or twice, and the men's conversation abruptly ended. One harsh voice finally reached out of the dimness, breaking the edgy silence.

"What's been keeping you, Mr. Tree? Those black duck vigilantes scare you out of Grant's place?" There was a husky laugh or two, but the laughter was uneasy and hedged with caution.

And again, the same voice: "Been expecting you, Mr. Tree. Hey, Cooke, how come you're serving up that good whiskey to an Injun man? Man alive, what's this place coming to?"

The barkeep glowered toward the long table. "Mind yer business, Gad! Who the hell you think yer talking to?"

"That half-breed there," the man called Gad replied sarcastically. "Ben Tree's his name. *Mr.* Ben Tree. It's him I'm talking to."

Ben stared down at his tin of steaming coffee, and without looking up he quietly asked Cooke, "Who's the mouthy one? His name?"

"Gad Moore . . . Drifter, works here and there. A roughneck." Cooke edged closer and whispered, "Look, if you're Ben Tree, for certain, then you'd bet-

ter move out. I hear those no-goods down at Alder
Gulch got five hundred on yer head.''

"Is the boy drunk?''

"Naw, he's a goddamned cocky rooster, that's what!
But he's armed, a brace of 'em. Never saw him use
them, so can't tell you 'bout that. Those other fellers
are no mind.''

Turning slowly, Ben addressed the back of the room.
His voice was easy, his body loose. "I'm afraid I don't
know you, son, only your poor manners, and I'm willing to forget that for this time.''

"My name is Gad Moore!'' was the sullen reply.
"Naw, you don't know me. Shit, no! There's some
that *do*, for sure. Now, I'd say we all know what you're
up to, coming back here among us white folks, Mr.
Almighty Tree. You're hunting a white man, ain't you?
An ol' man you been runnin' scared for years. Ain't
that right?''

One of the men said, "Sit down, kid, and play.''

Ben took a final sip of his coffee and slowly pushed
it aside. "My business has nothing to do with you,''
he quietly countered. "Like your friend says, I'd advise you to back off, play your cards. . . .''

"I'm *playin'* my cards,'' returned Moore. "Lemme
tell you something. . . . This ol' man you're picking
on, he's a friend of mine. Boone's a good ol' buddy,
you hear? But he's an ol' man down on his luck, not
what he used to be, you raggin' him'n all, drivin' him
crazy.''

"He's a bushwhacker,'' Ben said flatly.

"Well, now look who's talkin'!''

Cooke suddenly intervened again, speaking to the
back of the room. "Better do what the man says, Gad!
You settle down and shut up! Get back to the game
and mind yer own business, or I'll put you out.''

"*You* shut up!'' Moore cried out. "Hell, I know my
game! Goddammit, don't any of you bastards be tell-

ing me what to do! You think this breed's reputation scares me belly-up? Maybe he scares ol' men like Boone, but I ain't no ol' man, not by a damned sight!''

With that the other four men began edging away from the table, and the two women clambered into the nearest corner.

"You're a fool, son," Ben said. "It's not worth it, not to me or you." He spoke aside to the others. "You gentlemen are my witness. I'm ready to cache. I'll not pull down on this boy first. I'm going for the door."

At that point Gad Moore made one frantic lunge for one of his revolvers. The weapon had barely cleared the scabbard before a resounding blast staggered him back toward the fireplace. His own shot came a full two seconds later, splintering the boards at his feet. Clutching his breast, he fell to the floor. He was dead when they rolled him over, his outstretched free hand painted red with blood. The prophecy of Ten Sleeps.

Ben walked over and stared down at the youthful face, barely covered by a few sparse whiskers, a thin mustache. Cursing softly, he looked at the nearest man. "How old?" he asked. "How old is this kid?"

"Nineteen, maybe . . . twenty."

Ben slowly holstered his pistol. He groaned and whispered, "Barely a man. What a waste."

"Maybe," one answered. "Maybe not. Tell you this, mister, you did what two other fellers couldn't. They're dead and gone."

Pathetically, Ben turned away, saw the bartender pouring himself a quick drink. "I'm sorry for the trouble, Mr. Cooke. Had I known . . . Does the boy have any kin around?"

Cooke nervously gulped the liquor, grimaced once, and coughed. "Never heard of any. He's been hanging real close for a couple of days. Beds down in back of the store across the street. Funny, it's like . . . like he knew you was coming, just waiting. Didn't mention relations, though."

"Friends?"

"Down Bannack way. They come and go."

"It figures," Ben said, pulling on his coat. "They were trying to set me up. My apologies for the trouble."

"Hell," Cooke said, "you sure don't have to go feeling sorry about this. We all saw it, didn't we? No fault of your'n. The crazy kid dug his own grave."

Ben fingered the pouch inside his belt and fished out a twenty-dollar gold piece. "I'll allow he'll need some help back-filling his hole." Tossing the coin to the bar, he said, "This should help cover it."

Cooke protested gently, "Aw, there's no need for that. We'll put him—"

But the heavy door had already opened and closed.

Ben Tree bitterly traveled the old familiar country, changing now, the signs of movers and squatters everywhere, like insidious tentacles reaching out by the month to envelop the land. He saw the tracks of many horses in the snow, always shod stock, the telltale ruts of wagon wheels, a piece of discarded debris here and there, broken campsites and human waste, the white man's trail to the gold fields. And Grant had told him of the budding ranches in the cold blue valleys ahead. This was no longer a welcome land, not for Ben Tree. He prepared himself.

By necessity he had become a cautious man, and after the incident at Cottonwood he made his own evasive tracks, turning well away from the clutter along the established routes of the white man. His followed the pads of the coyote, the fox, and the wolf. By day, he circled the few ranches, rode the foothills of powdery snow; by night, he built his fire in the timber's protection, bundled himself to sleep in between his buffalo robes. Once he saw the smoke from a distant cabin, distastefully ignored the warming invitation, remembering that in bygone years such sign could have come only from his red brothers. They seldom passed this way anymore.

A few days later, toward mid-afternoon, he came down through snowcaps of sage and stared at the winding furrows below him. In the distance two wagons trundled up the road, teams laboring, mules' nostrils flared, puffing steam into the frosty air. Ben waited until the teamsters were nearly abreast of him before moving out to hail them. He wanted to test the winds, and palaver. He knew Bannack was only another day's ride over the hills to his right, and these men were freighters, merchants, down from the Grasshopper, obviously enroute to Virginia City.

This turned out to be a chance meeting, not too unusual for a constant wanderer who had seen many faces in his life. The man behind the reins on the rear wagon was a friend, James Stuart, Granville's brother, and Ben had crossed paths with the Stuarts several times, both in Fort Hall and on the Hell Gate. The other two men were hired hands, and ready friends when they saw their employer reach up and shake hands with Ben.

The ensuing conversation abruptly altered Ben's course, and his destiny as well. He listened to Stuart tell about the harsh days that had suddenly come to Bannack. Vigilantes. Sheriff Plummer was dead, hanged only yesterday; so were two other men, all three convicted of murder and complicity in a gang of outlaws called The Innocents. More astounding, Henry Plummer himself had been the secret leader. Some of the vigilantes had already ridden on ahead toward Virginia City to seek out other known roadsters. Stuart said that one of the Bannack dead was a deputy, Ned Ray, an old associate of Plummer's from the Oro Fino and Clearwater country. All of the men had been condemned on evidence from Red Yeager, one of the two outlaws apprehended earlier on the Beaverhead. Ben already knew that particular story, the Yeager capture, but Stuart further enlightened him: Yeager and his partner, Brown, also had been hanged by the avengers. True to Johnny Grant's prediction, the Laurin ranch had been the last stop for the two bandits.

Ben feigned some surprise at the developments, but Stuart knew better. The merchant finally said, "You had cards on Plummer all the time, didn't you? You were down that way looking things over. I remember when you came back and stopped at the Fork. Someone got the word around."

Ben brushed off the intimation. "I only knew of Plummer's troubles in Lewiston, only what I heard. By jingo, anyone can draw conclusions about a crooked sheriff. What's that worth from someone like me? The pot calling the kettle black?"

"Ah, but you told Digby, I know that. His word has authority. A couple of his riders were up here last month."

"I wouldn't know one of your Innocents if I saw one," smiled Ben. "Looks to me like Plummer was peached on by his own man, that Yeager fellow."

"Well, it's done," Stuart said, shaking his head. "A terrible sight, Ben, back there . . . those poor devils. Makes one wonder how many names Yeager pulled out of his greasy hat, just how many rascals are really in on this thing, how far it will go."

Ben shot a quick look at the merchant. "Makes me wonder if my man is on the list. What about Helm? Heard anything?"

Stuart shrugged. "I don't know. I'm not a member of the select committee, Ben; the 'ferreting group,' I think they call it. I've no way of knowing such a thing . . . how much evidence they really have. But I'll tell you this: Helm is in Virginia City. Perhaps I should say, *was*. Who knows now? This business has stirred up everyone in the district . . . men running for cover in every direction. I suppose if *I* had some notoriety I'd be looking for the nearest shebang, myself. Frightful, in a way.''

"Notoriety? Meaning . . . ?"

Stuart laughed indifferently. ''You? Oh, not necessarily. Rather far-fetched, don't you think? Since when have you ever taken to running with a murdering band of thieves? You're a loner. Folks hereabouts don't know you.''

"Seems like people just don't like my name," Ben said with a grin.

"Oh, hogwash! Why, there's more than ten thousand people in this district, now. Small chance that even a handful will remember you, much less recognize you. It's not a pretty sight around here, but it's easy to get lost in a crowd. That's one good thing about it, a point in your favor. Everyone is too busy these days in the digs.''

Ben dismounted and started to remove the hackamore from the paint. ''Small chance, huh? Well, let me tell you, Jim, my odds haven't always been the best.'' He gave Stuart a tired smile.

"Well, I'll vouch for you," Stuart said. "What are you planning?"

Ben nodded toward Bannack. "I have no business that way. Reckon I'll ride into Alder Gulch." He led his two horses behind the wagon and tied them on. Toeing up on the wheel spoke, he jumped aboard the freighter. ''Move over,'' he grinned at the storekeeper. ''Let's see if I can still handle these long-eared critters.''

So they traveled, lumbered down the Grasshopper Hills. They followed the deepening ruts to cross the icy Beaverhead and come up the Passamari, ultimately arriving in the Gulch, where Ben once again suffered civilization. And it was worse than Stuart had ever led him to believe.

If Lewiston had been confusion, the populous settlements along Alder Creek were outright abominable. Winter's harsh hand did little to help. Any clean touch of snow was soon obliterated by one great continuous movement of humanity, the laboring tread of plodding hooves and slogging boots that quickly fashioned man's ugliest carpet: trampled refuse, slush, and excrement. It was not a street. It was wallow. Calm was nonexistent, shattered from dawn to dusk by chaotic cries, the resounding clatter of the hammer and saw, and the braying of stock. Stuart had been much too kind! Virginia City was not pretty—it was calamitous. Its litter, its filth, its rank huts and shanties of mud and log defied description, creeping up both sides of the scoured creek like some alien, parasitic growth. And people again, always moving, crawling like an army of troubled piss ants.

But the gold! There was gold here, scads of it, bedrocked beneath the cold waters and lichenous crevices. And men to dig it, men to spend it, men to squander and steal it. It was a disease of madness, and in the confusion, Ben had to escape the insanity. He found quarters in the Virginia Hotel, where he vainly tried to adjust. The room was small, badly misused, and all the ugliness of this new world closed in upon him. He thought of Rainbow and the children, wondered at his own particular brand of cupidity, that which had drawn him from the pure mountains in the guise of a sacred quest. And with burdened heart, he buried his head in his hands and cursed.

James Stuart had spoken to Ben of chance, the barest thread of it that anyone among the hundreds of hairy, strange faces in the Gulch would recognize him. Not so. Within his first twelve hours two persons al-

ready had spotted him, and at the time Ben had been
totally unaware of it. In the fading light of evening,
his casual inquiries had taken him to the saloons, ultimately to the wooden stoop of one called The Shades,
a small, obscure gaming house down from the Virginia
Hotel. He had not found it necessary to enter, nor had
he particularly wanted to. The small paned window
next to the door was adequate, and the face of Boone
Helm on the poster was a familiar picture in his mind.

He pressed close, the squint of his eyes quickly
sweeping the small interior. Several men stood at the
bar. They were strangers like the rest, men with
beards, goatees, mustaches. He passed on to a nearby
card table, then hesitated. Three men sat there, one of
them a haggard specimen of a man named Helm, his
eyes hollowed discs of worry, his heavy jowls covered
by a growth of silver and gray. But to Ben, he was
beyond recognition. Ben had no idea this man was
Boone Helm, any more than he knew his two companions were Jack Gallagher, a Plummer deputy, and
Hayes Lyons, a gambler of some reputation. Ben gave
up for the night, his first search obviously a dry run,
and he turned away, back to the frozen planks of the
boardwalk.

Inside the Shades, however, it had been shockingly
different. Boone Helm's face went ashen at the eerie
sight of the face in the window. He suddenly faltered
and fumbled his cards. Visibly shaken, he had just
seen a ghost from the past, the Tree boy that he had
killed long ago, and the man he had fled from in Walla
Walla. But by the time he had rallied, blurting out the
name of Ben Tree, the frightening vision was gone
from the window. His two friends displayed no qualms
and wasted no time. Guns drawn, both of them madly
bolted for the door. It would be some coup to shoot
down Ben Tree, a feat that one of their companions,
Gad Moore, had been unable to accomplish several

days past. The two men leaped at the opportunity, but when they hit the chilly night air, Ben Tree had already become part of the night scene.

Others watched, too. Across the street in the doorway of a hardware store, two men had been stationed, keeping their eyes trained on The Shades. One of them suddenly moved out, following the shaggy buffalo-hide jacket that was disappearing into the crowd below. This man, too, had recognized Ben Tree.

Ben, meantime, returned to the hotel, where within five minutes he heard a soft rap at his door. Quietly slipping the latch, he stood aside, revolver at the ready. With a quick hello the stranger came bustling in, immediately shut the door, and extended his hand in friendship. He wore a greatcoat, which hardly disguised his short stature. He was whiskered, his hat black with a broad brim, and what he lacked in size was equalized by his reputedly quick hand. He was a gunman.

"The name is Biedler," he said crisply. "John X. Biedler—my friends call me X. I followed you. You'll have to excuse that, but I came to tell you, Mr. Tree, that you picked a helluva poor time to come to this town. Now don't talk, just listen." He shed his hat and unbuttoned his coat. Ben saw the revolver strapped to his side. Like his own, it was a .44 caliber Navy Colt.

Ben gave the short man a faint smile. The presumptuous attitude of the intruder was curiously amusing. "You seem to know me, Mr. Biedler," Ben said. "Should I know you? Your purpose in following me up here?"

"I used to ride for Digby . . . James Digby. Now, listen to what I have to—"

"Jim Digby! Well, by jingo!" Ben exclaimed softly. He fell back and relaxed.

"That's right," Biedler returned brusquely. "Stage

and freight. You *should* know me—in a way, I was working for you. The last time you came through Fort Hall the old man had me following you for half the night . . . scared some drunk or bushwhacker was aiming to put a slug in your back."

"Yes, that sounds like Jim," said Ben with a smile. "And you're still on the job?"

Biedler frowned at the casual levity. "Hell, no! I work for Peabody's line, now. My visit has nothing to do with the express. It's personal. Let's say, out of friendship for Digby and your own hide." Biedler motioned his thumb to the outside. "You almost spoiled our game out there, your infernal snooping around. You never should have come here. You're going to cause us trouble. You have to get out of here."

"Your game?" Ben asked. "And what might that be?"

"Look, Tree," he said stiffly, "I know all about this thing between you and old man Helm. I know your reputation, and the word's already come down from Cottonwood on that killer, Gad Moore. Are you daft? You think there's others around that don't know the same? Dammit, if you'd presented yourself in The Shades down there, all hell would have broken loose! His friends are in there. And right now, gun trouble is something we can't afford. We can't tolerate it."

Protesting gently, Ben held up his hand. "Hold on, Mr. Biedler, hold on. You're running ahead of me. Maybe you just better slow down and explain. What's all of this 'we' business? Who is *we*?"

Exasperated, Biedler replied, "Just stay off the street, will you? Do me that favor, or you'll likely wind up on the short end of a rope, or shot. Dammit, are you crazy? You don't seem to see the gravity of the situation here, what's going on."

"I think I do," Ben said. "I have a tight mouth, if you want to talk on the subject. What about this saloon? Since you're butting into my personal business, maybe you just better tell me what's going on . . . something I don't know.''

John X. Biedler drew a long breath and sighed. ''Look, I can only tell you that this confounded grudge you have with Helm is useless. It's a dead duck, now. The worst thing that you can do is go picking a fight with that cutthroat. Didn't you see him? He's sitting down there with those dandies, Gallagher and Lyons! I figured that's why you backed out—the odds. They're as thick as fleas on a poor dog's back, and like a den of rattlesnakes when they're bunched up that way.''

Ben pursed his lips in surprise. ''Well, now, I didn't know my man was sitting down there. You see, I've never met Helm in my life, not personally—a picture, that's all. Tell you something else: I'm not about to turn my coattail, not now, not for you or anyone else.''

''My God, man!'' exclaimed Biedler. ''Why, you *must* be crazy, gunning for a man you don't even know! What's come over you?''

Ben turned away, sat on the edge of the bed, wearily rubbed his brow. ''I know him well enough,'' he said bitterly. ''He killed my father and brother, but it's been a long time. I didn't realize.'' He pulled out the folded poster and handed it to Biedler. ''Is this my man? Boone Helm?''

The stocky gunman scrutinized the sketch, then cursed. ''Hell, you'd never know Helm from this thing. Why, this picture must be ten years old!''

Ben mused, ''Yes, I'm beginning to see . . . this boy, Moore, what he said . . . old man. This Boone fellow is getting along in his years, I reckon.''

''Yes, and you were damn lucky on that Moore affair,'' Biedler huffed. ''Gad was on the committee's list to be hanged until he crossed up with you. Quite a hand with a gun, too. By our accounts he's killed at least three, maybe four men.''

"He was a boy!" Ben retorted sorely. "A *boy*! Worse yet, he was slow . . . stupid and slow." And then he curiously stared up at the express man. "The *committee*? Well, well! So, that's it," he said. "The committee . . . vigilantes. You're a part of it, taking the law into your own hands. That's what's bothering you . . . Helm, those other men down there . . . ei, and me. You want Helm and I want him, but I go back a long time before the vigilantes."

Biedler hurried to the door, listened, hunched over, his loose coat dragging the floor like tent flaps. He stared back at Tree. "Dammit, even the walls have ears in this infernal place."

Ben nodded. "By jingo, I can believe *that*. I've never spread my blanket in a worse hole, and that's a fact."

Pulling the lone chair close to the bed, Biedler began to talk in low, hushed tones. He said that the situation in Virginia City was precarious—at that very moment, the Vigilance Committee was in secret session in the back of Pfout's store, determining the fate of another group of men, all reputed members of The Innocents. Helm, Gallagher, and Lyons were among the names presented by the investigating committee. By midnight it would be decided, finished. Both ends of the town would be blocked. The condemned men were to be trapped, tried, and without much doubt, hanged in the morning. It was that conclusive.

"You couldn't have come in here at a worse time," Biedler continued. "There's more than fifty of us, some I don't even know. If some flighty merchant or packer gets word that you're here . . . impeaches you in some way, what kind of weight do you think I can possibly swing? With your reputation, those are bad odds."

Resting back on the bed, Ben stared up at the short man. He said easily, "Mr. Biedler, I certainly appreciate your concern, but if your men are square, they should know that I'm no robber. I shot that Moore boy in a fair fight, too. Anyhow, Digby will vouch for me . . . so will Jim Stuart."

"Jim Stuart!" Biedler scoffed. "That's one man's word, one man! It would be like talking to a stone wall . . . some of the men involved in this make no distinctions about outlaws. And old man Digby is six hundred miles away. Dammit, why don't you talk some sense?"

"I haven't trailed west of the mountains in years, but I was here long before the diggers made this unholy mess you call a town."

"You're a renegade," Biedler said flatly, although without malice. "You already have a reputation. That's the way most around here will see it. Right or wrong, it doesn't matter. There's a few who'd put you on the list in a minute, if they knew you were holed up here. What's more, you're a half-breed, and that's reason enough to some of these fellows who've lost family and friend on the trails."

"You know better," Ben returned. "My game never has been on the Overland. You know the kind of men I deal with, and why. And don't blame your fool miseries on the natives. This is your creation here, and that of the scum outside."

Biedler scoffed back, "And you think you can convince the committee of that? Poppycock! You haven't the slightest idea who you're dealing with. I'll tell you this, they're not in any mood for moralizing."

"And if I'm a renegade," Ben went on, "I'll allow the likes of some of those outside had a hand in it. Ei, you talk about the trails. By jingo, you do have a short memory, Mr. Biedler. My whole family was wiped out on the trail—by whites, not Indians. And seems to me, you're forgetting who put this damned committee on to some of the roadsters in the first place. It was me!

No, it's not the likes of me and my brothers who've brought on your miseries; maybe up north on the Indian lands, or what's left of them, but not down here, no sir."

"As you will," Biedler said. "Your memory is just as short. You're forgetting your share in Digby's operation down at Fort Hall. I'd say you've been catering to the white traffic in your own way."

Ben nodded gravely. "Yes, and that part of it, I've lived to regret. But you know damn well I've never condoned the drummers or the interlopers. And as long as I can sit a horse and use a gun, I won't, either. They had best stay out of my path, and my country up north."

Biedler shook his head. "What you do up above is your own business, but this is free country down here. It has to be safe. We intend to make it that way in the Idaho territories, once and for all. There'll be no exceptions."

"Ei, free and safe for those of your own choosing."

Biedler threw up his hands in despair. "Dammit, Tree!" he fumed. "I didn't come up here to argue the sanity of civilization, or the plight of the Injun! I came to warn you . . . to try and keep you out of it . . . to get you out of Virginia City! Can't you get that through your hard head? And in the name of your partner, Jim Digby, and your own ornery hide, you *better* get the hell out of here before dawn." He straightened his short frame and offered his hand. Frowning again, he said, "The old man told me you were a silent partner. No offense, but I sure as hell understand why. You're too damned contrary. Damned if you aren't."

Ben shook Biedler's hand. "Yes," he said with a grin, "I've heard as much. Seems like years ago, an old medicine man told me a story. . . . Had something to do with a contrary goose, one that flew backward . . . got himself lost. I know that you're in a hurry, so

I'll not burden you with the details of the yarn. Superstition, understand, not too palatable for a white man.''

Biedler was at the door. He glared back. "Mr. Tree, you're impossible! I only hope you get some sense and take my advice. Get your tail out of town.''

"I'll sleep on it—if I can sleep at all.''

"You'll end up in a pine box, if you don't. You're no goddamned lost goose!''

The door closed.

Shortly after dawn, Ben was up. His sleep had been fitful, what with the night noises, Biedler's warning words, his own laboring mind, the constant mull over the decision that loomed. Once again that old feeling of futility, echoes of the past, lost causes, limp banners. Time, relentless time, had disintegrated his quest, time and fate. All these crumbling, wasteful years! How many times had he been close to Boone Helm, close yet unaware? Only a badly harried Helm could answer that. And that was part of the fate Tree had to accept: Helm *was* the waste, that pitiful shell of a man that he had unwittingly seen at the card table, perhaps playing his very last hand. Helm was already dead—decayed *inside*. Ben had ruined the man.

Tree's boots fell heavily on the crusted mud. It was a cold morning. Perhaps the chill of death made it worse. He packed the pinto, those few belongings that he had taken into the hotel, and saddled up War Paint. He came from the livery stable back into the bite of the morning air, rode up the frozen street toward the hotel. The sight above suddenly stopped him. He saw the small knot of men there, momentarily gathered, now moving hurriedly in his direction, only a heartbeat away. *Destiny*, he suddenly thought. Had he, too, become a part of it? Here they came, straight for him, and they had rope, hanging rope. And then, for the first time, he saw Boone Helm among them, the tired, gray man with the speckled whiskers. And Biedler was there, too, his stumpy figure boldly marching alongside, jaw outthrust in steadfast authority. On they came, and Ben Tree, hand near his holster, nervously watched the narrowing gap.

Then the momentary pause, the outbreak, the hoarse, hollow cry of a condemned man. Helm had thrown his bound hands to the sky, unexpectedly presenting himself to the mountain man, Ben Tree. "Look at me!" Helm screamed up. "Look at me! Look at me, you goddamned heathen! It's me, old Booney . . . my hair, the flesh and blood of me. You see what's left? They've got me for sure, and it'll be no Injun' job, not from you, Tree. You hear? Look at me . . . my hair, I still got it . . . my hair . . ."

Ben sagged in his saddle, sucking for a breath of the cold morning air. For one frightening instant he stared down at the stricken hulk, the hopeless face below him. Oh, how pitiful! Even in approaching death, Boone Helm pathetically had nothing to give, and Ben Tree's answering words unexpectedly spilled from his heart.

"Mr. Helm, I'm sorry . . . truly sorry for your miserable self. May God forgive you. May God Almighty forgive us all."

The anxious crowd, eager to witness death, crudely pushed on, ignoring the man in buckskin, overriding Helm's last few choking words, the shredded accusations against Ben muffled by the press of angry men. Someone close to John X. Biedler shouted excitedly, "Who's the stranger, X? Is he one of 'em? What the hell was that all about? Who is that man?"

Biedler marched ahead, his dark eyes on the distant gallows. "I don't know him," he replied. "Never saw the man before in my life, but he sure as hell talks like a God-fearing buster, doesn't he?"

Ben slowly threaded his horse through the wide-eyed miners racing around him toward the spectacle of the gallows. His direction was east, beyond the rivers, toward the legendary *Nah-Pit-Sei,* the highest and holiest of mountains, the very breast of Mother Earth, the place where the whole man is judged and saved at the same time, and where the troubled soul may plunge to eternal peace.

Ben Tree's eighth December had passed.

January, 1864

I am back with my brothers and my family on the Yellowstone. Hunting elk has kept me busy, and tending to my ponies is another chore. My soul still wanders, though, often strays from the path that the Great Spirit has set for me. But I am healing and my heart is full, for now I know I must put away my vengeance and trust that justice will be done by His hand alone. How can I explain this feeling of peace that swims in my renewed blood? I know there is no trail back to what once was, and I have no great medicine like Buffalo Horn to foretell the future. So, the land must change and all its many people as well. What I have written these long years on the trail has been from my heart, and this is all that I have come to believe, that some day the inherent goodness in all of us will prevail. This is my final wish, and I end this white man's journal now and forever. Some day it may speak well of me and my brothers, and what we have done in the name of justice.

Man Called Tree.

EPILOGUE

Because the journal of Benjamin Tree was so extensive and detailed, the New York *Herald-Tribune* reporter, Harold Stebbins, spent two days perusing it and taking notes. He thought he had the ingredients for a good series of articles on the legendary Ben Tree. On the third morning, Stebbins appeared once more at the door of James Bridger. He had come to return the journal and ask a few more questions. The old mountain man invited him in to parley and have some coffee. They talked most of the morning, and though Bridger was hesitant to answer all of Stebbins' questions, the young reporter did manage to garner a few missing details. Did Mr. Bridger believe that Ben Tree would reappear on the frontier?

"Mebbe yes, and mebbe no," Bridger replied. "If he does, won't be the one you been reading about in that book for the past two days. But if you see him, won't be no mistake knowing who he is. One good look into Benji's face and y'ain't liable to be forgettin', no siree, bob."

"I would very much like to meet this man."

"Not likely," Bridger said with a grin. He blew a stream of blue smoke toward the ceiling and watched it hover and slowly dissolve into haze. "Sorta like that smoke, ain't he? Here one minute, gone the next."

"Elusive."

"His medicine sign . . . coyote, sun, tree."

"Yes, I remember."

James Bridger's eyelids fluttered, and after a moment he said, "Keep the grit out of your eyes, Mr. Stebbins. Keep the stones out of your ears. Benji has those two boys up in the mountains, and the way I figger it, you ain't heard the last of this—not if they's the same cut as their ol' man, you ain't!"